Between the Lines

BRANDY PELLETIER

Developmental editor: Melanie Yu at Made Me Blush Books

Copy/line editor: Beth Lawton at VB Edits

Cover designer: Sam Palencia at Ink and Laurel

For Clara Jean, who gave me books.
And everything else.

BETWEEN THE LINES PLAYLIST

"Sweet Pea" - Amos Lee

"Start Nowhere" - Sam Hunt

"Everything Has Changed" (Taylor's Version) - Taylor Swift
feat. Ed Sheeran

"Dandelions" - Ruth B

"Peer Pressure" - James Bay feat. Julia Michaels

"Butterflies" - Kacey Musgraves

"Better Man" - James Morrison

"On My Way to You" - Cody Johnson

"Write a Book" - Maddie & Tae

"Speakers" - Sam Hunt

"Angel" - Aerosmith

"Strangers" - Maddie & Tae

"Set Me on Fire" - Estelle

"Try Losing One" - Tyler Braden & Sydney Sierota

"Great Ones" - Maren Morris

"What My World Spins Around" - Jordan Davis

CHAPTER ONE

LUKE

Secrets don't keep in small towns. Not forever anyway. And mine is one of *those* kinds. The kind that weighs a man down, makes his soul weary. No, it isn't scandalous. I haven't committed murder or robbed a bank. No defacing of beloved local landmarks or engaging in a torrid affair. Secrets don't keep; yet somehow, I've managed to keep mine for years.

It weighs heavy on my heart as I sit in my truck in the parking lot of my daughter's elementary school. My routine back-to-school conference with her teacher starts in exactly five minutes, and I can't bring myself to exit the truck. But Hannah Shipley is my entire world, all five-years-and-plenty-of-sass. And she has me wrapped like nothing else. So for her, I take a deep breath and step out.

The late-afternoon sun burns down on the asphalt as I make my way across the parking lot. August in central Georgia is brutal. I'm only halfway to the front doors when a bead of sweat makes its way down my spine and into the waistband of my jeans.

I pass two or three cars on my way in, and there are a handful of buses parked at the north end of the lot, baking in the sun after their afternoon runs. This is exactly why I chose the last time slot Mrs. Gibson had available. I don't have the capacity to be overly friendly today, even to people I've known most of my life. Not with this damn secret eating at me with such ferocity that there's a physical ache in my gut.

Bennett, Georgia, my hometown, is small. Not one-stoplight small, but in a town this size, it's hard not to know everyone—and most of their business. Though very few know my secret. My best friend knows, but Cordell is loyal to a fault. He's carried it with him for years, never pressuring me about it. And my parents, of course. But hell, I'm not sure they really know how bad it is.

The inside of Bennett Elementary smells like it did when I was a student here—like a mixture of Play-Doh, cleaning supplies, and kid. I chuckle softly at the wave of nostalgia it brings on as I head to the office window to sign-in. The office staff are gone for the day, but the visitor clipboard sits on the windowsill, so I grab a pen and scribble my name on the next available line, leaving the other two columns blank, even though the rows above have all been filled in.

The hallways seem so small. When I was a kid, this place felt massive, like I would never be big enough to leave it. Clothes-lines full of artwork line the halls, reminding me of the refriger-ator door at our house full of Hannah's scribbles and masterpieces. I pass by the wing that holds the second-grade classroom where I first met Cordell; his family moved to town a few weeks before school started that year. We bonded over a game of Jackpot at recess that first day, and we've been friends since. Other than my dad, he's the best guy I know.

Mrs. Gibson has been in the same classroom since before I started school here. She wasn't my teacher, but I definitely remember her. Her kids were a grade or two ahead of me in school. They're married up and moved on out; lots of folks get out of Bennett the first chance they get. Some just can't cope with the small-town vibes.

Taking my sweaty Braves cap off my head before I enter room four, I run my hand through my hair and give a courtesy knock before stepping through the open door. *Here goes nothing.*

"Lucas Shipley, get yourself in here, son!" Mrs. Gibson calls from a horseshoe-shaped table in the back of the room. She's the definition of an elementary teacher—maternal and kind but firm when she needs to be. Her light brown hair is cut short and styled, with streaks of gray showing through. She takes off a pair of reading glasses as I cross the room.

"Luke's fine, ma'am," I respond as I try to fit my six-one frame into a tiny red plastic chair across from her.

"Luke." She gives me a warm smile. "Gosh, I can't believe you have one in school this year. How're your mama and daddy doing?"

"They're good, thanks."

"They probably spoil Miss Hannah something fierce, right? She's the sweetest little girl."

"Thank you, ma'am. She sure does love school. A lot more than I ever did." Understatement of the century. Other than sports and Cordell, school was torture.

"I remember you as a little guy. Joined at the hip with Coach Watkins. Only one thing on y'all's minds: ball. He's doing such a good job with those boys up at the high school, isn't he?"

"Yes, ma'am, he sure is. Loves it." I take a deep breath, bracing myself for what comes after the small-talk portion of the meeting. *This is for Hannah,* I remind myself, knowing that my life is about to change. Because another soul is about to know my secret.

"Let's talk about how Miss Hannah is doing in school, shall we?" Mrs. Gibson pulls out paper after paper, showing me examples of Hannah's progress in kindergarten so far. The kids have only been in school for a couple of weeks, but she's got a whole stack of work to go through.

Knee bouncing, I try to nod in all the right places and return every smile she gives me, but I'm not focused on the school-work. Though I do take note of the smiley faces and check marks at the tops of several of the pages.

She takes a breath and continues. "Now, let's talk about Hannah's reading."

My knee stops its constant motion.

"She's making good progress with letters and sounds. And she's a little sponge when I read to the class."

I exhale a deep breath. "So she's—she's on track with her reading?" I ask.

Mrs. Gibson smiles. "She's doing well. Were you concerned?"

"Yeah—yes, ma'am."

"She's progressing as she should. You read to her at home, right? That will help build her vocabulary and comprehension skills."

She's likely expecting a straightforward yes or no so we can move on. But I can't lie to her. So I simply say, "Well, my mom does. When Hannah stays over there."

She pauses her shuffling and peers up at me. "But you don't at your house?" she questions. Her tone is not full of blame, just genuine curiosity.

"No, ma'am."

"Oh, that's an easy fix," she states, not knowing how very wrong she is. "She can bring home books from our class library or the school library. Add the book titles to this reading log so we can keep track of them all." She hands me a paper with a smile.

Gaze glued to the table, I stay silent, my knee bouncing again despite my best efforts.

When I don't answer, she goes on. "Make it a part of her

bedtime routine—a story with Daddy every night before bed." Like it's the simplest thing in the world.

Hannah is the most important thing in my life. And I'm all she's got. Her mom hasn't been in the picture since Hannah was two. I've been a solo parent for most of her life, and everything I do, every day of my life, is for her—to ensure she has every damn thing she'll need to grow up happy and healthy.

"Mrs. Gibson," I finally respond. "I want to give Hannah the very best of everything—"

"Of course you do, hon. I know you're the *best* daddy to her."

I clear my throat. "But to be the best daddy, to give her the very best, I have to be honest. The reading stories thing is going to be challenging for us."

She waves a dismissive hand. "I know families are busy these days. Just a quick bedtime story can make a world of—"

"No, not because of time." I take a deep breath and force myself to look this teacher square in her concerned eyes. This is the moment I've been dreading all damn day. My stomach plummets—if I say this, there's no going back.

"I can't read, ma'am." I drop my head and study the hat I've got crushed in my hands, my vision blurring with tears I refuse to shed. I take a moment to check my emotions after the bomb I just dropped, forcing air into my lungs. Because the secret I've kept for most of my thirty-four years has the power to impact Hannah's life in a negative way. And I just can't have that.

"What happened, Luke?" Her voice is soft and kind.

I shake my head, searching for the words to explain a lifetime of struggles and lies. "I..." I swallow down the shame threatening to pull me under. "I've always struggled with it. It never clicked for me, and I learned how to hide it, I guess."

When I finally meet her eyes again, I'm faced with a look of steely determination.

"Lucas Shipley, we need to fix this. And we can. But it's

going to take some work on your part. We'll have you reading to that girl, come hell or high water."

Now it's my turn to look shocked. I'm pretty sure this sweet kindergarten teacher just cussed. She strides over to her desk and rifles through a drawer. After a few moments and an "Aha!" she scurries back over, brochure in hand. Which I can't read. Perfect.

"The county library offers an adult literacy program," she says, pointing at the glossy paper in my hand. "You'll need to sign up with Mr. Weaver down there. They meet twice a week. Here, let me read it to you." She proceeds to read the entire brochure to me before passing it back. I commit as much of the information to my memory as I can, a skill I've gotten pretty good at over the years.

I squeeze my cap in my hand as I stand to face her, if for no other reason than to stop my damn knee from bouncing. She still has that determined look, and I'm torn between feeling grateful and ashamed. Though ashamed is slightly ahead.

"You're doing this, Luke. I know you can." She nods, smiling encouragingly. "In the meantime, be sure Hannah gets lots of story time with Nana. Marjorie will eat that right up."

"Yes, ma'am," I say, feeling like a kid in trouble. "Please, there aren't many folks who know about this, so—"

"Don't worry your head about that. Everything we discussed stays here. All of it."

I nod, take another deep breath. "Thanks for meeting with me. And for this," I say, waving the brochure. I hold tight to it like a lifeline all the way out to the parking lot. My life is going to be different, starting now. *I* am going to be different. I'll fix this damn secret, and there's no going back.

I pull up the gravel drive leading to my parents' ranch-style house just before dinnertime. My dad's out in the garage, working under the hood of his sixty-eight Camaro. Hannah is with him, no doubt telling her Papaw about every minute of her day.

Living on the same land as my folks means I have no shortage of support and help with Hannah. And what Mrs. Gibson said is true—they spoil her, but not in an obnoxious way. My parents are hard-working, honest people, and they raised me to be the same. Now they're passing those qualities on to my daughter as well.

"Daddy! Daddy!" Hannah yells before I've even turned off the ignition. She jumps up and down outside my door, eager for me to scoop her up. As soon as I step out, she's in my arms.

"Guess what," she says, her arms looped around my neck. "There was a *snake* on the playground at recess! Mr. Trey had to come get it so no one would get hurt!"

"A snake? Really?"

She nods, her lips pressed in a straight line and her big brown eyes solemn. *God, I love this kid.*

"Hey, what's this?" she asks, putting her little hands on my day-old scruff. "Your face is hairy again! I thought we talked about this." She rubs at the coarse hair with both palms; this is one of our many inside jokes, and she knows what's coming next.

"You know why. It's so I can do *this*!"

Her contagious giggles fill the air as I rub my stubble on her neck and under her chin. When the game is over, she takes my face in her hands again and plants a quick kiss to the top of my cheek, right under my eye.

"I love you anyway, Hairy-Face Daddy," she whispers so close I can smell her pre-dinner snack—Doritos.

"Love you too, Banana." I give her a squeeze and set her back on the ground. "Why don't you hang out here with Papaw for a few more minutes so I can talk to Nana real quick?" Her hand in mine, I lead her to the garage where my dad is still bent over the hood. "Hey, Pop. I need to talk to Mom for a minute. Keep Banana with you until dinner?"

"Sure thing, kid," he says as he straightens up and gives me a smile. *Kid.* Even though I'm thirty-four and three inches taller than him. I'd never admit it, but I love it. Shipleys are big on nicknames.

Mom's in the kitchen, standing over the stove, stirring what smells like spaghetti sauce.

"Hey, you! How was your day?" Her face brightens when I step through the door. "How'd the school thing go?" She doesn't stop stirring as I bend to kiss her cheek.

My parents were young when they had me, so in a way, we all grew up together. Though they made it clear from early on— they are my parents, not my friends. I didn't get away with shit growing up, and I still don't. The only area they were lax about, weirdly enough, was school. They expected me to be there, all right, but they weren't overly concerned about grades or tests or studying. Despite that, I don't blame them for my trouble with reading. They did the best they could as young parents, and I've never been in jail, so…

"It was good. Hannah's doing real good in school, Mrs. Gibson says. Showed me lots of her classwork and stuff."

"I knew my little June Bug would rock that school stuff. She's so smart!" she says, pulling four plates out of the cabinet— my cue to set the table.

I jump to it, grateful to keep my hands busy while we talk.

"Mrs. Gibson mentioned reading more here and at home, to help her learn and all." I don't look up from my task, but all movement behind me has ceased. "Yeah, so I had to confess that I'm not the best at that, you know. The reading thing."

Before I've finished my admission, my mom's by my side, pulling out a chair.

"I want to get better at it. For Hannah, you know? And…for me, too."

Marjorie Shipley is quiet for several moments as I continue to set out silverware and napkins. She's studying the table and running her hands through her dark shoulder-length hair. When she finally looks up at me, my heart flips at the tears shining in her eyes and the wobble of her chin.

"Luke, I know we've failed you—"

"Mom, no. I've never thought that," I say, taking the chair across from her, flipping my cap backward in frustration.

"No, it is true. We knew you struggled. Of course we knew. But I don't think we really understood what a disadvantage it would be for you. And a little part of me was in denial, too." A lonely tear rolls down her cheek.

"Mom, I hid it from you," I argue, her devastation eating at me. "I got really freaking good at hiding it, at finding a way to fake people out. This is not on you. I promise."

"It is, and I'll believe that to the day I die. All I can do now is tell you how sorry I am that I didn't fix it for you." She wipes at her cheeks. "And I'll do everything in my power to help you fix it now. We both will, your father and me." She reaches across the table, palm up.

I take it and hold on tight, soaking in all the love she's offering, hoping to ease the pain of regret she's drowning in. "Mrs. Gibson told me about this program at the library. They meet twice a week." I pull the folded-up brochure out of my back pocket and hand it to her. "I want to try this."

"Absolutely. Whatever you need." She nods and sniffles. "We can take care of June Bug those nights. I can switch my hours if I need to. I want you to do this for yourself."

"I will." I nod and give her a small smile. "Thanks for being there for Banana. And for me."

"I love you, Lucas. I'm proud of you."

After dinner, Hannah and I head back to our home. It's on the same forty acres of land that have been passed down through the Shipley family for generations. I honk the horn as we round the side of my parents' house. Then I take the gravel drive past the small pond, through a small group of pines, and around another bend to my favorite place in the world.

After her teeth are brushed, her pajamas are on, and she's chosen a sleeping buddy from her pile of stuffed animals (tonight it's a stuffed octopus), I get my girl tucked in under her butterfly sheets and kneel beside her bed for good-nights and sweet dreams.

"You know how I met with Mrs. Gibson at school today, Banana?"

She nods, clutching the octopus to her chest as her tiny face screws up in a yawn.

"She told me that you are so smart and sweet. You know what I said to that?"

"What?" she asks, tilting her sweet little head.

"I told her that you're the smartest and sweetest girl in the whole state of Georgia. And she couldn't argue with that."

She gives me a sleepy smile, and I lean over to kiss her forehead.

"Night, Banana." I stroke her dark hair, soaking in the quiet time with my girl.

"Night, Daddy," she whispers, her eyelids already heavy.

The girl likes sleeping as much as I do, so, in true Hannah fashion, she's out in minutes.

From my spot on the floor, I watch her dark lashes flutter against her round cheeks, her chest rising and falling with peaceful, deep breaths. And I know, without a doubt, that the shame and embarrassment I felt confessing my secret today were worth it. That what comes next—the struggle, the vulnerability, the hard work—will be worth it, too. Because this little girl deserves a hero who will face *anything* to make sure she has the best life possible. I'm going to be that hero for her. I'm going to learn how to read.

CHAPTER TWO

TESSA

Tuesdays have got to be the saddest day of the week. Monday has a certain edge, like it knows it's everyone's least favorite and it kind of revels in that. No one blinks an eye over a crappy Monday. Wednesday is like halftime; there isn't much to hate about making it halfway to the weekend. Thursday is Friday-eve, so by default, it's not so bad. But Tuesday? Sadsville.

As I go through the motions of getting ready for work on a Tuesday morning in late August, my mind bounces from the Tuesday blues to the list of things I need to get accomplished today. No time for sadness, really.

Thermos filled with coffee in one hand, I take a minute to scan my cozy apartment and ruminate again about how different my actual life is in comparison to the life that was expected of and planned for me. The life I'm living here, in a smaller-than-small town in the middle of Georgia, working as the children's library director for the county. My parents are still in denial.

Growing up in Atlanta, the only daughter of two no-nonsense attorneys, I had all the creature comforts one could supposedly wish for—a swanky house in an exclusive, gated community, private school education, weekends at the country club with fellow upper-middle-class offspring. And yet I never really fit in that world. I felt like an outsider, a fraud. My attendance was often required at social gatherings and parties, but I always found a way to sneak off with a book. My dislike of crowds goes *way* back. I always felt judged, looked down upon for being different. Though the people throwing shade didn't really *know* me at all.

I went along with a lot of things to keep my parents happy. As their only child, I put immense pressure on myself to live up to their expectations and demands. They didn't have a backup kid; they couldn't demand a do-over. I was it for them. Now, at twenty-six years old and with two degrees, I'm still a constant disappointment to them.

It takes every ounce of bravery I have to stand up for myself and my future, and I've been searching for more of it, hoping to replenish my reserves, ever since I left for college.

Patrick and Kathleen Burton are not and probably never will be impressed with me. And the weight of my choices sits heavily on my shoulders any time I'm in their presence. Which I avoid as often as possible.

I smile at the little space I've lovingly made into a home for myself. My apartment is one of four in a converted Victorian house a couple of blocks from the main street in town. (Which, incidentally, is called Center Street, *not* Main Street.) There are two apartments on the ground floor, and two above, one of which is my home-sweet-home.

At the door of my new place, I double-check that I have all the essentials for this Tuesday morning. Purse? *Check.* Lunch? *Check.* Coffee? *Check.* Cardigan? *Of course.* Cardigans are, in fact, the lab coats of the academic world. No matter that it's hot as Hades outside, even this early. Air conditioners in the south are legit powerhouses. So a cardigan indoors is a necessity.

On my way out the door, I swipe quickly through the photo

album on my phone to check that today's pictures are there. One of my hair straightener set to off. The second, the coffee maker, also switched off. And to complete the trifecta, I snap a picture of the doorknob as I stick the key in the keyhole. At some point during this Sadsville Tuesday, I'll panic. And these three pictures, all time-stamped with this morning's date and time, will give me peace of mind. I know; I have issues.

The library isn't far from the house, and in the fall and cooler months, walking to and from work will be good not only for my physical well-being but also for my mental health. But in late August, driving with the A/C blasting is a must.

As the children's director, I supervise the children's areas of all the public libraries in Macon County. It's pretty much my dream job. I travel to all the branches, verifying that programs are running smoothly and the staff is up to date on the shared calendars and class schedules. But my home base is here in Bennett, where the largest of our children's book collections is housed. This county is full of small-knit communities, and the libraries in each are the heart of them. Residents have access to everything from free Internet hubs to book clubs and story time and knitting circles.

Walking through the doors of the Bennett Public Library feels like coming home, where all of my book friends wait, ready to welcome me back. Books have always been an escape for me, an escape from the life I didn't feel I belonged in. Now I spend my days helping children fall in love with books the way I did so many years ago, introducing them to the plucky characters who still hold a piece of my heart. It's quiet this early in the morning. It's a library, so it's quiet most of the time, but now that school has started again, the only kids we see this early are the ones whose parents or daycare bring them for toddler story time.

I settle in at my desk and sip on my morning coffee while I check the latest email updates about the Kids' Zone plans I've been working on. The summary of said emails? We still don't have the money to get things underway. Isn't that always the problem? But especially in a small county like ours.

But I'm a firm believer that reading can change lives, so I'll find a way. First on my list of priorities is a partnership with the public school system, and we've been given the green light to get started. Some of the library staff will travel to the elementary schools this fall to encourage kids to talk to their parents about signing them up for library cards.

I'm sending a follow-up email to one of the staff at the Montezuma branch when my boss pokes his head in my door.

"Busy day, Tessa?"

"The usual, sir. What can I do for you?"

Phil Weaver is the director of all the Macon County libraries. He's a lifelong resident of Bennett, and his wife teaches at the high school. He's easy-going, where I am definitely not, but he's been encouraging and supportive of my ideas thus far.

He steps into my office and removes a stack of children's books from the only other chair so he can sit. "Remember when I mentioned having you take over the adult literacy tutoring program?"

"Sure, but I haven't heard anything since. Is it still an active program?"

"Technically, yes. But we haven't had any participants here in Bennett for over a year now. A couple of the other branches have active programs, but we kind of wait until we have a willing body to set any kind of schedule up."

"So there's someone here who needs it now?"

"Yep. Local boy came in last week and asked to speak to me about it. And to be honest, it slipped my mind until this morning. I told him to come in on Tuesdays and Thursdays at six." He ducks his head as he continues. "*So* he'll likely be here tonight. At six…"

The abrupt change in my daily schedule rattles me a bit, but I will not let it show. So I hold my chin high instead. "No problem. I can be here."

"I appreciate you being so flexible. I apologize for not mentioning it sooner." He smiles and considers me for a moment. "Fair warning, though. We've been offering this service for years, and not many participants actually follow through with it. Sure, they'll start like gangbusters, but after a couple of weeks, when the going gets tough, they skedaddle. Just don't want you to get your hopes up too high with this."

I can't imagine the bravery it takes for a full-grown adult to admit he or she can't read and then take the leap to learn how. I'm enthralled by stories I've read of people in their seventies and eighties learning after a lifetime of being illiterate. This is why I sought a master's degree in reading after completing my undergrad. This, along with introducing books to children, is my life's passion.

"I understand," I assure him.

"His name is Luke. Luke Shipley," Mr. Weaver says, standing and moving toward the doorway. "His mama works at Crazy Daisy's."

The florist shop owned by a woman whose actual name *is* Daisy. I haven't met her yet, but I hear she's the go-to source for any and all Bennett information.

"He's asked for our discretion, so I assured him that the only staff who would know about his visits would be me, you, and the front desk clerk."

"Of course," I promise him. I would never risk creating idle gossip and discouraging someone from learning how to read.

With a firm nod, he heads in the direction of the break room. No doubt in search of the donuts Mrs. Weaver sends with him twice a week. The man has a notorious sweet tooth.

In the early afternoon, a young mom comes in looking for early reading picture books. Late afternoon, a few middle school–age kids come in to do research on the library's computers. I get a chance to finish covering and labeling a box of books that came in last week and finally shelve that stack on my chair. All in all, it's a quiet day. Most days are, and I find myself breathing deep, relishing the slower pace of small-town life. And I only had to check the pictures on my phone once today. Progress.

I ready one of the two private study rooms for my session with Mr. Shipley and pull out the worn copies of the adult literacy workbooks and materials from where they were shoved into a storage cabinet under the main desk. The books are well-used and outdated, but they'll work for today. Next time, I'll come prepared with resources I can look up online and some odds and ends from grad school I stuck in a box in my spare closet.

A few minutes before six, I remind Shanice at the main desk to let Mr. Shipley know where to find me when he comes in, and I head to the study room. It's a small space with a window on the door, occupied by only a table and two chairs.

I'm studying a screening assessment I want to administer tonight when a slight knock comes from the doorway. Fixing an encouraging smile on my face, I lift my head to take in Luke Shipley for the first time.

Well.

He's tall and broad with wide shoulders and muscular arms encased in a gray T-shirt. His hair is the darkest brown, the ends curling up under his worn Braves cap. His left arm is covered in tattoos. The swirling, detailed grayscale designs start at his wrist and disappear under the sleeve of his T-shirt. I try not to stare, though I'm intrigued by the designs. But one detail sticks out to me during my brief perusal: the name *Hannah* in swirling cursive on his forearm. It blends seamlessly with the other designs that make up the tattoo.

"Mr. Shipley, hello!" I say, maybe a bit too cheerfully. "I'm Tessa Burton."

His eyes narrow as he takes my extended hand in a firm shake.

"You? You're my tutor?" he asks, his tone incredulous. Or possibly angry. Maybe a mix of the two?

"That's right," I say, settling in my seat again.

He's still standing just inside the threshold, that name on his arm jumping out at me. Hannah. A girlfriend? Or wife? He isn't wearing a ring, but that doesn't mean he isn't married. Judging by the look of his work boots and worn, slightly smudged jeans, there's a good chance he has a physically demanding job that wouldn't allow him to wear one at work. I give my head a little shake. Why am I putting so much thought into whether this guy is married? To recover, I extend my hand to indicate that he should take the chair across from me.

After a moment, he sits, a wary look on his face. We have one moment of direct eye contact, then he glues his eyes to the table and crosses his arms. He's tense, like he's ready to spring out of here at any moment.

"You're on the right path just by showing up," I encourage, remembering Mr. Weaver's advice. "I'm sure it's not easy to find the strength and time to do this, but—"

"No offense, but I don't need a pep talk," he grunts, never looking up from the table.

My cheeks flame, and I pull in a deep, calming breath. Okay, so he's got a chip on his shoulder. Understandable, given his circumstances. So rather than offering more platitudes he has no interest in, I jump right in.

"The first thing I'd like to do is assess your phonemic awareness. Your ability to hear and isolate individual sounds in words. I'm going to ask you to do some listening and answering, if that's all right with you."

"My hearing is fine. I can't *read*."

My heart breaks a little more for him. I can't imagine having gone through life without the ability to read signs, paperwork, owner's manuals, and the like. Reading is such a fundamental life skill.

"Right. This is more about your ability to break words down into individual sounds. A lot of people who struggle with reading have deficits in this area." I pause, giving him a chance to absorb the information. "It's painless, I promise," I say, offering a wide smile, hoping he'll take the bait and make eye contact again. No dice.

After several quiet moments, he huffs out a breath and grumbles, "Fine." He readjusts his cap, pulling it down lower on his head.

He's going to be a tough nut to crack, so I'll take any kind of affirmation I can get, even if it is unwillingly given.

The PAST assessment is given orally, and all Luke has to do is listen, think, and answer. We start with breaking compound words into syllables, then move into breaking multisyllabic words into individual syllables, too. He breezes through these first few levels, but I figured he would. When the tasks get a little more challenging, his deficits are revealed to me.

"Say *led*," I tell him.

"Led."

"Now say *led*, but instead of /l/, say /s/."

His response: "Sled." The correct response: *said*.

I don't indicate whether his answers are right or wrong. But this is giving me valuable information about how to help him going forward.

We move through a few more ask-answer items, and when he misses several in a row, I have my first puzzle piece in place. His phonemic awareness skills are matching up to those of a student in about the second grade. This is where we'll start when we work together in earnest.

When it's obvious Luke has reached max capacity of discomfort, I say, "We'll stop here for today. This has given me the information I need to know where we should start."

All I get in response is a gruff grunt. He does glance up at me, though, his dark brown eyes revealing his embarrassment before they dart away just as quickly.

"Same time and place on Thursday?" I ask, silently begging him to not give up on himself.

Finally, he looks into my eyes before responding. "Yep. We done?"

I nod and offer him another wide smile. He briefly studies my face before he nods once, his cheeks turning pink. And without another word, he stands and leaves.

Taking a deep breath, I gather up the materials to take back to my office.

While straightening my desk, images of Luke's tall frame in the doorway flash through my mind. The stretch of his T-shirt across his chest and upper arms. The designs in his tattoo.

I would love to lick those tats one day.

Um, what? Tessa Diane Burton, where did that filthy thought come from? My cheeks heat, even though I'm alone. And then my mother's unwelcome voice flashes in my mind. *Burtons don't like boys with tattoos.*

To rid my brain of her, I picture Luke's face—his scowling face. But it's a nice face, too. Masculine. Sharp jawline. Dark stubble. His skin is tan, like he spends his days in the sun. The perfect nose—I didn't know a perfect nose existed, but there it was, on Luke Shipley's face. His lips? Full, but not too full. Dark brown eyes framed by lashes thick enough to make any girl jealous. All of these features work together to create one of the most handsome faces I've seen in real life.

Get a grip, Tessa.

I shake my head and stride toward the exit. I can't let myself get distracted from my goal—teaching Luke how to read. That must remain the focus, no matter how handsome he is.

Though my Tuesdays just got a whole lot more interesting. Maybe not so Sadsville after all.

CHAPTER THREE

LUKE

I swipe the mirror to clear off the steam from my shower and take in the disappointment staring back at me. Damn, I was such an asshole to that girl.

That girl. *Tessa.*

My first thought when I stepped into the study room tonight: *Fuck, she's cute.* Then: *Fuck, I can't do* this *with* her.

No matter how uncomfortable I was, though, there's no excuse for my behavior. Yes, she's fucking adorable, and yes, it's been a long time since I've had such an immediate reaction to a woman. But I was raised better than that.

I shake my head at my reflection once more before aggressively squeezing toothpaste onto my toothbrush. The universe must be out to get me. Some kind of karma shit. Me, taking a leap and finally, *finally* admitting that I want to fix this issue, finding the boldness deep within to take action, and *she* is the one the universe sends to be my saving grace. Can I really be expected to be this vulnerable mess of a man—freaking illiterate, laid bare—with *this* girl? Who looks like an actual ray of sunshine, that smile lighting up her face and my darkest shame all at once? A cruel f-you from the universe, for sure.

Hannah and I are both grumpy bears in the mornings. Good sleepers usually are, so prepping the night before is a must. As I go through the motions of packing our lunches, tossing in a Cosmic Brownie, our favorite dessert, I picture that face once again. Big green doe eyes, probably sussing out my every imperfection. Pert button nose and full rosy lips. Straight white teeth that probably cost her parents a pretty penny. Smooth porcelain skin, begging to be caressed by big, callused hands. Thick brown hair, a couple of shades lighter than my own, falling to just past her shoulders. I only stole glances at her here and there, but I've memorized what I could see. And I like it. *All of it.*

Tessa Burton. She must be new in town. Because if I'd seen her before, trust me, I would remember. Why in the world did she move *here*? Most folks want out of Bennett, not in. I make a mental note to ask Mom to get the scoop from Ms. Daisy. That woman knows all the comings-and-goings. I'll just have to be careful to do it in a way that won't make my mom suspicious. She's always after me to "find a nice girl." But my focus over the last few years has been Hannah. Haven't found anyone who's interested me enough to make time for. Not that Bennett is offering up a whole lot of choices.

As I settle in for the night, I can't stop my mind from wandering: my confession to Mrs. Gibson, the talk with my mom, the discussion with Mr. Weaver. Tessa Burton. Tessa Burton's eyes. Tessa Burton's smile. Tessa Burton's lips working between mine…

I groan and turn over, bunching my pillow to fit under my head. It's going to be a long night.

I wake with an agonizing feeling in my gut. Because being vulnerable in Tessa's presence? I don't think I can do it. She's too distracting, yes, but it's more than that. I just can't let myself be as vulnerable as I need to be with her. I don't want her to have a front-row seat to my struggles or think of me as broken or less-than in any way. Call it stubborn male pride or ego, but I can't let this girl witness me stumbling through work my five-year-old can probably do. Nope.

I'll have to visit with Mr. Weaver again and demand a different tutor.

Mind made up, I head down the hall to wake Hannah, silently hoping for something easier than a stage-five, all-hands-on-deck situation this morning. I've had to call my mom down to intervene before. It isn't pretty.

Luckily, my Banana takes it easy on her old man. Once she's dressed in pink shorts and a flamingo T-shirt, she trudges down the hall and to the kitchen for breakfast.

"Oatmeal today, Daddy?"

"Yep, with a banana for my Banana."

She munches on the half I placed on a napkin at her seat while I slice the other half into my bowl of cereal.

"Why'd I have to stay at Nana and Papaw's after dinner last night?" she questions through a mouthful.

"Chew first, sweetheart," I tell her. "I had a meeting. I have more coming up, so you'll be with Nana and Papaw after dinner a couple times a week. That okay?" I rub at the spot in my chest that tightens with the lie. I hate being dishonest with her, but she thinks I'm the bee's knees who can do no wrong, so how do I tell her I can't read? *Please leave it at that.*

"Can I have two braids today?"

I let out a deep breath, freaking grateful for a five-year-old's ability to change the subject at will.

"Sure thing, Banana girl."

After our quick breakfast, we make our way to Hannah's bathroom. She steps up on the little wooden stool she uses to reach the sink.

Being a single dad, I had to learn real quick how to deal with my daughter's nearly waist-length "princess" hair. And after dozens of tutorials—God bless YouTube's voice search feature—

and practice sessions while watching cartoons, I can pull off a mean braid: french, fishtail, rope, dutch—I'm a braiding machine. And while I work on her hair, I tell Hannah a story of her choosing.

"Whaddya wanna hear today, Banana?" I ask as I separate her dark hair with a middle part. We're going with french braid pigtails today.

"Hmm." She yawns big and rubs her eyes. "What about the hospital one?" A favorite. The story of the first time I held my whole world in my arms.

"That's a good one. Let's see." I dive into the retelling. "You were *supposed* to be here on May twenty-seventh—"

"But I wasn't finished baking yet, right?"

I smile at her in the mirror. She's heard this story so many times she could retell the whole thing.

"Yep, my little Banana still needed some baking time. So we waited around for days, all of us—Nana and Papaw, Uncle Dell, Ms. Rhonda—waiting to meet our perfect little girl." She grins at me in the mirror, rapt. "Your mom and I went for a walk during the afternoon on the last day of May. It was hot, and we were both grouchy. Not grouchy at you or each other, but grouchy because we couldn't wait to meet you. It was like waking up on Christmas morning, but being told we couldn't open our presents yet."

She nods, the movement abrupt enough to tug the hair from my hand.

I snatch it quickly, thankfully before my hard work can be reversed. "So there we were on this hot May day, walking and talking about how ready we were to meet you. All of a sudden, your mom's shorts get dark, like they're wet."

"You thought she went potty on herself!" Hannah giggles.

"Yep. Sure did. I said, 'Shelley, did you wet your pants?' knowing she was going to be madder than a hornet if I laughed about it. She turned to me, this shocked look on her face and her mouth hanging open. Dumb ole me didn't even realize what was happening."

"Her waters leaked out, right?"

"Her water broke," I correct, hoping to God this will not be the day she asks *what* exactly that means. "She looked at me and yelled, 'Get the car, you idiot!' So I left her there, by the side of the road, and ran back to Nana and Papaw's to get the truck. I was in such a state, I forgot about your mom and made it halfway down the street in the opposite direction before I realized I left the most important parts of this adventure on the side of the road."

"Me and Mommy were the important parts, right?"

"For sure. So we got all checked in at the hospital, ready for Miss Hannah May to make her appearance. But…" I pause for dramatic effect and peek at her over her shoulder. "She had other ideas, right?"

My daughter giggles again, hugging herself. "Yep. I didn't want to be Hannah May. I wanted to be Hannah June!"

"Right. You waited until the early hours of June first to greet your fan club. When the nurse put you in my arms, I looked down at your wrinkly, red face, your head full of dark hair just like mine, and I fell in love."

"I fell in love with you, too, Daddy," she says, holding my gaze in the mirror.

And that right there—my daughter's sweet disposition—it's what keeps me going all morning.

After I drop her off at school, I head toward the jobsite. On the drive, I reaffirm my decision to demand a new tutor, vowing to do it on my lunch break and rip the Band-Aid right off.

My phone chimes as I'm parking at the site. A voice text message from Cordell. He's got a planning period first thing, so he's probably watching film or doing whatever it is high school football coaches do to prepare for the upcoming season.

Since I'm one of the first to arrive, I have time. I press the

Play icon to listen to his message. "Hey, bro. Just checking in to see how that library thing went last night. Hit me back when you can."

My inability to read affects my life in so many ways, including communicating with others, especially with how heavily we rely on texting. My parents and Cordell send voice texts or call, but now and then, I'll get regular texts from people at work and I panic.

"Hey," I respond, holding the microphone icon, "it was all right. Think I'm going to request a new tutor, though. Let's grab a beer soon."

The message disappears immediately, indicating that he's listened to it. And sure enough, my phone rings within seconds.

"What do you mean you need someone different? You're not backing out, are you? 'Cause I'll beat your ass if you try that crap." He says all of this before I can even say a word. "I've respected your privacy about this for years, but now that you've taken this first step, I'll be damned if I let you quit."

"Well, hello to you, too, man."

"I mean it. What's wrong?"

"I'm not quitting, so you can put the whoop-ass away." I let out a frustrated sigh. "It's the tutor. This girl."

"What? She smells bad? Has a big, hairy wart on her face? What's the problem?"

"She's young, for one," I hedge, avoiding the real reason. He'll tease me about it relentlessly.

"Oh no! Not young!" he says in mock outrage.

"Yeah, *young*. And, she's, you know…" *God, just say it.* "She's real pretty, man." I rub my eyes and hold the phone away a bit, bracing for it.

"*Oh*, I see," he crows, smug as hell.

"You don't *see* anything." I'm trying to hold on to a shred of my dignity here.

"Oh, but I do. You don't want this cute, young thing to get to know you in *this* way. This way that makes you feel bad about yourself." Damn it. He's spot-on.

"Okay, genius, you have me there," I admit. "But I'm heading up there at lunch to request someone new, and that's that."

A bell rings on his end of the line. "Dang, I gotta go. But you're not quitting this."

"Yeah, yeah."

He harrumphs. "Gotta run. Let's hit up Fuzzy's after work on Friday."

"Sounds good, man."

After hanging up, I gather all my gear and head out to start another grueling day with Statler Construction. My mind is occupied while I focus on the framing of a building that'll house a new business on the outskirts of town. It isn't until the manager signals lunchtime that I think about Tessa Burton again.

This is for the best, I tell myself ten minutes later as I open the door to the library and step into the cool, dark building in search of Mr. Weaver. No more big green eyes. No more perfect lips. No more excuses to avoid what I need to do for my daughter. *Yes, this is for the best.*

CHAPTER FOUR

TESSA

This Wednesday is giving Monday a run for its money.

I overslept, which I *never* do. And what's even more troubling is the *reason* I couldn't sleep last night.

Luke Shipley.

I couldn't stop thinking about him. I tossed and turned, agonizing over our first session. He was so uncomfortable. And I hate that I can't offer him a quick fix; there's no magic wand to wave or spell to cast that will take away his years of shame and illiteracy. I hate feeling helpless. And secretly, I also kind of hate how attractive he is. That's going to make this whole thing even more difficult because I cannot, *cannot*, like him like *that*.

And not just because he's my student and it would distract from the purpose of our sessions. But also—he's simply not the type of guy a girl like me *likes. Great, now I sound like a snob.*

So yeah, my Wednesday is not off to an auspicious start. On my way to Central to meet my friend Mel for lunch, I stop at the corner to wait for the road ahead to clear before I cross, and before I even realize what I'm doing, I'm scanning my camera roll for my morning pictures. *Boo.* Three times before lunch; that's gotta be a record. But there's no time to dwell because, moron that I am, I chose to walk the two blocks in the heat of the day. I'll be lucky if my makeup hasn't melted off my face before I get there.

DejaBrew is the only coffee shop in Bennett, and it's located on the ground floor of a two-story brick building downtown. There are large windows on either side of the door, and the word *COFFEE* painted directly above in white block letters.

The cool air and aroma of coffee hit me as soon as I step inside. Mel's already seated at one of the few tables, her lavender bob easy to spot. She's sipping on a green smoothie, and there's an iced mocha waiting for me across the table.

"Hey, hooker!" Mel whisper-shouts, looking up from her phone as I plop down in the chair across from her.

My cheeks blaze at the very inaccurate nickname. Never mind that we're the only ones in here besides Corky, the barista, who, unless he's waiting on customers, always has his AirPods shoved in his ears.

"Hey, yourself. Thanks for ordering," I say, taking a swig of the white chocolate mocha.

Mel "Only My Grandma Calls Me Melanie" Marshall is my only friend in Bennett. And we could not be more different. We met during my first week in town when she brought flyers to the library to advertise her yoga studio. She took one look at me as I reached for her stack of neon orange papers and said, "You're new here." I nodded sheepishly, and then she followed up with, "That settles it. We're going to have to be, like, best friends. You're looking at the only other single female under the age of fifty in this town." I highly doubted that was true, but I didn't tell her so.

Mel was aggressive with her friendship, but in a good way. She refused to accept that we wouldn't become best friends. Now, six weeks later, I can't imagine not having her and her strong personality in my life. She's good for me, even though my parents wouldn't approve. *Add it to the list, Tessa.*

Mel tucks a lock of her lavender hair behind an ear that holds several piercings. She's stunning, like a perfect mix of girly, rainbow, and emo, if that's even a thing. This hair color is the second shade she's sported since I met her. That first day, it was a bright turquoise. I like the lavender better, though. Today, she's wearing a black T-shirt that says *Perfectly Defective* in white letters over her dark purple yoga leggings.

"What's with your stressed face?" she asks after Corky has dropped off our sandwich orders. "Don't worry, I made sure he left off the sprouts." She sets about dunking her wrap in the vinaigrette and taking a big bite, her eyes locked on me curiously.

"I overslept," I explain, like it's a cardinal sin I'm confessing to a priest.

"Oh no, alert the media," she deadpans. Then she tilts her head and squints. "You know you're allowed to mess up, right? It's part of this thing called being human. The world won't spiral into oblivion if it happens. Frequently."

Her carefree attitude about life is one of my favorite things about her, and something I secretly envy. She truly marches to her own beat. Maybe some of that will rub off on me through our friendship.

"I know." I wave off her comment, eager for a deflection. "How was class this morning?"

Mel runs the yoga studio next to DejaBrew. Her family owns the entire building, and Mel's apartment is on the second floor. Mel's parents are what I would consider "Bennett Royalty." Her mom is the only doctor in town, and her dad is a successful real estate agent, also the only one in Bennett. Her older brother is a doctor in Columbus; he's married with twin sons Mel calls "Whosie" and "Whatsie," though she's crazy about those little boys.

Mel proceeds to tell me about this morning's senior yoga class—"Crazy Daisy in downward dog is a sight, I tell ya!"—her lighthearted story replacing my stress and self-loathing with warmth and delight. She's an incredible substitution for the therapy I really need to look into getting. One of the many things Bennett doesn't have? Mental health services. Time and time again, I've made a mental note to research therapists in nearby communities, but it always gets pushed to the bottom of the to-do list.

"Tessa." Mel's tone is abnormally serious.

And that can only mean one thing. She's going to say something I won't like.

"Drinks. After work on Friday. I won't take no for an answer this time," she states as we gather up our plates and napkins and stack them for Corky. I've jumped at every invitation Mel has issued since we met, except joining her at the local bar for drinks. Fuzzy's Tavern is packed on weekends. And crowds full of strangers make me anxious.

"I don't know," I hedge, my heartbeat accelerating as I scramble for yet another excuse for bailing on this particular activity.

Mel watches me with narrowed eyes. She's short, so the vision of her sizing me up while she's half a foot shorter than me brings a smile to my face. "I'll pick you up at five thirty. That should give you enough time to get home and change out of your librarian costume."

"Fine," I offer, secretly thankful that I still have two days to get out of it.

Mel blows me a kiss before we part ways at the door to Deja-Brew, and I stroll back down Central Street to the library. Mood elevated—because time with Mel is guaranteed to lift anyone's spirits—I'm thinking that this Wednesday just might be salvaged after all.

Once inside the building, I greet Shanice and start down the hall to my office. Before I can step inside, voices from Mr. Weaver's office, two doors down from mine, catch my attention.

Both voices are male, and one sounds frustrated. I drop my purse on the chair by my door and take a step toward the noise, already feeling guilty about eavesdropping.

"I'm telling you, I won't work with *her* anymore," an agitated voice spits out.

"I'm sorry, son, but we don't have the staff to accommodate that request. Tessa is the one who provides the service here in Bennett."

My stomach drops to my toes at the mention of my name, and my heart rate speeds up as it dawns on me who the other voice belongs to.

"There's gotta be someone at one of the other libraries. I don't mind the drive. I just don't think she's the right person to help me with this."

"All of our branches close at seven. By the time you get there, you won't get the necessary time in. And the Montezuma and Oglethorpe branches are already booked during that last block of time." Mr. Weaver's voice remains calm and collected. "Tessa is highly qualified for this type of work. She has a master's degree in reading. And since nothing negative happened during your first session, I truly don't see a problem with her being the one to help you."

"Look," Luke Shipley huffs out a breath. "I'm sure she's real nice and all, but it's not going to work. It's just not."

"I'm sorry, son. My hands are tied here."

The silence that follows has me panicking. I need to get back to my office and close the door pronto, before Luke comes out of the office and catches me.

Too. Late.

Luke, dressed in a neon yellow T-shirt that says *Statler Construction* on the front pocket, jeans, and work boots, comes barreling out of Mr. Weaver's door and freezes when he sees me standing in the hallway. Crap. From what I can see under the bill of that same Braves cap, he's angry, but he has the courtesy to drop his gaze, a guilty grimace replacing the scowl he wore when he halted in front of me. He's breathing heavily and massaging the back of his neck with one hand. He peeks up at me, the top half of his face in shadow, his mouth open like he wants to say something. But then he snaps it closed again. Because, after all, how does one explain the kinds of things he just said?

Me? In true Tessa form, I stand there, my mouth agape. *Say something!*

But I don't. Confrontation avoidance is my go-to strategy, and I shut down when backed into a corner.

Luke lets out a deep sigh that might be part growl and, head still down, storms to the front of the library. Frozen to the spot, I will my racing heart to calm, my feet to *move* already.

Fix it, Tessa.

I'm not sure where my body gathers this kind of moxie from, but instead of slinking into my office to cry like a baby, I turn and charge after him. I won't let him give up today.

Determined, I stalk out to the parking lot. His hand is already on the door handle of a navy crew cab pickup. It's now or never.

"Hey!" I yell across the lot.

He stops and turns, pinning me with those dark eyes. And that's when my mom's voice floats through my head, unwelcome as always. *Burtons do not confront people in parking lots.*

Shaking off the reprimand, I say, "You can't quit, okay?" I take a few steps closer, doing everything I can to hold on to the gumption that propelled me out here in the first place.

His eyes are mostly hidden by his ball cap, but I can feel them roving over me, even from several feet away. I will myself not to blush under his scrutiny, but my face heats anyway.

"Look," he says, rubbing the back of his neck again but not looking away this time, "it's not personal. I just don't think it's going to work."

Taking a chance, since I know little about this man or what

motivates him, I spit out, "You sure don't seem like a quitter to me, Mr. Shipley."

Welp, that did it. Maybe a tough love approach is *not* the way to go, because he narrows his eyes and jabs his pointer finger in my direction. "You don't know anything about my life. Yeah, I can't read. But I promise you the *last* thing I need is Ms. Ivy League thinking she can swoop in to save the day!"

"Ivy League?" I scoff. "UGA is hardly Ivy League!" I throw back.

Now it's his turn to scoff. And shake his head. And take a step closer.

Feeling bold for perhaps the second time in my life, I, too, step closer. Now we're only a few feet apart, the sweltering sun forcing me to shield my eyes with a hand.

Luke plants his hands on his hips, breathing heavily from his outburst. He drags his gaze from my face down to my espadrilles cooking on the hot concrete and back up again. That he's still standing here is a positive sign. I've *got* to convince him somehow.

"Look, Mr. Shipley—"

"It's Luke," he cuts in. "Mr. Shipley is my dad." Most of the vitriol is gone from his voice.

"Fine. Luke." I take a deep breath, calming and readying myself to make my best sales pitch. "I know this is overwhelming. It probably feels unattainable. And you're embarrassed. I get that. But you don't have to be embarrassed with me. I'm trained for this. Not *Ivy League* trained," I add.

At that, I get an eye roll. I'll take it. It's better than the daggers he was shooting my way.

"But I know what I'm doing. I can't promise you a quick fix. Or that you won't have frustrating moments. But I *can* promise that I will work tirelessly to get you where you want to be. You can trust me, Luke."

His internal struggle plays out across his face and body while

I watch him, waiting with bated breath. He stares at me for several moments, like he's weighing my words. Then he removes his cap and turns it backward. Hands back on hips, he kicks at the asphalt under him before letting out another sigh-growl combination. Then he looks up at me, squinting in the sun, and says, "All right, Ivy League. I guess I'll trust you, then."

It takes everything in me to not jump up and down in victory. Instead, I nod and offer him my biggest, most confident smile.

Stepping forward to shake his hand, sealing this promise between the two of us, I say, "Okay, Luke. I'll see you tomorrow night."

He dips his chin and turns back to his truck.

And I can't wipe the smile off my face all the way into my office.

Turns out this Wednesday isn't so bad after all.

CHAPTER FIVE

LUKE

pic. Fail.

That's the only way to describe my lunchtime visit to the library yesterday.

I went in determined not to leave without being assigned a new reading tutor.

I left with the same one.

And once again, Tessa saw me at my assholiest. (Nah, it's not a real word. But it should be.)

It's a wonder she doesn't want to quit on *me*.

And yet…

As we stood in that parking lot, something in her eyes made me take the leap. God knows why, but she believes in me. She really thinks I can do this, and her confidence in me filled me right up, coating my insides like warm, gooey syrup flowing from my core all the way down to my fingers and toes. For the first time in my thirty-four years, I feel like I have someone besides my parents and my best friend in my corner.

For the first time in my thirty-four years, I'm starting to believe in myself.

I've never doubted that I'm a good son, father, or friend. But in pretty much every other area of life? Yeah, not winning any awards. I'm not sure how I made it through school, to be honest. In high school, I had to pass my classes to play sports. I eked out a D average, and that was only because of Cordell's help. He'd complete assignments outside of class for me and slip me answers in the hallway between classes when he could. And somehow, I hid my troubles all that time.

I was just a kid who fell through the cracks.

In elementary school, it felt like everybody else picked up on how to read fairly easily. But I didn't understand how the words on the page didn't just pop into my head like they did for Cordell and the other kids. Didn't understand why I couldn't for the life of me remember words for spelling tests or how to put my thoughts to paper. I understood stories when they were read to me. But when it came time to read them for myself, I might as well have been looking at something written in a foreign language.

Now, though, I have hope that maybe Tessa can do what none of my teachers could.

After getting Hannah settled at my folks' place after school, I scarf down a helping of my mom's sausage casserole before heading back into town. My palms are slick on the steering wheel, not only from the heat, but because I've been such a jerk to Tessa both times I've been in her presence. And though she'd probably never believe it, the shitty attitude is out of character for me. But I can't help it. Because if I let my defenses slip? I don't even want to think about it.

I can't let myself think about how pretty she is. About how it would feel to run my fingers through her thick, silky hair. Or how perfectly her lips would feel brushing against mine.

Nope. Definitely not going there.

I make a promise to myself in the parking lot of the library: I absolutely, positively cannot allow myself to feel anything for this girl. My future depends on us keeping things strictly professional. Teacher and student. I've gotta keep my focus on the reason I'm here—learning how to read. So I can be a better father to Hannah. So I can help her as she grows. Hell, it might even mean a different job one day. Sure, I like what I do, but I imagine it might feel pretty incredible to have options.

I, Luke Shipley, do hereby promise to not let myself catch feelings for my reading tutor.

I'm resolute as I stroll through the front doors and past Shanice, whom I've known since kindergarten. Steadfast in my decision to stick with this, I don't allow myself to worry about whether she knows the real reason I'm here; if I do, I might bolt and never look back. Instead, I give her a quick salute and beeline for the study room we used on Tuesday.

Tessa's already there, hair pulled back in a low ponytail and smiling that sunshine smile in my direction. I want to punch parking lot Luke in the face. With a chair.

Nope. Professional adult student Luke is here to learn.

I take the chair across from her as she greets me with a hello.

I dip my chin in acknowledgment and lace my fingers, resting my hands on top of the table.

"Ready to get started?" she asks sweetly, pulling an alphabet strip out from between the pages of a notebook.

I nod. *Why can't I find my voice with this girl?*

"How do you feel about your letter-sound knowledge? Do you know the sounds that all the letters spell?"

Do I know my letters and sounds? Yes. The issue is everything that comes after that. But I don't elaborate. All I can do is nod mutely once again.

"Good," she breathes. "Just trying to get a baseline, see where we should start. This letter here." She points to the *E*. "How many sounds can it spell?"

She follows up with a few more examples, hitting the vowels and a few other random letters.

"So you're from Bennett, then?" she asks as she shifts papers around.

This is probably an attempt to draw me out since I haven't said more than five words to her this evening.

"Yep." I need to say more, give more than grunts and head nods to this girl, because I owe her for what a jerk I've been. She's taking time out of her day to help me. She deserves better, so I add, "Born and raised. But you're not from Bennett. How'd you end up here?"

She pauses and blinks at me. Probably a little shocked that so many words have left my mouth.

"I'm from Atlanta, but I went to school in Athens. I moved here six weeks ago to take over as children's library director for Macon County."

As she tips forward to place a laminated paper in front of me, I catch a whiff of her perfume or shampoo. It's coconutty, and I want to take in another lungful and keep it with me always.

But no. Professional adult student Luke would never. So to cut off that line of thinking, I ask, "How's Bennett treating you so far?"

"It's very different from Atlanta, that's for sure. But I like the slower pace. I like knowing my neighbors. Well, I *will* like knowing my neighbors once I *know* them. You know?" Her face quickly turns the sweetest shade of pink.

God, even this girl's blushes are adorable.

I offer a slight smile to put her at ease. "I know what you mean."

Tessa returns the expression and then proceeds to explain what she calls a "decoding screener." An activity that will help her pinpoint where I'm struggling.

"These aren't real words, so don't worry if they sound weird."

I struggle through the first three lines before she stops me.

She never nags me for having trouble with it, never loses her patience, never makes me feel slow or dim.

After the screener, she pulls out a handful of colorful plastic chips the size of poker chips. She explains that each one represents sounds in words and has me use them to count how many sounds I hear in words she calls out. She praises if I get the right answer and gently corrects and shows me *why* when I get them wrong. Finally, she uses the chips to change sounds in words. It's difficult at first, but as she shows me several examples, I start getting them all correct using the pattern of the chips' colors to help me remember the sounds. We do this for a big chunk of time, all without me seeing any actual letters or words.

Tessa glances at her watch and starts to gather the materials on the table. "Really good work tonight, Luke."

"Uh, thanks," I say, wishing desperately that our time wasn't up. I'm not ready to part ways, so in a rush, I say, "Listen, I'm sorry for being such a jerk to you. I promise my mama raised me better than that." I stand and push in my chair, then step around to the other side to do the same with Tessa's because she has her arms full of study materials. Being this much closer to her brings that coconut scent back.

She blushes again and shuffles the load in her arms. I extend my own arms in a silent offer to help.

"Oh, I've got it," she says, hugging the stack closer and padding toward the door. "And there's nothing to apologize for." She turns in the hallway that leads to the staff offices. "I understand how hard this must be for you. Just promise me, *promise me*," she emphasizes, "that you won't give up on yourself, okay?"

So I make my second promise of the evening, knowing damn well I'll probably only keep one of them.

～

Fuzzy's Tavern is crowded, even for an off-season Friday night. Cordell and I stand at the end of the bar that spans the whole left side of the room. Football season starts next weekend, so his Friday nights are about to be occupied until at least early December.

"Coach Watkins! Lemme buy you a beer!" a man yells across the space.

My best friend tips his half-full beer in the direction of the pool tables, his way of acknowledging that he's covered. To keep small-town gossip to a minimum, he usually sticks with the one beer when we come to Fuzzy's. No need to set the tongues wagging about the high school's head football coach getting wasted.

"How's Miss Hannah liking kindergarten so far?" he asks me as another tipsy resident gives him a high five on his way to the restrooms down the hall behind us.

"Loves it," I answer, scanning the crowd.

Ms. Daisy, my mom's boss, is cackling at a table with Ms. Rita Hewett, owner of the local thrift shop, and Cordell's mom, Ms. Rhonda. Rhonda gives me an enthusiastic wave when she sees me looking in their direction.

"Luke Shipley, man of many words." My buddy smirks and takes another swig of his beer.

"Ha" is my response, proving his point.

I feel good tonight, an unexplained excitement sitting in my gut. Feels like one of those rare nights where anything is possible.

A young couple vacates the stools we've been standing behind since we arrived, so we swoop in to claim them. I order another beer, vowing to nurse this one slowly since it'll be my last of the night. Cordell attacks a bowl of peanuts that Fuzzy's owner and resident barkeep places in front of us.

"How are the boys looking this season, Coach?" Gordon asks as he gets to filling a pitcher.

"Coming along pretty good, Gordo," he responds. "Spending a lot of time in the weight room, getting stronger. Getting faster. Looking forward to the season."

The anticipation the whole town feels for the upcoming season always pumps me up, almost like it did when we played ages ago. An end-of-season injury our senior year, coupled with the not able to read thing, dashed any football star dreams I may have had.

But Cordell lived those dreams, for a while at least. Not only was he a star wide receiver, but he's brilliant, so colleges were salivating over him like crazy during our junior and senior years. He was recruited by LSU and majored in kinesiology. With a 4.0 GPA, of course. After a star-making senior season, the NFL came sniffing around, and he was drafted in a late round to Tennessee, where he played for three seasons. An injury and his mom's breast cancer diagnosis brought him back home to Bennett. He nursed Ms. Rhonda through beating cancer's ass while coaching a winning season in his first year as head coach at Bennett High. He's a local celebrity and his mom's hero. He's pretty high on the top of my list, too.

The crowd groans as the jukebox plays "Come On, Eileen" for what has to be the fifth time. In a row. Pretty sure Ms. Daisy is responsible for that.

Cordell and I turn on our stools to people watch, chuckling at the back-and-forth between Daisy's table and a group of old timers who look like they've been here all afternoon. It's good-natured ribbing, the kind that happens when neighbors get together and alcohol is involved.

As the roaring laughter both groups join in on finally dies down, the air around me changes. A brisk, almost electric current courses through the place, making my skin prickle with aware-ness. And then? In walks Tessa Burton.

She's with Mel Marshall, who is pretty much her polar oppo-site. I've known Mel since we were kids, even though she's probably five or six years younger than me. Her mom is my doctor. And my parents' doctor. And Hannah's doctor. Pretty much all of Bennett sees Dr. Marshall.

Mel's hair is purple today; last time I saw her it was blueish. Then, like a magnet, my eyes are drawn back to Tessa. She's paused just inside the door, standing behind Mel like she's using her friend as a shield. Mel points to an empty booth beyond the pool tables and heads that way, and Tessa obediently follows with her head down.

On her trek to the table, I scan her from head to toe. She's wearing a pale yellow dress that's fitted at the waist with a flowy skirt that hits just above her knees, showing off smooth, shapely legs, and the same strappy shoes she was wearing when she chased me out to the parking lot. Tessa's got real-woman curves, and this dress highlights them perfectly. It's sleeveless, and as I trace my eyes along her bare arms, a shiver racks through her, like her body is responding to my inspection. Her thick brown hair is down, but it's not pin-straight like I've seen before; tonight, it's styled in gentle waves that are begging for my hands to run through them.

"Who's that with Mel?" Cordell asks, thankfully oblivious to the way I've been ogling.

Tessa darts a quick glance in my direction, a blush I can see from all the way across the bar staining her cheeks.

Fuck. Why do I find that so freaking adorable?

It pains me to look away, but I force myself to before I give the girl hives or something. And before I give Cordell the ammo that could wreck my whole professional adult student persona.

In my periphery, as more people approach Cordell to talk football, a waitress drops off a pitcher of beer and two glasses at Mel and Tessa's table. No fruity cocktails for my library girl.

No. Not *my* library girl. Not *my* anything.

We continue in this manner for a while. Me, nursing my beer, trying to keep my eyes from wandering back to that table, trying to keep my best friend from noticing how often my gaze lands there. And Cordell, throwing out comments here and there, sipping through a straw. He switched to Coke a while back.

"Want to order something to eat? I'm famished," he says, elbowing me.

Wanting any excuse to stay longer, I agree immediately even though Fuzzy's only serves nachos and wings. They're decent, though, so we each order both.

For the next little while, I try to pretend like Tessa Burton isn't sitting yards behind me, like I'm just here to scarf down nachos and wings with my best friend like it's any other night at Fuzzy's. All too soon, we're finished and Gordon is dropping off bills. We pay up, and while we're waiting to sign receipts, Cordell heads to the bathroom. As I'm standing behind the stool, making room for folks waiting for a seat and watching the baseball game on the TV above the bar, a feminine voice behind me says, "Well, aren't you a tall drink of water, Lucas?"

I spin around and tilt my head, looking right into Mel Marshall's hazel eyes. She's a lot shorter than me, so I have to practically tuck my chin to my chest.

I smirk, but before I can respond, a voice from my left says, "Nah. Mr. Six Feet Tall has nothing on me. All six feet and *four* inches of perfection right here." It's Cordell, back from the bathroom and in full flirt mode. It's his default when he's around Mel.

"Hey," I mutter, "it's actually six-one, thank you very much." As the words leave my mouth, Tessa sidles up to her friend. She gives me a shy smile and a slight nod in greeting.

"*One inch*? Like one inch matters," Cordell says with an eye roll.

"It matters," Mel chimes in, crossing her arms as she glares at Cordell, madder than a hornet.

"She gets it," I say, tipping my head in her direction. She's so short, I'm sure she hoards every single one of her inches.

In a flash, her angry eyes soften, and she pulls Tessa into her side, their obvious height difference comical. Tessa's got a good half a foot on Mel.

"Cordell, Luke, this is Tessa Burton. She moved to town a few weeks ago. She's my friend, so be nice to her. Or else."

Cordell shakes Tessa's hand. "Watch out for Ms. Marshall, here. She's trouble."

Mel's hands fly to her hips, and she gapes in mock outrage.

"Cordell is the head football coach at the high school," I explain to Tessa.

My best friend's eyes are on me, boring holes into the side of my head. "Well, aren't you going to be neighborly and introduce yourself to our new friend?" he asks me, tipping his head in her direction.

There's an awkward beat while I fumble for words, but Tessa beats me to it. "Oh, we've met before."

"Have you, now?" Cordell questions, that stare of his only intensifying. I feel it; the moment he realizes how we know each other, our conversation from a couple of days ago coming back to haunt me.

"Wait, you have?" Mel asks, her eyes darting from me to Tessa and back again.

"Y-yes," Tessa stutters, probably trying to work out an explanation that won't spill my secret. Just that little hesitation proves that I can trust this girl.

"We met at the library," I answer, my tone leaving no room for further questions.

Mel keeps squinting at us, one brow cocked , but eventually shrugs and moves on. "Well, boys, we best be heading out. We're having a best friends' sleepover at my place tonight. I even bought us matching unicorn pajamas." She says that last part with her hand bracketing the side of her mouth in a mock-whisper, like she's letting us in on a big secret.

I find myself trying very hard not to think about what Tessa Burton sleeps in.

The girls wave their goodbyes and head toward the exit. I want to offer to walk them to Mel's, but I don't need Cordell reading any more into the situation than I can guarantee he already is. And it's a short walk. Before she crosses the threshold, Tessa turns back, makes eye contact, and smiles shyly. The expression is so quick, I almost miss it.

For a moment, all I can do is stare at the space she just occupied.

"*Hmm,*" Cordell drags out obnoxiously beside me.

"What?" I groan. But I *know* where this is headed.

Instead of waiting for an explanation, I take a step toward the exit, but his big hand clamps down on my shoulder, stopping me. "Luke Shipley, I do believe you are crushin' on your tutor."

CHAPTER SIX

"Remember to sweep all the way through the word, beginning to end. Don't just guess based on the first letters' sounds."

Luke now knows I expect him to go back to the beginning of the row when I stop to correct him. The first few times it happened, he stiffened and almost shut down, like he couldn't stand to make a mistake. I imagine that's what he's done in the past when things got difficult; it's easier to give up than push through. So each time he flubs a word, I remind him: "Mistakes are another opportunity to learn."

Now, he just rolls his eyes good-naturedly at me.

We've been working together twice a week for a couple of weeks, making our way through the adult literacy workbook steadily. For the most part, he's been a model student, even if he's not very forthcoming some days. There are times when he can barely shake the frustration, and then there are moments when he's shocked himself with his progress. We've moved on from simple consonant-vowel-consonant words to words with beginning and ending consonant blends. He's doing well decoding, or "sounding out," the words in isolation but gets overwhelmed when faced with several lines of text on a page. He has a few high-frequency words already mapped in his brain: words like *the* and *have* and *you*.

Finding adequate decodable text for him to practice reading is a challenge, though. The workbooks are great but only provide fluency drills and word chains. There isn't any real-world text in them. And I don't want to embarrass him further by using actual children's decodable text; having him read *See Spot Run* at this point would be demeaning, even though the ability level would be appropriate. So I write out decodable sentences for him on a whiteboard and have him read them out loud to me. Often, I'll compose personal questions that he must answer in order to "unlock" the next sentence of text.

After he finishes the drills in the workbook, I ready the first whiteboard question.

"What deep, probing questions do you have for me tonight, Ivy League?"

Oh yeah. That nickname stuck. It's been Ivy or Ivy League since our third session.

Now it's my turn to roll my eyes, making his mouth lift on one side.

I bet his full smile is devastating. The real thing has eluded me so far, but I'm constantly on the lookout for one to light up his face. It's like gazing up into a clear night sky, wishing for a shooting star. I'm going to feel so absolutely honored if I get to witness one.

After I flip the board around so he can see it, he studies it for a moment, his eyes narrowing as he works to match symbols with sounds. "Wh-what is the b-e-st, best, tr-trip you have had?" He repeats it again, more fluently this time. "What is the best trip you have had?"

He purses his lips and pushes them to the side as he thinks this over. He's not wearing his usual Braves cap tonight, and his rich brown hair looks like it's been cut. The stubble on his face is shorter than I've seen it, too.

"Got it," he declares, sitting back and lacing his fingers across his torso. "My family didn't take many trips when I was a kid, but one summer we went to Myrtle Beach. I think I was eight—no, nine? My parents let me use my allowance to buy hermit crabs at the cheesy tourist shop on the beach. And my dad let my mom and me bury him in the sand. I think that's my favorite."

I love getting little glimpses of his life like this. He always lights up when he talks about his parents. He hasn't ever once mentioned a wife or girlfriend. I still don't know who Hannah is, and I haven't asked, scared I won't like the answer.

"Then again, I visited Cordell when he was at LSU once. That was a pretty fun weekend, even if it took me forever to get there in the beat-up pickup I had at the time. No air conditioning. Miserable. Plus, not being able to read street signs made that an interesting trip."

"Ugh, I can't imagine. He played football there, right?"

"Yep, he did." He tilts his head to the side and asks, "What about you, Ivy? Best trip ever."

He does this, volleys my reading practice questions back to me. But it doesn't feel performative, like he's just asking to fill an interpersonal expectation. It's like he genuinely wants to know.

But how do I answer this question without sounding obnoxiously pretentious? Do I mention the two-week European tour with my parents after I graduated from high school? Or the Hawaiian getaway when I was twelve? The many skiing trips to Colorado?

My cheeks and chest burn as I ponder my answer. He's watching me intently, those brown eyes taking in every part of my face, which makes me blush even harder.

"Let's move on to your next question," I say, quickly erasing the whiteboard so I can write the next one down.

"No way, Ivy. I want to hear it." He's smirking at me, like he knows exactly why I want to deflect. "Let me guess…African safari? Beach hut in the Caribbean? No, I've got it!" He snaps his fingers and points. "It was an expedition to the moon." He's making fun, but his tone also feels kind of…flirty?

Is he flirting with me?

Surely not.

I sigh heavily. "Fine," I give in. "Banff, Canada. My parents took me for my sixteenth birthday. I'd always wanted to see the mountains and crystal clear lakes. It was everything I hoped it would be."

"Outdoorsy, huh? Thought an Ivy League girl like you would pick Hollywood or something like that." He's still teasing, but not in a mocking way. Still with that undercurrent of flirtation.

"Enough with the Ivy League, Mr. Shipley," I say, giving him a mock glare.

His lips twist up like he wants to smile, but he's fighting it. I watch closely to see if it spreads into mega-wattage territory.

I can't help but feel a sliver of disappointment when it doesn't.

As I'm copying the next question onto the whiteboard, he asks, "It's just you and your parents, then? No brothers or sisters?"

"No, just me," I chirp, like the weight of carrying that burden doesn't plague me. "You? Do you have siblings?"

"No, just me," he parrots my answer back. "My folks tried for years and years to have another. When I was seven, my mom had a miscarriage. I asked Santa for a little brother every Christmas, but it just didn't work out." His voice is low, heavy with this confession.

My heart aches for him. And for his parents. "Oh, I'm so sorry, Luke."

He shrugs it off, almost like he's physically trying to shake the sadness off himself. "I guess you can't really miss what you never had."

Looking up at his handsome, solemn face, I know in my heart that isn't true.

September's heat carries on, the sticky mornings and sweltering afternoons making me restless. I'm ready to experience small-town life in the fall: pumpkins on porches and hayrides and cool nights. I go on about my days as usual: working at the library, checking in with each branch, binge-watching Netflix with Mel, and on Tuesdays and Thursdays, ending the day with Luke. I'm starting to like those days most of all.

We've stitched together a semblance of a friendship over the past few weeks, unraveling pieces of our personalities one thread at a time. He's stoic and proud, and like me, just wants to blend in.

Growing up, I never wanted to be seen as different from my peers, even though I most definitely was, so I kept to myself. I didn't have many close friends in high school, and only a couple in college. Letting Mel get so close, so quickly, has been difficult for me. I wouldn't change it, but it was hard to let her see the imperfect parts, hard to deal with the worry that she would find me lacking.

Luke is the same. He doesn't trust easily, but when that trust is earned, he becomes a rock-solid support. I want to be rock-solid for *him*.

As a friend. *Only as a friend*, I remind myself for the eleventy-hundredth time.

This afternoon, I finally get what I've been dreading for weeks—a phone call from my mother. The sight of her name and picture flashing on my phone screen triggers immediate stomach pain.

"Hello, darling, we haven't heard from you in a few weeks. Tell me you've got Internet service in that place." The disdain in her voice is hard to miss.

"Hi, Mom. Yes, we have most of the modern conveniences here in Bennett," I say, suppressing a sigh. "Sorry I haven't called. I've been busy settling in."

"Hmm, well, your father and I have been worried about you. We'd appreciate a check-in here and there so we know that our only daughter is alive and well, living in the middle of nowhere, Georgia."

"I'm fine, Mom, really." I bite back a huff. "I love my job. I love my apartment."

"We're so glad you're renting. How long is the lease? A year? No sense in putting down roots in that place, Tessa. You'll be ready to move on before we know it, I'm sure."

I hold my phone away, fighting the urge to groan. This is an ongoing argument with them. They think that my move is a grown-up tantrum on my part.

It's not.

I never want to go back to that life, but no matter how many times I try to explain this to them, they're not convinced. They argued with me for weeks about renting versus buying a home here. Though I hate to admit it, they won that battle.

Before we can get sucked into it again, I shift the conversation away from me. "You're probably gearing up for the big fall fundraiser with the Junior League about now, right?"

Success!

For the next several minutes, my mom goes on and on about the theme for the Halloween masquerade and the costumes she's picked out for herself and my father. My stomach remains a bundle of nerves while she goes into detail about table centerpieces and catering options and the latest gossip about people I grew up with.

"Guess who's moved back to Atlanta."

Oh no. I can guess where this is headed.

"I couldn't possibly guess, Mom." I need to end this conversation. Now.

"Tyler. Davenport." She pauses, probably waiting for me to respond.

I stay silent.

"You remember Tyler, don't you? You two practically grew up together."

Untrue, but I don't say so. The Davenports are wealthy friends of my parents'. Tyler and I went to high school together, sure, and we attended many of the same functions over the years, but we were not friends. He was a pompous jerkface, but I keep that to myself, too.

"That's great, Mom," I finally say, knowing she'll keep going whether I acknowledge her or not. I squeeze my phone in my hand, bracing for what's coming.

"He's so handsome, Tessa. He finished his MBA at Wharton and moved back home so Rich could groom him to take over the family business. Rebecca is still at Notre Dame. You remember her, don't you?"

"Mm-hmm."

Of course she'd focus on their college choices. The reputation of one's alma mater is more important to her than just about anything else in this world. Both of my parents and all but one of my grandparents attended Emory, so naturally, I was expected to follow suit. "It's the Burton legacy," they would say. Imagine their horror when their high school senior announced—at the last minute—that she would be attending the University of Georgia instead.

I can still hear my mother's response after minutes of stunned silence: *A public school? Tessa, don't be absurd!*

On top of that, I majored in library science instead of the expected political science, the gateway to the revered law school.

My dad's response to that one? *I think you're confused about your sciences, there, sweetheart.*

Oh, there were arguments. I was on a never-ending push-and-pull those last couple of months I lived at home. It was clear then that nothing I did going forward would be enough to atone for the choices I'd made.

"Anyway, I was talking to Helen at the club last weekend, and we were thinking that when you come back home for the holidays, you and Tyler should catch up."

And there it is.

I swear my mother's mission in life is to marry me off to the son of one of her rich friends.

Never mind that I'm never interested in them. Ever.

"We think you two would get along so well—"

"Mom," I interject, massaging the bridge of my nose with my free hand. I've got to nip this in the bud now.

"You have shared history, so that could be the basis for building—"

"*Mom.*" Forcing more strength into my voice gets her to finally stop talking. "I'm not going out with Tyler Davenport."

"Tessa Diane, why not?"

"First of all, I don't live in Atlanta. I don't plan on moving back. Why would I want to date someone who lives over two hours away? Also, he's not a nice guy."

"He's perfectly nice, Tessa. You have to stop being so picky. Maybe he was brash as a young man, but he's matured over the years, I'm sure."

"It's a no, Mom."

"But—"

"Mom. Stop."

She huffs an exasperated sigh, the sound crackling through the line. "Well, I need to run, darling." She might be giving in for now, but I know Kathleen Burton, and this is not the last time I'll hear about Tyler Davenport.

We say our goodbyes, and I feel—as I always do after a conversation with my mother—like I've just finished one of those high-intensity workouts, but without any of those feel-good endorphins that make the agony worth it.

I give myself a few minutes to shake off the disappointment that every one of her words was dripping with, then set about straightening up my apartment in preparation for a girls' night in with Mel. I bought all the ingredients to make our own pizzas, and she's bringing dessert. She's always in charge of dessert. She loves to bake the most bizarre cupcake flavors she can find. Most of the time, they're delicious despite their dubious combinations. Sometimes, though, they're disturbingly disgusting. I can only hope that isn't the case tonight.

Mel arrives a little after six with her lavender hair in pigtails and wearing cut-off jean shorts and a gray T-shirt that says one bold word: *Pants*. She's carrying a container filled with cupcakes in one hand and a bottle of Tito's in the other.

So it's going to be *that* kind of night.

She kicks off her Birkenstocks by the door and sweeps into the kitchen, immediately going for the glasses in the cabinet next to the sink.

"Okay, don't hate me, but I didn't have it in me to go off the deep end of cupcake mountain today. I went with dark chocolate bacon again."

I breathe out a sigh of relief. My favorite. This feels like a win after the phone conversation with my mom.

"What else did you do today?" I ask as she helps me set out ingredients for homemade pizza. I roll out the dough as she tells me about her day.

After another laugh-out-loud senior yoga story, we place toppings on our individual-size pizzas. Ham and pineapple for Mel and boring old pepperoni for me.

Boring and consistent—that's me.

The first time we made pizzas together, Mel teased me about my bland choices. And *old* Tessa would've taken it, laughed it off good-naturedly like it was no big deal. But *newish* Tessa, the one who took a deep breath for the first time in her life the second she stepped out of her Audi in Bennett, Georgia, looked straight at Mel, a very new friend at that point, and said, "Don't yuck my yum, and I won't yuck yours."

She regarded me for a long moment, sizing me up, before she said softly, "You know what? You're right. I'm sorry."

And it might be a tad overdramatic to think this, but that was a pivotal moment in our friendship. Mel learned that I won't *always* be a pushover, and I learned that Mel, though a force to be reckoned with, could admit her wrongs and apologize authentically.

It's during the pizza topping placement that I tell Mel about my conversation with my mother. She's never met my parents, but she's already not a fan. Her own parents, though as successful and career-driven as mine are, are warm and down to earth. Mel and her brother were raised to forge their own paths in life.

"So your mom is trying to play high-society matchmaker to get you to move back to the A-T-L?"

I turn on the faucet to rinse my hands and peek at her over my shoulder. "Pretty much."

"Ugh, that's gross. You're not a broodmare, T."

"Well, thanks, I think," I snort.

"That's the exact opposite of the type of man you need in your life," she says, leaning back against the counter as I place the pizza pans in the oven.

"Do tell. What type of man do I need, Mel Marshall?"

"A real man. A manly man. One who will treat you like a princess in public but ravage you in private."

He sounds perfect.

Refusing to let her see how red my heated cheeks must be, I focus on wiping up the mess we made on the counter. "Let me know where I can get one of those."

"Oh, I happen to know where you can find one."

When I turn back to her, she's still propped up against the counter, one foot crossed over the other. She's considering me carefully, holding her half-empty glass of Tito's and Sprite.

"Yeah, where's that?" I ask, crossing my arms and copying her stance.

Mel gives me a smug, *smug* smile and singsongs, "Ri-ight he-re. In Bennett."

I think I know where she's going with this, but I refuse to let her. I can't let her go there, because I can't let *myself* go there.

However, if Mel *is* thinking what I think she is, that means *he* is indeed unattached.

"So you met him at the library, huh?"

Dang it. She's not going to let me off the hook.

"Yep," I confirm, turning back to the kitchen counter clean-up.

"What was he doing there?" she asks behind me.

"Oh, you know…" I trail off, grasping for a reason.

Just say he was getting books, Tessa, like any other person would at a library.

But Mel snorts before I have a chance to respond and sidles up next to me. "He's not the adult literacy student you're working with, is he?"

Her question was posed innocently; she would never expect Luke Shipley to be the one I've been tutoring, but my cheeks flame as soon as the words leave her mouth.

"Oh shit." All the color drains from her face, and my brash friend's expression turns uncharacteristically bewildered. "Oh damn, Tessa." I watch as she collects herself and nods as if she's trying to work out the details.

All I know is I need a subject change—and fast. Thinking

quickly to divert her attention, I cry, "Ooh, it's your turn to pick our Netflix binge tonight. What's it going to be? Comedy or drama?" I push off from the counter, grab my drink, and head to the living room, hoping she drops it.

Please let her drop it.

I sit on my favorite corner of the couch, pulling my feet up under me, and grab for the remote. Mel's watching me from the kitchen, I'm sure, but I refuse to look her way, instead busying myself by pulling up Netflix on the TV.

But she doesn't drop it. Of course she doesn't drop it.

"That would be like a kick-ass way to fall in love, right? Boy meets girl, girl helps boy. It's like one of those meet-cutes in the romance books you like to read."

"Hmm" is all I can manage at this point. This conversation has me reeling. And worrying, because now she knows about Luke's reading difficulties. All I can do is scroll through the options on Netflix, hoping the promise of entertainment will distract her.

Finally, she pushes off from the counter and heads over to join me on the couch. When she rounds the trunk that serves as a coffee table, I finally peek up at her face. She's giving me that smug, knowing smile again.

But she doesn't say a word.

Taking advantage of the reprieve, I relax my tense muscles and settle into the couch cushions.

But I know Mel. She might have conceded tonight, but she will *not* let this one go.

I just pray I can hold her off a while longer.

CHAPTER SEVEN

LUKE

"**B**anana! I have to go, honey! I'm going to be late for my meeting!"

I'm standing at the door to the garage, hurrying my five-year-old along so I can drop her off at my parents' on my way back into town. The job I'm assigned to this week has become a bigger headache than we anticipated, and I didn't get out of there until after five.

Hannah's upstairs, whining about not knowing which toys to bring to her grandparents' house, like she doesn't have a million options waiting there for her already. I will myself to stay calm with her, even though this has been a day from hell and her five-year-old antics are wearing my already thin patience to a razor's edge.

"Hannah! *Now*," I bellow, using my I-mean-business voice.

She calls it my "Grumpy Daddy voice."

Accurate.

Finally, she stomps down the stairs as loudly as her little feet can actually stomp. I'd chuckle if I wasn't in such a foul mood.

"Fine," she snaps when she finally turns into the short hallway leading to the garage. Her appearance is in direct opposition to her mood—she's wearing her ladybug rain boots, even though it hasn't rained here for days. "I guess I'll just be *bored to death* at Nana and Papaw's." Her little arms are crossed and her lower lip wobbles.

Taking a deep, calming breath, I say, "Banana, you have every kind of toy imaginable up there. You'll have plenty to do. And I'll only be gone for about an hour." I glance down at my watch, cringing at the time.

There's no way I won't be late to meet Tessa. And I don't want to lose one minute of time with her.

I tell myself that it's because I want all the learning time I can get. That more time equals more reading practice, more sounds and letters and syllables. More time to grow into the reader I want to be.

You're a fucking liar, the devil on my shoulder whispers into my ear.

"I said *fine,*" Hannah huffs, glowering at me from where she waits by the back door of the truck cab.

I shake my head. The attitude on this one.

Hannah is the sweetest, most pleasant kid on the planet. She's full of joy and happiness most of the time. But when she's *not* that way…

"Lose the 'tude, ma'am," I tell her, lifting her up into the truck. She can heft herself up into it on her own, but we don't have time for that now. She settles in her booster seat and refuses to look at me, arms crossed again.

I hop in and waste no time throwing the truck into reverse and speeding down the gravel road. The door to my parents' garage is lifted, and before I'm even stopped, my mom is stepping out through the mudroom door. Normally, I park and walk Hannah in, but my mom probably realizes I'm running late, so she hustles out to get Hannah from the back.

"She's already had supper," I say over my shoulder. "And she's in a *mood,*" I add in a lower voice.

"Well, we'll cheer this June Bug right up!" Mom cheers, helping Hannah hop down from the cab.

I holler out a quick goodbye and pull away before they've even gone back into the house. The clock on the dash reads 6:02. It usually takes me a solid fifteen minutes to make the drive back into Bennett, but tonight, I do it in ten.

Wiping at my dirty Statler Construction T-shirt, I try my best to transform from dirt-covered, sweaty construction worker Luke into professional adult student Luke as I make my way into the library. I'm so flustered by the time I sit down with Tessa that I already feel like calling it in for the night.

But one look at her sunshine smile has me digging deep for the will to follow through.

"Hey, glad you're here!" she chirps. She doesn't question why I'm late or comment about my grungier-than-usual appearance.

"What's on the agenda for tonight, Ivy?" I ask, loving the way her nose scrunches just a bit when I use that nickname.

She starts off taking it easy on me, doing what I call her "listening games," where she'll say a word and I have to change, add, or take away a sound to make a new word. I don't really get how this helps with reading words on a page, but Tessa does, so I'll just have to trust her process. Even though I'm usually quick to answer these exercises, and answer them correctly more often than not these days, that's not the case tonight. It's like I brought the bad juju into the room.

But Tessa? She never gets frustrated or impatient with me. Even when I slap my hand on the table after getting yet another answer mixed up.

"Hey," she breathes, pausing the work. "You okay?"

"Yep." It comes out gruffer than I intended. But I don't apologize.

"Let's move on to fluency drills." Great. I hate these. Lines and lines of words to read in a row. Not sentences that make sense, just words that look similar that force me to really concentrate on the letter and sound combinations.

If I miss a word, I have to go all the way back to the beginning of the row. I could be on the very last word in the row, and if I miss it, I have to start all over again. Normally, I don't mind.

Tonight, it's agony.

A red-hot ugliness bubbles up from somewhere deep within, growing with each mistake I make. I'm so overcome with it, my hands shake, so I fist them tightly and hold them against my legs under the table. And to make matters worse, my ears are ringing and my heart is racing, like I'm a shaken-up soda set to go off.

And the very next time Tessa tells me to go back and try again, it spews out.

"I'm done here!" I yell, pushing back from the table so forcefully that half a stack of papers slides off the other side.

"Luke, mistakes are another—"

"Opportunity to learn. So you've said! A million times. And I keep messing up. All I do is mess up! I don't want to hear that crap anymore, Ivy! I'm sick of it! I'm sick of feeling stupid!" As soon as the words leave my mouth, I regret them. Not because they don't describe exactly how I'm feeling, but because my volume and tone cause Tessa to flinch. She doesn't say anything, just keeps her green eyes focused on the booklet in front of her, pressing her lips into a thin line, a flush slowly spreading over her face. Great. Now I've made her uncomfortable. I *yelled* at her, for Christ's sake, and I hate myself even more.

This self-loathing runs deep. How could it not? I can't even *fucking read*. Something so necessary to being a freaking adult, and I can't do it. I'm so buried under this enormous burden that I'll never claw my way out.

But, God, I'm so *freaking* angry. Angry that I've made it all the way into my thirties without these skills. Angry that I spent years suffering in school, absolutely miserable and embarrassed, without access to the proper help. Angry at myself because I should've done this years ago. Just angry at the whole damn world sometimes.

I tip forward, resting my elbows on my knees and dropping my head to my hands, willing the beast inside to calm the hell down. "I'm sorry," I mumble to the carpet.

She's quiet for so long, I almost look up to see if she's still in the room. Then her soft voice, a voice so kind and patient it makes the shame from my outburst burn in my gut, says, "Look at me, Luke."

I can't. I have to get these wild emotions running through my body under control first. My eyes fill with tears that I refuse to let spill.

"Please," she begs several long moments later.

I finally lift my head, finding her green eyes instantly. She's not looking at me with pity, thank goodness, but with understanding.

"You need to hear this, Luke Shipley, so listen up." That sweet, soft tone morphs into a no-nonsense one. "You. Are. Not. Stupid. You have reading deficits, yes, but that does not make you less intelligent than people who learned to read when they were six." She tucks a stray strand of hair behind her ear and scrutinizes me, one brow arched.

What does she want me to say to *that*?

I force down a swallow. "Tessa—"

"Nope. I want to hear you say it."

"What?"

"That you're not stupid. You need to say it, and you need to believe it."

"It's not going to change any—"

"Say it, Luke. Or we'll be here all night." She leans back in her chair, crossing her arms like she's issuing a challenge.

What is it with these girls crossing their arms at me today?

Not willing to call her bluff, I do as she demands. "I'm not stupid," I force out, the words feeling like a lie as they pass my lips.

"Hmm. You said it, but I'm not sure you believe it. *Yet*. But you will, Luke. I promise you will."

She collects the study materials from the floor and even the ones on the table. Panicked, I check my watch. We still have twenty minutes left. I don't blame her for wanting to cut this short, but I can't stand the thought of us ending this way.

"So we're done, then?" I ask.

"Nope, you still owe me twenty minutes, mister. We just need a change of scenery." She pops up out of her seat. "Help me lug this stuff to my office, would you?"

Change of scenery? What does she have in mind?

Trailing behind her, I'm struck with several inappropriate images of Tessa and me in a *very* different setting. Lips. Tongues. Hands. Limbs. Lots of smooth skin.

Dang, get your shit together, man.

I shake my head to clear those thoughts. Tessa is standing in her office, wearing a puzzled frown. Now it's my turn to look flushed.

I clear my throat and ask, "What did you have in mind, Ivy?"

That frown morphs into a grin. "Let's see what words this town has to offer us this evening, shall we?"

Confused, I follow behind her anyway. I would follow her anywhere at this point.

We say goodnight to Shanice, who's closing up shop, on our way out. Stepping out into the muggy evening air feels like stepping into a different world. I feel ten pounds lighter already.

The businesses that line Central Street, with the exception of Ruth's diner, are empty. The sun sits low in the sky, casting long shadows and making the town around us look like it's ready to tuck in for the night. Tessa drifts to the corner, heading toward downtown. I take a couple of long strides to catch up, then fall in step silently beside her.

I give her a puzzled look when she stops in front of Mr. Rusty's hardware store. Pretty sure Mr. Rusty closes up at five every day.

"Tell me what words you see," she says, lifting her hand in the direction of the door. There are words painted on the glass, as well as flyers taped in the windows. I catch sight of our reflections in the windows, and *damn, we look good together.* Tessa is wearing a flowy floral skirt that skims her knees, topped with a tucked-in maroon short-sleeved shirt. The cream-colored sweater thing she was wearing in the library is now draped over her arm with her purse. Me? I look like I just crawled out of the nearest dirt pit. Which is not that far from the truth, actually. But even though she's polished and shiny, and I'm dingy and dirty, we fit together somehow. Like a meant-to-be opposites-attract fairy tale.

But I'm definitely *not* the prince in this scenario.

Tessa's waiting patiently for me to focus on the words. I point out the few I know automatically, and she points to a few others so I can use what she's taught me so far. She praises my attempts, then turns, so I follow, continuing our journey down Central. We stop and do the same thing at several more businesses.

At the end of the last block, we cross over to the other side of the street and work our way back up in the direction of the library. As we approach Ruth's, I get an idea.

"Hey, Ivy, how do you feel about pie?" I ask.

"I'm generally in favor. Why?" She scrutinizes me, a little wrinkle forming between her eyebrows that I'm tempted to smooth away with my thumb.

Miraculously, I refrain. "Tell me you've had Ruth's pie, then."

"I have not had the pleasure, I'm afraid."

"That won't do." I scoff. "Ruth's is a Bennett institution. Got the best pie in the state of Georgia. The peach is a town favorite, but it's out of season, so you'll have to make do with either strawberry or chocolate, but I promise you won't be disappointed."

I pull the door open and dip my chin, gesturing for her to enter first. She hesitates for a moment, her lip caught between her teeth, before stepping inside the empty restaurant.

Ruth's Diner is the only actual sit-down restaurant here in Bennett. Sure, the coffee shop serves food during the day and a couple of food trucks pass through pretty regularly, but Ruth's is it if you want dinner in town. It's been owned by the same family for generations. The actual Ruth passed away when I was a kid, but I remember the way her white hair matched her white apron when she would wait on tables back then. Her two sons, who are a few years older than my parents, run it now.

"Looks like we have the place to ourselves. Counter or booth?" I ask Tessa, who still has an unsure look on her face.

"Booth," she answers, and I mentally fist pump. A booth means I'll have an excuse to look at her gorgeous face.

We settle into one along the front windows and pluck the laminated menus from behind the napkin holder at the end of the table.

"I've only been here once, with Mel. For breakfast one Saturday. It was good," she says, her eyes never leaving the menu.

"Everything here is good," I tell her. "My mom waited tables here as a second job when I was in school. I guarantee I've tried everything they serve."

While her eyes are still cast down, I take the opportunity to study her some more. Today, she's wearing her hair in a side braid draped over one shoulder. I'll have to ask Hannah if she'd like to try that one day.

Ms. Peggy comes out from the kitchen area and jumps when she sees us sitting at a table.

"Luke, I didn't realize anyone was out here waitin' on me!"

she hollers, pulling her notepad from the apron around her waist as she hustles over to us.

"No worries, Ms. Peggy. We're just here for pie."

"Always a good choice." She looks from me to Tessa and back again, the wheels no doubt turning in her mind.

Ms. Daisy will be getting a phone call tonight.

Weirdly enough, I *want* to be town chatter if Tessa Burton is involved in it with me. I *want* people in this town to assume things about us. That way, no other local bumpkin gets a wild hair to swoop in and steal her out from under me.

But I don't want Ms. Peggy to mention *anything* like that in front of Tessa, so I hurry this process along. "I'll have a slice of strawberry, Ms. Peggy."

"And for you, sweetie?"

Tessa wrinkles her nose in indecision. Her little button nose might be the cutest damn thing I've ever seen.

Other than my Banana.

"I can't turn down chocolate," she finally states, placing the menu back behind the napkin holder. Now that she doesn't have it to distract her, she has to look me full in the face.

"So," Tessa says, lacing her hands together on top of the table once Ms. Peggy has dashed off to slice up our pie. "Other than Ruth's eclectic offerings, what else do you like to eat, Mr. Shipley?"

"The better question is what *don't* I like to eat? That list is much shorter."

"What would you want for your last meal, then?" she asks, tilting her head and keeping her gaze right on me.

I soak up every inch of her face, starving for it.

Fuck, but she's beautiful.

"My mom's meatloaf, without a doubt. Mashed potatoes. Green beans. Cornbread." I list off my favorites without hesitation. "Oh, and Ruth's peach pie. Rounded out with a jug of sweet tea."

"I take it you've thought about this before?"

"For sure. Construction site conversations. I know *way* too much about the guys I work with."

She breathes out a soft laugh, the sound a buoy tied to my heart.

"What about you, Ivy? Last meal?"

"Hmm." She taps her lips with a finger, her chin resting on her hand. I think about those perfect lips way more than is decent, how the top one's slightly smaller than the bottom one. How I'd love to taste them. "I'd have to go with a breakfast-for-dinner situation. Eggs and bacon. Grits, hash browns. And biscuits, of course. What southern girl doesn't like biscuits?"

She says *biscuits*, and my mind goes straight to thinking about how I'd like to make her breakfast.

And bring it to her.

In my bed.

After a night where we don't do much sleeping.

Ms. Peggy rescues my brain from further torment by setting our plates in front of us. Tessa digs right in, taking a bite of her chocolate cream pie, closing her eyes, and letting out a little moan.

Shit.

Mind back into the gutter.

I shove a big forkful of strawberry cream pie in my mouth to distract myself. Again.

And again several silent minutes later when her tongue darts out and swipes a chunk of whipped cream off her fork. That's when I know I have to break the spell. Otherwise, I'll be in big trouble when I stand up from this table.

Nothing more sobering than talking about why we're really here, right?

So I offer Tessa another piece of my story as a way to make amends for losing my temper earlier.

"I never go to restaurants I haven't been to before," I confess.

She pauses mid-bite and surveys me patiently, waiting for me to continue. "Yeah, I can't read the menus, you know? So I hate going anywhere new because I have no idea what to order. If the menu has pictures, I end up pointing to one that looks good. But if there aren't any pictures? That's when my chest gets all tight, and I break out into a cold sweat, like I'm going into panic-mode or something."

Telling her that leaves me feeling exposed. But I want her to know these things about me. The hard things.

The things I've never told another soul.

Tessa sets her fork down, swallows, and takes a breath before saying, "I can't wait for you to discover all the new things this world has to offer you, Luke. I'm so proud that I get to be part of your journey."

Now my chest is tight for a totally different reason, and I have to duck my head to keep from giving away just how much those words mean.

We finish our pie quickly after that. By now, it's dark out, and I need to get home to get Hannah in bed.

"This is I'm-sorry-for-being-a-total-jackass pie," I tell her when she tries to pay for hers. She pushes back a little on it, but I come out the winner.

Our steps back to the library parking lot are a lot less leisurely.

"Thanks for the pie," Tessa says as she opens her car door.

"Any time, Ivy."

She gives me that little nose scrunch and half-hearted eye roll as she gets into the car. Before she closes the door, she calls out, "See you next week!"

All the way back to our land on Thigpen Road, I rub at the tightness in my chest that's been present since Tessa's last comment at the diner.

And I can't find it in myself to worry about how *right* that tightness actually feels.

CHAPTER EIGHT

TESSA

I wanted pumpkins. I've got pumpkins.

With a smile, I take in my surroundings. Pumpkins everywhere.

Appropriate for October. And appropriate for a fall carnival at an elementary school.

Shanice and I have just finished setting up our table. The surface is covered in library flyers about the services the county offers and clipboards with application forms for obtaining library cards. Secured to the front is a banner that reads *Carve Out Time to Read* with *Macon County Libraries* in smaller print beneath a picture of a friendly jack-o'-lantern.

I debated about that slogan for weeks.

In a chair next to the table, I've placed a life-size posable skeleton holding a book, with a sign around its neck that says *Dying for a Good Book*. Shanice keeps calling the skeleton a he, but I've secretly named her Scary Poppins.

Halloween is seriously my favorite.

Like, my love for it borders on unhealthy.

Growing up, I often wanted to morph into someone else because of how little I fit in with my peers. Donning a disguise for Halloween was a perfect little escape for me. October first is like Christmas morning to me because I get to spread Halloween happiness all over the library. Pumpkins and bats and witch hats and cauldrons and skeleton cats, everywhere.

This library sign-up event is one I've been looking forward to since I was hired. It's part of the library's initiative to partner with local schools to foster a love of books and reading in the places that reading happens most often. We've already held sign-up events at the one other elementary school in the county. Today, we're at Bennett Elementary's annual fall carnival.

I check the time on my phone, then force myself to lock it down again before going to my morning pictures. My Saturday routine feels off. This morning, I even had to go back upstairs to check that I remembered to lock my door, even though I'd already snapped my daily picture. I take a deep breath and slip my phone into the back pocket of my jeans.

As a family of four approaches and Shanice launches into our typical sales pitch, I observe the goings-on of the carnival from where I sit. The majority of booths are set up outside. But according to Shanice, the cakewalk is always held in the gym, and it's a must-visit activity. Mel even baked four dozen cupcakes to donate for the event, even though she doesn't have kids. That's one lovely thing I've discovered about small-town living: neighbors always willing to help each other.

Spread out across the playground are several typical fall carnival staples: a hayride that Mr. Rusty is running using his tractor and trailer, a hay bale maze, and the jack-o'-lantern carving station, among others. To our right is a face painting booth next to another that sells shirts that feature the local schools' logos. There's a coffee station set up by DejaBrew, and the delicious savory scents of Mel's favorite food truck waft through the air. Taco Tuesdays serves the best street tacos in the south, according to her.

Kiddos of all ages are dressed in their Halloween costumes.

Tiny Batmans and princesses and witches and ninjas dart from one booth to the next in excitement. Being around kids all the time brings about an odd kind of nostalgia. Not so much for the childhood I had, but for the one I *wish* I'd had.

Then *those* thoughts make me feel like a selfish cow, because I wanted for nothing as a kid. Materially, at least. Emotionally is a whole other matter.

Shanice's husband and son come by to show off his face painting choices. They're a precious family, and just looking at them makes my heart pang in an unwelcome way.

Will I ever have that?

Will I ever be loved the way I long to be?

Will a man ever look at neurotic, stressed-out Tessa Burton and want *her*, flaws and all? Or will I be forced to settle for someone of my parents' choosing, destined to live a life exactly like the one I've tried so hard to leave behind?

Calm down. You're only twenty-six. Plenty of time to worry about that.

Right.

Shanice's voice breaks into my thoughts. "A little bird told me you were on a date with Luke Shipley a few weeks ago."

My face blazes with the heat of a thousand suns.

"Wh-what?" I stutter.

Shanice smiles like the cat who got the cream. "Yep. Darrell heard it down at the station. Said Mikey heard it from his Aunt Daisy."

I glance around, making sure no one is within earshot. "Um, no. That is *not* what happened."

"So you weren't eating pie together at Ruth's?"

"Um, we were, I guess," I stammer. "But it wasn't a date. Not even close. It was just a friend thing. Like two friends getting pie. That's a thing, right?"

Shanice presses her lips together and squints. "It might be a thing where you're from, but here in Bennett, if you have pie with a boy, it's serious."

No. This cannot happen. I cannot let my professional and personal boundaries get crossed. I'm Luke's tutor, and it's my job to give him the help he needs. Nothing more.

I open my mouth to say all this to Shanice when she prattles on. "You could do a lot worse, you know. That white boy is *fine*."

I gape in shock. I can't even find the words. But all she does is give me a smug smirk.

Finally, I recover and sputter out, "Please. It's not like that. I can't have people thinking that about us." Realizing how utterly snobbish that sounds, I follow up with, "He's great, like really great, but it isn't like that. I'm helping him, that's all." I keep it vague. Shanice works at the library, so she knows why Luke comes in to work with me twice a week, but I don't want to betray him by talking to others about our meetings. It's bad enough that Mel figured it out because of me.

Shanice's smirk is replaced with a warm smile. She sways closer, places her hand on top of one of mine, and says, "It's just small-town gossip; it'll blow over in no time. I've known Luke since kindergarten, and he really is a stand-up guy. Comes from a wonderful family. But I respect your professionalism, girl. Won't say anything more about it."

I give her a grateful smile and take a few long breaths, reining in my out-of-control heart rate.

Crisis averted? Gosh, I hope so.

But I can't help but give in and pull my phone out to check the morning pictures after that bombshell.

The next couple of hours pass by quickly. Our booth is nowhere near as busy as the others, though, so around lunchtime, I shoo Shanice off to spend time with her family. She offers to bring me back a funnel cake, and then she disappears into the crowd.

I'm lost in rereading one of the picture books I brought for our display when the shuffling of little feet snatches my attention. And when I close the book and look up, the cutest little girl stands on the other side of the table, perusing the items I've laid out with a serious furrow to her brow.

"Hey there, Jelly Bean," I say. "Whatcha looking for?"

She gives me a big smile, cheeks rounded, and says, "What kind of game is this?"

"It's not a game like the other booths. It's a place to sign up for a library card. So you can come visit us and borrow books."

She tilts her head thoughtfully, her attention back on the books on display. Her long dark hair is styled in a perfect french braid, topped with a thick fabric headband in Halloween colors.

"Your hair sure is pretty," I tell her. I glance around the area but don't see a grown-up in the immediate vicinity.

She grins and gives a little giggle. "My daddy did it!"

"And I love your outfit!" I exclaim, wanting to keep her here until a parent or school official comes this way.

She steps back from the table, pointing one miniature black Converse to the side to give me a better peek at her ensemble. Her purple T-shirt features a glittery black cat, and when she twirls, her black ruffle skirt flares, showing off her lime green and black striped leggings.

After the spin, she puts her hands on her hips and looks me up and down like she's taking in my outfit as well. I've paired my boyfriend jeans with a Halloween graphic tee and an orange three-quarter length sleeved cardigan.

Can't leave home without one.

She nods appreciatively at what I'm wearing. "I like your outfit, too," she says, her voice a little flatter, like she's not quite impressed but she's already learned how to be polite.

I'm about to ask where her parents are when a deep voice several yards away shouts, "*Hannah!*"

Luke Shipley gently pushes his way through a crowd of

stragglers and stops when he lays eyes on the little girl standing in front of me. An immediate look of relief takes over his face, and he strides to the table.

Going down on one knee to get eye level with her, he takes her shoulders in his hands and says, "How many times have I told you not to wander off like this? You had me scared to death, Hannah!"

Hannah.

So *this* is Luke's Hannah.

"I'm sorry, Daddy," she says in her sweet voice.

He huffs out a deep breath and pulls her in for a hug. "It's okay, Banana. Just don't do it again, okay?"

"Yes, sir."

Luke finally looks up in my direction. His frantic expression brightens when he catches sight of me.

"Looks like you made a new friend," he says, standing. Though I'm not sure whether he's talking to me or his daughter.

He takes Hannah's little hand in his large one and gives her arm a little shake. "This little fugitive is my daughter, Hannah. Also known as Banana." He smiles at me, then looks back down at his daughter. "Hannah, this is my friend Tessa."

Hannah is the spitting-image of her dad. Same dark hair and eyes, same perfect nose. She's absolutely precious.

Her father is absolutely precious, too. But in a much more grown-up, manly way.

Today, he's wearing jeans, like usual, but these are not his dusty work jeans. Oh, no. These are fit-him-just-right, lived-in-but-not-ratty jeans, and they are glorious. Instead of his typical T-shirt, he's got on a plaid button-down. It's untucked, and he's got the sleeves rolled up to his elbows, showing off strong fore-arms and that tattoo sleeve that does funny things to my belly. His thick hair is styled in a haphazard I-didn't-try-to-fix-it way that just *works* on him. That chiseled jawline sports just a hint of growth, enough to make me wonder what it would feel like under my fingers.

To quote my friend Shanice: that white boy is *fine*.

And at that moment, the professionalism that I've been clinging to for dear life slips. Just a little.

No, I tell myself. *Rein it in.*

"Nice to meet you, Hannah Shipley," I say, rounding the table and crouching to offer her my hand. She takes it and knows exactly what to do but smiles shyly at me as she does it.

It's then that I notice Luke is carrying a goldfish in a clear plastic bag.

"Oh, did you win a fish?" I ask the little girl.

"My daddy won it for me!" she exclaims, her chest puffed out and her eyes alight with pride.

I drag my attention to him, finding him watching me, his gaze laser focused. And that's when I know without a doubt that he's heard the gossip about us, too. He blinks a couple of times as if he's trying to clear his mind and says, "Yeah, nothing like a temporary new pet, huh?"

I regard Hannah, hoping to soften the future blow, and say, "You know those guys can only be your pet for a few days, right?" Just thinking about all the kids taking home a goldfish today is kind of depressing.

"Yeah, Daddy warn-ded me already." Her hand still locked in her dad's, she swings her arm back and forth. "Daddy, Ms. Tessa says we can get li-berry cards here. Can we?" She turns those wide brown eyes to him.

Oh, he's a goner with this one.

"'Course, Banana."

Hannah takes a clipboard from the table and hands it to her dad, and when he's got it clasped in his hand, his attention fixed on the form clipped to it, panic flashes across his face.

"Here, why don't you tell me your information so I can get this filled out for y'all?" I say, holding out a hand.

Luke nods, one side of his lips kicking up. "Sounds good, Ivy."

Luke relays the information for the forms, including his address and phone number, and I get all the necessary spaces filled in.

"Okay, Jelly Bean, we'll stick your library card in the mail, and you should get it in a couple of days. Sound good?"

Hannah nods, her hands clasped in front of her chest like it's Christmas morning and she's just opened the gift she asked Santa for.

"And talk your dad into bringing you to some of our Saturday story times, okay?"

"I will," she promises. "Daddy, can we go carve my jack-o'-lantern next?"

"Sure thing, Banana," he says, searching my face again.

At his inspection, my face, neck, and chest grow hot. Darn it. This blushing is out of control.

Hannah chimes in, "Can Ms. Tessa carve pumpkins with us?"

"Oh, I'm pretty sure she's busy, honey," he tells her, but his eyes never leave mine. It's like there's an invisible force keeping us from looking away.

Hannah continues, "*Please*? Ms. Tessa, you want a jack-o'-lantern, right?"

I finally find the willpower to drag my attention away from him and focus on the little girl at his side.

"You want to know a secret?" I lower my voice and whisper, "I've never carved a pumpkin before." It's true. As a child, my parents never allowed such messy activities, and when I was finally on my own in my dorm room, I didn't really have the space to go about it.

I've lived on this planet for twenty-six years, and I have never carved my own jack-o'-lantern.

It's a travesty, really.

Luke widens his eyes at my confession. "That needs fixing, pronto," he says.

I hold my arms out and shrug in a what-are-ya-gonna-do gesture right as Shanice steps up to the table.

Oh crap.

"Hey, Luke. Hey, Miss Hannah," she greets them.

They say polite hellos, and then we all stand and look at each other awkwardly for a moment.

Hannah, bless her heart, breaks the silence. "We need Ms. Tessa to come carve jack-o'-lanterns with us. Right, Daddy?"

Shanice turns her head in my direction but doesn't take her eyes off Hannah. "Well, that's fine with me. I can hold down the fort for a while."

Silently, I will her to look at me so I can try to telepathically communicate what a bad idea this is, but she's not biting.

Oh crap.

"Looks like we're going pumpkin carving, Ivy." Luke's deep voice pulls my attention back to his face, and what I see almost knocks me back a step.

A smile.

A full, uninhibited Luke Shipley smile.

Straight white teeth. Tiny laugh lines crinkling the corners of his brown eyes. The barely

there indentation of a dimple peeking through the stubble in each cheek.

I was right.

It's devastating.

I'm so hypnotized by it that I don't realize Shanice is guiding me out from behind the table until I'm standing just a few feet away from Luke and Hannah.

"Lead the way," he tells his daughter, and I numbly follow behind.

And it isn't until I'm seated at one of the cafeteria tables that's been placed outside that I shake loose of the spell that smile put me under.

Luke sets about choosing two perfectly proportioned pumpkins, then talks me through how to cut a top in mine. As we get both tops cut and work on pulling out the "guts," as Hannah calls them, I find myself stealing glances at Luke. The way the muscles in his forearm bulge when he scrapes the inside of Hannah's pumpkin to loosen things up for her. The calm, sure way he directs her, making sure he handles all the dangerous parts himself. He consults her about what kind of design she wants and then draws it on with ease. The quintessentially traditional jack-o'-lantern face is perfectly symmetrical.

When I ask if he'll draw on mine, too, he obliges and offers me another knock-my-socks-off smile. Then he spins my pumpkin around, searching meticulously for the best side to carve the face.

I love that he takes jack-o'-lantern-ing so seriously.

Hannah, of course, becomes bored during the tedious process of carving out the design and asks to join the bouncy house line that's set up to our left. He gives permission but makes it clear he will have his eyes on her the entire time.

"So you have a daughter," I say casually as I start on my pumpkin.

"I do."

"She's precious, Luke."

He gives me a wry smile. "She knows it." But there's a sense of pride in his voice.

He's a good *daddy*, I think wistfully.

"How old is she?"

"Turned five in June. She started kindergarten this year. That's why I'm doing what I'm doing, you know. For her."

I pause my carving to search his face. He's still concentrating on his own work, but he nods determinedly as he continues.

"Hannah and I have been on our own since she was two. My

folks help out a ton, but I'm her only parent. And I hate the idea of not being able to help her with schoolwork and stuff."

"Where's her mom?" I ask softly, immediately cringing. I'm probably being too nosy.

"Her mom." He pauses like he has to build himself up to continue. "Shelley and I were not a good fit from the start. Honestly, I don't know that she's a good fit for anyone. But we met at Fuzzy's one weekend; she was staying in Oglethorpe with a cousin at the time. She was young, but I..." He trails off, staring at the pumpkin in front of him, carving tool in hand. "*I* should've known better. I was six years older than her, and I was lonely. My best friend, Cordell—you met him at Fuzzy's—he was helping his mom through her chemo treatments, and we never saw each other. Not that I'm blaming him, but he probably could've talked some sense into me. My mom tried. She met Shelley once and knew it wouldn't last. But I was an idiot—we both were because we weren't careful." He places the lid back on top of Hannah's pumpkin and slides it back, inspecting it. "When she told me she was pregnant, I offered to marry her, but she refused. Said she didn't want to be tied down. Like having a kid won't force that on you anyway.

"After Hannah was born, we lived with my folks. She didn't really like being a mother, but she stuck it out as long as she could, I guess. She started going out again around Hannah's first birthday, not coming home some nights. I wanted to be done, but she's my kid's mom, so how could I kick her out? But even when she was there, she wasn't really *with* us, you know?"

I nod, taking in his downturned lips, the soft, sad eyes he keeps focused on the table, wishing I could grab for his hand, comfort him. But I refrain. Professionalism, ladies and gentlemen.

"A couple of days before Hannah turned two, Shelley came home after being gone for two nights, told me she felt like she was suffocating here, with us, and packed up her stuff."

"I'm so sorry, Luke. Has she seen Hannah since then?"

He shakes his head. "Signed away her parental rights and everything. But I guess I'm okay with that. I don't want an unreliable, unstable adult in Hannah's life. I can be everything she needs."

"She's a very lucky girl," I tell him.

He gives me a small smile in thanks, then says in a much brighter tone, "So, Ivy, how was your first pumpkin carving experience? Everything you hoped it would be?"

"More." I spin my pumpkin so he can check out my finished product.

And there it is. Luke Shipley smile number three.

Luke's easy, loving interactions with his daughter revealed a whole new side of him today. As the weeks have gone by, I'm finding myself deeply drawn to every facet of him. Today compounded my intrigue tenfold. And that can't be good for my professionalism.

But I'll let Future Tessa worry about that.

CHAPTER NINE

LUKE

"I want to name him Nemo," Hannah tells me from her perch up on my shoulders. She's resting one hand on the top of my head, and she's got the goldfish in its bag gripped in the other. Very tightly, I hope. I'd hate to have to witness a skydiving goldfish today. But I have to trust her with it, considering I'm carrying a pumpkin while simultaneously keeping a Banana balanced.

"Remember what we talked about. Nemo will probably be a short-term guest only."

"And then we send him back to the ocean?" she asks.

Well, that's one way of looking at a flush down the toilet.

"Sure, honey."

Please let this damn fish die overnight so I can get rid of the evidence before she wakes up.

We're almost to the truck when Hannah pipes up. "The li-berry lady called me Jelly Bean and said my hair is pretty."

"Yeah, she's nice, huh?" I say, instead of what I'm really thinking.

Which is: *Yeah, Banana, I like that li-berry lady, too. Maybe too much.*

Hannah chatters all the way back home. This was her first school carnival, and to her, a visit to school over the weekend is magical. I listen to her stories and respond in the right spots, but my mind is on someone else.

Someone whose natural caramel-colored highlights caught the autumn sunlight while we carved jack-o'-lanterns. Someone whose big green eyes are hard to look away from. Someone who would probably never go for a guy like me.

Single father.

Blue-collar job.

Tattooed.

Can't read.

The deck is stacked against me. At least I'm working on that last one.

What could someone like *me* possibly offer someone like *her*?

I don't know what possessed me to open up to her about Shelley. I could've just given her a short answer that invited no further questions. But again, I find myself wanting her to know *all* of me. Even the not-so-favorable parts.

When we pull into my parents' drive, my dad's outside working on the Camaro again. He raises a hand in greeting but doesn't remove his head from under the hood.

"Can I stay out here and talk to Papaw?"

"For a bit. Let's see what Nana has planned for dinner." We don't eat at my folks' every night, but they'd love it if we did.

Mom's in the kitchen slicing tomatoes. I give her a quick peck on the cheek in greeting and grab a stool at the bar that separates the kitchen from the dining area.

"How was the carnival?" she asks, spinning toward me, knife still in hand.

I hold up Nemo's bag as an answer.

She rolls her eyes. "Oh great. That thing won't last the weekend."

I grunt in agreement and set the bag on the bar, being sure to arrange it so it won't fall off.

"We're having sandwiches for supper. You and June Bug gonna stay?"

"Yeah. Thanks, Mom."

"Of course." She turns back to the cutting board, but not before giving me a long once-over. Which means she's got more on her mind.

And sure enough, she says, "How come I have to find out from my boss that my own son is seeing a girl these days?"

Yeah, I've been waiting for this since that night at Ruth's. Why it's taken her a couple of weeks to bring it up is the real question here.

"Been holding on to that one for a while now, huh?" I smirk.

"Lucas William Shipley, don't sass me. Tell me about this girl. Daisy heard from Peggy that the two of you had pie together." She says *had pie together* like it's code for something scandalous. "And yes, you know I heard about it the very next day. I thought I'd give you a chance to tell me about it yourself. But here we are, weeks later, and I haven't heard a peep about it from you. So spill it—before your father comes in and tells me to stay out of it."

"Slow your roll, Marjorie," I say, chuckling. She pretends to hate it every time I call her that, so I make sure to do it at least a couple of times a week. Then, more subdued, I add, "There's nothing to tell. We're not dating. She's my reading tutor at the library. And no, I'm not going to ask her out. And we aren't going to get married and have a million babies or live happily ever after, so let's just put this to rest already."

She glares. "Lucas."

"Mom." I mimic her expression.

She stomps her foot just a little. Now I know where Hannah gets that from.

"Why not?" she asks with a whine.

"Drop it, please."

"Daisy says she's single and new in town. She's renting one of the apartments in the old Schubert house."

Great, now I know where Tessa lives.

Enter: me, finding any excuse to drive by every time I'm in town, hoping to catch a glimpse of her coming or going.

"She sounds like all kinds of good for you, Luke. So what if she's your tutor?" She tilts her head, dark eyes that match mine full of hope.

"Mom. Seriously. She's my tutor. And she's younger than me."

"Pfft. I'm younger than your father. So what?"

"A *year* younger. Tessa's like *eight* years younger than me." I run a hand through my hair, frustrated. I cannot let my mom get her hopes up about this.

Just like I can't get *my* hopes up.

"Look, she's a nice girl, but she's not the one for me." The words taste bitter coming out.

I don't make a habit of lying to my mother. But self-preservation demands it this time.

"Fine," she finally responds, her voice resigned. But she's got a steely look in her eyes as she plates the tomatoes and lettuce for sandwiches.

I might have shut her down for now, but I know Marjorie Shipley. She's like a dog with a bone.

And there's no way she's giving up so easily.

Chants of "Go, Eagles!" carry through the air as Hannah and I make our way up the bleachers to where my parents are already seated. The stadium is mostly full tonight, spectators in red and white shirts and hats crowded together on the metal bleachers.

My family has season tickets, so we never have to worry about finding a seat. The Shipleys have attended every Bennett High home game since Cordell took over as head coach. Tonight's homecoming game is bound to be even more crowded than usual.

A wave of nostalgia hits me like it does every time I take in the field. It's the only place I ever felt like I belonged when I was a student here, the only place where I could show people my worth. I was the starting quarterback for the Bennett Eagles for two seasons, and Cordell was the star wide receiver who caught pretty much every ball I put up.

Now, I get to watch my best friend coach a new batch of knuckleheads to greatness. And I couldn't be prouder.

"There's Uncle Dell!" Hannah yells when the Eagles take the field. Like always, as soon as he gets settled on the sidelines, he finds us in the stands and raises a hand in a salute before turning back to get down to business.

"Can I get nachos?"

Before I can respond, my dad stands to make his way down the aisle. If Hannah asked him to jump, he'd ask how high.

"You want something, kid?" my dad asks. After we all relay our concession stand orders and decide he probably can't carry all of it by himself, so I follow him down the metal steps. The line is frustratingly long, and I'm mentally cursing about missing so much of the game when my attention snags on the figure in front of me.

Before I make my presence known, I take advantage of my position and let my eyes travel from the wavy brown hair to the jean-clad curves to the red Chucks and back up again.

Damn. This girl can wear some jeans.

Stepping closer, I get a whiff of that coconut-rich scent of her shampoo, then, in a low voice, right next to her ear, I say, "They don't serve pie here, Ivy."

Tessa startles, then spins wildly to see who's creeping in on her personal space. Her hand flies to her chest and her face matches her shoes when her eyes meet mine.

"Luke! Gosh, you scared me!" At the exclamation, Mel Marshall, who's standing next to her, turns and gives me a big grin and a high five.

"Happy homecoming!" she says.

"You too." I nod in her direction. My focus, as usual, finds its way back home almost immediately, and I'm soaking in the warmth of Tessa's shy smile again.

Mel greets my dad in about the same way, then introduces him to Tessa.

"Good to meet you, Tessa," he says, taking her offered hand in his.

"You sittin' in your parents' seats tonight, Mel?" he asks her as we all shuffle forward a few steps. Mel nods, sending a wave of mixed emotions coursing through me. Because the Marshalls sit in the row in front of us, right next to Cordell's mom. While I'm excited about the prospect of being so close to Tessa for the next couple of hours, my mom—if not the whole town of Bennett—is about to have a field day.

Mel and Tessa make it to the front of the line, collect their orders, then give us little waves as they head back to the stands. Once the girls are gone, my dad's eyes are locked firmly on me. Keeping my attention trained on the cashier in front of me, I rattle off our order, worried that if I make eye contact with him, he'll know.

Hell, he probably already knows.

"That the girl your mama wants you to date?" he asks in a low voice, leaning in close.

Still not looking at him, I nod.

"She's cute, kid."

"Pop—" I start, turning his way.

He holds up both hands in surrender. "Just sayin'. You been alone since Shelley ran off. Just thinkin' it might be nice for you to have someone sweet to spend time with. But I won't bug you like your mama. We just want you to be happy."

"'Preciate it, Dad." When the teenager returns to the counter with two armfuls of snacks and drinks, I snatch up as much as I can carry and step to the side, desperate to end this father-son bonding moment. My dad takes the hint, paying, then following suit with silently collecting our concessions. He's good at giving me space to sort out my thoughts and feelings—unlike Mom, who just can't help herself.

Hannah, of course, has already gravitated to the row in front of us when we return. She's standing in front of Tessa, rocking her little body side to side shyly. Tessa's holding Hannah's hand in hers, inspecting the nail polish my mom painted on last night while I had tutoring.

That not unpleasant tightness hits me in the chest at the sight of the two of them like that. I shake it off as best I can and open my mouth, ready to demand that Hannah let them watch the game in peace, but then my little girl catches sight of me and shouts, "Daddy, it's the li-berry lady!"

Soft laughter trickles out around us. Ms. Rhonda has taken her place directly in front of us, and Ms. Daisy and Ms. Peggy are in their usual spots to her left. Looks like this meeting of the Bennett Gossip Club has been called to order. The whole lot of them are exchanging not so sneaky looks, raising brows, and grinning like fools. Even Mel shoots my mom a smirk.

Let's just say that there are a *lot* of eyeball conversations happening around me.

"Banana, let's leave Ms. Tessa and Ms. Mel alone so they can watch the game. And your nachos are here, too."

Mom swats at my arm playfully and scolds, "Oh, let her be. It's not every day my June Bug gets to make new friends." Mom smiles their way and shoves her hand in front of me toward Tessa. "Hello, dear. I'm Marjorie Shipley. Luke's mama and Hannah's nana."

"Mrs. Shipley, so nice to meet you." Tessa smiles that sunshine smile in my mom's direction, the look making my chest constrict that much more.

"Luke's sure enjoyed getting to know you, Tessa. Glad to have you here in Bennett."

Tessa raises a brow in my direction. With a boldness I don't expect, she says, "You've been talking about me, sir?"

God, please let the earth swallow me up right now.

I'm racking my brain for words to explain, to downplay, when Ms. Rhonda joins in on the fun. "Here, sweet girl." She pats the metal bleacher beside her. "I bet Ms. Burton and Ms. Marshall wouldn't mind if you sat with them." She twists at the waist and takes the nachos from my hand and smiles at my daughter. When Hannah is settled between her and Tessa, she hands the tray to her and whips out a napkin, too. Hannah, of course, swings her legs, dipping chips into the cheese sauce in the tray.

"We don't mind at all, Ms. Rhonda," Mel crows, looking over her shoulder and sending a wink my way.

What the hell is going on here?

Mouth agape, I turn to my mother, but she's busy exchanging smug looks with Peggy and Daisy. These women are relentless.

Throughout the game, I sneak my own glances to where Hannah sits by Tessa and Mel. She basks in their attention, showing off her version of the cheers the cheerleading squad is performing down on the track in front of us. Tessa and Mel offer praises for everything she does, answer all of her questions patiently, and share their popcorn with her at halftime.

Me? My leg won't stop bouncing on the metal under our feet. Twice, my mother reaches over and taps my thigh while giving me her patented mom look.

Every once in a while, Tessa looks back in my direction and gives me a reassuring smile, like she's making sure I know she doesn't mind Hannah keeping them company tonight. She's so *good* with my kid.

And it's like she knows exactly when *I* need comfort, too. Like it just comes naturally to her. Every time I see this girl, I'm more drawn to her, and I'm so torn over what to do about it.

Not that I'll really have the opportunity to *do* anything about it.

Hannah's bottom lip wobbles when she has to say goodbye to Tessa and Mel shortly before the end of the game. But Tessa, of course, kneels to look my daughter in the eye. She playfully pinches Hannah's round cheek and says, "Hey, Jelly Bean, no tears. We'll see each other again."

"Promise?" Hannah whispers, wiping one eye with the heel of her palm.

"Pinkie promise," Tessa declares, holding up her hand. Hannah locks pinkies with her, then throws her arms around Tessa's neck in a tight hug.

My heart might up and burst out of my chest right here in these bleachers.

More than likely, though, it's just gonna follow that girl home.

Mom nudges my side and gives me a told-you-so look as the crowd around us waves and calls out goodbyes to the girls.

After the game, Hannah and I step out onto the field for our traditional celebration with Cordell and the players. They won big-time tonight.

As soon as my little girl's feet touch the grass, she takes off in Cordell's direction, yelling, "Uncle Dell!" the whole way. He sweeps her up in a hug when she reaches him.

As I'm approaching them, Hannah's saying, "Good game, Coach."

"Thanks, Banana." Cordell passes my daughter back to me, probably eager to get to the locker room for his post-game rituals. But instead of jogging back to the field house like I expect, he sizes me up and says, "Hey, I need a favor."

"Whatcha got?"

"Don't laugh, okay? But I got a couple of guys who need to work on their balance and flexibility, so I signed them up to take a yoga class in the morning."

"Yoga?" I huff out. "Like at Mel's?"

He nods. "Yeah, but here's the thing: these tough guys keep whining about it being all girly and whatnot, so I'm going with them to put that incorrect assumption to rest."

"And what does this have to do with me?"

"I figured that if they saw us doing the same thing, like a couple of *real* men taking on these poses, they'd feel more comfortable."

Pretty sure my best friend has been possessed. I don't know the first damn thing about yoga, and I have stepped foot in Mel's place exactly zero times.

"You're serious?"

"Yeah, man, I know it sounds crazy, but I need you." He puts a hand on my shoulder and gives it a little shake. "Plus, uh, a little bird told me that a certain pretty, young librarian takes this same class."

"You been talkin' to my mama?" I accuse, shifting Hannah to my other hip in frustration. She rests her head on my shoulder, probably minutes from conking out.

"Nope," he says, letting the ending sound pop out of his lips. His face is all innocence, not a sign of a smirk in sight.

With a scoff, I say, "Just coincidence that you need your players to go to the same class *she* happens to go to, huh?"

He sighs. "Look, I'm doing this thing with these guys tomorrow. Just thought you'd jump at the chance to participate, knowing you'd get to see your crush in yoga pants." His eyes take on a mischievous glint.

I scan our surroundings to make sure no one overheard, even if he did say it quietly. We're in the clear.

"Man—"

"Hey," he interrupts, shrugging. "If you feel like helping me out tomorrow, the class starts at nine. And I'll owe you one. A *big* one." He then turns and starts for the field house with a few of the stragglers, leaving me standing in the middle of a football field, my five-year-old on my hip, wondering what in the hell a dude is supposed to wear to a yoga class.

Feeling ten kinds of foolish, I'm outside Mel's yoga place at ten minutes before nine. The place is called Go with the Flow-Ga, which sounds just about right for a place she owns. I look down and worry for the millionth time that the clothes I'm wearing aren't right, that I'm an idiot for doing this, that the reason I'm here is all too obvious.

I'm considering bailing and making a detour into the coffee shop next door when Cordell wanders up with his starting running back and cornerback, though the boys look like they'd rather be pretty much anywhere else.

Cordell's shaking my hand and patting my back when Mel turns the corner like she's running from a fire.

"Late!" she hollers breathlessly. "Late, so late," she chants as she unlocks the door. Once she steps inside, she turns to the small crowd that's now waiting on the sidewalk, points in my best friend's direction, and growls, "I don't want to hear it, Cordell Watkins. Not. a. word." Then, in a more friendly tone, she turns to the rest of us and says, "Sorry, guys. Just give me a couple minutes to get set up!" With that, the front door swings shut behind her. Next to me, Cordell's holding both palms up like he has no idea why he was singled out.

"Coach, what'd you do to *her*?" Jesse Lewis, the cornerback, asks his coach.

"Yeah, Coach, she looked like she was gonna kick your—"

"Porter!" He barks out the running back's last name using his coach voice. "Don't even think about finishing that sentence." Both boys look equally reprimanded, but Jesse elbows Kobe Porter in the ribs, and they're working to stifle their laughter. Cordell ignores it, or maybe he doesn't notice.

Because he's too busy dodging the daggers I'm shooting his way. He scans the small crowd, and his eyes go wide.

Tessa is not here.

Mel comes back to the door to wave us all in, and I roll my eyes at Cordell before following the boys through the open doorway. We gather next to a small counter inside, and Mel instructs us to remove our shoes and socks and shows us where to store them.

"Any of you need mats?" she asks, giving Cordell a look again.

"We do, Ms. Marshall," he says with a charming smile.

She glares his way for a second before ducking into a closet to the left of the counter. She comes back with a tall tub holding several rolled-up purple mats.

"If this becomes a habit, *Coach* Watkins, you'll need to use those booster funds to buy your boys their own mats." Her tone is full of snark, but he's looking at her like he could eat her right up.

Huh. Glad one of us is enjoying this morning.

Mel leads us into a dimly lit room with no windows. The walls are painted a soft gray and adorned only with a few light fixtures that cast a warm, welcoming glow. There are lines on the hardwood floor to show where to place the mats. We get settled, Cordell herding the boys to the first row so he can set up behind them, no doubt in order to make sure they take this seriously. I take the space next to him in the middle spot of the middle row.

Mel turns on quiet instrumental music, then she gives directions in a soothing voice I've never heard from the wild woman before.

We're all seated on our mats in what Mel calls child's pose when the door from the front foyer swings open.

My heart rate speeds up when I turn and find Tessa standing in the doorway, backlit by the bright lights in the foyer. Mat in her arms, she looks flustered and very adorable. Her brow is furrowed as she scans the space. She rears back a little when she lands on me, and she brings her hand to her chest when she realizes everyone's staring at her.

"Um, Mel, this is the flow class, right?" she asks in a shy voice.

"You're exactly where you should be, Ivy," I tell her.

Mel rushes over to usher her friend into the room. She takes Tessa's mat from her arms and places it on the floor.

Right next to mine.

And on her way back to the front of the room, she shoots me a look that says *your move* before she resumes instruction.

"Now relax and sink deep to feel grounded in this pose. While here, connect with your breath."

In my periphery, Tessa's taking deep, frantic breaths, her eyes closed. No one else is speaking except Mel, but I can't stop myself from tipping closer and whispering to her. "Ivy?"

She doesn't open her eyes, doesn't look at me right away, just continues with her deep breathing. When she finally does side-eye me, I give her a soft smile and whisper, "You're good," trying to reassure her.

She nods, her lips barely turning up, then focuses on the front of the room, where Mel is providing instruction and gentle feedback to all of us as a group.

No offense to Mel, but there will be no connecting with my breath with this woman beside me. She's wearing her hair in a side braid again, and it's taking every ounce of my willpower not to openly gawk at her curves in those skintight black leggings. The upper part of her body is encased in a tight black tank top that shows me exactly how perfectly her tits would fit in my hands.

I'm having extremely naughty thoughts about this girl, so I run through the list of all the reasons I can't want her again and again.

She's my tutor.

She's too young for me.

She's probably not looking to settle in Bennett long-term.

She's not going to date a tattooed construction worker.

She's never going to want someone who can't read.

Mel's voice cuts into my thoughts. "Now exhale. Send your hips up for downward facing dog, chest pushing toward your thighs…"

I'm doing my best to follow the movements of the others. This position has me wishing Mel had placed Tessa's mat in the row in front of me so I could get a really good look at her perfect ass in those leggings.

God, I'm such a horndog.

I shake my head to clear those thoughts. Again.

And again, it only works for a minute or two.

But my thoughts about Tessa don't all revolve around getting laid. Lord knows, I want that pretty fucking badly, but I want more than just that with her.

I want all of it.

I want all of *her*.

I want to be the one who calms her storms, who takes care of her needs, who holds her when she's sad and laughs with her when she's happy.

I want to *make* her happy. Every single day.

But if I've learned anything in my thirty-four years, it's this: wanting something doesn't mean I can have it.

CHAPTER TEN

TESSA

"Let's move into Savasana." Mel's melodic voice floats through the air, but it does nothing to calm my thoughts as they flit from one topic to the next in rapid succession. I try my best to relax into this pose, stretched out flat with my body on my mat and my arms out to each side.

This is the corpse pose, though there's nothing corpse-like about how my body reacts the moment I feel a light touch on my right hand.

Luke's fingers brushing mine.

Even though his touch is featherlight, a bolt of electricity arcs down and through my body, all the way to my toes. I'm terrified to look his way, but I can feel his gaze on me like a spotlight, even though we're supposed to have our eyes closed so we can focus on our breathing.

Neither of us breaks the connection until Mel directs us to sit with our hands at our hearts. My heart, of course, is thumping so hard I'm afraid it's going to tear through my workout tank.

Why is my body reacting like this to one simple touch?

My brain is still trying to catch up when Luke stands up next to where I'm still cross-legged on my mat. He extends his hand to me, but instead of grabbing it, all I can do is gawk up at him.

Handsome. Determined.

Finally, I take his hand and let him help me to my feet.

He doesn't let go right away. In fact, he pulls me close and murmurs in my ear instead. "Good workout, Ivy?"

His scent's intoxicating, masculine—woodsy and spicy, mixed with something fundamentally *him*.

I cut my eyes over to where Mel and Cordell are talking to the teenage boys who were in the row in front of us. Thankful they aren't paying us too much attention, I turn back to Luke. But all my brain can think to say is, "Y-yes." I look down to where my hand is still clasped in his strong, callused one.

At the sound of laughter from the front of the room, the spell is broken, and I instinctively pull away.

"Wh-why are you here?"

Get it together, Tessa.

He's still standing so close I have to tilt my head back to make eye contact. His warm brown eyes crinkle in the corners as he grins sheepishly. "Gotta strengthen my core. You know, in case I need to spend lots of time on my knees."

At his words, my face, neck, and chest flame so hot I'm surprised I don't melt into a puddle at his feet.

"Laying tile, you know? Gotta have a strong core for that."

Luke pats his abdomen and smirks, hesitating a moment at my still slack jaw before dragging his attention to the bare skin above my breasts, which has got to be as flushed as my face. "Do you get this red all over, I wonder?" he asks in a low, husky voice, tilting his head to the side and keeping his eyes where they definitely shouldn't be.

But then his features even out and his eyes are back on mine. He's biting back a smile, probably at my obvious reaction to his innuendo, and I find myself wanting to smack him with my rolled-up yoga mat. I tuck my chin, searching for the strength to collect myself, my gaze snagging on Luke's bare feet, the sight doing funny things to *my* core.

Who has attractive feet, for goodness' sake?

Girl, you need serious help.

I'm saved from further embarrassment when Mel, Cordell, and the teenagers join us. I force myself to dig deep to calm the red wave that's taken over my body.

"Tessa, nice to see you again." Cordell tips his head in a friendly way.

I smile in return, noticing, though, that Mel is not so charmed by him. She has her eyes narrowed in his direction. But he has a great smile, too, his teeth blindingly white against his rich, brown skin.

What is it with this town? They grow them *real* cute around here.

Because Luke? He's wearing a fitted T-shirt that shows off his impressive biceps, and he's paired it with gray sweatpants.

Gray. Sweatpants.

The audacity.

I've read enough contemporary romances to know that those things should be considered weapons of mass destruction.

"You, too, Coach," I say, vowing to get my mind out of the gutter. "Did you guys enjoy the class?"

"Sure enough, when it finally got going." Cordell is giving Mel some serious side-eye, though his tone is teasing.

Mel, on the other hand, is fuming.

"Thanks for your patronage, *Coach* Watkins. You make sure to leave the mats in that bucket there by the door so I can fumigate them. Especially *yours*."

I've never heard Mel's voice sound so antagonistic before. I look to Luke like maybe he'll have an explanation, but he's focused on the floor, shaking his head, a small smile curving his lips.

Cordell has a smug look on his face as he considers Mel's

angry words. "Let's go, guys." Then he turns to me. "Tessa, a pleasure, as always. Ms. Marshall, it was real…something." He pats her head as he walks by, the boys following closely behind.

"Ivy," Luke says in farewell, making his way out the door behind the others.

Mel's still staring after them several seconds after they move out of sight. Her glare softens after a moment, and a thoughtful look settles on her face.

"That man is delicious" is all she says.

At first, I think she's talking about Luke, and a sharp sting of jealousy hits me. But then Mel turns to me and elaborates. "No, silly. Not talking about the yummy boy with the tattoos. He *is* hot, but he's clearly on the Tessa Train, going full speed ahead with no stops along the way."

I shake my head in denial but can't fight the feeling of warmth that settles in my chest and on my cheeks. Again.

Dang blushing. Gives me away every time.

Mel smirks at my reaction. "And since you're *clearly* all aboard the Luke Express, Imma need you two to *ride* each other already."

"Mel," I admonish. "He's my student. It wouldn't be appropriate. At all."

"Screw appropriate." She taps a finger to her lips. "Better yet…screw *him*!" She cackles.

"I can't with you!" I shake off my scandalized expression and narrow my eyes at her. Now I'm desperate to get the focus of this conversation off Luke and me. "If you weren't talking about Luke being delicious, that could only mean you were referring to a certain football coach…"

"Uh-uh, T. Not going there." She shakes her head as she makes her way over to the pile of yoga mats.

"Melanie."

"Hey! Only my grandma!" she says forcefully, pointing a finger at me. After a beat, we both break out laughing.

"So what's with him calling you Ivy, anyway?" she asks after we've sobered.

A little part of me doesn't want to tell her, like the story of his nickname for me is a sacred little secret meant only for the two of us. However, I know Mel, and she won't accept the brush-off. I haven't told anyone about overhearing the conversation Luke had with Mr. Weaver when he demanded a different tutor, so I go with an abbreviated version of the truth. "He called me Ivy League when we first started working together. I guess because he thinks I'm smart or something. He shortened it to just Ivy, and it's stuck." I play it off with a shrug. "And yes, I did explain to him that UGA is *not* Ivy League."

Mel gives a little *hmm*, but thankfully doesn't push any further. I don't know why things have felt different between Luke and me lately, and I don't want to analyze it too closely.

After that, we work in silence, getting the mats sanitized before Mel's next class, which happens to be senior yoga. I usually bring a book to read out front and wait for her so we can have lunch after she's done for the day. Today, though, I can't focus on the storyline and spend most of that time mentally replaying the class and conversation with Luke after. I also check my morning pictures twice.

"Oh, hon," Ms. Peggy says when she stops by our table at Ruth's to take our order, "you just missed that good-lookin' fella of yours!"

"I'm sorry?"

"Your fella! Luke. Came in with Coach Watkins for breakfast."

My face heats again. I swear I'm in permanent tomato mode today. "Oh no. He's not my fellow," I explain, looking across the table to Mel for backup.

She ignores me, instead studying the menu like she hasn't had the whole thing memorized since childhood.

Thanks for nothing, Melanie.

Ms. Peggy plants her hands on her hips and studies me. "Could've fooled me, hon. That boy is sweet on you. You think you're too good for him or somethin'?"

I'm taken aback by her question. It's not so much an attack on me, but more of a protective measure to defend one of her flock. One of her fellow townsfolk.

"Oh, no, I promise that's not it at all," I tell her, putting every bit of genuineness I possess into my response. "We're just friends. He's wonderful, though." I offer her a weak smile, which is all I can manage at the moment.

With a nod, she says, "Don't you go breakin' that boy's heart, missy."

"I would never," I tell her, slapping a palm to my chest.

That must appease her, because she instantly switches back into waitress mode, taking our lunch orders.

Mel has mercy on me and doesn't mention Luke once during our meal.

I make sure to return the favor and don't mention Cordell either. But there's a history between them I'm dying to uncover.

After lunch, we part ways. Mel heads back across the street to her apartment while I wander down Central toward my own home.

Along the way, I revel in the touches of fall brought on by the late-October weather. Halloween is right around the corner, and though I'm giddy about passing out candy to kids for the first time ever, I've already checked with my neighbors and each one declined to join me on the porch to greet the trick-or-treaters. Mel says businesses downtown pass out candy, too, so many local families end up down here to socialize.

The day before Halloween, I put the finishing touches on both of my costumes. I'll wear one to work at the library and one for the trick-or-treating festivities.

Halloween is on a Monday this year, my least favorite day of the week, but at least it elevates a typical Monday into something worth looking forward to.

I start my favorite day of the year as Hermione Granger, curling and teasing my hair into a mess to complete the look. The local daycare brings in their preschool class for Halloween story time and treats, and I take my role as academic witch very seriously as I give them a special potions presentation that would make the real Hermione proud.

Seeing children and adults alike come into the library in their costumes all day long reinforces my decision to move here; these people take Halloween as seriously as I do. Shanice, dressed like Cruella De Vil, is perfectly in character the whole day, and both Mr. Weaver and I take delight in watching her interact with the few kids who are dressed up as puppies or dogs.

We close the library early today to give employees time to get ready for trick-or-treating.

"Cruella, make sure y'all bring DJ by my place tonight! I've got special treats for my friends!" I call out to Shanice as she gets into her car.

"You got it, Hermione!"

I'm so excited about tonight I catch myself wanting to skip home in my gray uniform skirt and knee socks. Trick-or-treating starts at five thirty and lasts until seven thirty, so I only have a half hour to make my costume change and lug my tubs of candy and treats down to the front porch.

I tame my hair as best I can, then don my pointy witch hat and give myself a once-over in the full-length mirror in my bedroom. The long-sleeved black dress is fitted on top but flares out into sparkly fullness at the waist, stopping mid-calf. I slip my feet, purple-and-black striped socks and all, into the black buckle shoes that look like they were made exclusively for a witch.

The transformation from daytime witch to nighttime witch is complete.

With my broom under one arm, I lug the black plastic cauldron full of candy and the pumpkin tub full of special treats down the stairs to get my candy-passing station all set up, remembering to light the candle in my jack-o'-lantern on the porch railing.

As the sun casts longer shadows over sleepy Bennett, Georgia, the town's residents come out in droves. Costumed kids scurry from house to house, and most of the adults accompanying them are dressed up, too. Familiar faces, including the football players from the yoga class, appear here and there, calling out greetings to neighbors, stopping in the middle of the streets to catch up until the kids they're chaperoning tug on their sleeves, anxious to get to the next house.

It's like a scene right out of a feel-good movie, and I get to live here.

Shanice stops by with DJ, who's dressed like Captain America, and along with a handful of candy, I give him a treat bag with a Halloween pencil and Monster Mad-Libs inside. Shanice is always retelling the hysterical stories the kid comes up with, so I thought the Mad-Libs would be perfect for him.

The stream of trick-or-treaters is steady. So much so that I have to break into the extra bag of candy I purchased just in case. Several kids who frequent the library make appearances on my porch in their adorable and sometimes scary costumes. Even Ms. Daisy, dressed as the bride of Frankenstein, and Ms. Peggy, dressed as herself, stroll down the street together arm in arm, observing the festivities. Mel leaves her parents stationed in front of Go with the Flow-Ga to visit me for a few minutes. She's dressed as a goth rag doll, with her purple hair pulled up in high pigtails and fake stitches lining the skin around her mouth and eyes.

"Looks like you've been busy tonight, T," she says, peering into my half-empty candy cauldron.

"There are so many of them!"

"Yeah, lots of families who live out in the country drive in to bring their kids." She flops onto the top step and turns so she can see me where I'm sitting in one of the rocking chairs on the front porch. We chat between trick-or-treaters, and Mel gives me a rundown of her favorite costumes of the night.

Fluffing her ruffled skirt on her thighs, she looks at me slyly. "*So*, had any interesting visitors tonight?"

I know who she's referring to but refuse to acknowledge it. "Sure have. Robots and superheroes and skeletons and princesses and monsters and—"

She cuts me off as she stands to leave. "Just keep your eye out for someone wanting to round to third base." With a wink, she skips down the steps and onto the sidewalk to make her way back to her studio. And I sit, shocked at her innuendo. I stay that way for a solid twenty seconds, contemplating how I'm going to convince her that there is nothing going on between Luke and me.

Because there can't be. He and I have built a solid foundation for a friendship, but it can't go any further than that, no matter how my traitorous body reacts to his touch and his scent. I'm his reading tutor and friend. That's all.

Once the darkness is good and settled around us, the foot traffic slows considerably. I peek into my now almost empty candy cauldron as the minutes of trick-or-treating tick down, and a deep melancholy washes over me.

Why am I so sad all of a sudden?

Surely, it's not because a certain someone didn't bring his daughter by for candy.

Just friends, right?

I glance over at the book waiting in the pumpkin bucket. The one I picked out just for Hannah.

No, silly, you're sad because your favorite holiday is winding to a close.

I've almost convinced myself of it when the sweetest voice shouts, "Trick-or-treat, Ms. Tessa!"

And there she is. Hannah Shipley is skipping up the front walk, decked out like a tiny Rockford Peach.

She is an absolutely adorable little baseball player. Red knee socks and white tennis shoes. Pinky-peach uniform dress and a red baseball cap pulled over long pigtail braids.

I stand and wave. "Hannah, happy Halloween! You look perfect!"

She pauses halfway up the front walk, pulling her skirt out to the side to show it off. "My nana sew-ded it."

Behind her, at the end of the walkway, is the rest of her family, big smiles on their faces. Luke is wearing a white-and-red baseball jersey, a red ball cap that matches Hannah's, and his fit-just-right jeans. Whew. My heart cannot handle the adorableness of this scene—he and his daughter in matching costumes—or the cuteness that is *him*, in general. But now Mel's third base statement makes a lot more sense.

Just friends, Tessa.

Luke's parents are just as festive, both wearing clothing that would be stylish in the 1940s, like they're spectators at a baseball game where Hannah is playing and Luke is the manager. The whole scene causes a yearning pinch to squeeze my heart.

What would it be like to have a family like this? One where parents are active in their kids' lives rather than being too busy keeping up with the Joneses to even know their children?

Hannah climbs the few steps up to the porch confidently. "Pretty witch," she murmurs wondrously when she pops up that final stair. She scans me from head to toe, reverently taking the sparkly skirt of my dress in the hand that's not clutching her plastic pumpkin bucket. Then she gives me a grin that's both wide and shy at the same time. "You look beautiful," she breathes.

"She sure does," a deep, male voice chimes in.

Luke. Standing in front of the porch steps, hands in his pockets. Looking at me like Hannah is—like I'm a wonder to behold instead of a boring, neurotic librarian.

Heart fluttering like mad, I give him my biggest smile. "You guys look amazing, too."

He shrugs one shoulder like it's no big deal. He's got his lips still quirked, and he doesn't take his eyes off my face. I wave to his parents, who are still standing at the end of the front walk, chatting with one another, though they're both laser focused on us.

Like a magnet, my attention is pulled back to Luke, and we stand there, me a foot or two higher than him on the porch, him rocking back on his heels, watching each other for several long moments. It should feel awkward, but it just…doesn't.

I'm afraid to delve into why that is.

Hannah pipes up then, finally breaking the spell I must have accidentally cast. "What kinda candy do you have, Ms. Tessa?"

"Manners, Banana," Luke corrects gently. "It's not polite to ask that."

"I bet you'll find something in here you like," I tell her, offering her the candy cauldron. She reaches her little hand in to dig around in what's left, pulling out a fun-size packet of peanut M&M's moments later.

"My daddy loves these," she tells me.

"Oh, don't you know? Jelly Beans get to pick out more than one thing."

She giggles and dives back in. Bucket still held out, I straighten and fix my gaze on Luke again. Not even trying to stop myself. He's watching us, his attention bouncing from me to his daughter and back. Hannah takes out a fun-size candy bar and adds it to the plastic pumpkin that's almost filled to the top.

"Jelly Beans also get a special prize," I explain, pulling my eyes from Luke's once again.

"They do?"

"Absolutely, they do." I take the book out of the other bucket and hand it over to her. She gives a little gasp, like I've just given her a treasure, as she takes it in her hand. "It's called *Happy Halloween, Biscuit*. Have you read any Biscuit stories before?"

"I have! Mrs. Gibson reads them at school."

"Well, he's one of my very favorite characters. He's such a cute little puppy, don't you think?"

She nods and studies the book's cover. "I love puppies. But Daddy says we can't get one," she pouts, lower lip stuck out and everything.

I know I shouldn't encourage her, but I can't help myself. "Maybe ask Santa instead," I suggest, stealing a glance at Luke, hoping he's not angry that I went there.

The look he gives me says *gee, thanks for that.* I offer an apologetic smile and a shoulder shrug and turn back to his daughter.

Hannah nods like she'll take my advice into consideration, then totally changes the subject when she asks, "Daddy, can you take my picture with Ms. Tessa?"

Without argument, Luke pulls his phone from his back pocket and aims it in our direction; I kneel next to this sweet girl, making sure the brim of my hat doesn't hit her in the face, and hold on to her tiny waist in a side hug. Luke snaps a few, then holds his phone down to study them before nodding.

"June Bug, if you want to finish this block, we best get goin'," Mr. Shipley calls up the walk.

"Oh!" she cries, turning back to me and sticking out her pinkie finger. "Pinkie promise I'll see you again?"

"Promise, Jelly Bean," I swear, linking fingers and tugging.

Satisfied, she rushes down the steps and past her father to where her grandparents are waiting. Mrs. Shipley crouches low and whispers in her ear, then Hannah's calling out, "Thank you for the book, Ms. Tessa!"

"You're welcome!" I wave.

Luke's still standing at the bottom of the steps, lips pursed and tugged to the side, hands back in his pockets. Like he's not ready to say goodbye yet.

And neither am I.

"Luke! We'll take June Bug on down the street. Meet you back here in a few minutes?" his mom offers.

"Yeah," he calls, not bothering to turn around. "Sounds good."

He takes a step closer, the toes of his boots almost touching the bottom step, and a thousand butterflies take flight in my stomach.

Just friends. *Just friends.*

Taking what I hope is a subtle deep breath, I sit on the top step and pat the space next to me.

When he settles his tall frame on the concrete, he turns to me. "You didn't have to get something extra for Hannah, you know. But thank you. It sure made her feel special."

"I'm happy to do it. And she is special."

He watches me for a moment, his eyes bouncing between mine. "You are, too, Ivy," he murmurs, his tone sincere, vulnerable.

My initial reaction is to deny, deny, deny. "I'm really not," I huff out.

"You absolutely are. You'd have to be to put up with my stubborn ass."

I snort-laugh and look out toward the street. The night brought along a cool breeze that wasn't present when the sun was out. Most of the revelers have made their way back to their homes, and it's quiet now, the laughter and shouts and whoops from earlier in the evening fading into the moonlight. I take in a lungful of the cool night air, and a sensation of rightness sweeps over me, like I'm exactly where I'm supposed to be at this moment in my life. It's so profound, I shiver.

"You're not that bad, Mr. Shipley. You've accomplished so

much already." I never pass up a chance to encourage his progress, knowing he thrives on it. And it's true—he has made incredible progress in the two-and-a-half months we've been working together. He could read that Biscuit book to Hannah if he wanted to, but not wanting to put undue pressure on him, I didn't mention that to her.

"All because of you." His brown eyes roam my face and land on my lips for a moment before moving on.

Dangerous, Tessa. This is very dangerous.

Needing to dispel the weight of the moment, I change the subject. "I love that your whole fam dressed up together tonight. And *A League of Their Own*? Love that movie."

"Pretty sure it came out before you were born, Ivy League." His tone is teasing.

"So," I scoff, teasing back. "You say that like I'm too young to drive or something."

"Wait, you have your license already?" he asks, his brows arched in mock surprise.

I swat at his arm. "Ha ha. I'm not *that* young."

"No, not too young to drive." He sobers. "But for other things, maybe."

Alarm bells ring in my head. *Flirting! This is flirting!*
Just friends. Just friends. Just friends.

"You'd be surprised what kinds of things a twenty-six-year-old can do. I know it's been a *really* long time since you were one yourself."

"Hey, respect your elders, Gen Z."

We're grinning like mad at each other and startle when his mom calls to us from the sidewalk. "Hey, you! Ready to go?"

"Yep." Luke stands and starts down the steps. When he gets to the front walk, he turns back to me. "So, Ivy, how was your first Halloween in Bennett? Was it everything you hoped it would be?"

My heart squeezes at his question. He asked me the same question after pumpkin carving.

"More," I answer.

He gives me another of his devastating smiles and turns to join his family. I watch them until they turn the corner onto Central Street and disappear from view.

And darn it, I can't fight the smile that takes over my face as I gather up my trick-or-treating supplies.

Because my first Halloween in Bennett?

Pretty sure it might be the best one of my life.

CHAPTER ELEVEN

TESSA

"This dang tail keeps knocking things over!"

Shanice laughs at me from her post at the main desk as I head back toward the Kids' Zone. The tail of the blow-up dragon costume swings back and forth behind me as I shuffle-step as best I can to get to my destination.

She doesn't have time to keep teasing about my costume, though, because a mom and her little boy step up to the desk to check out books.

Story time on Saturday is usually one of our busiest times, but today's crowd is setting records. Probably because of the book we've been promoting.

Dragons Love Tacos.

I'm set to read it to the group congregating on the bright rug in the Kids' Zone in exactly five minutes, and wrangling this huge blow-up costume into submission is proving to be a challenge. After story time, we'll direct families to the parking lot, where the Taco Tuesdays food truck is setting up, with a line already stretching down to the corner of Central.

Wishing I had made a more low-key dragon costume instead

of buying this ridiculously cumbersome thing, I make a mental note to learn how to sew.

Add it to the long list of things I want to accomplish in life.

Mr. Weaver makes his way through the crowd to where I'm fighting not only the tail, but also the head of the costume. My face is visible in a cut-out hole in the dragon's neck, which means the creature's head and ferocious mouth are bouncing around up on *my* head. Since it's a blow-up costume, I've got a battery pack tucked inside somewhere and air circulating around my body to keep it inflated. Despite the airflow, I'm glad I chose leggings and a T-shirt today, because I'm already sweating bullets.

"Tessa, you ready?" Mr. Weaver asks in a soft voice. It's difficult to hear him, what with the costume and the fan inside it and the crowd that's gathered in the Kids' Zone. Every fold-up chair we set out this morning is occupied, and kids are seated several rows deep in front of them on the colorful rug.

I take a couple of deep breaths to calm my anxiety. Large crowds of strangers make me nervous. They have ever since I flubbed my entrance at a debutante ball my mother made me attend during my sophomore year of high school. Every eye in that room was on me, judging me. Of course, as a librarian, I've read stories to crowds before—both kids and adults—but never one this size. In a space this cramped.

I nod my response and do my best to shuffle up the side of the crowd, trying to keep the dragon's tail from knocking children over in the process.

Finally, I'm at the front, ready to personify the fiercest dragon I can muster.

Story time is probably my favorite part of my job, even with my crowd issues. Adopting book characters' voices, making stories come alive for children, has got to be the most fulfilling thing I've done in my twenty-six years. Until recently, maybe.

Because tutoring is quickly pushing story time out of that number one spot.

Dressing up in a costume while doing this? Yeah, it's the icing on the cake.

Although I'm majorly rethinking costumes of the blow-up variety for future read-alouds.

I won't be able to hold the book while reading thanks to the T-rex arms, but thankfully, I've read this story so many times that I practically have it memorized. Mr. Weaver stands beside me in the cramped space, holding up the book so the audience can see the illustrations.

I launch into the story, using my best intimidating dragon voice. And these kids *eat it up.*

Much like the dragons eat up the tacos in the story.

I'm nearing the end of the book, feeling good about how it's going, when two familiar faces in the audience jump out at me.

And my face flushes as red as the fake flames coming out of the costume's toothy grin.

In the back of the room, Hannah Shipley is perched on her dad's shoulders so she can see above the crowd. She gives me a shy wave when I look in her direction.

I refuse to look at her father's face for longer than a second.

Since our Halloween porch conversation a couple of weeks ago, I've only seen Luke while working hard to help him decode one-syllable words in the library study room. There have been no more flirty, teasing comments. No smirky looks. No intense eye contact.

He's been serious about his progress. Courteous and friendly and nothing more.

Which is how it should be.

Because we're friends.

Just friends.

No matter how attractive he is, no matter how much I look forward to our next session or how many times I've thought about the way his hand brushed mine during yoga class, all we'll ever be is friends.

And I have to be okay with that.

Even if my stomach hurts every time I remind myself that I can't get swept up in the idea of him.

I end the story with a big, dramatic "The end!" and am immediately swarmed by kids and parents wanting to take pictures with the dragon. The initial rush of the crowd sends my heart beating double-time, but I plaster a smile on my face for the dozens of phones directed at me. The temperature inside this costume has to be reaching triple digits, but I soldier on, refusing to disappoint the kids by skipping out to change and cool down.

This is the first truly cold weekend we've had here in Bennett, and Mr. Weaver finally resorted to turning on the heating unit this morning. If only he'd waited one more day. Add the warm air blasting from a nearby vent to the heat radiating from the tightly packed bodies around me and my anxiety about crowds, and it's like the perfect firestorm igniting inside my body.

I'm pretty certain all my makeup has melted off my face by the time Luke and Hannah reach where I'm corralled against a bookshelf. Desperate for a cool breeze, I will my heart rate to slow and my lungs to work properly, but I definitely can't let down the little girl peering up at me.

"Hello there, Jelly Bean. Did you like my story?" I ask, sticking with my dragon voice but probably sounding like a banshee.

Hannah nods so enthusiastically she looks like a bobblehead and says, "I love tacos as much as those dragons do!"

"I bet you do," I choke out, blinking hard, because all of a sudden, the Hannah in front of me has split in two. The floor beneath my feet rocks, and black spots dance in front of me, blurring both Hannahs and the rest of the folks still mingling. My chest squeezes, like a dragon's decided to use it as a seat, crushing my lungs so I can't get enough air. And I'm so hot I might as well *be* a fire-breathing dragon.

Then I sway, panicked, because I imagine the end result would make me look like a turtle on its back. But I don't topple over. Instead, I'm propped up by strong, solid support.

A strong, solid support with a deep voice that says, "Ivy?" The voice sounds concerned, but then again, all the sounds entering my ears are traveling down a long, long tunnel to reach me, so maybe I'm imagining it.

Other disembodied voices drift through the tunnel, and then I'm moving. Almost floating yet still on my feet.

"Get her some air…"

"In here…"

"Need to get this damn suit off…"

The familiar walls of my office come into view as my vision starts to clear and the ringing in my ears lessens. Strong, steady hands peel the dragon's head off mine, then they're sliding the suit down my body. A cold bottle of water is pressed into my free hand, and something cool and wet is draped along the back of my neck.

Luke's face appears before me, and he's squeezing my knee. "You okay, Tessa?" He's kneeling in front of me, worry etched in the lines around his deep brown eyes. He rarely uses my real name, and I loathe myself for how much I like when he does.

An intense need to check my morning pictures hits me, and I grip the arms of the chair I must have been guided to.

"My phone!" I shout, scanning the room wildly.

The person holding the cold, wet something to my neck pulls away and gives my shoulder a gentle pat. I'm being handled with kid-gloves right now, and I don't like it.

I don't ever want to be a burden, and feeling like one now sends my anxiety spiking and the dragon weighing on my chest into a deeper rage.

"Hang on a sec, girl. We'll get your phone." It's Shanice, the one behind me. She snatches my purse from the bottom drawer of my desk and rummages through it beside me. Mr. Weaver is also here, standing at the door with a concerned look on his face.

"I need it now!" I'm still burning up, and my clothes are so soaked I feel like I've wet my pants.

Oh God. What if I wet my pants?

"Hey." Luke's deep, strong voice cuts through the chaos swirling in my mind, but his tone is gentle and patient. "Look at me, Ivy." He's still kneeling in front of my chair, his thumbs rubbing soothing circles on the insides of my knees. "Hey," he says again, even softer this time. "Breathe."

I pull in a deep drag, expanding my lungs as full as they'll go. Then, slowly, I let it out, never taking my eyes off Luke's handsome face.

"Good. Again," he instructs. So I do it again. And again. And again, until my chest feels looser and my body sags into the chair.

Shanice hands me my phone, and I instantly navigate to my camera roll as Luke takes the forgotten bottle of water out of my other hand to open it for me.

Hair straightener, off.

Coffee pot, off.

Front door, locked.

My heart rate slows even further as I quickly swipe to close the photo app.

"Girl, you gave us a scare!" Shanice chides sweetly. "You feeling better?"

"I-I think so," I croak. Now that the panic has mostly passed, the mortification moves right in and takes up space. Now, how can I remove myself from this room without causing these people who are staring at me like I'm broken more concern?

No. Maybe the broken thing is all in my head.

Your thoughts are not your reality, Tessa.

It's concern I see in the way they watch me.

Abruptly, I sit up straight, my hands gripping the armrests of my chair. "Hannah?" I gasp.

"She's with DJ and my mom," Shanice answers before Luke can. "I'll call Darrell. He's at the station right now. He should check your vitals."

"No!" I implore, not wanting to burden anyone else. "Please. I promise I'm fine. Just got overheated in that dang dragon suit." I wave at the wilted nylon puddle in the corner.

She tilts her head and frowns, but I give her my best calm face, and she finally relents with a nod.

Mr. Weaver speaks up for the first time since we've been in my office. "I'll stay here with Tessa, Shanice. I'm sure you have a crowd at the main desk."

I smile at him gratefully and take a sip of the water that Luke keeps prodding me to drink. "I'm really okay."

Shanice gives my shoulder a final squeeze and scoots her way back out into the hall.

"Really," I say to Mr. Weaver, who's still looking at me with a concerned frown. "Just too much dragon excitement for one day."

"I'll stay until—"

"I've got her." Luke cuts him off, making it clear he'll brook no argument on this.

Mr. Weaver glances between the two of us for a moment, finally nodding as he says, "I'll bring Hannah back."

"Thanks" is Luke's only reply. He hasn't left his position in front of me, his hands still on my knees.

"Your car here?"

"No. I walked this morning."

"'Kay. Banana and I will walk you home."

I open my mouth, ready to argue, but the scowl he gives me has me snapping my jaw shut again.

"It's happening, Ivy. You know how stubborn I am. We're. Walking. You. Home. End of discussion."

Hannah appears in the doorway, hesitant to come all the way inside. "Daddy?"

"Yeah, Banana, come on in. We're gonna walk Ms. Tessa home. She's not feeling good."

At that, Hannah lifts her chin and approaches me. She takes my hand in hers and looks at me with an expression far too mature for her age. "My daddy will make you feel better, Ms. Tessa. He always does when I'm sick." Her quiet confidence in her father tugs at my heartstrings. Every little girl should think that her daddy can fix everything.

I grew up feeling like my daddy wanted to fix *me*. To mold me into his vision of a perfect daughter.

"I'm sure he does, Jelly Bean," I tell her.

"You got a jacket, Ivy? It's cold outside."

I slowly stand, hesitating in front of my chair to make sure I've got my legs under me before I pull open the tall cabinet in the corner. I remove the sweatshirt I wore this morning, but before I can pull it on, Luke yanks it out of my hold and bunches it up. Then he's pulling it down over my head. I manage to push my arms through myself before he gently tugs the bottom down to rest on my hips.

A small part of me wants to balk at being treated like a child.

But mostly, I relish in the feeling of being taken care of.

Just friends. Remember that.

We weave through the throngs of people still crowded inside the library. Outside, the brisk air cools my overheated skin quickly. The sensation is incredible, but I need to get indoors soon since my clothes are still damp from sweat.

As we shuffle down the street in the direction of my place, Luke softly asks, "That happen often?"

"Oh. Um…" I'd rather find a rock to hide under than talk about this with him. Yes, we can only be friends, but I hate that he's gotten a glimpse of my issues.

He doesn't push, though. He stuffs one hand in his pocket and glances down at Hannah, who's walking quietly beside me.

But I need to give him something. And he's been so vulnerable with me. I owe him at least a sliver of the truth. "A few times over the years. Usually in private instead of in front of a whole dang town, though." I try for a self-deprecating laugh, but it falls flat. I haven't had a panic attack in years, but when I do, it has to happen in front of half the population of my new hometown, where I desperately want to belong.

"Hey." Luke puts a hand on my arm, stopping my forward progress. He turns to face me on the sidewalk, peeking over to where Hannah is distracted by the colorful leaves on the ground a couple of feet away. "This town has seen way worse, believe me. I bet it's already forgotten, especially because those damn tacos are good enough to make people forget their first names."

Despite my embarrassment, I can't hold back a smile. "They are good, aren't they?"

"The best," he says. Then he's waving at Hannah, and we're walking again. When we're a few houses away from my place and he hasn't brought the incident up again, I think I'm in the clear, but then he asks, "And the thing with your phone? The pictures?"

Ugh. Now I *really* want to find a rock to live under for the rest of my days.

My steps slow as I steel my spine. "It's this dumb thing I do." I keep my eyes downcast, studying the sidewalk in front of me.

Luke stays silent, again giving me time to collect my thoughts.

"Every morning, before I leave my apartment, I take pictures of my appliances set to off and one of me locking my door. So that when I have a moment of panic during the day, questioning whether I turned my hair straightener off, things like that, I have a way to check without making a return trip home."

"Hmm."

"Once, when I was in high school, I forgot to lock up at home." Oddly compelled to offer him further explanation, I continue. "The housekeeper noticed and mentioned it to my parents. Of course, they read me the riot act. I was terrified of disappointing them, so I promised myself I'd never let it happen again."

"Tessa," Luke says when we're a few steps from my walkway. My name in his deep, gravelly tone causes flutters in my core. "I'm probably the last person who should be offering you advice on this, but..." He shrugs. "There are folks who can help you, you know. If you feel like you want to talk about it."

"Like therapy?" I question.

Dipping his chin and rubbing the back of his neck, he gives me one quick nod.

"Yeah, I know it would be good for me. It's on my to-do list, I promise."

He smiles in response and gives me one more nod. Then he calls Hannah over from where she's using her collected leaves to make a design on the sidewalk a few feet away.

"Hey, what's this about?" I ask. Taking an opportunity to change the subject, I give the sleeve of Luke's hoodie a little shake.

His eyes crinkle as he stuns me with one of his devastating smiles. "It's purple and gold on Saturdays in the fall for us, I'm afraid."

I scoff teasingly and point to my black and red sweatshirt. "I didn't think those colors were allowed in the state of Georgia."

"Uncle Dell went to LSU!" Hannah pipes up. She's smiling adorably as she tugs on the front of her own sweatshirt.

"That's right. I'm so sorry," I tell her, my voice full of sympathy.

Luke chuckles. "We're meeting up at his house to watch the game tonight." The way he says it has me dragging my attention from Hannah back to his handsome face. There's a question in his eyes, and I'm suddenly afraid that he'll voice it.

"Well, may the best team win," I say, taking a step back toward my walkway.

Luke opens his mouth but closes it again without saying anything. Then he smiles down at the ground before meeting my eyes again. "We'll let you get inside, then. You need *anything*, Ivy, I want you to call me." He stands with his hands in his pockets, and Hannah loops her arms around one of his, pulling herself off the ground and swinging as best she can.

"I'm fine, I promise."

With his free hand, he takes his phone out of his back pocket. "Tell me your number."

Just. Friends. And friends have each other's phone numbers, right?

Luke taps away for a few seconds, then holds up his phone so I can see what he's entered. A new contact.

My first and last name. Spelled perfectly.

I'm struck again with pride. At how far he's come. At how hard he's worked these last few months.

"Number?" he questions, a brow cocked.

I recite it for him, and he immediately calls my phone so I'll have his number, too.

"Anything, Ivy League. I mean that."

"Anything," Hannah parrots in her little voice.

Unbidden, my eyes well with tears, but I refuse to let him see yet another weakness today. Hannah bounds over and silently offers her pinkie; I take it in mine and shoot her a wink.

"Thanks for walking me home, Jelly Bean."

"Welcome!" she chirps. "Daddy, can we get tacos now?"

He shakes his head like he's exasperated, but with a smile on his face, he tells her, "Sure thing, Banana."

With a final wave, I turn toward the house, feeling like I could sleep for eleventy hours. I quickly shuck off my damp clothing and slip into my pajamas from the previous night, fore-going a shower for a nap, even though it's three on a Saturday afternoon.

I've just finished adjusting my weighted blanket and I'm snuggled in deep in the middle of my bed when my phone dings.

It's a text from a number that doesn't have a contact name listed yet. One with a central Georgia area code.

Have a good nite ivy.

Smiling, I settle into the softness surrounding me and promise myself I won't dream about brown eyes and strong, comforting hands.

CHAPTER TWELVE

LUKE

"So, Ivy, I need to ask you something."

When Tessa peeks up at me from across the table, the tightness in my chest I've been experiencing for months comes back. My heart squeezes, sending a lightning bolt of a message to my brain. It says: This girl. This is *the* girl.

And, like it's been doing for months, my brain shuts that shit right down. What I refer to as The List spirals through my mind once again.

She's my tutor.

She's too young for me.

She's probably not looking to settle in Bennett long-term.

She's not going to date a tattooed construction worker.

She's never going to want someone who can't read *well*.

That last excuse on The List has undergone a change since we started meeting up at the library. Because I can read now.

Sorta.

I can read easy things. Things Hannah will probably be reading herself in a couple months. I still get overwhelmed when there are a lot of words on a page, but Tessa breaks them down for me into what she calls "manageable chunks." And she showed me how covering up lines of text, only revealing a little at a time, can help. But I can help Hannah with her kindergarten homework now, and as simple as it sounds, that right there feels amazing. My mom still reads me notes from the school, just so I don't miss anything important, though.

But yeah. It's December, and I can fucking *read* stuff.

I am so much more aware of words these days. They're everywhere, all around me. On the drive to work, on random boxes and packing slips at jobsites, on Hannah's papers from school, the ticker on the bottom of my TV. Sure, they've always been there, but now that I can read many of them, it's like I'm an addict. I can't get enough of them.

Like I can't get enough of *her*.

She's looking at me now, with those big green eyes that have become as familiar to me as my kid's, waiting for me to ask my question.

I'm kinda nervous about asking this. Because it's a big deal.

But I've come this far in my reading journey, and I feel hopeful that the hardest part is over. The part where I actually had to admit the problem and start the damn process to fix it.

If I can do *that*, I can do this.

"Hannah's teacher is looking for mystery readers to come in after Christmas. To read to the class. And I'd really like to sign up. If-if you think I'm ready, I mean." I hold my breath, waiting for her response.

Her eyes light up, her sunshine smile on full display. "Luke! That's so wonderful! I love that idea, and yes—you're ready."

Relieved, I blow out a long breath.

"In fact, we can choose your book now so you can practice before the big day."

Her belief in me makes that squeeze in my chest just a little tighter, though I try my best to ignore it.

I've been ignoring a lot of things since Halloween. After our porch conversation, I told myself that I needed to stick to the parking lot promise I made months ago: Tessa is not meant for me. No matter how badly I want her. No matter how great she is with my kid. No matter how much being around her just feels *right*.

I want this girl so bad I ache for her.

But she hasn't given me any indication that she might feel the same way, other than that adorable blushing she does when I flirt with her. But she blushes in response to other people, too.

Then there's The List.

I haven't let myself flirt with her or touch her at all for weeks. Except for last month when she almost passed out at the library and I felt a fear I've never experienced before. Seeing her that way made me crazy with worry, and I couldn't stop myself from stepping in to help and comfort her. Since then, I've only brought up the incident once. During our next tutoring session, I wanted to make sure she was okay. Though I'm curious about whether she's found someone to talk to. I feel protective of Tessa, like I want to be the man who fixes all the things for her.

But I can't be. So my brain has become MVP of this whole dilemma, shutting down the feelings my heart has gotten caught up in. We've worked together at the library twice a week every week, since then—only tutor and student behaviors allowed.

"Luke?" She's looking at me, waiting for an answer to a question I totally missed.

"Sorry, what?"

"What's Hannah's favorite story? Or is there a topic or animal she loves to learn about? We can choose a book for the mystery reader thing today if you want."

I want to do everything with you, Ivy.

"Oh, uh, sure. She likes horses. And fairies, and not just the tooth variety—all fairies. Big fan of cats and kittens. Puppies. Oh, and butterflies."

Tessa grins at me, no doubt thinking that a grown man talking about fairies and shit is hilarious.

"What? She's five," I defend.

"Oh, I'm aware. But it's cute that you can rattle off all of her favorites so easily." As soon as the words leave her mouth, that adorable blush spreads across her skin.

Wait. Did Tessa Burton just call me *cute*?

No, you idiot. It's cute that a dad, probably any dad, knows his daughter's favorites, dumbass.

I don't offer a comeback, and she stammers a little when she makes a suggestion. "Y-you know," she clears her throat, "*The Very Hungry Caterpillar* is a classic. That might be a good choice."

"Oh yeah, the one about the caterpillar who eats a bunch of stuff before turning into a butterfly, right? Sounds like a good one, Ivy."

"Great. Let me grab it real quick." She leaves me in the study room, and though I'm expecting to be on my own for several minutes while she hunts the book down in the library, she's back in seconds.

"Here it is," she says, carefully opening the front cover. "This is my personal copy. I keep it in my office along with my other childhood favorites." She's quietly thumbing through the pages, the soft look on her face reminding me of how one would look when being reunited with an old friend.

God, I want to know everything about this girl.

Before the MVP can step in to make the save, I blurt out, "Why'd you want to become a librarian?"

She presses her lips together, focusing on something over my shoulder, like she's recalling a memory. "Books." She smiles her sweet smile. "They've been my best friends my whole life."

"How so?" I can't help myself. I might die if I don't know more about her.

Her cheeks are pink again. "I was a bookish, nerdy kid.

Shocker, right? I didn't fit in at school, or anywhere really, so books became my constant companions. They never judged me or let me down or made me feel like an outsider. They were always welcoming. Taught me new things, took me on grand adventures." She's wearing a dreamy look, like she's thinking about one of those fictional adventures. The way she talks about books like they're friends, like they're real and special and hold a place in her heart, is fascinating. Personally, I've never thought of books as anything other than complicated, discouraging obstacles that popped up at every turn, determined to make me feel bad about myself.

But *she* makes me want to love them as much as she does.

"I was expected to go to law school because my parents are lawyers, but when it came time for me to declare a major, I couldn't go through with it. I knew I'd be miserable for the rest of my life if I didn't forge my own path. And I just couldn't live that life anymore." She trails off, her focus locked on the table. After a moment, her expression clears and she looks at me again. "So, here I am, surrounded by my best friends every day."

With a trembling hand, she tucks a strand of hair behind an ear. She's waiting for me to respond, to give her a piece of my own truth, but I'm afraid that if I dig into that vulnerability right now, I'll confess what's in my heart—that *I* want to be her best friend and be surrounded by *her* every day.

That I'm a grown man who's kinda jealous of some damn books.

Instead, I ask, "Will you read it to me, Ivy?"

Nodding, Tessa turns to the first page again and reads in a soothing, songlike voice.

She comes alive when she's reading the words on a page, lit by an internal glow, the sunshine in her soul shining just for me.

It's the most beautiful thing I've ever seen.

And my heart tells my brain to take a hike.

On a brisk December Thursday, the week before Christmas, I'm loading a wooden structure into the back of the truck when Hannah blurts out, "Can I go to the li-berry with you this time?" She's been riding her bike around in circles in the driveway while I put the finishing touches on the piece.

"Not this time, Banana. Sorry." Her bike tilts on one training wheel for a moment as she takes a turn too sharply.

"Why?" she asks, her breath coming out in little puffs in the cold air.

"Kids aren't allowed at this meeting."

Hannah stops her circling and scowls. "You're hoggin' all the time with Ms. Tessa. I haven't seen her in a jillion days." Balancing on her bike seat, she crosses her little arms and harrumphs.

Somewhere along the way, Hannah found out that I see Tessa at my meetings. And she hasn't stopped lecturing me about how unfair it is that she doesn't get to join us.

My kid is half in love with Tessa Burton already.

Like father, like daughter.

"You'll see her again, kiddo. I'll take you to story time after Christmas."

"But I don't wanna wait until Christmas. That's forever away!"

The sass is in full force today.

"Hey, no whining. And Christmas is in three days, so stop with the forever nonsense."

With her bottom lip stuck out, she pouts. Her hair has started to come unbraided after playing outside at my folks' house all afternoon, tiny wisps surrounding her head like a halo. Her big brown eyes laser in on me, like she can change my mind by sheer force of will. These are not please-feel-sorry-for-me puppy eyes, they're give-me-what-I-want-and-no one-gets-hurt eyes. Though the message is softened a bit by the ladybug rain boots on her feet.

God, I love this kid.

"Daddy," she says, going for reasonable again.

"Banana."

"Pleeease?"

It breaks my damn heart, but sometimes saying no is the right thing to do.

"Not happening this time, honey. You know how you have to follow the rules at school?"

After a long hesitation, like she doesn't want to admit it, she nods.

"I have to follow rules, too. And there is a no-kids-allowed rule for my library meetings."

"The li-berry made that rule or Ms. Tessa did?"

Damn, this kid is determined.

"Library."

She doesn't let up on the stare-down, probably racking her brain for a loophole. But finally, she concedes. "Okay." Her voice and the dejected look on her face are pitiful. And without another word, she walks her bike back into the garage, head hanging sadly. Once her bike is parked, she drags herself over to the truck, ready to get loaded up to leave.

I swing her up into a hug, planting a noisy smack on her little cheek that makes her giggle despite her disappointment.

"I love you big, Banana girl," I say to her as she places her hands on my cheeks to rub at my stubble.

"I love you, Hairy-Face Daddy."

Tessa's driving home to Atlanta for the holidays and won't be back in Bennett until after the New Year, so I won't see her for close to two weeks. The reminder causes a twinge in my gut that I'm pretty sure won't go away until our next session.

I back the truck into a spot near the front door and scramble out, my melancholy overtaken by a hit of nervous excitement.

She's already in the study room, wearing a festive red and green plaid sweater that looks so soft and cozy I have to fight the urge to reach out and pet her arm.

"Hey! You ready to get started?" she asks as I step into the room.

"In a minute. First, I want to show you something outside."

"Okay." She tilts her head and studies me, but without another word, she follows me through the library and out the front door. Like usual, at this time of the day, the lot is mostly empty. And since it's already dark outside, I rush to grab a heavy-duty flashlight from the back seat of my pickup so she can see what I brought.

I shine the light on the structure I have strapped to my truck bed, but I keep my focus firmly on her face, anxious to see what she thinks.

She steps closer, scans the wooden structure, and finally, her face lights up in recognition. "Is that—"

"A puppet theater. For the kids' area. I hope it's what you were looking for."

"Luke." She runs her hand down one painted panel of the wooden structure, a look of pure wonder on her beautiful face. "It's…it's amazing. I'm—I can't believe it. You *made* this?" She turns to look at me then, her green eyes glittering in the moonlight.

"Yeah."

She takes the flashlight from me and steps up to the tailgate so she can get a better look. Slowly, she scans the sturdy frame. The decorative loops and dips I painted on the front to look like curtains, the fabric covering the window I had Mom sew to match the paint scheme. She studies every facet, even swallowing roughly and blinking away tears, I think. Though it's hard to tell for sure in the dark. The only sounds coming from her mouth are little squeaks and sighs.

Just the reaction I was hoping for.

About a month ago, she mentioned how she was hoping to purchase a puppet theater for the kids' area, but the library didn't have the funds for it. She'd talked about hitting up garage sales and scouring online second-hand sales sites but explained that there probably wouldn't be much available until the end of the school year, when teachers were shuffling classrooms or retiring.

I went home that night and searched how-to videos on YouTube, but it was a relatively easy build once I found the proper dimensions.

"I can't believe you did this," she says, her eyes on me again. "You *built* this. Like from scratch."

The innuendo slips out before I can stop it. "I'm really good with my hands, Ivy."

Tessa fumbles with the flashlight and juggles it a couple times before she catches it, and I know without a doubt that her cheeks are burning.

But then she surprises the hell out of me.

"I'm sure you are," she says, boldly studying my face.

The tension between us pulls taut. I *like* it. I *crave* it. Like I crave running my fingers through her silky hair and pressing my hard body against her soft one and making her blush all the way down to her toes.

This has gone farther than it ever has before, because this time, she's actively participating in it—the flirtation. And she sees it, too, but not for a moment. When she does, though, it's like a light switches off, and a look of regret crosses her features.

But I refuse to let her feel bad about it, so I snatch the flashlight from her and say, "Let's get it inside before you freeze out here."

Tessa helps me carry the heavy wooden structure into the library, and we place it in the kids' area. Once it's situated the way she wants it, she steps back and admires it again, this time in the light.

"Luke, it's perfect. Truly. I don't know how I can ever thank you for this."

I can think of a few ways.

"It was my pleasure, Ivy. Merry Christmas."

"Merry Christmas to you, too."

For the next hour, we review syllable types. Then she has me work on what she calls encoding multisyllabic words, which is a fancy way of saying that she calls out words, and I have to spell them out on a whiteboard, one syllable at a time. We even have a little time to practice *The Very Hungry Caterpillar* before our time is up.

As I stand to help her collect her supplies, Tessa calls out, "Oh! I almost forgot! Hang on!" She leaves the room in a rush but is back moments later with two wrapped gifts in her hands. "Christmas presents. For you and Hannah," she says, her chin tucked shyly.

Hang on, heart.

"Wow, Ivy. You didn't have to do that." I hold them carefully, not wanting to mess up the fancy bows she's tied them with.

"Oh, I wanted to. You've become such a good friend to me, Luke."

Friend.

I hate that word right now. I want to erase it from her vocabulary.

"You want me to open mine now or—"

"Oh, no!" she interrupts, looking flustered. "No, you can wait until Christmas."

Stalling for more time, knowing it's going to be weeks until I see her again, I ask, "You all packed up?"

She offers me a little smile. "Yeah. I'll drive up tomorrow."

"Y'all got big plans for Christmas?"

"Ugh." She huffs, but an instant later, she's frowning, like she feels bad about her reaction. "I talked to my mother yesterday, and yes, she has our every minute planned out. My parents host a Christmas Eve dinner at their house every year and invite all their snooty friends. It's miserable, believe me."

"Good food, though, right? That's something to look forward to."

"Yes, I suppose that's true."

We trudge out to the parking lot, her feet dragging just as pitifully as mine.

"Hang on," I tell her before we part ways. "You walked here?"

"Yeah."

"I'm walking you home," I say, opening the back door of my truck and setting the gifts on the seat. "Or I could give you a ride since it's so cold."

"Oh, you don't have to—"

"Ivy," I growl, opening the passenger door. "Get in the damn truck."

She sighs dramatically, sounding eerily like my pint-sized roommate, but she shuffles over to the truck.

Inside the cab, her scent takes over. Her coconut shampoo combined with something soft and feminine. Jasmine maybe?

I want that scent all over me.

In my bed sheets.

I'm spiraling, my promise to keep her at an arm's length dying a slow, painful death. But I can't find it in myself to care.

Maybe it was her brief, unguarded reply to my flirty comment. Or her genuine emotion at seeing my gift. Or her thoughtful Christmas gifts for Hannah and me.

But I'm caring less and less about the boundaries I've placed on myself about this girl with every passing block.

Like a thoroughbred at the starting gate, I'm ready to break free and run straight to the finish line. Straight to *her*. Consequences be damned.

Tessa's voice breaks me out of my trance. "Luke?"

"Oh, sorry," I tell her, pulling into her driveway. I put the truck in park and shift in my seat so I can see her better in the dim glow of the Christmas lights from the porch of the Schubert place.

"Your Christmas plans?" she questions.

"Oh yeah. After Banana discovers her surprises from Santa, we'll head to my folks' for the day. My mom always makes my favorite—"

"Meatloaf and mashed potatoes?"

"Right. And Cordell and Ms. Rhonda come over for dessert. It's real low-key."

"Sounds perfect."

"Almost," I say, because this year, one integral thing, one person who's becoming more important to me every day, will be missing.

"I can promise it'll be way better than what I'll be doing."

Before I can ask what she means, the cab of the truck is illuminated by something in the bag at Tessa's feet. Her phone. She huffs out an apology as she grabs for it.

I don't mean to be a nosy ass, but, unbidden, my eyes home in on the screen as she holds it in front of her. She declines the call, but the image is there, burned into my retinas.

I see red, my head spinning at the urge to pummel something that takes over.

Because the name on Tessa's screen was a guy's name. I didn't catch the last name; it was long, and it still takes time to decode unfamiliar words. But I definitely made out the first name: Tyler.

Who the *fuck* is Tyler?

"Sorry." Tessa apologizes again as she fumbles with her bag and stuffs the phone back into it.

And I know, *I know*, I have absolutely no right to ask her. That by asking, I'm showing my hand. But the not knowing would eat at my gut for days, so before I can convince myself otherwise, I blurt out, "Who's Tyler?" My voice comes out gruffer than I mean for it to. But it's out there now. No takebacks.

Tessa's eyes widen, then roam around the cab, like she's searching for the answer, before they land on me and she sputters out, "N-no one."

I hold her gaze, not backing down. Who is this guy to her really? I need to know.

She slumps and closes her eyes for a beat as she sighs. "We went to school together. His parents are friends with mine. I always thought he was a jerk, but he moved back to Atlanta recently, and my mom is determined to set us up, even though I told her I'm not interested. Repeatedly."

Gripping the steering wheel, I work to keep my breathing nice and even.

Tessa continues without a clue that I'm about to have a coronary. "Apparently, what I want doesn't matter."

Fuck. The way her voice dips when she says this kills me. Makes me want to follow her to Atlanta and stand up to her parents for her, but it's not my place.

Not yet, anyway.

"My mother arranged for him to be my date for this New Year's Eve gala I have to attend. That's probably why he's calling me." She dips her chin and fidgets with the hem of her jacket. "I hate going to those things, by the way. Fake people with fake intentions. They only care about appearances, not the things that matter." She shrugs, one side of her mouth ticking up like she's forcing herself to smile, attempting to lighten the mood, but all it does is make me angrier.

Makes me want to hunt down this Tyler dude and do awful things to him.

This khaki-wearing, country club card–carrying douche canoe who gets to take *my* girl to a lame-ass party. Gets to put his hands on her for some waltzy dance shit. Gets to lean in and breathe in the scent that's invading my senses right now.

Brain: *Slow your roll. She's not your girl.*

Heart: *Like hell she's not.*

"I should get inside, I guess," Tessa murmurs. She opens the door but turns back to me, giving me that sunshine smile that lights up my world. "Merry Christmas, Luke. Tell Hannah, too, please? And your parents. Thank you again for the puppet theater. It's absolutely perfect."

I ball my fist in my lap to keep myself from dragging her over to me so I can press my lips against hers. So I can claim her for myself before Tyler-the-douche has a chance.

"Yeah. Merry Christmas, Ivy. And you're very welcome." Miraculously, I keep my voice calm, even though, inside, I'm a rage monster.

She hops out and strides for the front porch. After she opens the door, she turns and waves, then pulls it closed again, disappearing from my life until after the holidays.

My jaw is clenched so tightly all the way home I'm convinced I'll wake up with a headache. And I can't shut down the images assaulting me. Of Tessa and a rich jackass flirting and laughing and falling in love. Doing all the things *I* want to do with her.

Suddenly, all the reasons on The List seem ridiculous. Answers for each excuse slot into place for me, like pieces of tile fitting together perfectly.

She's my tutor. *Not forever.*

She's too young for me. *Does age really matter?*

She's probably not looking to settle in Bennett long-term. *I can convince her to stay.*

She's not going to date a tattooed construction worker. *She just made it very clear that she's not into all that hoity-toity bullshit.*

She's never going to want someone who can't read well. *I'm not that guy anymore, thanks to her. She's going to want* me.

As those negative thoughts are replaced with more agreeable solutions, I make a new promise to myself—I'm going to win this girl and keep her. Forever.

Operation Win Tessa Over will begin in the New Year.

And it'll be a fight I refuse to lose.

CHAPTER THIRTEEN

TESSA

I feel eleventy pounds lighter when I pass the *Welcome to Bennett* sign and slow as I roll through town.

My body, so tightly wound for the past three hours (three hours *plus* two whole weeks), finally abandons that fight-or-flight mode, and the tension in my shoulders eases immediately.

So this is what "coming home" feels like.

It's been a long, *long* two weeks, and all I want to do is unpack my car, then sink into my couch with a book. Tears prick my eyes when I turn into the driveway of the Schubert house and peer up at the window overlooking the street on the second floor.

My window.

I've missed this place so much. I've missed Mel. And Shanice and Mr. Weaver. And the library and Ruth's Diner and DejaBrew and the yoga studio and…

Him.

I've missed him most of all.

But since I left Bennett, I've refused to let myself dwell on those thoughts for long.

That look of hopeful nervousness on his handsome face when he brought me out to see the puppet theater.

His look of shock when I called his bluff with his flirty comment about working with his hands.

I'm really good with my hands, Ivy.

I'm sure you are.

I went *there*. I still couldn't quite believe it.

But…it was fun. To flirt back.

Made me want to do it again. *A lot.*

I force all thoughts of Luke away, like I've been doing for two weeks, as I haul my suitcase and bags up the stairs to my apartment. Once inside, I suck in a deep breath and take in the cozy space. It's still decorated for Christmas, even though it's January sixth. Deciding I've earned a few twinkle lights for what I had to endure in Atlanta, I turn on the Christmas tree lights and bask in their soft glow for a long moment.

Atlanta. What a cluster that was.

My parents were ruthless in their pursuit to convince me to move back, even going so far as to call in favors from friends who have a family member who works for the Fulton County library system. Likely hoping that if they found a job for me at a library in the area, the battle to get me back into their sphere of influence would be half-won. And if they could make that happen, I'm sure their next step would be to chip away at my resolve to remain a librarian. No doubt they'd religiously drop hints about going back to school for poli-sci.

Then there was the Tyler Davenport setup.

The New Year's Eve charity gala for children's healthcare was a worthy cause, to be sure. And one my family has contributed to for years. But there was absolutely no need for me to attend on the arm of one of Atlanta's most eligible twentysomethings except that my mother (and by extension, my father) liked the optics. Wanted her only daughter to be seen being wined and dined by the Davenports' oldest son, the one being groomed to take over his family's corporation.

Though teenage Tyler could be cruel to outcasts and outliers, the version of him I spent hours with on New Year's Eve was mature and gracious to everyone he came into contact with. He dazzled my parents all night long and tried his hardest to do the same with me.

He had a hand on me all night, lightly resting on the small of my back or at my elbow in a gentle, albeit possessive grip. We danced together, and he was attentive when I needed a drink refill or to excuse myself to find a restroom. He seemed genuinely interested in me, asking questions about my work and about what I've done since high school.

And he was flirty.

In a way that made me think that *maybe*, had I not moved away for college or work, he might be someone who I could see myself wanting to spend more time with. Someone I could find myself falling for.

"Tessa, you are divine. Have dinner with me tomorrow night," he'd said in that slow-as-molasses drawl as he swept me around the dance floor for the final time that evening, grinning down at me with that playful mouth full of perfectly straight white teeth. Confidence oozed out of him, and I knew he would have a hard time taking no for an answer. He was a man who was used to getting everything he wanted.

But he wouldn't be getting *me*.

After the gala, my mother raved about what a "striking couple" we made, about how we were a "perfect match" in all the right ways. I didn't dare tell her the *real* reason I refused a second date with Tyler despite his persistence.

Because Tyler Davenport isn't *him*.

The man with the dark, disheveled hair he hides under a Braves cap. The man with the deep brown eyes that brand me when he looks at me. With the devastating smile that makes me want to melt into the floor. Whose masculine scent is a thrilling combination of woods and sawdust and sweat. Whose muscles were honed from hours of hard labor outdoors, not a member's-only elitist gym. Whose tattoo sleeve—detailed, intricate whorls and designs in black and gray ink—begs me to trace it with my fingertips. The man who is a stand-up friend and loves his family devotedly.

The man who, when he's near, makes a million butterflies take flight in my belly.

Tyler Davenport is no Luke Shipley.

But I couldn't tell my mother anything like *that*. So I used the *long-distance dating never works* argument when questioned over breakfast the day after the gala. But she was as persistent as Tyler was. She claimed I was throwing my life away in "that tiny, podunk town" and that I would regret letting a catch like Tyler slip through my fingers when I found myself bitter and alone in a few years' time.

Subtlety has never been in Kathleen Burton's wheelhouse.

Somehow, I managed to extricate myself from that breakfast slaughter by claiming a champagne headache, but all that did was put the conversation on hold.

But I'll let Future Tessa deal with my mother's ridiculousness. That's a problem for another day.

After unpacking and throwing a load of laundry into the washer, I make good on my plan to curl up with a good book, soaking in one final day of Christmas coziness in the place I've made a home.

Those butterflies are primed and ready for our first tutoring session after the holidays. I've had all weekend and yesterday (a true-to-its-nature Monday if there ever was one) to prepare myself to see Luke again. During all those hours, I undecked my halls, finished up the laundry, and watched a few documentaries on Netflix, all in hopes of keeping myself from obsessing over him. But despite my best efforts, every time I turned around, my mind was drifting to Luke's smile or his eyes or his strong hands.

It's like Santa brought me a Luke fixation for Christmas.

I took extra care getting ready this morning, second-guessing every article of clothing or swipe of lip gloss, then spent a good ten minutes berating myself for it. Still, it's five minutes before six, and here I am, in the staff bathroom, taking in my reflection in the mirror, nervously tucking pieces of my hair into place and double-checking that my makeup is still intact after a long day. And naturally, because it's too late to do anything about it, I scan the hunter green and navy plaid dress I've paired with navy tights and brown leather ankle boots and wonder if it looks like I'm trying too hard.

Trying too hard for what, exactly?

Shaking off the thought, I wrap the hunter green cardigan tighter and force myself to leave the safety of the bathroom.

When I get to the study room, Luke is already there.

"Oh…hi," I rasp and freeze in the doorway, my cheeks already going hot and my heart galloping away from me.

"Ivy." Luke turns and gives me a once-over. "It's really, *really* good to see you." And then he smiles one of those radiant smiles I've been missing and darts forward like he's going to wrap me up in a hug, but when he's a foot away, he practically skids to a stop and sticks out his hand instead.

Brushing off my disappointment, I force myself into motion and shake his hand, then take my usual place at the table. I've already set up all the supplies we need for our lesson today, including my copy of *The Very Hungry Caterpillar* so he can practice the read-aloud again.

"How's Hannah? How was Christmas? Santa was good to her, I hope."

He nods at my rapid-fire questions. "Yeah, he was. No puppy, though. She didn't even question that, thank goodness. But Christmas was good. How about you?"

"Yeah. Good, I guess." I shuffle through the stack of papers in front of me, hoping to avoid elaborating on my two weeks in Atlanta.

When I finally work up the nerve to peek up at him, his throat bobs. Then he's saying, low and rough, "God, I missed you, Ivy."

And just like *that*, all the oxygen is sucked out of the room.

Cue the butterflies. Millions of them.

His jaw is set, and those chocolate eyes are molten as they search my face, like he's memorizing every inch of it.

Luke's not wearing the Braves cap today, and his hair's disheveled, like he's run his hands through it several times. His plaid button-up shirt is rolled up so that the tattoos on his left arm are on full display.

"So." His voice takes on a sharp quality, and he works his jaw from side to side. "How was that date?"

Wait. Is he jealous?

My heart hasn't stopped beating double-time since I entered the room. I open my mouth to answer but can't find the words.

Why is he asking about my date?

I clear my throat and try again, my voice as shaky as I feel. "It was fine." God, I wish he didn't even know Tyler Davenport existed, let alone that I was forced to go on a flipping date with him.

Am I brave enough to tell him that Tyler means nothing to me? That the whole time *that* man was working to impress me, I was thinking about *him* instead?

"Just 'fine,' then." It's not a question. He's nodding, like he's making up his mind about something. "You plan on seeing him again?"

"No," I whisper, studying my clasped hands on the tabletop, fighting the urge to fist them tightly so I don't pull out my phone and check the pictures from this morning. I want so badly to question why he cares, why he's taken a sudden interest in my love life, but I can't seem to find the nerve.

At my soft answer, a deep breath escapes his lips, the sound loud in the silent space. Then, after what feels like an eternity, Luke's inching a hand toward mine on the table. I suck in a breath when he hooks his pinkie around mine. He stays like that, promising, pledging, but I refuse to look up, even as he says, "I can't fight this anymore, Ivy. I don't *want* to."

I remain silent, terrified that this is really happening.

Terrified that I might do something to *stop* it from happening.

"Tessa."

My name is a plea, but my eyes are still glued to the table, my heart still pounding.

"Will you look at me?"

"Fight what, Luke?" I croak as I lift my head.

The look in his eyes just about takes my breath away.

Fierce determination.

"You know what," he challenges. His pinkie is still wrapped around mine, and he gives our intertwined fingers a small shake.

How are you going to handle this?

I know how I *want* to handle it. I *want* to tell him that I feel it, this indescribable *thing* between us. That I have for weeks and weeks. How I've fallen asleep at night running through scenarios where he becomes mine somehow. Where he takes me in his big, strong arms and kisses away every bit of anxiety and doubt taking up space in my body. Where we fall in love and never look back.

I've imagined it all. A hundred different times, in a hundred different ways.

But just because I've dreamed about taking this further doesn't mean I should. I certainly do not want to start something that has the potential to derail any future progress Luke can make with his reading ability.

Not to mention one very sad, embarrassing fact: Tessa

Burton, at the ripe old age of twenty-six, has never had a *real* boyfriend. Sure, I've gone on dozens of dates, mostly arranged by my mother, but all with guys I'd never choose for myself.

Luke would be the first.

And not only do I want to choose Luke Shipley for myself, but I want to choose him for more than just a few dates. I want to choose him to be mine.

All mine.

Six little words—*I can't fight this anymore, Ivy*—and all the excuses I've made about why we have to keep our relationship platonic fade into oblivion, floating away like balloons released into the sky.

Another gentle shake of my hand pulls me out of my reverie.

"Where'd you go?" Luke murmurs. "Tell me what you're thinking before I go crazy here," he says.

There's a vulnerability in his voice that I want nothing more than to reassure. But I'm still absolutely terrified. And so unsure myself. I search his gaze, absorbing the honesty I find there.

He'll keep you safe.

It's that thought, so steadfast and true, that causes the word to break free from my lips. "Okay."

He closes his eyes for a second and inhales, then lets it out in a whoosh. "Yeah?" he asks softly.

"Yeah." And I can't hold back a grin.

Luke pulls my hand up to his mouth and places a soft kiss across my knuckles. "I've been wanting to do that for weeks," he says, turning my hand over and placing another kiss in the middle of my palm. His lips imprint his intentions on my skin, leaving fire in their wake and causing an involuntary shiver to work its way down my body. Luke smirks at how obviously affected I am, his expression reminding me of a rake in a historical romance novel.

Oh. My. Goodness. I just gave this man a green light. Did I agree too quickly? Should I have made him work a little harder for it? Would I take it back if I could?

No—it feels like we've been on this path since we met. We might have delayed the inevitable, but there's no denying it anymore.

"So," I clear my throat. "Um, what now?" The weight of my inexperience feels insurmountable. I'm trusting Luke to do the heavy lifting for now.

"Now, Ivy League," he says, all confident and handsome, "now you let me take you out."

"O-okay."

"And you let me hold your hand."

"Sure." He hasn't let go yet.

"And there will be other things later."

"Other things?" My heartbeat speeds up again, butterflies swarming.

"Yep," he says, one side of his mouth twisting up. "But for now, how about you just take a page from Banana's book and pinkie promise that you'll come to the mystery reader thing? I'd feel a hell of a lot better if I could look across the room and see your beautiful face."

Whether he senses my nerves or inexperience, I don't know. But he's taking it easy on me. Asking me to start with an activity that's 100 percent in my wheelhouse.

"I mean it, you know. You are beautiful, Tessa."

My face flames at his compliment, but I thank him anyway.

"Welcome," he says, brown eyes lingering on my lips before finding my eyes again.

I extract my hand from his and stick my pinkie back out to him. "I pinkie promise I will be there when it's your turn to be the mystery reader," I swear.

"Good."

"O-okay, let's get some work done, shall we?" As much as I'd love to sit here and stare at Luke without having to be covert about it, we've got a lot to cover. I'm giddy as a schoolgirl, but I miraculously channel the literacy coach inside me and work through the activities I planned. And although Luke works with determination, everything he does is with a hint of flirtation. When the alarm on my phone goes off at seven o'clock, I find myself somewhat relieved to know I'll soon get a reprieve from the tension in the air.

Not because I don't like it.

But I'm itching to get home and have a proper freak-out. To call Mel and hash this out ad nauseam.

As usual, Luke helps me put away all of our study materials before he walks me out. Shanice has already gone for the evening, so after locking up, I join him in the parking lot, where his truck is the only vehicle left.

"Walked again, huh?" he asks as he takes my coat from where it's draped over my arm and helps me put it on.

Head down, I work on the buttons. "Yeah, I love the cold." Georgia's winters are mild, but it's cold enough to make me wish I had grabbed my gloves when I left this morning.

"Truck or walk?" he questions, tilting his head, raking his gaze all the way down to my boots and back up again. Slowly. Like he's taking the time to appreciate the whole package.

I like that a lot, too.

There's no point arguing that he doesn't need to see me home, so I reply with "walk."

"You got it, Ivy," he says, ducking his head and holding out an arm, silently telling me to lead the way. Once we're on the sidewalk, Luke laces our fingers together.

The action is so natural. Like they were made to fit together like this.

Butterflies. All the butterflies.

We walk in silence the whole way to my place, floating in a bubble of contentment. Luke walks me all the way up the porch steps and turns to face me when we reach the front door.

Oh God, is he going to kiss me?

A rush of emotions courses through my body: panic, elation, excitement, nervousness, anticipation. I might melt into a puddle on the cold concrete this instant.

But he surprises me. Of course he does. Because he's been doing it since we met. He brings my chilled hands to his mouth, blowing warm air into the cocoon his big, strong hands make around my smaller ones.

Then he's watching me, those chocolate eyes so soft and earnest. "I can't wait to see you again."

All I can do is gawk. He's so flipping cute, standing on my porch, smiling that devastating smile down at me. This man— tall and strong and handsome and kind and hard-working —likes *me*.

So I say the only thing I can manage. "Okay."

"Hmm. That might be my new favorite word." He steps closer, his woodsy, masculine scent wafting around me, short-circuiting my brain. "Text me before you go to sleep."

"Okay."

He chuckles as he angles in and places a soft, sweet kiss on my forehead, his lips lingering there for a moment before he pulls away.

Stepping back, he tilts his head to the door, reminding me that I actually have to open the dang thing. Somehow, I manage it without embarrassing myself.

"Night, Ivy," Luke says in a low, husky voice before he jogs down the stairs. I get inside as quickly as I can and slump against the door once I close it, forcing air into my lungs. I belatedly realize that I never said good night, but I remain frozen where I stand, mentally replaying the highlights of the evening in rapid succession.

He said he can't fight this thing between us anymore.

He held my hand all the way home.

His lips touched my face.

He wants to do other things *with me.*

It takes a minute to collect myself, to convince myself that tonight wasn't a figment of my overactive imagination. Because only in my wildest dreams would a man like Luke Shipley like a girl like me. A stress ball of a girl with a myriad of issues—anxiety, parental disappointment, feelings of inadequacy, inexperience with romantic relationships.

But despite all that, Luke really likes *me.*

I climb the stairs to my apartment, smiling the whole way.

And the expression remains on my face the rest of the night, through my phone conversation with Mel, my good-night text to Luke, and my nighttime routine. And as I drift off to sleep, snuggled deep in my soft, comfy sheets, I have no doubt it'll still be there in the morning.

CHAPTER FOURTEEN

LUKE

Kindergarten teachers are saints. There's no doubt about it. Right now, Mrs. Gibson's got one little guy following her as she moves between the small tables scattered around the classroom, directing kids this way and that, putting out fires as she goes. As she turns to deal with a mishap involving a pair of scissors, her little stalker runs right into her gut, forcing an *oof* out of her. She calmly walks him back to his seat and continues wrangling a classroom full of tiny humans like the miracle worker she is, never once losing her patience or raising her voice.

When I arrived, Mrs. Gibson had me and two other adults wait in the hall so she could introduce us one at a time by reading clues to the class. The kids called out their guesses using what I'm sure aren't inside voices as each one of us made our way into the room.

When it was my turn, Mrs. Gibson went through her speech again, this time using the clues Tessa helped me prepare. "Our final mystery reader is the father of one of our special kinder friends." Voices rang out once again, one shouting, "It's my daddy!" as another announced, "My dad is at work today!"

"Here is your next clue, friends!" Mrs. Gibson's voice rose above the chatter. "He is very good at building things." That led to another handful of guesses from the five- and six-year-old audience. "And your last clue: This mystery reader loves sports. His favorite team is the Atlanta Braves." After she gave the kids another minute to make guesses, she said, "Okay, mystery reader number three, come on in!"

The look on my little girl's face when I stepped through the door is one I'll remember for the rest of my life. The pure joy and pride that radiated from her as she shouted, "That's my daddy!" and ran into my open arms makes everything I've endured these last few months worth it. Every moment of struggle, every frustration, every ounce of shame.

She's sitting obediently at her little table now, listening as the first guest reads her story at the front of the room, but every few minutes she peeks back at me wearing a big grin, checking that I'm still here.

I give her a reassuring smile every time she looks my way, but on the inside, I'm a nervous wreck. Because the *other* reason I've pushed through the discomfort and shame is not here like she said she'd be.

I pull my phone out of my back pocket again to make sure I haven't missed a text or call from Tessa. I've been second-guessing myself since I got settled here in the back of the room. *Did I tell her the right date and time?* I scroll back through our text messages; there aren't many because I'm still not great at typing out words, but the last I got from her came last night before I fell asleep:

See you in the morning!

Where is she?

I've taken things *very* slowly since the night we decided to explore this thing between us, not wanting to spook her. Like she's a skittish animal and I'm carefully reaching out a hand, hoping and praying I don't frighten her off.

If it were up to me, we'd be well into the *other things* I promised her that night. But I haven't even asked to kiss her yet, though I'm dying for a taste of those lips.

I'm dying for a taste of *every part* of her.

When I came up with Operation Win Tessa Over, I told myself I'd give it a few weeks, turn on all my Shipley charm, and ease her into the idea of an *us*.

But I took one look at her in the doorway of our study room after two long weeks without the sight of that sunshine smile or those green eyes or those luscious curves, and I thought: Fuck. That.

So I jumped. And by some heavenly miracle or stroke of luck, she jumped with me.

We're still wading in the kiddie pool these days.

With floaties on.

But at least we're both in the water.

Together.

However, I feel all kinds of alone right now, a trickle of sweat sliding down my back. If I was sitting, my knee would be bouncing like a spring. Maybe I should have skipped my morning cup of coffee. I flip through the caterpillar book I'm holding in a death grip but freak when the words blur together and swim across the page.

God, how am I going to do this?

I'm racking my brain for ways I can get out of it when Mrs. Gibson calls my name. The sound of her voice forces my attention to her and the dozens of eyes watching me.

From the front of the room, she nods and gives me an encouraging smile. "You ready, Luke?"

Shit.

Swallowing the lump in my throat, I push off the wall, the only support I've had while I've been freaking out, and shuffle to the front of the room. The action is more of a death march than anything.

I'm just clearing my throat to introduce myself again when the classroom door flies open and my saving grace peeks her head in, looking anxious and out of sorts, her eyes huge and her hair a little wild. The attention she garners from the classroom full of people brings a pink flush to her cheeks.

Hannah whisper-shouts, "Ms. Tessa!" and in return, Tessa gives her a quick wink and small wave, juggling her phone, coat, and purse in her hands.

Tessa mouths, "I'm so sorry" to me before she tiptoes to the back of the room, Hannah waving at her the whole way.

Her brows are furrowed and those green eyes dim. I have to stop myself from marching back there, pulling her into my arms, and vowing to take care of what's brought that anxious look to her face, no matter what it is.

But in true Tessa fashion, despite whatever she's been through this morning, she gives me a smile and a head nod, then mouths, "You got this."

And then, like magic, I *do* have this.

I clear my throat once more and read.

"Ms. Tessa, can you come over to my house today?"

We're standing beside Hannah's table, telling her goodbye after the mystery reader event. Tessa looks more at ease than when she first burst through the door, but she keeps fiddling with the hem of her sweater.

Hannah has no idea that her favorite librarian and I are dating; this is nothing more than a little girl innocently asking her new bestie to come see her house so she can show off her toys and then convince her to play Barbies. Or Legos.

"Not today, Banana. But I'm sure Ms. Tessa would love to

come see your room another day," I say, giving her ponytail a jiggle.

Tessa smiles at me gratefully before turning her attention back to the disappointed five-year-old peering up at us. "Sure would, Jelly Bean." She crouches so she's eye level with Hannah, like she always does, and once again, my heart swells at the sight of the two of them together. They formed a bond the moment they met, and I can't wait to watch how it grows.

It's enough to make me weep with happiness.

You know, if I was the weeping kind.

Hannah offers her pinkie to Tessa, and they seal the deal.

Before I'm able to slip out the door, Mrs. Gibson pulls me aside and squeezes my arm. "I knew you could do it," she murmurs, tears welling in her eyes.

My own emotions almost get the better of me, so all I can do is swallow down the lump in my throat and nod.

Hell, maybe I am the weeping kind.

Tessa's quiet as we wander out to the school's parking lot. I take her hand, lacing our fingers together as soon as we step out into the cool January air. I don't want to push her, but I need to know what has her so frazzled this morning. Once we've made it to her car in the back of the lot, I pull her into me and wrap my arms around her body tightly, not saying a word. She rests her cheek against my chest and inhales deeply a couple of times. I hold her like this, my chin resting on top of her head, until the tension in her body starts to ebb. I will hold her like this all damn day if she needs it.

After several long moments, she loops her arms around my waist and tilts her head so she can see my face. "I am so, so, *so* sorry, Luke."

"Hey," I murmur, "There's nothing to be sorry for."

"I almost missed it. I almost missed you read the heck out of that book."

"I did read the heck out of it, didn't I?" I grin, pride coursing through me. I never thought I'd get here.

"You *so* did. I'm very proud of you."

"How proud?"

"Immensely," she says.

"Mmm, I love it when you use big words, Ivy League."

She coughs out a quick laugh, but her face sobers again quickly.

It's time to do a little pushing.

"So, beautiful, what happened this morning?"

She lets out a sigh, returning her forehead to my chest, like she wants to hide from what's chasing her today.

"Mmm, you smell good," she says, avoiding my question.

I know what game she's playing, so I let her indulge a little longer. "So do you," I breathe into her hair. "You always smell good. Like coconut and sunshine and *you*. I want to bottle it up and keep it with me. But since that's not possible, I'll just have to carry you with me instead, maybe get you a backpack carrier or something."

Her body bounces a little, like she's laughing silently. "Luke—"

"Baby, you can tell me."

"I know." After another long pause, she finally huffs out, "My mother called me just as I was getting ready to leave the library." That's all she says at first, but I know from the few times she's mentioned her parents that she doesn't have the best relationship with them—nothing like what I have with my folks. She's hinted that they're unhappy about her chosen profession and that she's settled in Bennett. And she's made it obvious that she doesn't want anything to do with their lifestyle. "We got into an argument," she finally whispers. "Same old stuff, really. She's disappointed in me, disappointed that I won't move home, that I won't agree to see Tyler again. Just disappointed in general. *Immensely*, to use that big word again."

The mention of douche canoe Tyler makes my blood boil, but

all I can do is continue to hold her tightly and let her unburden herself in my arms.

"I just can't win with her."

"What about your dad?" I ask, giving her a squeeze.

"He's…he's not as vocal as she is, but he shares her opinions on the train wreck that is my life. He just shakes his head at me like he can't believe his only daughter turned out like *this*."

"Your life is not a train wreck, Ivy." I hate that she's let her parents' warped view of happiness taint her self-worth. I know a lot about self-loathing myself, and from where I'm standing, there is not one aspect of Tessa's life that she should be ashamed of. "You're the most responsible, put-together twenty-six-year-old I've ever met," I tell her. "You've got two freaking degrees, for Christ's sake, and you've got a job—heck, a career—you love. And you know what?"

"What?" Her voice is muffled against my shirt.

"Happiness. That's the ultimate goal in all this, right?"

With a shrug, she mutters, "I guess."

"It is," I retort. "And from now on, we're going to focus on the things that make *you* happy. So tell me, baby. Tell me something that makes you happy."

She pulls back again, giving me a wobbly smile, her eyes shiny with unshed tears. "Bennett," she says.

"Good. What else?"

"Books. And the library."

"Excellent. Next?"

"Hannah and our pinkie promises."

Whoa. Heart, buckle up.

With my thumb, I wipe away the single tear that escapes and rolls down her cheek. "Anything else?" I whisper, splaying my palms on either side of her beautiful face.

"You," she whispers back.

Heart, it's time to surrender. You never stood a chance.

I am so gone for this girl.

Somehow, I find my voice. "Can I take you on a real date, Ivy?"

"Okay," she smiles softly.

"Good," I rasp. "Good."

Knowing I might die if I don't get my lips on hers, I finally work up the nerve to ask, "Can I kiss you now?"

"Here?" she squeaks out, probably not expecting our first kiss to be in an elementary school parking lot.

As I scan the lot to ensure we're alone, I'm reminded of another monumental moment that started with me in this parking lot. When I worked up the nerve to be transparent with Mrs. Gibson.

Feels like a full-circle moment to me. What better place to give my girl our first kiss than the place where I resolved to change my life?

"Right here." My voice is determined, my stance ready. I push my hands deeper into her hair so I can angle that beautiful face exactly where I need it.

Tessa's cheeks are flushed, her thick lashes still wet, but she's not afraid. If anything, the resolute set of her jaw makes her look as determined as I feel. "Yes."

As soon as she breathes the word, my mouth is on hers, my lips brushing hers in a series of soft, slow pecks. We both grow more confident, the pecks transforming into open-mouthed kisses that get my blood rushing south. Her lips are soft and fit against mine perfectly.

She lets out a contented moan, and I take that as a green light to delve deeper, swiping my tongue against her lips once before she opens farther for me, letting her own tongue flirt back with mine. Tugging her as close as I can get her, I drag the hand in her hair to her nape. Her fingers trail up my chest, over my collarbone, and around my neck, where she plays with the ends of my hair. She nips my bottom lip, pulling a growl from me. I need her closer. One arm still wrapped around her, I caress the small of her back, then slip under the hem of her jacket and grab a handful of her perfectly round ass. I pull her more firmly into me so she knows exactly what she's doing to me as these kisses get more and more intense.

Kissing Tessa Burton is a religious experience. And if this is what kissing her does to me, I can't imagine how incredible those *other things* will feel.

God, I'm a lucky bastard.

My brain finally registers that this is probably *not* appropriate for an elementary school parking lot. Hers must send the same message because we pull away simultaneously, both heaving ragged breaths through our reddened, swollen lips.

With my forehead pressed to hers, I whisper, "five months" into her mouth. "I've been wanting to do that for five months, Ivy."

"Luke," she pants, her emerald irises glittering.

I place soft kisses in response—to her cheek, forehead, the corner of her mouth, and finally, to her button nose. Her skin is flushed that shade of pink I love so much.

She finally clears her throat, like she's coming out of a fog. "I should get going. I've got to be at the Montezuma branch in an hour."

I squeeze her hips and tug her close again, not ready to let her go.

"Luke," she tries again, laughing and patting my chest.

I let out a grunt and finally release her.

She offers me a consolation prize by asking, "When are you taking me out on that real date, handsome?"

I pull her open jacket tighter around her and drag her in for another soft kiss. "Soon, Ivy."

"Hmm. I'm thinking I need a specific date and time."

"Do you, now?"

"I do, Mr. Shipley."

Wide-eyed, she watches me tenderly. I take a mental picture

of this moment, knowing I'll want to remember it forever—my girl, looking freshly kissed, with affection written so clearly on her face that it takes my breath away.

Though I don't want this moment to end, I remind myself that we're just getting started, that we'll have many more moments as special as this one.

"Let me take you to dinner tomorrow night." I cage her in with my arms again, and she automatically slips her hands up to the back of my neck, the soft touch sending a shiver down my spine.

"Okay."

"Okay," I repeat before leaning in for one final kiss. This one is sweet and slow, our lips joining in a way that already feels familiar. I revel in it, wishing I could kiss this woman all day, every day.

All too soon, she pulls away. With one last longing look, she gets into her car and buckles up.

I motion for her to lower her window, and with my hands in the pockets of my jacket, I bend at the waist so I'm eye level with her. "How was that first kiss, Ms. Burton? Everything you hoped it would be?"

Her smile is wide and there isn't a trace of doubt on her face as she says, "More."

We're both grinning like fools as she raises the window. Then she shifts into reverse and backs out of the spot. And with one final wave, she takes off.

When her car is out of sight, I make the trek to my truck, Tessa's lips, and how they taste, the only thing on my mind.

They taste like *mine*.

Once I'm settled in the driver's seat, I send a quick voice text to Cordell, asking him to call me when he's out of school this afternoon.

I need my best friend to help me plan the perfect first date for the girl of my dreams.

CHAPTER FIFTEEN

That. Kiss.

I can't stop thinking about it.

Was it even real? Because it was so perfect, there's no way it could have been, right?

I've kissed boys before. Mostly one time make-out sessions at the end of dates that my mother set up. Sometimes, I was into it, and sometimes, it served to get the night over quicker.

But *never* have I been kissed the way Luke Shipley kissed me yesterday in the parking lot of Bennett Elementary School.

The way he held my head while controlling the kiss, tilting it to take over and run the show with those soft lips and that sensual tongue. How he grabbed my backside and pulled me closer so I could feel how turned on he was. The way he strategically took the kiss from soft and sweet to hot and demanding...

Intoxicating. He tasted like coffee and mint and everything I shouldn't want but long for anyway.

I must have brushed my fingertips over my swollen lips a dozen times on the drive to Montezuma yesterday. Just to remind myself that yes, it *had* really happened.

And today, I'm still replaying every detail while I wait for

Mel. She's coming over to help me get ready for my first official date with Luke.

In the couple of weeks since his confession at the library, we've done nothing more than hold hands and banter over study materials at the library, along with a few phone calls after Hannah's bedtime and maybe a flirty text here and there.

Until yesterday, that is.

A huge part of me wants to go all-in, force my doubts to take a back seat, and enjoy every minute. But then there's a part that warns me to be cautious. To take it slow. This man has a daughter, and I'd never want to do anything to cause turmoil in her life. Or in his, for that matter.

Never mind the deep-seated instinct to protect my own heart at all costs.

Tessa Burton doesn't jump into romances with single fathers.

Sometimes my mother possesses my inner voice.

Will I ever be free of her influence?

"He-ey!" Mel singsongs when she steps into my apartment, forcing my worries away—for now. She gives me a quick hug and then tugs me by the arm to the couch and forces me onto the cushions beside her.

"Okay," she says, pulling her legs up and turning so she's facing me. "I want every last detail. Every single one."

I texted Mel last night and dropped the "he kissed me" bombshell. Seconds after I hit send, my phone was ringing in my hand. But she refused to let me tell her the story over the phone, claiming that I would "shortchange" her by leaving out the "juicy parts." She declared that our best friend status entitles her to a play-by-play retelling. She pretty much demanded everything except a reenactment.

Thank goodness for small mercies.

"Wait!" Mel forces out, pulling one of the throw pillows into her lap. She's still dressed from her yoga sessions today, but she's covered her workout tank with a sweatshirt that says

Hedgehogs: Why don't they just share the hedge? above a cartoon hedgehog holding a protest sign that says *No!*

Not for the first time, I wonder where she finds these things.

Mel tightens her short purple ponytail like it will help her focus, then says, "Go! I want every excruciating detail, T."

Mel Marshall is literally the only person in my life I'd be willing to be excruciatingly detailed with, so I hold nothing back. She's rapt. Her eyes widen at the kissing part, and she has a smug grin on her face the whole time.

"I *knew* it!" she cheers when I'm finished. "I *knew* he'd be a bomb kisser and I *knew* you two would be fire together!"

"Oh, you knew, huh?"

"Sure did! He's a Leo, and you're a Pisces. A passionate sign mixed with a sensual one, my friend. When you two finally bang, it's gonna be explosive!"

"Whoa, there, Madam Mel!" My face flames. "This is our first date, so there will be no *banging*."

Mel's eyebrows are practically in her hairline. But then, because she's Mel, she changes the subject without pressing me further. "What are we thinking for tonight's outfit? Did Luke tell you where he's taking you or what y'all are doing?" She stands and strides toward my bedroom, but not before mumbling, "Other than banging?"

"Mel!"

In the doorway, with her back to me, she raises her hands in surrender. "Okay, okay. I can wait for *those* excruciating details. But don't make me. Or *Luke*"—she spins and dips her chin, giving me her narrowed, I-mean-business look—"wait too long."

Good golly, that's a Future Tessa issue for sure.

I don't have the mental capacity right now to focus on anything after tonight.

Mel forces me to model a couple of outfit options and offers advice on hair styling and makeup tips. And though I roll my eyes every time she needles me about *banging*, I soak in the way it feels to have a close friend like her. One who's here because she wants to be, not because of what I can do for her or out of obligation to her family.

Once Mel leaves, I still have a couple of hours to kill before Luke is supposed to pick me up. Although it won't take me all that long to get ready, I go ahead and shower and start the process, just to give myself something to focus on.

And even though—much to Mel's chagrin—there will *not* be any banging tonight, I buff and scrub all the things and shave my legs.

You know—doesn't hurt to be prepared.

While styling my hair into soft waves, my phone rings from my bedroom. I can't fight the smile that takes over my face when Luke's name appears on the screen. "Couldn't wait two more hours to hear my voice, huh, handsome?"

Luke groans. "Ugh, you're killing me, Ivy."

"Well, that won't do. I need you alive to take me on this hot date, mister."

"Yeah, about that." He lets out a deep sigh, the phone line crackling as he does. "I'm afraid I need to reschedule our date, baby. I'm so sorry."

My heart plummets, and I drop onto the edge of the mattress, but I affect the most chipper tone I can. "Oh, that's fine." I refuse to give in to the urge to ask why.

"Liar," he says, his voice so deep and husky it rumbles straight through the phone line and into my core. Then he's huffing a regretful sigh again. "Banana's sick. Started running a fever this morning, and I just can't leave her. My mom is helping Daisy set up for a wedding in Macon and won't be back until late, and my dad is out of town. I'd ask Cordell and Ms. Rhonda to watch her, but her temp was at 103 earlier, and I just can't pawn her off on them this sick. I put off canceling with you all day, hoping she'd turn a corner somehow or that my mom could make it home in time, but it's not working out."

"Aw, poor Jelly Bean. Can I do anything for y'all?" I'm hit with a wave of relief that his reason involves parental duties, then immediately feel horrible because it means Hannah is sick.

"You're the sweetest thing for asking, but we're set here. I'm rotating meds to keep her fever down, and Doc Marshall is just a call away. I think this just needs to run its course. Feel terrible that my Banana is so puny, though." He lets out the lowest growl. "And it's killing me that I can't get my hands on you tonight." His words make me flush from head to toe, that heat in my core burning hotter.

I clear my throat and pull my shoulders back, shaking off the sensations. "Call me if you need anything. And keep me updated, too. I hope Hannah feels better soon."

"Will do, Ivy. Let's try again next weekend, yeah?"

"Yeah," I say softly, my heart heavy.

After we've hung up, I bring my legs up onto the bed and allow myself to have a mini pity party. I bite the inside of my cheek, phone in hand, ready to call Mel and break the news to her, but as I hover over her contact, an all-consuming need to see Luke tonight washes over me. His daughter comes first and always should, and I feel awful about her being sick. But I don't want to be alone tonight. I could probably talk Mel into coming over for a binge night, or we can hunt down Taco Tuesdays' location and go on a road-trip taco run. There's always drinking away my disappointment with her at Fuzzy's. But every idea I come up with pales in comparison to spending the evening in Luke's company.

Ugh, when did I become such a simp for this man?

I wallow for a few more minutes before an idea comes to mind. Maybe there's a way I can see Luke tonight after all.

~

I almost miss the turn at Thigpen Road, and as a result, I hit the brakes a little too hard and crank the wheel, wincing when the paper bag on the floorboard of the passenger seat slides. I say a silent prayer that the items inside make it without too much damage.

About a mile down Thigpen, the disembodied voice coming from my phone tells me my destination is on the left.

All those butterflies are swarming like crazy right now.

Am I stupid to do this? What if he doesn't like unannounced visitors?

I consider turning around and heading back to Bennett, but the part of me that made the very bold decision to do this tonight won't let me turn tail and run.

So I press on.

I stop at the end of a long gravel drive that leads to a cozy-looking ranch-style house with a vintage muscle car parked next to the closed garage. The sun is preparing for its nightly slumber, and I can just make out the details of the property in the twilight as I step away from my car. It's quiet out here, even more so than in Bennett, which is saying a lot because that place is pretty dang quiet. Even though it's the end of January, the weather is mild.

I step up to the front door and tug on the hem of my sweatshirt to straighten it out. After a deep, calming breath, I ring the doorbell and wait to see whether my appearance will cause happiness or frustration. After a minute or two without even a shuffle or a peep from inside, I ring the bell again.

Nothing.

I'm struck with a terrible thought: Luke Shipley lied to me.

If his daughter is so sick, why isn't he here?

Then I vacillate in the complete opposite direction. What if Hannah got so bad that Luke had to take her to the hospital?

But then I'm back on the he-is-a-lying-scumbag train, so torn about what to think.

Tears well in my eyes on my way back to my car. Am I

reading things with Luke all wrong? Am I so desperate for affection that I've fallen too quickly for someone I barely know?

Back in the driver's seat, I give in to the urge to check my camera roll, then remember that I left in such a hurry this evening, not wanting to lose my nerve, that I didn't snap a picture of the turned-off straightener I used, nor did I take the time to capture the moment I locked my door before rushing down the stairs. Panic threatens, roiling low in my gut and radiating out to my limbs and up to my chest and neck.

Calm down. You know you did those things without seeing photographic proof. It's fine. It's all fine.

With nothing left to do except go home and cry, I put my car in reverse and back down the long gravel drive. As I do, I notice that it continues on past the left side of the ranch house and beyond a pond, where it curves before disappearing behind a copse of pine trees.

Curious.

What if—

I shake my head and scold myself for being nosy, but just as quickly give in to my curiosity and put my car back into drive. I stay on the path as it winds past the pond, through the pines, and around another sharper turn until the trees open up to another clearing. And then I'm gasping at what I see through the windshield.

In the middle of the clearing is a modern white farmhouse, complete with a large front porch. The flat roof of the porch is supported by three thick, square columns, and two rocking chairs and a hanging swing beckon invitingly. The windows on the front of the house are framed by black shutters that match the front door.

It's the most precious, perfect little house I've ever seen.

I drive all the way up to the open garage on the left, where Luke's navy truck is parked.

I'm embarrassed at the level of relief coursing through me. Because Luke is *not* a lying scumbag.

There's no going back now, Tessa.

Hefting the brown paper sack on one hip, I head to the front of the house and up the porch stairs. The design of the half lite door means there will be no doubt about who is standing on the porch once I knock. Also, no hiding his initial reaction when he realizes I'm here, interrupting his Saturday night.

Butterflies fluttering like mad, I tap lightly on the window that takes up the top half of the door, hoping I don't wake Hannah if she's sleeping. I heft the paper bag higher up on my hip and wait.

Moments later, he's there. Striding toward the door with a look of surprise on his handsome face.

Please let it be a good surprise. Please let it be a good surprise.

He pauses in the entryway, gaping at me through the windows for a long moment. The surprised look on his face morphs into one of his devastating smiles as he gives me a thorough once-over. Then the door swings open, and there he is, barefoot and looking adorably disheveled in plaid pajama bottoms and a gray T-shirt.

"You're really here?" he asks softly, scanning me for a second time.

"I hope it's okay," I answer, giving him a one-shouldered shrug.

"It's more than okay, Ivy League. It's the best damn surprise I've had in a long time." He grasps my free arm and pulls me over the threshold.

Right into his strong arms.

Luke Shipley gives the best hugs on the planet, hands down.

A girl could get used to a greeting like this.

"You're here," he whispers, shaking his head. Then he nods at the bag pressed to my side. "Whatcha got?"

"Oh," I say, holding it out. "Chicken noodle soup from Ruth's for Jelly Bean. And dinner for you."

Luke takes the bag and peeks inside.

"And pie. Couldn't forget the pie."

"Strawberry?"

"Of course."

"God, you're something else," he says, shifting the bag to his side so he can step closer and kiss my lips.

Once. Twice. Three times.

"Banana's finally asleep, but I know she'll love the soup when she wakes up."

"Good."

"You're not worried about our germs?"

"Nope," I say, and I mean it. A little sickness would be a small price to pay for getting to spend time with Luke tonight.

"Come on in, Ivy."

I finally manage to pry my eyes away from him long enough to take in the inside of his house. It's homey and bright, with crisp white walls and weathered gray hardwood floors. In the open-concept living room, a plush navy couch and loveseat sit around a neutral-colored area rug centered in front of a fireplace. There's a brown leather recliner on the other side of the rug, angled perfectly toward the flatscreen TV above the mantel. It's easy to see traces of the little girl who lives here, from the doll stroller beside one end table to the naked Barbie lying forgotten on the brick hearth and the stray crayons scattered on the coffee table.

"It's perfect," I tell him honestly, because it is. Luke's home is perfectly cozy and perfectly him.

He rubs the back of his neck, suddenly looking so very shy.

"It took long enough to get it that way. That's for sure." He motions toward the wall to my left, where an entryway table is positioned just inside the door. Above the table, there's a mirror and several framed prints.

One of those prints is a replica of this house, painstakingly drawn and colored, down to the last detail.

Then it dawns on me. Why he's being unusually bashful.

"You drew that?" I ask.

"I did. That's the first drawing I put together. It's what I wanted this place to be."

"Wait." I gawk, understanding dawning on me. "You mean that you—"

"Built it, yeah. Built my dream house."

Speechless, I step closer to the framed drawing, taking in every line and every angle. "You're brilliant." The words leave me in a breathless rush, and I turn back to him to repeat them, louder this time. "You're brilliant, Luke."

He gives me another aw-shucks smile, rubbing his chest with the hand not holding the bag of food.

"How?" I ask, desperate to know more about this piece of him.

"Come eat with me and I'll tell you," he says, holding out a hand.

I let him lead me into the kitchen, drinking in every detail along the way—Hannah's adorable kindergarten artwork on the refrigerator, the white cabinets, dark countertops, and gleaming farmhouse sink. The Atlanta Braves hand towel hanging from the oven's handle, children's Tylenol and Motrin bottles on the otherwise clear countertop. Luke keeps hold of my hand and guides me to a round rustic wooden table. I run a hand over the smooth surface, marveling at its craftsmanship, thinking that there's a good chance he built it as well.

Luke Shipley—constantly surprising me.

"So that picture," he says, pointing to the frame by the door. "I drew that when I found out Shelley was pregnant. This land has been in my family for generations, and my folks have always told me I could build a place of my own here. So the idea had been bouncing around my brain since I was a kid. I started saving for it in high school." He pulls containers from the paper bag as he's talking and sticks the soup in the refrigerator. From the cabinet over the dishwasher, he pulls out two white dinner plates and then portions out the meal I brought for him from Ruth's—beef tips over rice with green beans, macaroni and cheese, and cornbread. "In my line of work, it's easy to find guys who'll help. So I drew up the plans, had an architect friend of my boss's look at my drafting sketches, and then recruited some buddies on my crew to help out when they could. Paid them in beer and my mom's meatloaf, believe it or not. My dad is an electrician, so he did all the wiring, and Cordell's uncle in Americus is a plumber. It was like a community build. My dad helped as much as he could, so it was just the two of us out here a lot. We'd spend hours framing, putting up sheetrock, tiling, you name it, until Mom called us in for dinner."

"How long did it take?"

He chuckles softly. "Longer than I wanted. We cleared the land when Hannah was three months old, and we were finally able to move in this past June, right after her fifth birthday." By now, he's brought the plates and silverware to the table and has taken the chair beside me. I can't help but examine him, mesmerized by the talent he possesses.

He built a house with his own two hands and some help from friends. From start to finish. All while not being able to read.

Brilliant can't even describe Luke Shipley.

I have so much I want to say to him. My heart feels so full of pride, admiration, and affection for the man sitting beside me it's almost overwhelming. But I don't know where to start, so for a few minutes, I let the silence between us take hold and dig into my dinner.

"Luke," I finally say when I've got my thoughts in order. "I just...this house is absolutely beautiful, and it's even more special because it came from you, from your heart."

"I'm glad you like it, Ivy." He smiles at me softly and brushes a wave of hair behind my ear.

"You're amazing," I whisper, taking that same hand and holding it tight, marveling at his callused palm and tracing his strong knuckles. This very hand I'm holding built the room I'm sitting in.

"Come here," he says roughly, pushing his chair back from the table. He tugs on my hand, forcing me to stand. And then he pulls until I'm seated on his lap, my legs hanging over one side of his thighs. "Looks like I'm getting my hands on you tonight after all." His deep voice sends a shiver down my spine, and that shiver multiplies as he loops his arms around me to hold on to my hip and upper thigh, then buries his face in the space between my neck and shoulder, just resting his head there and inhaling deeply before placing a kiss on the side of my neck.

Mel's words from earlier come back to haunt me, and suddenly, my internal temperature ratchets up.

Luke pulls back and tilts his head so he can make eye contact. "How'd you know how to find us out here?"

"Don't make me say it," I whine, putting my head in my hands.

He chuckles and pulls my hands away from my face, giving me a teasing pointed look.

So I blurt it out. "The library card application we filled out at the carnival."

"That was months ago, Ivy."

"I memorized it. The day I typed it all in."

"Hmm. That's a little stalker-ish of you."

"I know!" I wail, slapping my hands to my face again.

Luke's body is shaking with laughter as he once again pulls my hands away, this time capturing my face between his palms before I can hide again. "I don't mind being stalked by you, baby." He's turned serious now. Those brown eyes search my face before landing on my lips. My body responds, flushing all over, and that deep throb low in my core revs up, liking where this is heading."

Luke's lips brush mine, and my hands instinctively move to his hair, my fingers running through the soft strands. He deepens the kiss, his tongue seeking mine.

I moan into his mouth at the sensation, at the way Luke grips me tighter to him.

But then a sleepy little voice croaks, "Ms. Tessa?"

Luke and I pull away from each other like we've been scalded, but when I try to stand up to put some distance between us, his grip on me doesn't lessen enough to allow it. When we turn as one, Hannah's standing on the bottom stair across the living room, watching us with a brown stuffed dog clutched tightly to her chest. She's wearing strawberry-print pajamas. Her long hair is down and unruly, her big brown eyes are wide, and her little face looks paler than normal.

"Banana, sweetheart, you shouldn't be out of bed. You're still sick, honey."

"Why is Ms. Tessa sitting on your lap?" She completely ignores Luke's comments.

This time, when I try to stand, he lets me, but he fastens me to him with an arm around my back and a hand on my hip when he stands beside me.

Okay, so we're going there already.

"Ms. Tessa was sitting on my lap because that's something that grown-ups sometimes do when they like each other."

I try to offer her a smile, but it's a wobbly facsimile. I've never been caught by a five-year-old in the middle of making out, so I'm feeling a little out of my element here.

But Luke's totally composed. "Ms. Tessa and I like each other. More than friends like each other. Like Nana and Papaw like each other."

"You mean like she's your girlfriend?"

"Yep," he answers, offering no further explanation. And if he's shocked by her question, he doesn't show it.

She yawns big, apparently satisfied with his answer, then says, "I'm hungry."

This jump-starts Luke. "Right. I'll bring a bowl of soup to your room. That way you can rest while you eat." He turns for the fridge and calls back to her over his shoulder. "It's almost time for your medicine, too."

I'm frozen in place, feeling all sorts of awkward. Hannah spins on the bottom step and trudges back up, but she stops after a few stairs and says, "Are you and Ms. Tessa having a sleep-over?" Her question is totally innocent, I know, but I can't help the wave of mortification that crashes over me.

"No!" I blurt out at the same time Luke says, "Not tonight." I turn to look at him, my jaw at my feet, and he just gives me a wink.

Tessa Burton, you are in trouble.

With a shrug, Hannah continues up the stairs.

I can't even touch the "not tonight" comment, so I step closer to where he's heating the soup on the stove and murmur, "I should head home."

Lips pressed together, he nods. "Let me walk you out." On our way to the front door, he stops at the foot of the stairs and hollers up to Hannah, "I'm walking Ms. Tessa out to her car! I'll bring your soup in a minute!"

"'Kay!"

Barefoot and silent, he walks me out, hopefully not regretting his decision to out us to his daughter.

Like he's reading my mind, he clears his throat and tells me, "I'm glad Hannah knows about us."

"Really?" I say, unable to hide my surprise.

"Absolutely. You're special to me, and it makes sense that the other special person in my life knows about you."

"If you're sure—"

"I am." No wavering, no hesitation.

"Then I'm sure, too." The butterflies go nuts again, but despite that, it feels *right*.

"Good," he confirms, pulling me in.

I hold on to his waist as he threads his fingers into my hair and kisses me.

Once. Twice. Three times.

"I should get back in there," he says, stepping back. "I can't tell you how happy I am that you came to see me. I'm sorry our first date ended up this way, but I'm not sorry about anything that happened tonight."

"It was the perfect first date," I tell him, meaning every word. It really was perfect.

Except for getting caught red-lipped by the five-year-old.

"I'm taking you out for real next weekend."

"You better, handsome."

Luke smiles before giving me one last slow kiss. He opens my car door and waves as I take off down the gravel road.

As I drive away, I look back at the perfect farmhouse glowing in my rearview mirror, and my heart warms at the realization that this won't be my last visit out to Thigpen Road.

CHAPTER SIXTEEN

LUKE

Tonight's the night.

My first official date with Tessa.

Hannah's all set for a Saturday night sleepover at my folks' place. Not that I expect to be having my *own* sleepover, but I'm not sure how late I'll be out. Better to have my Banana settled in for the night than to risk waking her to carry her home. She's back to feeling like herself again after the crud she dealt with last weekend, thank goodness.

Hannah's question about Tessa and I having a sleepover last weekend makes me chuckle even now.

My girl was embarrassed as all get-out.

Me? I can't wait to have a *real* sleepover with her.

One that *doesn't* include a whole lot of sleeping.

She's not ready for that, though. And I can be a patient man.

Even though these blue balls might kill me while I wait.

Even though it gives me and my dick lots of *together time* in the shower these days.

When she showed up on my front porch last Saturday night, looking all kinds of nervous and cute, it did something to me.

The *you're brilliant* she murmured when she realized that the vision for my home came from my own head and from my own hands? That comment made that tight knot in my chest grow so big it pushed against my ribcage.

No one has ever said something like that to me before.

And having her in my home…God, that felt so *right*. Like written-in-the-stars, meant-to-be kind of stuff we all grow up hearing about but, deep down, doubt will really happen. Even though my own parents are great examples of what it means to love for the long haul, being burned and left high and dry made me wonder if I'd ever experience that kind of magic.

But I'm here to tell you—that shit really happens.

Tessa Burton is that kind of magic.

What we're doing feels like the most natural thing in the world to me. The List that troubled me for months? A long-forgotten fever dream.

I'm ready for a heavy dose of that Tessa magic tonight. Cordell helped me run through my options, but our choices are pretty slim here in Bennett. If we want to go somewhere fancier than Ruth's, we'd have to drive a bit. But Tessa's made it clear that she's not impressed by fine dining.

I pull up to her house and park along the curb. I'm so revved up I forget about the bouquet of wildflowers lying on the passenger seat, and I have to jog back across the yard to get them. Then I'm hoofing it, climbing the stairs two at a time up to the second floor. When I reach the door to apartment four, I take a deep breath before knocking.

I'm blown away by the vision that answers the door.

My girl, sunshine smile in place, looking like all my wildest dreams come true.

She's wearing black jeans that hug all her curves just right and a black and white checked button-up shirt under a loose tan sweater. Short tan boots complete the look. Her hair is styled in those loose waves she was sporting when she came over last weekend. Her makeup, like usual, is light. It's just enough to highlight her natural beauty.

But her lips? Tonight, her lips are red. I've never seen her wear a lip color this bold before.

God, I want those lips all over me some kinda bad.

I can't fight the grin that's eating up my face as I look her up and down, counting my lucky stars that this girl is *mine*.

"Hey, handsome," she says, opening the door wider for me to enter.

"God, Ivy, I'm not gonna make it to dinner without kissing your face off."

She laughs, big and carefree, and steps back.

I follow her inside and pull the flowers from behind my back.

"Oh, Luke! They're beautiful."

"Perks of having a mom who works for a florist," I tell her with a shrug.

She takes the wildflower bouquet and holds it up to take a whiff. "I don't think I have a vase," she says, rounding the kitchen counter. She opens cabinet after cabinet, searching, and finally, she pulls out a white pitcher that'll work. She goes about arranging the flowers as I take a look around the space she calls home.

It's totally Tessa. Books everywhere. Stacks of them on end tables by the couch. Two bookshelves full of them on either side of the TV stand. A teal couch and a multicolored rug on the floor. She has several house plants, too, all green and healthy, like they thrive on her sunshine smile.

Finished with my quick inspection, I join her in the kitchen, where she's inspecting her arrangement.

"I'd best be getting you a vase then. I have a feeling you'll be getting flowers again soon."

She presses her lips together and turns back to the bouquet, but not before I see the pink creeping up her cheeks. I can't help myself. I sidle up behind her, snag her around the middle, and hug her to me. I pull her in so her back is to my chest and I can breathe in her scent. She relaxes into me, like she finds comfort from simply being in my arms.

Makes a man feel damn good.

"Where are you taking me tonight?" she asks softly.

"Nowhere if we don't get out of here soon. Those red lips are way too tempting."

Tessa runs her hands down my arms and laces her fingers with mine where they're still pressed to her abdomen. "Let's go, then, handsome."

I manage to pull myself away, but I keep hold of one of her hands and lead her to the entryway.

I help her into her jacket and usher her into the hall. After she closes the door and locks it, she hesitates, her attention locked on the knob.

"Ivy?" I ask after a long moment.

"Yeah," she says, still facing the door. She glances at the phone in her hand, then shoves it into her purse. "Yes," she says, more firmly, finally turning my way and giving me a smile. "Let's go."

"Proud of you for that," I tell her as I take her hand again to lead her down the stairs. In response, she offers me a smile that takes my breath away.

We talk and laugh and flirt during the thirty-minute drive. I can't seem to keep my hands off Tessa these days, so I rest my palm on her thigh and give it a squeeze now and then. And my chest constricts every time she leans her head back against the headrest and looks over at me with a smile on those red lips.

Restaurant is a loose term for the place I'm taking her. It's a hole-in-the-wall down a back road. A place Cordell and I discovered a few years ago while out looking for new fishing spots. But the Smoke Shack serves the best barbeque in the state of Georgia. It's literally a wooden shack with a pit barbeque out back where all the magic happens. There are only two four-top tables inside, and food is served in Styrofoam or cardboard. But what it lacks in decor and seating, it makes up for in quality.

When I pull into the gravel lot, Tessa looks over at me with a tiny crinkle between her brows.

Yes. I'm taking my dream girl to a shack on our first date.

I toss a smirk her way as I unbuckle her seat belt and pull her hand to my lips. "Yep. This is the place," I tell her and plant a kiss on her knuckles.

She narrows her eyes in a playful bring-it-on way and says, "I love it."

This. Girl.

I hop out of the truck and round the hood to Tessa's side to open her door.

"You don't have to—"

"Uh-uh," I cut her off, taking her hand as she steps down. "I know you're capable of opening your own doors. But I want to do it for you, so let me. Please."

She huffs a little and rolls her eyes, but then she's smiling. "Fine. Thank you."

"My pleasure, Ivy."

"So what's good here?"

"Hell, it's all good. Brisket, pulled pork, sausage. But the ribs are my favorite. Second only to Mom's meatloaf," I tell her as we step inside and the sweet, smoky scent fills our lungs.

Luckily, one of the two tables is available. We step up to the counter and place our orders—ribs for me and a brisket sandwich for Tessa.

During dinner, I can't keep my eyes off my girl. That's pretty much been the norm since I met her, but now I don't have to be so covert about it. I love watching the way she lights up when she talks about books or reading or her job. How she tosses her head back in laughter when she jokes about her friendship with Mel. And the soft expression she wears when she asks me about Hannah's first years.

I'm addicted to her every expression, and I'm already so familiar with her body language that I can tell exactly what she's thinking without words. And I'm obsessed with how her blush spreads across her face and upper body when she's embarrassed or shy.

I think I'm falling in love.

There's no falling *involved, dumbass. You crash landed there months ago.*

It's dark when I pull onto the road that led us here, but instead of heading back to Bennett, I drive west, toward our second stop of the evening. The farther we go, the smaller and windier the roads become. The scenery outside, though cloaked in darkness, is increasingly overgrown.

Ten minutes in, Tessa jokes, "Is this where you hide all the bodies?"

I laugh in response but give nothing away.

Then we're approaching the turnoff, a rocky dirt road that winds through the trees until it leads us into a clearing along the bank of the Flint River.

This spot is the best kept secret Cordell and I share.

Other than *the* secret that's not so secret anymore.

We lucked upon it the same day we found the Smoke Shack, while we were looking for a fishing spot that wasn't crowded. It's the perfect hideaway. Where the forest meets the flat, solid riverbank. It's an easy spot to launch Cordell's fishing boat without the crowds or the parking chaos at the popular boat launches in the area.

I park near the river and turn to look at the gorgeous woman sitting beside me. The moon is full tonight, not a cloud in the sky, and its light lines her features in a soft, silver glow.

"What's next, Luke?" she questions quietly, twisting at the waist to face me. When she smiles, my heart rate races like a thoroughbred leaving the gate.

"You and me. The moon. The river. Thought we could enjoy

nature for a bit, seeing as it's not too cold. What do you say, Ivy? Will you sit with me awhile?"

"Okay," she whispers, a little breathless.

God, I want this girl so bad.

I want to kiss every inch of her, get her twisted up in pleasure as our bodies become intimately acquainted, leave no room for doubt about how I feel about her. I want to trace all her soft curves, memorize each bend and dip, discover the sounds she makes when she reaches that peak.

But tonight is not about that.

I lean over and place a soft kiss on Tessa's full lips, still red and begging for mine.

After helping her out of the truck, I open the back door and remove the supplies I packed. Even though the temperature is warm for late January, I lay a thick wool blanket on the lowered tailgate, keeping a second blanket folded up on the bed liner to wrap around my girl if she gets a chill. The full moon gives us just enough light to see each other, to see what's right in front of us. I get her settled on the end of the tailgate, her shapely legs swinging off the end, and steal another quick kiss before going back for the other items I brought.

I bring the small cooler around to the back of the truck and hop up next to her on the tailgate. Her eyes dart from the cooler to my face and back to the cooler, a question swimming in those emerald irises. Before she can voice it, I hand her a plastic fork.

"What kinda first date would this be if we didn't have pie?"

"From Ruth's?"

"Where else?"

I hand the container holding a slice of chocolate pie to Tessa and chuckle when she shimmies her shoulders at the first bite. I can't help but fixate on how her red lips wrap around the plastic fork and the soft moan she emits as she chews thoughtfully.

Great, now the front of my jeans is growing tighter and I'm jealous of a damn plastic utensil. I need to gather some self-control before I chuck my strawberry pie and maul her like a freaking animal.

After chewing another bite, she scrutinizes me and says, "Question time."

I nod and shove another bit of pie in my mouth, doggedly ignoring the hormones coursing through me at this moment.

"If you could change anything about your childhood, what would it be?"

"Getting deep right off the bat, huh, Ivy?"

She takes another bite of pie, some of the whipped topping sticking to her top lip, like an open invitation for me to lean in and take care of it.

So I do. Taking her chin gently in one hand, I place an open-mouthed kiss on that sweetness, the tip of my tongue darting out to lap it up. When I pull back, she gives me a shy smile, then sticks her own tongue out to lick the same place.

Holy hell, I'm in trouble.

An inferno ignites in my gut, so I shuck off my jacket and tug at the sleeves of my Henley. If this doesn't cool me down, a dip in the river may be next.

The beautiful girl beside me remains unaware of the way my body reacts to her every move. It's an amazing kind of torture.

"Luke?"

"Ah, yeah, sorry." I clear my throat. "My parents are pretty damn great, but I wish they could have had more kids. Would've loved having a younger brother or sister. But if I could go back and change one thing, I wouldn't have kept my reading problems a secret. My parents knew I struggled, but I should've talked to them about it more, you know? Made sure they really understood how bad it was instead of sweeping it under the rug."

"I get that," she says, swinging her legs and looking out into the night. "But it can be hard for kids to advocate for themselves. Don't be too hard on little Luke for that. It takes a village, as they say, but sometimes that village lets a person fall through the cracks. Not because they don't care, but because with so many neighbors to care for, it's a numbers game. Plus, there's a lot more research about brain development and reading out there these days." She's looking at me, honesty shining in her eyes. "You've done something about it now, and it's never too late to learn how to read. So give yourself some credit for taking the hard steps when you did. And give yourself some grace for not knowing better when you were younger."

Incredible. This girl has a knack for knowing exactly what to say to make me feel better. She's done it time and time again since we met.

Like a magnet, my lips find hers for a grateful kiss.

"Okay, you know the drill, Ivy." During our study sessions, I'm sure to toss her whiteboard questions back to her, and tonight is no different. "If you could change anything about your childhood, what would it be?"

Tessa lets out a soft *ugh*. She doesn't like to talk about her parents, but I want to know every single thing about her. The good and the bad. I want to give her the same kind of support she gives me on the regular. She looks off into the distance, like she's gathering which pieces she wants to reveal to me tonight. Finally, she offers me a tight-lipped smile and says, "Would I sound like a terrible, ungrateful brat if I said everything?"

"Nope."

"Well, that's my answer, then."

"Uh-uh. I want more, baby." I lace my fingers with hers for support and bring our joined hands to my thigh while she talks.

"Aren't we focusing on what makes me happy, handsome?" she asks, trying to deflect. She's throwing my own advice back at me, but I won't let her off the hook that easily tonight.

Give me all of you, Ivy. I want it all.

"We're focusing on that, yes," I tell her. "But being your man means I get to know about the things that make you unhappy, too. So I can make sure they stay the hell away."

"*Luke,*" she drags out my name, tries to tug her hand back.

But I refuse to give in, so I hold on to her hand, raising an eyebrow.

"Fine," she huffs, picking an imaginary piece of lint from her jeans. That wrinkle between her eyebrows is back, but I resist the urge to smooth it away. "You know how my parents are really into their social status, right?" She peeks over at me, and when I nod, she continues. "I would change that, for starters. I love my parents, I really do, but I wish they had been more present in my life when I was growing up. And that they saw and appreciated the *real* me, not the me they expect me to be. I wish they could've been happy that I found my own path in life, instead of being disappointed that I chose one different from theirs. I wish a lot of things when it comes to them, honestly." She's looking down at her lap, tears glimmering in her eyes.

"Thank you for telling me, Ivy," I say softly, giving her hand a small squeeze and shake. "And you might feel like you're a disappointment to them, but you are anything but that, baby, I promise you. You are smart and kind and so, so precious. You're kicking ass at a job you love. One you're good at. Maybe once they see how much you're thriving here, they'll come around."

"Maybe." Though she doesn't sound so sure.

"And if they don't, if they never see the real you, accept the life you've chosen for yourself, then that's their loss. Because they would be missing out on someone pretty damn incredible."

"Luke—" she starts. But she doesn't finish. Instead, she chooses to show me her feelings by leaning in to press her lips to mine sweetly. I pull her closer and deepen the kiss, letting go of her hand to place both of mine on her cheeks and hold her tenderly while our mouths explore, eager. She slides her hands up to my shoulders before draping her arms over them and playing with the ends of my hair, driving my lust higher.

Higher. I'm so high on this girl, I might as well be on the moon.

Before I know it, I'm half lying on Tessa on the blanket beneath us, trying to keep my very noticeable erection from digging into her hip, and she's delving her hands into my hair with more fervor, her short fingernails raking my scalp in search of a better grip. I manage to pull my mouth away from hers, but it doesn't go far, because I'm planting kisses along her jawline, under her chin, down her throat, up to her ear.

"Ivy," I rasp. "Give me a second," I beg, knowing I have to rein myself in. I finally pull my lips from her skin and rest my forehead against hers, breathing hard. "God, I love kissing you. And I want you so bad, beautiful. But I think we should pump the brakes."

"Yeah?" she asks, also breathing heavily. She takes my face in her hands, watching me with eyes as lust filled as mine probably look right now. "Yeah, okay." She smiles, rubbing my stubbled cheeks with her thumbs, then placing one more long, lingering kiss on my lips. "I want you, too, Luke," she whispers into my mouth.

I let out a groan and bury my face in the space between her neck and shoulder, taking deep breaths of her scent until I'm drunk on her. "Baby, I don't want this to happen in the back of my truck," I mumble, nuzzling into her one more time before lifting my head to look into her eyes. "I want it to happen, like you have no idea how bad, but not here."

"Okay," she says again. "So our date is over, then?" she asks innocently, but her eyes narrow as she sizes me up.

I grin down at her. "Not a chance, Ivy League." I sit up, pulling her with me. She remains on the end of the tailgate as I hop to the ground and move back to the cab of the truck. I turn the key in the ignition so just the battery is on and turn up the volume on the country station so we can hear it at the back of the truck. Once I've got the windows down, I jog back to where Tessa waits.

The end of a fast song plays out, and like some kind of divine intervention, the next song is a slow one. One perfect for what comes next.

Tessa gives me one of her sunshine smiles as I stand between her legs and slide my hands up and down her perfectly thick thighs. As the song plays on, I take her hand and pull her off the tailgate and into my arms, our bodies touching at every possible point. She wraps her arms around my middle and places her cheek on my chest. Her head fits under my chin like she was made to be there.

Like she was made just for me.

"What are you doing?" she asks as I sway to the music.

"Dancing with a beautiful woman."

She says nothing but lets out a soft, contented sigh. So I hold her close and dance with the girl who has captured my heart so completely.

The song ends, but we keep swaying, lost in one another. Dipping my chin, I bring my lips to the shell of her ear and whisper, "So—first real date, Ivy. Was it everything you hoped it would be?"

"More," she breathes into my neck.

At this moment, just the two of us out here under the stars, I have everything I've ever wanted.

And it feels like magic.

CHAPTER SEVENTEEN

TESSA

The past few weeks have been a dream. I find myself literally shaking my head in disbelief all the time. When Luke calls me baby. When he gives me three perfect kisses in a row. When he runs his fingers through my hair. All of it feels like it should be happening to another girl.

But it's happening to *me*.

And every moment has been perfect.

Like that first date? Most romantic night of my life.

Since then, we've been inseparable. Dinners at his parents' house. Happy hour with Mel and Cordell at Fuzzy's. Park visits with Hannah on the weekend. Two slices of pie in a booth at Ruth's.

Luke always holding my hand or gripping my thigh in a possessive way that sends a thrill through my body. Kissing my forehead, or nose, or lips, or fingers. Smoothing his hand down the back of my head. Every time we're together, he finds little ways to touch me, like he can't quite believe I'm real either.

I love all the ways he shows that he cares about me.

The bouquets of wildflowers on my porch before work, a little white note stuck between the blooms that says *Have a good day Ivy* in his still-wobbly handwriting. Or the way he calls me every night after he tucks Hannah in, just to tell me good night and to have sweet dreams. How he watches me, brown eyes full of desire and something else I'm afraid to label so soon.

I'm afraid to label it, but I feel it, too.

And that terrifies me.

Maybe that's why I haven't mentioned Luke to my parents yet. And why I haven't allowed myself to move past making out with him like a couple of teenagers past their curfews.

I think about him nearly every second of the day.

Like right now, when I should be helping Shanice shelve books. Instead, I'm lost in thoughts of Luke. His lips. His strong arms. His devastating smile that makes my butterflies swarm. His voice when he answered Hannah's question about me being his girlfriend, so deep and confident.

"Mm-hmm-hmm," comes from behind me. It's Shanice. I'm reluctant to turn around, knowing my face will be as red as the copy of *The Maid* I've been holding for the past several minutes. "Girl, you gonna shelve that book or read it?" Her voice is all knowing and teasing.

"Right." I say, finally managing to put it in its proper place. Then I take a moment to compose myself before turning to face her. When I do, she's giving me a smirk that tells me she knows exactly where my mind was vacationing.

"Why don't I finish up those last few?" She nods to the four books on the book trolley I've been aimlessly pushing around for a solid hour. The old Tessa would be mortified to be caught giving less than 100 percent on the job. Today, I'm grateful for a friend who remembers what it's like to have one's thoughts consumed by a boy.

"Yeah, thank you."

"No problem. You and Luke got big plans tonight?" she asks as she takes over the trolley and deftly shelves the next book in a matter of seconds.

Tonight. Right. It's Valentine's Day. Hence the glittery cupids and hearts hanging from the library ceiling over the main desk. I told Luke I didn't want anything special, and since it's a Tuesday, that I would expect him in the study room at six on the dot. We've finished the adult literacy workbooks, and he's come so far with his reading skills. But I'm reluctant to wrap up our sessions just yet because he still has trouble decoding longer words when he's reading text. We've been working on word morphology and vocabulary so he can also use his knowledge of what word parts mean to help him with unfamiliar words.

We're still working at the library, but it might be time for us to move our sessions to my place or his because of our relationship. I don't want to make anyone uncomfortable here. Shanice knows what's going on, and I'm pretty sure Mr. Weaver suspects something is up, but I've managed to maintain professional behavior in the study room. Even if Luke is incorrigible with the touches and flirty comments. I expect strictly above-board behavior when we're in study room two.

On the drive or walk home, on the other hand…

"Not really. He's coming in for his session as usual. What's Darrell got planned for you tonight?" I ask her.

She gives me a *hmph* while she continues down the row of shelves to place the last book. "When you've been married this long *and* you have a kid, you don't really make a big deal about Valentine's Day like in those lovey-dovey days. I'll be happy if we get DJ to bed at a decent time so we can watch an episode or two of a show together before we pass out on the couch."

"That sounds like its own kind of perfect, too," I tell her honestly.

She pushes the trolley past me, smiling and nodding. "You know what? You're right." She gives my arm a squeeze. "You enjoy that fine white boy tonight, you hear?" she says, giving me a wink over her shoulder.

Miraculously, I make it through the rest of the day without

daydreaming. But I do get in some heavy-duty second-guessing about sticking with our tutoring session tonight. It's our first Valentine's Day as a couple. Should I expect him to plan an elaborate date? Should *I* have planned one? Does he expect a surprise from me, or will he be expecting *other things* because of the holiday? Should I have gotten him something more than the gift wrapped in shiny red paper sitting on my desk?

I'm not very good at this girlfriend thing.

These thoughts plague me for the rest of the day, so much so that my stomach aches each time I glance at the clock.

During this afternoon freak-out, I open up my camera roll, only to realize that I didn't take my morning pictures. This is not the first time I've forgotten in the past month, but it's the first time I've panicked about it. It takes all my self-control not to sneak out and run home to check.

By the time Luke's tall figure appears in the doorway of the study room, I'm convinced that I'm going to let him down. And burn my house down because I left the straightener on.

"What's wrong, baby?" he asks. This man can always tell when my anxiety is flaring. In a heartbeat, he's in front of me with his hands on my upper arms, rubbing up to my shoulders and down to my elbows. His eyes are full of concern as he crouches to search my face.

But my thoughts are a jumbled mess, so in a breathless rush, I blurt, "I'm so sorry I'm a sucky girlfriend and I made you come in for this on our first Valentine's Day instead of going out. And I said I didn't need anything special, and that's the truth, but then I realized that *you* might need something special and I—"

"Whoa, whoa, whoa, Ivy. Take a breath, darlin'."

He's still rubbing my arms in that calming way, so I focus on that sensation instead of the heavy weight pressing in on my chest or the nauseous ache in my stomach.

"Baby, you gotta breathe for me," he reminds me again. He guides me back to sit in a chair and crouches in front of me, the same way he did when I panicked on the day of the dragon costume incident.

Deep breath in. Hold it for four. Out for four.

It's a breathing technique my therapist suggested. I've been meeting with her for the past few weeks; Mel discovered my morning picture stash on my camera roll one night about a month ago and gently suggested trying online therapy since Bennett doesn't have a local office.

I repeat this breathing sequence a couple of times, mortified about getting so worked up. Luke waits patiently, coaching me through my breathing, not taking his hands off my thighs.

"I'm so sorry." I groan, ashamed that he has to put up with me like *this*. Wondering why he'd choose to date a girl so riddled with anxiety she might as well lock herself in a bubble and never leave. A girl who needs constant reassurance.

It must be exhausting to date me.

"There's nothing to be sorry for." He gently lifts my chin so I'm forced to look at him instead of down at my lap. "You are not a sucky girlfriend. Not even close."

"But—"

"Nope, I won't let you talk about my girl that way." He eyes me, his stare boring into me like he's trying to figure me out.

Like he wants to know where *this* all stems from.

I latch on to the arm he's holding my chin with, trying to push it back so I can hide. Retreat. But he won't budge.

"Where'd this come from?" he implores. "All this nonsense about something special for Valentine's Day? Ivy, the only thing I want for Valentine's Day is *you*."

"I was afraid that I'd messed up. That you would be disappointed."

"Have I ever done anything to make you think you're a disappointment to me?" he asks. When I shake my head, he continues probing. "So where is this coming from?"

"*Ugh.*"

But Luke isn't backing down. He lets go of my chin and gives me time to collect my words, but he doesn't stop his rhythmic, soothing caresses.

"My parents," I force out.

Luke clenches his jaw and fixates on something over my shoulder.

"One year I offered to plan an anniversary dinner for them. Except when I called, their favorite restaurant was booked. So I had to go with plan B. They never said they were upset, but I could just tell. I could always tell…"

When his eyes find my face again, they've softened. "You could never be a disappointment, Tessa. To me or anyone else."

"Luke, I'm a hot mess—"

"You're *my* hot mess," he interrupts me again. He sounds so certain. I have no choice but to believe him, right? Plus, he's shown me more than once that my issues don't scare him off.

"Okay," I croak out, fighting the tears that threaten to spill.

How on earth did I end up with this man? He's so steadfast and good and strong and capable and sweet.

And *hot*. Lordy, is he hot right now, looking at me with those deep brown eyes, the ends of his hair still damp from his after-work shower, the perfect amount of stubble on his handsome face. Wearing the heck out of a gray thermal Henley and those jeans that fit him just right.

I don't know what I've done in this life to deserve him, but I'm keeping him.

Despite my best efforts, a few tears slip out and course down my face, even though I'm calmer now.

Luke swipes his thumbs across my cheekbones as he drags out, "Ba-by, my heart can't take it when you cry." He leans in to kiss my lips. Once. Twice. Three times. "I know you said no kissin' in the study room, but I'm breaking the rules tonight."

A watery laugh escapes. "I'll let you."

"Good. Will you also let me skip the lesson so I can be with my girl on Valentine's Day?"

I gasp in mock horror. "You have a girl on the side, Mr. Shipley?"

"Nah, I'm a one-woman man. She's got me wrapped, though."

"Does she?"

"Hell yeah, she does." He's watching me so intently, like he can see right down to my soul. Like he can see everything I have to give, and he doesn't find me lacking. He kisses me again, this one slow and languid. I feel it all the way down in my core, between my thighs, melting away the last shreds of self-doubt.

And just like that, my mind is clearer, and the mental whiplash is replaced with peace and quiet. Even the heaviness in my chest has disappeared.

Luke Shipley, my own personal weighted blanket.

"What do you say we get out of here?" Luke asks, standing and pulling me up at the same time. Once we're both upright, he drops his hands to my hips and tugs me into him. We stay like that for a moment, just holding each other, my cheek against his chest and his chin resting on the crown of my head. He's so warm. His woodsy, manly scent surrounds me, breathing life into me, and his heart beats steady and true beneath his shirt.

My voice is muffled against him when I say, "Since we've broken so many of the study room rules already, I guess taking the night off won't hurt."

His answering chuckle comes from deep in his chest, making my head bounce a little. Then he kisses the top of my head and pulls away, his phone already in hand. "Pizza sound like a good plan?"

"Pizza is always a good plan."

While he's ordering, I put away my materials and collect my things from my office, including the gift wrapped in shiny paper. I refuse to let those feelings of inadequacy from earlier reappear.

So I remind myself that he will love the gift no matter what, because I chose it for him.

The nearest pizza place is in the next town over, so we have to drive out to pick it up, and Luke keeps me entertained with Hannah's impressions of her first school Valentine's Day party the whole way there.

Turns out, Jelly Bean has an admirer. In her Valentine box, there was a total of five cards signed *Love, Chase* in big, uneven letters. The little rule follower was indignant because they were instructed to give one and only one card to each classmate. I can imagine Hannah complaining to her father in her sweet little voice. The thought of the two of them talking about their day in this truck warms my heart, even while wishing I could've been there for the ride.

I find myself wishing I was with them all the time these days. I don't want to miss a thing.

We make our way back to my apartment, and when we get out of the truck, Luke hands me the pizza box. He emerges from the back seat with a huge vase of gorgeous red roses and a flat, wrapped present.

"Happy Valentine's Day, Tessa," he says, standing on the sidewalk under the streetlight, looking so perfect I want to cry.

"Happy Valentine's Day, Luke."

For a long moment, all we do is stare at each other, lips curved into smiles. My belly flutters when he gives me a slow perusal.

"You're the best Valentine present I've ever gotten, by the way," he says, deep and husky.

The ache in my gut throbs at the sound of his voice alone. I want to go to him, fold myself into his arms and never let go, but a dozen roses and a large pepperoni pizza stand in our way.

Upstairs, Luke sets the vase on my small kitchen table while I pull out plates, napkins, and beer. We're quiet while we eat, and a weight I haven't felt before settles in the air between us. Like it followed us up here from our moment on the sidewalk. It's not unpleasant, but it feels significant. Luke's brows are drawn in as he stares at his plate, and I can't help but study his face and body language, hoping for a clue about what he's thinking.

When we're finished eating, he rinses our plates and loads them into the dishwasher, then grabs two more beers. After he passes me one, he smooths his hand from the crown of my head down to my neck; the motion simultaneously soothes and scorches me.

I can't get enough.

"Present time, Ivy?" he asks, dropping back into his seat. Canting forward, he tugs the leg of my chair closer to his so we're facing each other and my knees are tucked between his.

Set on making him go first, I hold his gift out. He doesn't take his focus off me until he's got it completely unwrapped. Once the paper falls to the floor at his feet, he finally peeks down at it.

A book.

He's achieved so much in our time together, and I'm so ready for him to experience all the things that books have to offer— adventure, knowledge, romance, differing points of view. I want him to fall in love with reading the way I did when I was a kid. To know he changed his world by taking the leap to learn how to read. Of course, his future is bright because of *who* he is, and I have no doubt that he'll accomplish anything he desires.

And I hope I'm there to witness every moment.

"A Spl-splin-splintered History of Wood." He reads the cover and looks up at me, a question in his eyes. Not about the gift itself, but about his reading of the title. Once I confirm that he's correct, he thumbs through the pages.

"I thought that since you love working with wood, you might enjoy reading about its uses throughout history. It even has a section on baseball bats."

He's studying the book's cover again, flipping it over to look at the back, then scanning the front once more. I can't read his expression, and I'm starting to worry he doesn't like it.

"I wrote a little note on the inside," I explain tentatively.

He searches my face for a moment, then opens up the front cover. "To Luke. I'm so pr-proud of you and your de-de-deter—determination…" He looks at me for confirmation again. "Determination to 'build' a better fu-future for yourself. Ivy." I agonized over what to write and how to close the note for hours, settling on simply signing it with his nickname for me.

"You know," I say, my nerves getting the better of me, "I just thought you'd enjoy learning more about the history of something you li—"

"Ivy. It's perfect," he says, smoothing a hand over the front cover reverently before setting the book on the table. Then he takes my trembling hands in his steady ones and pulls me in until our faces are inches apart. "You're perfect." He breathes the words into my lips before capturing them and kissing me senseless. The way his lips pull and twist mine, the way his tongue confidently caresses mine, the way he makes a little growly noise when the kiss gets more intense—all of that is also perfect.

When we finally pull back to catch our breath, Luke pushes up the sleeves of his Henley, as if the temperature in the room has suddenly risen. And instantly, I trace the lines and swirls of the tattoo on his forearm, the black and gray design a welcome distraction from the need coursing through me right now.

He's watching me, studying me, yet I keep tracing, keeping my head down in concentration. He wants to say something, I'm certain of it. Internally, I'm begging him *not* to say the thing—the thing I'm pretty sure describes all these too-big emotions.

"Tessa, I—"

"Don't," I whisper, a plea.

And I instantly regret it.

As much as I want him to say the words, I'm terrified. Asking him not to say it probably makes me a coward, but it feels like what my heart needs at this moment—a reprieve from the overwhelming sensation of leaping out of an airplane without a parachute.

That's what falling for this man feels like.

Finding the courage to finally look up, I take in his handsome face, those brown eyes locked on me. His jaw is set in a determined way, like he's ready to make the declaration I'm both terrified *and* impatient to hear. But the moment passes. His expression softens, and something like disappointment sweeps over his face as he nods subtly.

I want to let out a sigh of relief while simultaneously screaming *no*.

"I was just going to ask if you wanted to open your present now," Luke says with a slight smile. Not a devastating one, but a resigned one.

I take the box from him, trying to hide how my hands shake. "My mom wrapped it for me," he says, leaning back in his chair like he's settling in for a show.

"You outsource your wrapping, Mr. Shipley?" I ask, my voice wobbly from the panic and emotion of Luke's almost proclamation.

He just smirks and lifts his chin, urging me on.

I pull the paper away, an audible gasp escaping at what's inside.

It's a framed drawing. A riverbank, detailed browns and blues and greens of the real place. A navy pickup sits off center but prominent, its tailgate down and covered in a plaid blanket, with a small Yeti cooler on the edge. The background is brighter than our surroundings were that night, but the moon is drawn high in the sky and the scenery is heavily shaded. To the left of the truck, a couple stands with their arms wrapped around each other. Their faces are abstract ovals, but her hair is light brown and wavy while his is darker and mussed. Their clothing matches what we were wearing that night, right down to the tan suede booties on the girl's feet.

It's the most meaningful gift I've ever received.

But I can't find the words to tell him this. All I can do is let him see the tears in my eyes and pray he can sense the emotion and sincerity I feel.

"Baby," he whispers, instantly cupping my face, his thumbs swiping away the tears that are already falling. But the deluge becomes too much for him to wipe away, so he takes the drawing from me and places it on the table next to his book. Then he pulls me into his lap so my legs straddle his and lets me bury my face in his shirt. His strong, warm arms wrap around me and hold on tightly while I soak his shirt.

I want to stay here forever.

I want to stay buried in the comfort of Luke's embrace for a lifetime, because these tears are about more than his wonderfully touching gift. They're a product of the emotions raging through me after his near confession. I know exactly what he wanted to tell me, but I shut him down.

You are a fool, Tessa.

After several minutes, I croak out, "Luke, it's the most wonderful gift anyone has ever, *ever* given me."

Still holding me close, he rubs soothing circles on my upper back. "Just wanted you to have a way to always remember our first date. I'm glad you love it, beautiful," he whispers in my ear before kissing my wet cheek. Once. Twice. Three times.

I drop my forehead to his so my lips are hovering millimeters from his, a shuddered breath escaping me, an aftershock of my melt-down. Our noses graze, and Luke presses a tender kiss to my mouth, holding there for several long seconds before pulling away an inch.

"I know you're not ready for me to say it. So I won't tonight." His words are hot against my skin even as a chill races down my spine. "But I *will* be saying it. Soon." His voice is unwavering, the words strong and resolute. There will be no reasoning with him on this; his mind is made up.

I only wish my own mind would stop making me second-guess things. It's not that I don't feel the same way about Luke—I absolutely do. But that inner voice that constantly makes me question myself is hard to drown out. Combine that with my parents' expectations and disapproval of my life choices, and it's enough to cause a girl to doubt even when the answer is staring her in the face.

Luke wipes at the remnants of my tears, his strong, callused fingers leaving a warmth on my damp skin.

"Looks like I've set the bar *real* high in the gift-giving department," he teases. "How am I going to top this when it's your birthday or Christmas?" His certainty about his need to buy me a Christmas gift ten months from now sends a rush of giddy excitement through me.

That giddiness smothers out most of my regret.

We have plenty of time.

That realization has my whole body sagging with relief.

"I bet you'll think of something, handsome."

"Mm-hmm. You're easy to impress," he jokes.

I swat his arm playfully and stand from his lap. I was getting way too comfortable there.

Once I'm settled in my chair again, with Luke's hand latched on to mine, he does his best to lighten the mood after my pendulum swing of emotions. He's so dang good at handling me with care. Like he's memorized some Tessa instruction manual that details how to defuse every form of my anxiety.

When I yawn for the third time, Luke says, "I guess I should head home. Work in the morning for both of us."

I'm exhausted, both physically and emotionally, so I acquiesce. At my door, he sweeps me up in a goodbye kiss that has my toes curling in my shoes.

Just before he opens the door to leave, he turns and says, "Oh yeah. I forgot about the other part of your gift."

"What? You've spoiled me enough for one night, I promise."

But he ignores me. He pulls his wallet out of his back pocket and slides out a folded piece of paper. Once he's got his wallet tucked away again, he unfolds the paper and hands it to me.

At the top are the words *Bennett Family Medicine* and then the address and contact information for Mel's mom's office.

"Statler makes us get a physical once a year."

I look up at him and then back down to the paper.

"You'll see down there that this year, I requested additional blood work."

Confused and overwhelmed by the medical jargon, I tilt my head and squint at him. "Okay?" It comes out like a question.

One side of Luke's mouth curls up in a smirk. "See all these tests Doc Marshall ran?"

My face flames when I catch sight of the list of sexually transmitted diseases he's pointing at. Every one of them has the word *negative* beside it.

His smirk turns into a confident smile that makes me clench my legs together when I work up the nerve to peek up at him again. "Just wanted to be prepared," he says, tucking a strand of my hair behind my ear. And just when I think he's going to wrap me up in another embrace, he does the opposite. He steps back and pulls open the door, and all I can do is watch him, my mouth agape, the sheet of paper still gripped in my shaky hand.

Out in the hall, he turns back, his hand on the doorknob and his mouth poised to say the words that will sear me from inside out. That will send shivers of excitement dancing over every part of me.

"I'm ready when you are, Ivy."

CHAPTER EIGHTEEN

LUKE

I'm ready to put all my cards on the table. Lay my heart on the line. Use every cheesy saying imaginable to describe how I feel for the girl I left standing open-mouthed in her doorway.

I'm all in.

Tessa Burton is *it* for me.

Is it crazy that I want to tell her I love her after only a month? Maybe. Do I care? Fuck no.

But she does.

She's worried we're moving too fast. She hasn't said the words, but I know she's thinking them. And not just because she had a minor meltdown when those three little words were ready to slip past my lips like my heart couldn't contain them anymore. I know it because I *know* her. Inside and out. Even though we've only been dating for a month, I've attended the Tessa Burton school for six months now. Studying every expression and voice change. Memorizing her face, her curves, and the feel of her soft skin. Testing her boundaries and limitations. Taking mental notes of her likes and dislikes.

Not only have I learned how to read over the past six months, but I've learned everything about *her*. And I've earned myself an A-plus in that class, damn it.

So I'm not surprised that she stopped me from saying *the thing* tonight. She over-analyzes everything and lets her doubts and insecurities hold her back from so much living. I want to desperately break her out of the cycle of those negative thoughts, but I can't force her to change. She has to want it for herself. Starting therapy is a start for sure; I'm so damn thankful Mel convinced her to give it a try.

Changing oneself for the better—I know a little something about that. It took me a hell of a long time to get here, but I had to be the one to take the first step.

I'll be as patient as she needs when it comes to her anxiety. But when it comes to expressing my feelings for her? I meant what I told her—I *will* be telling her how I feel, and soon.

But that unconditional love that my parents have given me every damn day of my life? My girl didn't get the same treatment from her folks. And no amount of material items can make up for that. It's gonna be real hard for me to remain civil when I finally meet the Burtons face to face.

But even if she never finds a way to set her negative thoughts free, even if I have to talk her down every time she gets worked up for the rest of our lives, I'll fucking do it. I'll be her calm in the storm. I love this girl, every part of her, even the parts she wants to keep hidden.

I'll be her champion, because that's what she's been to me. She believed in me and pushed me when I wanted to quit, when the road to reading seemed too hard to travel. She's what kept me going all these months. My girl never backed down, and I'm going to return the favor.

Hannah is the spark that ignited the flame, but Tessa is the kindling that's kept it going.

My mom's watching TV in my living room when I get home.

She watched Hannah here instead of at their place so my little girl could sleep in her own bed on a school night.

"Hey," I say, roughing up her hair before dropping next to her on the couch.

"Hey, you." She's already wearing her pajamas and has a bathrobe tied around her waist. My folks are early-to-bed people. She's probably ten minutes from falling asleep. "How'd Tessa like the roses? And your drawing?"

"She loved them. Tell Ms. Daisy they were a hit, will you?"

"'Course." She tries to hide a yawn behind a hand, then waves it off like she isn't exhausted. Working in a florist shop at Valentine's Day is brutal.

"Want me to call Pop to come get you?"

"Nah." She hauls herself up, and I follow. "Hope you kids had a nice Valentine's Day." She leans in to give me a quick hug, but I hold on to her tightly before she can pull back.

Sometimes a boy just needs to hug his mom.

"Thank you for watching Banana tonight. And all the other times, too." With my hands on her upper arms, I pull her back so she can see how sincere I am. Tessa and I wouldn't be happening if my parents were not kick-ass grandparents to my kid. There wouldn't be any riverbank dates or happy hours or Saturday night Netflix make-out sessions on Tessa's couch if they weren't available to keep Hannah.

"Hey," Mom murmurs, squeezing my biceps. "This one is different, Luke. I've known that since the first time I saw her with you. And with June Bug." Her brown eyes are watery, making me force down a hell of a lot of emotion before I can answer her.

"Yeah, Mom. She's different."

She nods. "Good. Don't fuck it up." She pokes a finger in my chest for emphasis.

I huff out a shocked breath. I don't think I've ever heard my mother drop the f-bomb. Other swear words? Yes. But never this one. "Mom!" I finally force out, my eyes still bugging.

She raises her brows innocently. "What?" She pats my arms with both of her hands, turns to grab her keys off the end table, and heads to the kitchen to leave through the garage door. And I'm still standing in the living room, struck dumb by my mother's word choice.

The sound of her tires crunching on gravel jolts me back to life. I make sure she's shut the garage door, and then check in on Hannah before heading to my room to get ready for bed.

Sitting on the edge of my bed, I flip through the book Tessa gave me tonight. It'll take me a really long time to get through it because I still have to stop and sound out (or what Tessa calls "decode") long words. But I'm armed with knowledge of the six syllable types, so I know I can figure them out. Turning back to the inside of the front cover, I smooth my fingertips over her note, and that familiar tightness in my chest flares. She wouldn't have given me this if she thought for one second I couldn't read it. Knowing her confidence in me is true, I place it on my bedside table and admire the way it looks there. It's the first time I've ever had a book in that spot, ready and waiting for me to pick it up and get lost in its pages.

Words on pages. I never knew how powerful they could be.

But I fell in love with a girl between the lines of the words she taught me to read.

A girl whose patience and sweet spirit gifted me with the tools to make those words come to life, changing my whole damn life for the better.

"We're going to be late." Tessa's breathless, her hands tangled in my hair as my lips devour her neck. I'm *this* close to giving my girl a hickey like some horny teenager.

"Mmm" is all I can muster, lost in her scent and the sensation of her skin. I work my way to her collarbone, leaving a trail of kisses across and down to the neckline of her sweater.

I'm so fucking hard it's painful.

A soft moan escapes her lips, and that pain in my groin throbs.

Shit, the blue balls are real tonight.

Even though I told her I was ready over two weeks ago, we still haven't taken things farther than this. And that's okay.

Well, my brain says it's okay. My dick? He has a different opinion.

No way I'm pressuring this girl, though. I care about her too damn much, and I'd hate like hell for us to get going and then have her panic about it.

"Luke…" She's straddling my lap, her soft breasts pressed up against my chest.

I squeeze the round globes of her ass in response, pulling her closer, making sure to slide her along the hardness between my legs.

"*Oh,*" she breathes out, the movement spurring her to take the reins. Her hands leave my hair, and then she's got her palms on either side of my face, forcing it up from her chest and planting her mouth on mine.

Now it's my turn to let out a moan from deep in my chest. Tessa's tongue slides along mine, her lips sucking and pulling, her hands angling my head just where she wants me.

Fuck, it's so hot when she takes over.

After a few more breathless moments, she finds the willpower to pull away, breathing hard like she just ran up three flights of stairs. Her swollen lips tilt into a smile as she scans my face and brings her hands to my shoulders. "We have to stop."

She's winded and wound up and so damn sexy I want to rip this damn sweater off her body. Instead, I drop my head to the back of the couch in an attempt to control my breathing and the raging hard-on in my jeans.

"We told Mel and Cordell we'd meet them at six. And it's…" She swipes her phone from the end table. "It's five fifty-five."

"Ugh." That's all I can manage at this point.

I love our friends. I really do. But I love this girl in my lap so much more, and I want to hoard every damn second with her.

"Sorry, handsome."

I study her face for the millionth time, soaking in her smooth skin, those big green eyes framed by long dark lashes, her thick brows just a shade darker than her hair, that button nose she likes to wrinkle up to drive me wild, her rosy cheeks and kissable mouth. I press a thumb lightly against her lips, and she rewards me by puckering them and giving it a kiss.

God, I love this girl.

Just when I think our intense eye contact is going to lead to make-out session number two, Tessa's phone lights up next to us. When I see the name that flashes on her screen, every muscle in my body goes taut.

Tyler. Davenport.

"Why is that dou—uh, *dude*—calling you?" I ask more harshly than I mean to.

"No idea," she says, her brows furrowed in genuine confusion.

As the ringing continues, I have to clench my fists to keep from answering it and telling him to fuck right off. She's looking at it like it will magically reveal the reason for his call, but then she swipes it up and stands from my lap, leaving me to deal with the stiff third member of our little make-out party.

"Hello?" Tessa shuffles to the window to peer out. She listens for a moment, then glances my way to give me a small smile before she says, "I can't, Tyler. But thank you so much for asking." She's quiet again.

I want so badly to rip the phone out of her hands and tell Douche Canoe to lose my girl's phone number.

"No, I understand, and really, that's nice of you to think of me, but I can't. Mm-hmm." Then she draws a deep breath and says, "Um, I can't because I'm, uh, I'm seeing someone." More silence. "Yes, yeah, he's-he's totally wonderful." She looks right at me as she says this, and my heart swells in my chest. "Okay, then. You, too. Bye." Then she closes her eyes and takes in another deep breath.

Probably because she knows Tyler will say something to her parents. Who I'm pretty damn sure have no idea I exist. I wait for anger or hurt to surge to life as that understanding forms. But they don't. The only anger I feel is for that jerk on the other line.

"Ivy, talk to me." I stride to where she's standing.

She opens her eyes, lashes fluttering and fear shining in her irises. "Th-that was that guy I went out with when I was home in December." She's twisting her hands, nervous. *About my reaction or her parents?* "He asked if I would go with him to this fundraiser thing his family's company is hosting in a couple of weeks." She's searching my face, trying to read my reaction. But I keep my expression neutral. "You heard me. I told him no." When I don't answer, her brows draw together and she plants her hands on her hips. "Well, are you going to say something?" she demands.

Damn, she's cute when she's angry.

"Luke, *say* something. I told him no. You *heard* me," she repeats. But I keep quiet, sizing her up. We're so close I can see her pulse throbbing in her throat.

Finally, I can't keep it up any longer. "C'mere," I growl, linking two fingers in the belt loops of her jeans and pulling her body into mine. The move elicits an immediate sigh from her as she sinks into me. "Totally wonderful, huh?"

"Shut up."

Her face is hidden in my shirt, giving me the perfect opportunity to run my hands through her thick, silky hair.

"You know what, Ivy?"

"What?" The word is smothered against my chest.

"I think you're totally wonderful, too." I palm her cheeks so I can pull her off my chest and plant a kiss on her still-swollen lips. "Now, let's go. Our friends are waiting. And we're late."

It's a cool night, but we walk anyway. Mel and Cordell are already inside, seated on stools at one of the high-tops next to the pool table area. I keep my hand on the small of Tessa's back as we walk through the busy bar, because I know crowds can make her nervous. When I sneak a look at her by my side, though, she's wearing a soft smile.

Ms. Daisy and her posse are in their usual booth. She and Ms. Rhonda and the other ladies wave enthusiastically at us when we pass by.

"Cordell, I think your mom is here more than you are," I tell him, helping Tessa remove her coat before sliding my stool closer to hers and settling in. Then I drop my hand to her thigh under the table, where it will stay.

I only need one hand to lift my beer, right?

Cordell shakes his head at the table of middle-aged women. "I know. I swear her social life is way more exciting than mine." He reaches across the table for Tessa's hand and plants a quick kiss on her knuckles. "Looking beautiful tonight, Ms. Tessa," he tells her with that damn charming grin on his face. He's the only joker I'd let get away with shit like that.

Tessa's requisite blush spreads up her neck to her cheeks. The reaction is obvious even in the dim light of the bar. "Thanks, Cordell," she says, dipping her head.

A waitress takes our orders, and Mel and Tessa get lost in a conversation about cupcake flavors. Cordell gives me a questioning look to check in, probably because we were a good fifteen minutes late.

I just nod and say, "Yep." That's all he needs. He knows me that well.

The waitress returns with our beers, plus a huge plate of nachos that we all dig into.

"Sweet Emotion" blares from the jukebox, and through a mouthful of chips, Mel shouts out, "Oh, favorite Aerosmith song!"

Cordell groans, and I tip my head back with a huff. Every time we get together, Mel questions us about our favorites in as many categories as she can think of—favorite ice cream flavor, favorite nineties sitcom (which resulted in a heated argument between Mel and Cordell), favorite underdog story, favorite episode of *The Office*—if it's a subject that can possibly have a favorite, she's gonna ask it.

"C'mon, don't let me down now!" Mel wails. She takes a swig of her beer, then points at Cordell. "Go!"

"*Uh*," he thinks, his eyes closed tight. Then he snaps his fingers and says, "'Walk This Way.'"

"Nice," Mel agrees. Which is shocking. They never agree. Mel points to me next.

"I dig 'Angel' a hell of a lot," I say, giving Tessa's thigh a squeeze in a subtle secret message, "But my absolute favorite is 'What It Takes.'"

"Ugh, Luke, you do that every time!" Mel complains.

"What do I do?"

"You cheat by picking more than one favorite. And it's always phrased like that. 'I like blah-blah, but blah-blah is really my favorite.'"

Cordell cracks up at her attempt to imitate my deep voice, but he backs me up. "It's not cheating, Marshall. This isn't a real game. There's no winner or loser, so get over it." He raises his beer to his lips, not even looking her way.

Mel, on the other hand, looks downright furious. She opens

her mouth, no doubt to set him straight, but I speak up before she can.

"What can I say? I like what I like." I angle in to peck Tessa's cheek. How this girl manages to look simultaneously sexy and bashful, I'll never know.

Mel's watching us, a huge smile lighting up her face. "*Aww.* You two are disgustingly adorable." To Tessa, she says, "Your turn, T. Favorite Aerosmith song."

I'm wondering if my born-in-1995 girlfriend even knows who Aerosmith is when she blurts out, "Dream On."

"Takin' it *way* back," Cordell says, nodding like he's impressed.

"I like what I like," she replies, giving me a teasing smirk that makes me want to grab her up and get somewhere private.

"Well, before you two eye-bang each other right here at the table, come help me pick out some tunes before Ms. Daisy beats us to it." Mel grabs Tessa's hand and all but drags her off the stool and in the direction of the jukebox on the back wall.

Cordell spins on his stool and watches them until they reach it, then turns back to me, eyeing me over his beer bottle as he takes a pull.

"Mel's hair has been purple for a while now. Doesn't she usually change it every few weeks?" I ask, watching the girls lean in closer to the jukebox.

Cordell lets out a choked laugh, his lips curving into a sneaky smile. "She does. But a few months ago, I told her I hated the purple, so she's kept it to spite me."

"You didn't."

He grins and nods, tipping his beer my way.

"You really hate the purple?"

"Nah, just like riling her up." Then he sits up straighter, his expression turning serious. That's the signal. He won't give me more, even if I ask for it. He and Mel Marshall have been circling each other for years, and as his best friend, I'm wondering if I should encourage it or let it be, seeing as how they argue more than anything.

"Everything still going good there?" he asks, hiking a thumb over his shoulder in the direction of the girls.

"Better than good."

Maybe I've got hearts in my eyes or something because his face softens. "She's *it*, isn't she?"

I have absolutely zero doubts about us. But I find myself scared to answer my best friend's question. Not because I don't trust him—I trust him with my life. In fact, if anything were to happen to me and my folks couldn't care for Hannah for some reason, she's going to her Uncle Dell.

Unless you wife up that gorgeous woman standing over there.

But if I tell him how deep my feelings are, I'm worried he'll tell me to slow down. He's always been my voice of reason, my sounding board, my go-to when I need advice. If he tells me to pump the brakes, it will crush me.

He doesn't push for an answer, though, just swivels on his stool so he's facing me head-on and says, "You know, I had a teammate once who gave the best advice about how to know if you've found the one."

"Yeah, what's that?"

"If she's your very best friend, but you also want to fuck her? That's how you'll know."

"Huh." It's all I can think to say.

Tessa Burton has become my best friend. And I most definitely want to fuck her.

"You know what I think?" he asks, slapping me on the shoulder. "I think my days as your very best friend are coming to a close."

"Naw, man, that would never—"

He cuts me off with a shoulder squeeze. "It's okay, brother. It's how it should be. You and me? We'll always be best friends.

But the girl you spend your life with? She should be your *very* best friend."

Until now, my attention has been glued to the table, but when I look at the man who is one of the best people I've ever known, who kept my secret for years and has done everything he could to help me my whole life, I see nothing but pride and love shining back at me. My throat is tight, and I hope like hell I don't shed freaking tears in this damn bar.

For a second, his eyes are shiny, too, but then he clears his throat and says, "Best friends with fucking benefits. You know I love you, man, but I can't offer you that."

I choke out a laugh but sober quickly. "You know no one could ever replace you, right? You're stuck with my sorry ass until we kick it."

"Yeah, I know. Like you're stuck with mine." Cordell taps the neck of his bottle against mine, and we each take a deep pull.

We sit in comfortable silence for a few moments, finishing our beers and watching Tessa and Mel laugh in front of the juke-box, pushing buttons and swatting each other's hands away.

"Yeah, you best stick with that one. She's good for you." He tips his bottle in Tessa's direction.

He's got his eyes on them as I look at his profile. "I hope you find it one day, too, brother."

He sighs and never turns away from Mel, who tosses her purple hair over her shoulder and throws her head back in laughter. "Yeah, me too."

As if they sense us watching, the girls turn back; Mel winks and sticks her tongue out at us, while Tessa's sunshine smile lights up her face.

Damn, I'm a fucking lucky man.

CHAPTER NINETEEN

LUKE

"No, Daddy, like *this*." Hannah takes the bottle of sprinkles from me and violently shakes it over the cupcake, the bright green projectiles raining down on the lighter green icing until the top of the cupcake is covered. Then she carefully picks the whole thing up by the wrapper and places it in the plastic carrier I borrowed from Mom. She repeats the process on the next cupcake in line. The look of pure concentration on her little face about does my heart in. She's so into this task, I can't even make a fuss about the hundreds of sprinkles that miss their target and land on the countertop and roll off onto the kitchen floor.

My little Banana has done some major growing up since she started kindergarten seven months ago. She's much more independent and confident, wanting to do things her own way and not needing me nearly as much as she used to. She can tie her own shoes now, for heaven's sake.

How can something break a person's heart and make them so damn proud all at once?

She's standing on the wooden stool I built so she could reach the countertops, her dark hair in one long braid resting over her shoulder. She requested that style this morning so she could look like her bestie on such an important day.

St. Patrick's Day—Tessa's twenty-seventh birthday.

Hannah finishes sprinkling the last cupcake, then places it in the final spot in the carrier and takes care of the mess of icing on her fingers by licking them clean. I lock the lid in place and hand her a wet paper towel so she can work on cleaning up the wayward sprinkles that litter the counter while I get the Swiffer to capture the ones on the floor.

I want everything tonight to be absolutely perfect. Including the cleanliness of my kitchen.

"When will Ms. Tessa get here?" Hannah asks for the fifth time this afternoon.

"You missed those over by the sink, Banana." I'm so distracted sweeping up the floor that I don't answer her.

Still on the stool, she puts her hands on her hips and waits for my response. The same one I've given her the previous four times she's asked. "I told you. She's coming over at six thirty. All the other guests will get here at six so we can get in position."

"What is position?" she asks, wrinkling up her little nose.

"In place. Everyone will hide until she comes in—"

"And then we yell 'Surprise!'?" She throws her arms in the air like she's practicing for the surprise right now.

"Yep. Now, we gotta get this kitchen cleaned up before Nana and Papaw get here."

"'Kay, Daddy."

I picked Banana up from school early, and she spent the whole trip home complaining about Chase. More specifically, about Chase *chasing* her at recess.

The kid's name is on point.

"I told him to stop. Chasing. Me. But he said I'm not the boss of him. And he called me bossypants! And then he runned away."

"Ran away. So what did you do after that?" I'm working hard to hide my laughter behind my hand, turning to the window so she can't see my face.

"I chased him to the swings, and I told him that if he didn't stop chasing me, I was gonna tell the real *boss of him and he would get in big trouble."*

"Who's his real boss? Mrs. Gibson?"

"'Course, Daddy. She's the real boss of all of us."

Miss Bossypants's stories about Chase are a highlight of my week, especially because Tessa finds them as amusing as I do. Hannah tells her all about Chase when they talk on the phone—which is pretty much any time I try to have a phone conversation with Tessa in Hannah's presence. She walks around the house with my cell pressed to her ear, like she and her best friend are simply catching up about their days.

It's so fucking adorable it hurts.

So is seeing the two of them together. I've never given any real thought to finding a "new mom" for Hannah. Never wanted to change our dynamic or replace Shelley in her life. But when Tessa and Hannah are together, it feels *right*. Like it's meant to be. That magic that flows between Tessa and me also exists between her and my little girl. They adore each other, and I adore them. That longing I get in my gut when the three of us are together, the desire to make us a *real* family, overwhelms me.

If it wouldn't make me look like a total fucking lunatic, or send Tessa running for the hills, I'd get down on one knee tonight and ask her to marry me in front of the people who love us best.

That would be one hell of a memorable birthday.

But I won't be proposing tonight. Or any time soon.

Finally, the rogue green sprinkles seem to be contained. The rest of the house, however, is covered in green decorations, from the balloons tied to the backs of the chairs at the kitchen table (thanks to my mom and Ms. Daisy) to the streamers twisted along the tops of the windows to the *Happy Birthday* banner spanning the length of the mantel. The table is set with green paper plates and plastic utensils. Hannah even made her own banner and taped it to the windows that look out onto the back porch, the crooked green letters spelling out *Happy Birthday*.

Even the food matches the green theme. All except for the steaks. My mom's homemade mashed potatoes have been dyed green. We have green fruits—grapes, kiwi, honeydew—on a tray, guacamole and chips (not green, unfortunately), and the cupcakes that Hannah and I whipped up when we got home this afternoon. Mel assumed she'd be in charge of the cupcakes, telling me on the phone that she has a green tea recipe that's really good, but when I told her that Hannah has been set on making them, Mel graciously left the dessert to us, choosing to bring the ingredients for a lime punch instead.

Tessa has made it very clear for weeks that she doesn't want me to make a fuss over her birthday.

Oops. That's not how we roll in the Shipley family. At all.

Birthdays have always been a big freaking deal to us. So my girl will just have to get used to it.

It was Hannah's idea to make it a surprise party. We only invited a small group of friends, plus my parents. Hopefully, she'll see it for the loving gesture it is and won't get anxious or overwhelmed.

My folks arrive before the other guests, so I get my dad set up out at the grill. He'd be content to stay there the rest of the night, "manning the meat," as he says. Pop considers himself a grill master, so I leave him to it. Mom busies herself around the kitchen, setting the food out on the counter and sending Hannah to her room to change into her party outfit—a green shamrock dress with rainbow-striped leggings, plus glittery gold Mary Janes. She then shoos me off to get a quick shower, promising to take care of any early arrivals.

My stomach is a jumbled mess of nerves and excitement, so

it takes me no time at all to shower and change. I'm just rolling up the sleeves of my green-and-white checked button-down when the doorbell rings. Cordell and Ms. Rhonda are already stationed at the bar in the kitchen, and my mom is ushering Mel through the front door.

Her hair is still purple. Kinda disappointed she didn't change it to green.

"What are you gonna do if Tessa hates this?" she asks me with a smirk, jerking the grocery bags Cordell is offering to take from her closer.

He just rolls his eyes and returns to his seat. Mel pulls out Sprite and lime sherbet and frozen lemonade and sets them on the last empty spot on the counter. Mom wordlessly hands over the punch bowl she brought from their house, and Mel gets to work.

"She won't hate it," I say, totally unconvinced.

God, please don't let her hate it.

"Eh, she'll *probably* forgive you." Mel tosses a wink over her shoulder.

"She'll love it," Ms. Rhonda chimes in, patting my arm and giving me an encouraging smile.

I nod numbly, hoping like hell she's right. I don't have too much time to let my doubts run away with me, though. Shanice, Darrell, and DJ arrive next, and Hannah is so excited to show her friend her room, she drags DJ up the stairs, leaving the adults behind to finish last-minute details. Before I know it, the clock edges toward six thirty. Hannah and DJ pass out leprechaun hats to everyone and then keep watch for Tessa's car by the front door. Everyone except my parents parked around the back of the house so the cars wouldn't be seen when she pulls up. She expects my parents to be here, so that won't give anything away.

I'm wiping my sweaty palms on my jeans when Hannah squeaks, "She's here!"

And then the guests are scrambling like mad to find hiding

spots and I'm headed to the foyer to welcome the guest of honor. As I pass the kitchen, I see Mel's phone peeking up above the counter she's hiding behind.

Great. If Tessa freaks out, we'll have it on video.

With a big ball of nerves knotting in my gut, I open the door. Tessa's climbing the porch steps wearing a green dress that wraps around to tie at her waist, making her tits look fucking fantastic. Making the rest of her look fucking fantastic, too—all her curves are on display, and now I'm regretting my decision to have company over.

"Happy birthday, Ivy." I drag her in for a hug as soon as she steps into the house. She loops her arms around my waist, and her body relaxes into mine like it does every time I hold her. A perfect fit.

"Thanks, handsome," she whispers.

I take a moment to breathe in her coconut-and-sunshine scent, bracing for a whole lot of voices to shout out any second now. When she pulls away, I take her hand and guide her farther into the house, not taking my eyes off her face so I can see her reaction.

"*Surprise!*" The party guests hop up from their hiding spots, Hannah and DJ jumping up and down like they have springs in their feet. Tessa's face goes from shocked to panicked to teary, all in a matter of seconds. "Happy birthday, Tessa!" echoes around us, but her focus is locked on me.

"Luke," she says softly, then she's rolling her lips to keep the tears at bay.

I haul her to me again, letting her hide her face in my chest long enough to get her emotions under control.

In her ear I whisper, "I know you didn't want us to make a big deal. But you deserve a special night."

She just squeezes me tighter. Then she lets out a deep breath before she steps back and turns to greet her guests.

"Happy birthday, Ms. Tessa!" Banana's at her feet, grinning like a fool.

Tessa drops into a crouch and wraps my daughter in a hug. On the other side of them, Mel's capturing a picture of the two of them.

Okay, so maybe she's on to something, documenting every moment.

"Thank you, Jelly Bean. Did you help with the party?"

"Yep! I even helped Daddy make the cupcakes!" Hannah cheers.

"You did? I bet they taste delicious!"

My Banana takes Tessa's hand and leads her farther into the house. "Come and look at all the green stuff!"

Our friends circle around the two of them. Their laughter and smiles and love fill my house. The house I dreamed about for years.

I want it to be full of this kind of happiness for the rest of my life.

Around the table, our guests gather, asking Tessa about how her birthday has gone so far. Every time the conversation shifts and someone interjects, she finds me across the room and gives me a small smile. One meant just for me. It's a sweet smile, but despite its innocence, it heats my blood and makes my heart beat something fierce.

We still haven't done the *other things*.

We've come close a few times—including a hot-and-heavy dry humping session on her couch last weekend—but she's pulled away each time we get to the point where our clothes need to come off.

Patience, Lucas.

She's still in control. Though the anticipation is so amped that I worry that once I finally get inside her, I won't last more than a couple of minutes.

Fucking blue balls. Should've had a blue-themed party dedicated to the ache in my pants these days.

Pop steps in through the back door, announcing that the steaks are done, and a collective cheer rings through the crowd.

During dinner, the dining room is filled with laughter, green food, and Mel's ridiculous favorites game. She's really in her element with so many people to survey. Tessa sits beside me, Hannah on her other side because she insisted she had to sit next to the birthday girl. Though the room is full of all the people I love, I worry about whether the absence of Tessa's parents bothers her. As we eat, I watch her facial expressions for any flickers of sadness or regret, but my girl simply smiles her sunshine smile the whole evening, blushing when I lean over to kiss her cheek or whisper in her ear.

"Oh, I got one, Mel," Pop says between bites of steak smothered in green potatoes. "Favorite western?"

"Pop, no one watches—"

"*Tombstone*!" Mel and Cordell shout at the same time, then stare at each other in shock.

Tessa gives my leg a squeeze under the table. Though from the way everyone else is nodding in agreement or calling out their own favorites, it looks like we're the only ones who think anything of it.

"That's a good one," Darrell offers.

"Nothing beats *Butch Cassidy and the Sundance Kid*," Mom pipes up. "Robert Redford and Paul Newman in the same movie? Mm-mmm. I would watch them paint a wall. I tell you."

Mel and Tessa giggle at that, and Ms. Rhonda nods in agreement but then says, "How about Denzel in that remake of *The Magnificent Seven*?"

"Ooh, he's good, too. I really liked him in *The Preacher's Wife*. So handsome," my mom says, turning to her friend.

My father stops eating long enough to scowl at my mother, who's completely oblivious to his displeasure.

Mel cackles. "Mr. Shipley, I don't think that went the way you wanted it to!"

"Nah. I'll just work extra hard tonight to make my wife forget all about Robert, Paul, *and* Denzel."

God, strike me down right now.

"Pop!" I holler at the same time Mel shouts out, "Woo!"

The laughter and shouting get louder, but I want nothing more than to crawl under the table. Next to me, Tessa's red with second-hand embarrassment, but she wraps her hand around my bicep and holds on in support.

Pop sits back and crosses his arms smugly. My mom just swats at him playfully, but when she notices me dying a slow, painful death down the table, she sits up straight and squints. "Don't be a prude, Lucas William Shipley. How do you think you got here?"

I clear my throat and stare down at my plate, silently begging her *not* to say anything about Tessa and me being intimate.

Ms. Rhonda comes to my rescue. God bless this woman. "Tessa, hon, you want to open your gifts? Marj and I can clean this up and get dessert ready."

"I'll help y'all with that," Tessa says, pushing her chair back.

"Nonsense," Ms. Rhonda says, using the tone that makes Cordell and me fall in line like soldiers. "It's your birthday. You will *not* lift a finger." The tone works on Tessa, too. She sits obediently and takes the first gift from Hannah, who's been waiting not so patiently for this portion of the evening.

The big smile on Tessa's face doesn't dim once as she admires each gift and thanks each gift-giver earnestly. Shanice and her family gift her books. So do Cordell and Ms. Rhonda. I guess it comes with the territory when you're a librarian. My folks give her a soft throw blanket and an Amazon gift card. Hannah's bouncing in her seat when Tessa picks up the gift from her. Before Tessa even has the paper all the way off, Hannah blurts out, "It's butterfly socks!" She's so proud, having picked them out herself. "'Member when Daddy read that book to my class about the fat caterpillar turning into a butterfly? They 'minded me of that story!"

Tessa turns the colorful socks over in her hands. "Oh, Jelly Bean, they're the best pair of socks I've *ever* seen. I will wear them all the time and think of you when I do."

"And Daddy, too? Will you think of him, too?"

Tessa's eyes find mine, so full of emotion it about takes my breath away. "Yeah, I will," she says, her voice barely above a whisper.

If I don't get to show this girl how much I love her soon, I think I might die.

"My turn, Jelly Bean!" Mel calls out. Jeez, even Mel is calling Hannah by one of her many nicknames.

Banana, June Bug, Jelly Bean—this kid has won the nickname lottery.

After removing the colorful paper from the gift bag, Tessa peeks inside like she's scared her present will jump out and bite her. "Mel!" she shouts, slamming the bag shut and squeezing it tightly to her chest. Her face and chest turn that adorable shade of pink.

"What is it?" Hannah asks innocently.

"Nothing, Jelly Bean. Ms. Mel just likes to give joke gifts, and this one is private."

Oh hell, I'm dying to know what's in that bag.

Mel just grins like a crazy person, laughing and winking at Tessa like they're sharing the best secret ever.

When it's time for dessert, Hannah and DJ pass out cupcakes, and then the whole room fills with an off-key version of "Happy Birthday." I watch Tessa's every expression, drinking in the way the candle flame makes her skin glow, how her smile wobbles a bit when the song gets going, the unshed tears of joy brimming along her lower lashes when the homemade cupcake is placed in front of her. After the last words are sung, Tessa and Hannah lean in to blow the candle out together. The action knocks me in the gut, and visions of future birthdays in this house flash through my mind like pictures in a slideshow.

Then one single thought enters my mind: I'm going to make Tessa a Shipley.

I want it more than I've wanted anything in my life.

Hannah jumps into my lap, scattering my thoughts and bringing me back to the present. "Daddy, can DJ and I color while the 'dults clean up?"

"*Adults*. And yes, but only for a little while. You're spending the night at Nana and Papaw's, remember?"

"I 'member!" she says, skipping off to dig her crayons and coloring books out of the drawers in an end table.

I slide my chair back, ready to help with clean-up, but Tessa shoots to her feet, grabbing my hand and holding on for dear life.

"Hey," she calls out. "Um, sorry, uh, I just want to tell all of you—thank you so much for tonight. I'm beyond blessed to know all of you. And you've made this the best birthday I've ever had. So, um, thank you. Again."

The table erupts in applause and cheers, and Mel hugs her dramatically. I'm still locked in Tessa's death grip, so I bring the back of her hand to my lips and press a kiss to it.

With everyone pitching in, things are cleaned up and cleared away in no time. Shanice, Darrell, and DJ are the first to leave, followed by Ms. Rhonda and Cordell. Mel hangs around to color with Hannah for a few minutes, but then doles out hugs and collects her things. She and Tessa exchange a few whispered words before she leaves, no doubt about the gift, and the red that paints Tessa's face once again makes me even more determined to find out what was in that damn bag. My dad gets busy loading their car with all the supplies I borrowed from them.

"That was a success!" my mom says triumphantly, finishing up the last of the dishes. I'm leaning against a counter but reach out to snag Tessa as she walks by and tow her in for a hug from behind. As casually as I can, I inhale the scent of her shampoo, then rest my head on the top of hers, my arms wrapped tightly around her middle. Mom turns off the faucet and spins to face us, a towel in hand. She watches us for a moment and then says, "You two should get busy making me another one of those." She tilts her head toward where Hannah is still happily coloring at the coffee table.

Tessa's whole body locks up tight. I hate that I can't see her face to interpret what she's thinking.

"Mom—"

"Just sayin', Lucas." She holds her hands up in surrender, then steps forward to pull Tessa from me, her hands framing Tessa's face. "Happy birthday, sweet girl."

"Thank you so much. For everything."

They hug, making that tightness in my chest flare again.

"It was our pleasure, dear."

When Tessa steps back, she's still tense. Meaning Mom's comment is still messing with her head. It's confirmed when she spins around and says, "I think I'm going to head home. It's been a long day. Wonderful, but long."

I force myself to swallow the words I want to say, to push down the need to beg her to stay, to reassure her that we're still moving at the speed she's set. But instead, I croak out, "Of course, Ivy. Let's get your things, and I'll walk you out."

Tessa says goodbye to my parents and makes her parting pinkie promise with Hannah, then she leads me out through the garage and into the driveway.

Disappointment eats at me, despite my efforts to choke it back. I saved my gift for when we were alone, and now I'm going to have to give it in a rush, standing in the gravel next to her car as she prepares to run away from her feelings.

Away from *me*.

Mom and Pop stay inside with Banana as I load Tessa's gifts and the leftover cupcakes into her car. She's quiet, watching as I put her things into the back seat. When I shut the door and turn to face her, she's frozen in place, like she doesn't really want to go. The sky is bathed in the pinks and purples of twilight, the sun not quite settled for the night yet. She looks like a dream standing before me in that green dress that makes her emerald eyes even brighter than usual.

I want to draw this in my memory and keep it forever.

We're frozen still, just looking at one another for a full minute. Until I know that I must be the one to move us forward. I rub the back of my neck, not really knowing what to say. "Ivy—"

Before I can get another word out, she grabs the front of my shirt, pulling me to her so she can crash her lips to mine. I open for her instantly, taking everything she's willing to give. One of my hands finds its way to the small of her back while the other grips her perfect ass.

Too soon, Tessa pulls her head back and whispers into my lips, "This really has been the best birthday of my life."

"Even better than Canada?" I ask.

"You remember that?"

"I remember everything about you, Ivy."

My feelings for Tessa are so raw, so powerful, and I want to *tell her*, damn it. Instead, I put a little distance between us and reach around to my back pocket, where her gift has been hidden all night. She takes the small, thin box from me and searches my face in wonder.

"Happy birthday."

She smiles softly and opens the box, letting loose a tiny gasp when she sees the necklace.

It's a thin gold chain with two simple hearts intertwined at the center. I bought it a month ago, when I knew I was going to confess my feelings to her. Now it finally gets to make itself at home against her skin.

"Luke. It's beautiful. Help me put it on?" She spins and lifts her hair off her neck.

I don't hesitate. I pull it from the box and latch it behind her neck. With my fingertips, I brush over it gently where it lies against her skin, and I know, *I know*, it's fucking now or never. I force a swallow around the freaking bowling ball in my throat.

Eye contact, voice steady.

"I love you."

Tessa sucks in a breath and holds it as she studies my face. I take her right hand and place it over my heart so she can feel it galloping like mad, so she knows exactly how I feel about her.

Freaking. Finally.

"I love every part of you, Tessa," I continue, threading my hands in her hair so she can't escape this. "I love your incredibly smart brain, with its big words and brilliant ideas." Leaning in, I press my lips to her forehead. "I love your beautiful green eyes that see and accept every part of me." I place a soft kiss under one. "Your sunshine smile and how it lights up my whole world." A brush of my lips against hers. "I love your big heart and how kind it is." Head lowered, I place a kiss on the swell of her left breast. "I love every inch of you, inside and out. You don't have to say it back if you're not ready to. Just know I'll wait forever if I have to. I've never felt like this before, and I'm not willing to give it up."

"Luke..." Tessa's breaths increase, her teary eyes searching my face like she can find the words she wants to say hidden in it. But instead of words, she shows her feelings with action. Her lips brush mine again, softly at first, then hungrily as we let the weight of my words guide how we react physically. Before I know it, I've got my girl backed up against her car with her head tipped back as my lips map the skin of her jaw, neck, and chest.

My fucking hard-on is straining against the zipper of my jeans. I make sure Tessa can feel how badly I want her, pressing my hips into her, leaving no room for doubt—her man is turned *all* the way on. She whimpers as I roll my hips a couple times, simulating what I'd like to be doing without these layers of clothing between us.

"Luke." Her tone is full of warning, even though her hands are still firmly gripping my hair. Everything inside me is screaming for me to take it, to take what's mine. To throw her over my shoulder and stomp into the house and lock her inside. To refuse to let her go until I've had my way with her. Let her have her way with me.

But I tame my inner caveman and rest my forehead against her chest, right beneath the tiny gold hearts, as she rubs circles against my scalp and the back of my neck. She holds me like this while she says, "I'm not quite ready yet, handsome. I want to. I really do. It's just…it's been a while." She's never said a word about past sexual experiences, but maybe not being able to see my face right now has given her the courage to do so.

I want to plead with her, to ask her to spend the night with me. To beg on my knees if that's what it takes.

But that's not what my girl needs. She needs to be the one to initiate this.

So I do what I've been doing for weeks—I pull away and resolve to let my hand take care of my problem later.

"I'm sorry." The words are so faint I barely hear them.

"Nothing to be sorry for, baby," I tell her with more conviction than I'm feeling.

We hug once more. Tighter this time. Then I brush Tessa's hair out of her face and plant a lingering goodbye kiss on her lips.

"Thank you again for everything. I'll never forget this night."

"You're so welcome, beautiful."

And moments later, I'm watching the girl I love drive down the long gravel driveway that leads her home to Bennett and away from where she belongs—beside me.

∼

An hour or so after the party, I'm alone in the dark and feeling sorry for my damn self. Hannah and my folks left a while ago, my dad promising his only granddaughter he'd take her to get fresh donuts in the morning, and my mom giving me a sympathetic smile that makes me suspect she knows the cause of my sudden not-so-great mood.

I should go get a drink. Or go take care of the ache in my jeans.

But I sit and stew, mad at myself for letting my horniness ruin the end of what was otherwise a perfect night.

Perfect because I finally laid myself bare to my girl. Perfect because she enjoyed every minute of her birthday celebration. Because I caught glimpses of the future we could have together. Here. And I got to hold my girl and kiss her and make her breathless.

I'm just starting to turn my mood around when my phone lights up with a call.

Just seeing her name on the screen gives me a boost, motivates me to start moving.

"Hey, baby. Make it home okay?"

"Yeah." She sounds stuffy, like she's been crying.

"What's wrong?"

"Nothing. I just wanted to hear your voice. I'm sitting here thinking about how perfect tonight was. How perfect you are."

Chest tightness activated.

"Thank you, Ivy," I rasp, wishing like hell I'd convinced her to stay.

"I didn't have a chance to tell you that I talked to my parents today."

"Yeah? How'd that go?"

"Okay, I guess. They called to wish me a happy birthday. But, of course, it turned into the usual—asking when I'm coming home or if I want them to look into a library job in Atlanta." She sighs, the sound crackling through the phone.

"Hmm." I keep my opinion of her parents to myself. Along with what I think about their attempts to ambush her life.

"Then my mother asked me about Tyler Davenport and the conversation we had a couple of weeks ago."

At that, my whole body goes rigid. Shit.

"So I told them. I told them about you today." I knew she was keeping me a secret from them, protecting her life here in Bennett as best she could. For her to tell them that she's in a relationship with someone here…that's huge.

I have to proceed with caution, so I keep my voice as neutral as I can. "Wow. What did they say?"

"They asked for a copy of your CV and your social security number." She huffs a humorless laugh into the phone.

"CV?"

"Stands for curriculum vitae. It's like detailed documentation of your academic history."

Shit. There's no way I'll ever get these people to like me.

When I don't respond, she rushes out, "I'm kidding, by the way. They did ask me lots of questions about you, but not for anything like that."

"Did they ask where I went to college?"

She's quiet for a beat too long. Then, "Yeah."

I close my eyes and let out my own big sigh.

"You know I don't care about that, Luke." The softness is gone, replaced by a resolve that proves her belief in me.

"Yeah, baby, I know."

I try like hell to keep things quiet on my end, to not give away what I'm doing. After a few more silent moments, she changes the subject, surprising the hell out of me.

"I want to tell you about the last time I…well, the last time I slept with someone."

"You don't have to—"

"I know," she cuts me off. "But I want to. I've only ever done it one time."

My heart is picking up its pace, but I remain silent, knowing she needs to get this out.

"I was a senior in college. Still a virgin, and like, ashamed of it for some reason. All of my sort-of friends had already…you know. I felt like I was starting out adult life way behind my peers, which I know now is ludicrous. Anyway, my best friend in college was a guy."

I clench my hand around my phone, bracing myself to hear about the asshole who got to share this part of her life before she met me.

"His name is Nate. He was a virgin, too. We weren't attracted to each other. But one night, after too many beers, we both admitted that we hadn't done it yet. A few weeks later, he asked me if I wanted to try it—with him. With someone I knew as a friend, so we'd both feel safe and could get some experience together. I shouldn't have done it. I knew it immediately after. Not that he did anything wrong; I never felt pressured by him or anything." She clears her throat. "He finished in like two minutes, while I just lay there on the couch in his apartment, too nervous to move or to ask for him to help me get there. I remember lying there thinking, *Is that really it? This is what I've been missing?* Since it wasn't life-altering or anything, I've really never felt like I needed to again, you know?"

Shit, no wonder she's so reluctant to try again. Her first time was a joke. My voice is gravelly when I finally ask, "So you've never…you've never come, Ivy?"

She inhales sharply. "I…um. I mean, I have. Yes."

"By yourself?"

"Yes." Breathless and whispered.

"How, baby? How do you make yourself come?" We're on dangerous ground here. I'm ten seconds away from pulling my cock out and stroking it while listening to her voice.

"Um…with my, with my hand usually. And Mel gave me a vibrator for Christmas."

I can't help the groan that escapes from deep in my chest as images of Tessa touching herself invade my mind. My poor dick is cursing me out right now. I can hardly believe she's being this candid with me. I also need to give Mel Marshall a high five the next time I see her.

At the sound of Tessa's heavy breathing after her confession, my brain has only one thought: *Faster. I need to go faster.*

"Do you want to touch yourself right now, Ivy?"

"No."

"Why?"

Several moments of silence pass before she says, "Because I'd just be wishing it was you."

Fuck.

This girl—the perfect combination of sweet and smart and sexy. I *need* to know what she tastes like so fucking bad.

"Do you want me to come over and touch you, baby?" The words sound like they're coming from deep in my body, rough and low and full of desire.

"Luke..." She's still breathless. Is she as wet between her legs as I'm imagining?

"Tell me."

"Y-yes. I want you." I have to physically restrain myself from doing a ridiculous fist pump. She wants me, but does she want it to be tonight? I need her to say it, to leave no doubt between us.

"Say the words, beautiful."

She knows exactly what I need to hear. "I'm ready, Luke. I trust you."

The words are reminiscent of what I told her that day in the library parking lot when she convinced me to not give up on myself. Months and months of tutoring and friendship and longing and feelings have led us to this moment. Tonight.

"Good." I tell her. Then I end the call. And knock three times on Tessa's apartment door.

CHAPTER TWENTY

TESSA

He's here. Now.

Standing in my doorway, looking like he's ready to devour me.

I'm still holding my phone in one hand, reeling from the fact that he hung up on me.

He hung up on me…because he was already at my apartment door.

My brain feels like a pinball machine, my thoughts pinging around as quickly as that little silver ball flitting from one slingshot to another. I take in the sight of him in my doorway. His chest is heaving as if he's just run a race—a race to get to *me*. His tall, solid body looks poised to pounce; he's still wearing his jeans and boots from earlier, but he's changed his shirt. I inspect the way the material of the white Eagles alumni T-shirt hugs his hard muscles, how the short sleeves stretch tight around his biceps and his tattoo sleeve beckons me like a siren's call. And I'm transported back to the first time I saw those black and gray designs inked on his skin, to the naughty thought that invaded my mind: *I would love to lick those tats one day.*

Oh, Past Tessa, you sweet summer child.

"You gonna invite me in, Ivy?" Luke's gruff voice snaps me out of my reverie.

"Yeah, uh, yes. Come in." I sound like *I've* just finished a race. Blushing, I dip my chin, inspecting my own attire.

Crap.

When I told him I wanted him to come over, I thought I'd have time to change out of the black leggings and ratty gray library T-shirt I threw on when I got home from the party. I don't have too long to dwell on this, though, because as soon as the door is shut and locked behind him, he has me pressed against it and he's kissing me ravenously.

His hands are everywhere—in my hair, grasping my chin to tilt my head just where he wants it, squeezing my hip, kneading one butt cheek roughly. He is a man possessed, and I...I want him to possess me.

I feel the same intense throbbing between my legs and dampness in my panties that I always feel when we get going like this. My own hands sneak up under his shirt and caress the hard planes of his abdomen and chest. I can't get close enough to him. And he must have the same thought, because then he's pressing even harder into me, pinning me against the wooden door at my back, his erection straining against his jeans.

Oh my God, this is really going to happen.

Then he's pulling away. And of its own volition, my mouth chases after his as though we're connected there. It takes my brain a moment to catch up.

"What's wrong?" I pant out.

"Just...hang on, baby. I want to savor this." He's panting, too, his pecs heaving as he gasps for air.

I press kisses to the muscle over his heart, soaking in the way the warmth of his skin seeps through his T-shirt and his woodsy, manly scent draws me in.

Luke lets out a groan and pulls me away from the door. "I'm

sorry I attacked you like that. If we don't slow down, I'm going to fucking come in my jeans before we get started."

"S'okay," I tell him, going for reassuring, when honestly, I just want to rip his clothes off and climb him like a tree. I've never in my life felt as turned on as I do with Luke.

He gives me a thorough once-over, those brown orbs darkened with so much desire they're practically black. But there's something else shining back at me from their depths.

Love.

Tonight, Luke Shipley told me he loves me.

And I wanted to say it back so badly it made my heart ache with longing.

Because I *do* love him. I love him so much it's like a physical ache when we're not together. But, coward that I am, I couldn't work up the nerve to say it back.

"Baby. Where'd you go?" He's peppering my face with soft kisses, and I've been so in my head the last few seconds that I'm missing this.

"I'm here," I whisper. "I'm right here."

"Good." Then he takes me in a languid kiss that makes my nipples tighten, makes that dampness turn wet. His tongue plunders my mouth, coaxing mine to slide and twist against it sensually.

And now I'm imagining how that tongue will feel in other places.

This kiss goes on for so long, it feels as though he's sucking my soul right out of my body. And I'm more than willing to let him.

He finally breaks the connection, but his lips don't go far. He trails them along my jaw and down my neck, inhaling when he reaches the spot just below my ear. The action sends a surprising burst of heat to my core. When his deep, rough voice joins in with words of praise, my whole body is set aflame.

"Mmm." Kiss. "Ivy." Kiss. "You." Kiss. "Are." Kiss. "So." Kiss. "Fucking." Kiss. "Beautiful." Kiss.

"Luke…" I tug his hair, holding him close.

"Hey," he says, pulling back. "What was in that bag from Mel?"

The question throws me. "Wh-what?"

"The gift. From Mel. What was it?"

"Oh." That all-too-familiar warmth infuses my cheeks. "It was a book. A, um, sex book."

Luke's eyes widen as he coughs out a deep chuckle. "Yeah, she's definitely getting a high five," he mumbles before diving back in to suck on my neck.

"Huh?"

"Never mind. God, I need to be inside you so fucking bad." He rubs circles across my back but stops abruptly the moment he realizes it—I'm not wearing a bra. "Fuck, Ivy." He takes a small step back, but his hands never leave me. He fists my T-shirt at the small of my back, pulling and stretching the material until the obvious outline of my very tight, very sensitive nipples can be seen through the thin cotton. Then one hand is sliding around and up, palming my left breast, gently kneading.

I clench my thighs in anticipation as his thumb makes an agonizingly slow sweep across my nipple. Once. Twice. Three times, sending sparks arcing through me.

"Can I see them?" he asks, his voice a low growl.

At my nod, he grips the hem of my shirt and drags it up my torso. I lift my arms for him as he draws it over my head, then he's tossing it somewhere behind me. His breaths are ragged as he looks his fill, and it takes all my self-control to not cover myself.

I want to be brave for him.

So I stand still, hands fisted at my sides, letting him inspect me.

"Fucking perfect," he whispers, this time molding both

hands to my breasts, massaging and squeezing gently. When he dips to take one nipple into his warm mouth, my head instinctively falls back. He teases the hard peak with his tongue before sucking and pulling. The action causes a mewl that should be embarrassing to escape my lips, but right now, I find it hard to care.

"I can't wait to taste you everywhere," he whispers against the wet, swollen bud before moving over to give my other breast the same attention. This time, I swear my soul does leave my body. When Luke pulls off with a pop, I let out a whimper. He works his way up my shoulder, my neck, my jaw, and then his mouth is on mine again, his hands replacing his mouth on my boobs.

This man is determined to have me melted into a puddle on the floor.

I'm halfway there already.

Luke mutters out a muffled *fuck* and takes two steps back, raking his hands through his hair.

At the sight of the hard bulge in his jeans, I feel a momentary flicker of panic. Am I doing enough to satisfy *him*? I want him to love every minute of this as much as I do. I open my mouth to voice this concern, but Luke speaks first, the words grating out roughly. "Stop it."

My stomach drops. "Wh-what?"

"Whatever you're thinking that made you panic just now."

I can only stare at him, open-mouthed, naked from the waist up. How on earth did he pick up on that?

"The lie you're telling yourself right now has no place here. Got it?"

I'm taken aback by the bossiness of his tone. He's not being rude or dismissive, just determined. Insistent that I don't overthink this, don't let my mind wander off to a place where I can't enjoy what's happening between us.

Oh my heart, I really do love this man.

"Good. Now"—Luke licks his lips, the need radiating from him so strong the air is filled with it—"can I touch you, baby?"

I nod once, and he hooks a finger in the waistband of my leggings and tugs me closer to him. That same hand slides down the skin below my belly button, into my panties, all the way down, down, down. To *there*.

Luke closes his eyes and lets out a ragged breath when his fingers encounter the wetness gathered there. I instantly flush, embarrassment burning me from the inside. When he opens his eyes, he rakes his gaze from my face down to my chest, probably taking in the evidence of my abashment.

"Uh-uh," he growls with a shake of his head. "Don't ever be ashamed about being wet for your man."

"Luke—" I force out as the tips of his fingers brush along the wet skin, sliding up to softly rub at my clit with a featherlight touch. I wrap my hands around his forearm and squeeze as his touch increases slightly. And just when I think my knees will buckle under the weight of the passion burning through me, he pulls his hand out of my panties and hauls me up by my butt. I wrap my legs around his waist and my arms around his neck and rain kisses all over his face and jaw as he starts toward my bedroom.

"Now I get to teach *you* some things, Ivy."

Yes, please.

He squeezes my backside before lowering me to the floor beside the bed. I go for the hem of his shirt and tug it up, needing to feel his skin against mine. At the same time, Luke attempts to toe off his boots. We're all tangled up for a moment, laughing at our eagerness to get him undressed. When we finally wrestle his shirt off together, I step back and let my eyes rove over his body hungrily.

This man is *mine*.

Luke's body is not cut like a man who spends hours in the gym, but days spent on construction sites have honed it into perfection. He's covered in muscles defined from hour after hour of physically demanding labor. He's all tan and tattoos, with a light smattering of dark hair on his chest.

I step up to run my fingers along the upper portion of his tattoos that are usually covered by sleeves.

"Like what you see?" he asks gruffly, watching me survey his upper body.

"A lot," I breathe before I kiss the muscle over the heart that's beating wildly just for me. My fingers find their way down to the waistband of his jeans, and I take a page from his book and ask, "Can I touch *you* now?" The rough words that escape don't even sound like me.

"Baby, you can touch me everywhere."

With a boldness I wasn't sure I had until this exact moment, I pop the button on his jeans and lower his zipper slowly, staring into his eyes as I do. I slip my hand into his jeans and rub along the hardness I find there, over his underwear, loving the way his eyes roll in pleasure. Impatient, I push his jeans down to his thighs and almost come undone at the sight of his hunter green boxer briefs.

When my eyes find his again, he shrugs and dips his chin sheepishly. "St. Patrick's Day."

"You're definitely getting lucky tonight, mister," I tell him, blushing at how brazen my words are.

"Tessa, fuck," he groans, raking a hand through his dark hair. "You're killing me here."

I slip a shaky hand into the band of his underwear, past the trail of dark hair below his belly button, and wrap my fingers around his warm, hard length. For a second I worry about not knowing what I'm doing, but when I slide my hand up and down slowly, the noise Luke makes tells me I'm on the right track. There's a bead of moisture at the tip, and when I rub it with my thumb, circling the head, his reaction causes the warmth in my core to spread, heating me from my toes to my fingertips.

He lets me explore for a minute more but then pulls my hand out. "Baby, I'm gonna come if you keep that up. Let me take care of you now."

His hands dip into my panties again, this time gliding to my butt. The feel of his rough hands sends a shiver down my spine as he kneads and squeezes the round globes.

"I've been wanting to get my hands on this Georgia peach for months."

Then, in a flash, he lifts me and tosses me onto the bed. I squeal in delight as I bounce on the mattress. Luke's watching me with a cocky grin on his face. His eyes never leave mine as he peels my leggings and panties off in one smooth move. That grin slowly fades as he stands at the side of the bed and scans every inch of my body laid out before him. I swear I can feel the path his gaze travels over every curve and dip.

He's looking at me like I'm a masterpiece.

Me. Tessa Burton. Nerdy, timid, anxiety-riddled librarian, who is neither skinny nor sexy.

How can a girl not feel beautiful when the man she loves is admiring her so reverently?

When his focus returns to my face, he swallows hard. "Can I taste you now, Ivy?"

I can only nod and watch as he kneels beside the bed and runs his hands from my thighs all the way to my feet. I prop myself up on my elbows to get a better view as he grasps both calves and tugs me toward the edge of the mattress. He places a sweet kiss on one ankle, then the other, before placing my heels on the edge of the bed, spreading my thighs apart in the process.

Oh. My. Goodness.

Luke Shipley is staring at the most intimate part of me.

"Just look at you," he whispers, as if he's talking to himself.

I fist my hands in the quilt as he uses his thumbs to spread me open, and my back arches off the bed at that first slow swipe of his tongue. My thighs instinctively squeeze together, so he grips them to hold them still.

"Fucking heaven," he mutters before his tongue returns to incinerate me. He takes his time, exploring every hill and valley between my legs before reaching the peak at the top and flicking and circling my clit in a rhythm that makes my head thrash.

Then he slips a finger inside me at the same time he sucks on my clit.

"*Lucas*!" I gasp, my hands finding his head and holding on for dear life.

He smiles against me, his lips brushing my sensitive skin. Then he dives back in, torturing me in the most delicious way, adding another finger to rub inside me.

My orgasm builds and builds, tightening down deep, and I can't control the moans and hums escaping as he brings me to that glorious release. "Yes, don't stop," I encourage. And then, like a sudden detonation, I'm there. Wave after wave of intense pleasure ripple outward, my heart racing and my thighs shaking.

When my orgasm ebbs, Luke rises onto his knees, wearing a smug smile. "God, you're beautiful when you come." He bends to place tender kisses beneath my belly button as I let my eyes drift closed, sated and relaxed.

"You know what I love?" he asks.

I open my eyes again. He's on his feet now, looking down at me and pushing his underwear down. I drink him in, *all* of him, but I can't formulate words.

He continues anyway. "I love that I'm the only one who's made you come like that—with my mouth." Then he's looming over me, lifting me, shifting my body so my head is on a pillow. "And I love that I'm about to do it again—with my cock." He puts one knee to the bed, then the other, and prowls up my body, dropping open-mouthed kisses as he goes. When he gets to my breasts, he teases my nipples with his tongue, then sucks them so fervently a throb builds between my legs again. When he settles his weight on top of me, he says, "I think I've got you all ready, Ivy." He kisses me deeply a few times, sliding up and down my body, his erection gliding along the wetness between my legs. "Can I come inside you, baby?"

"Y-yeah. I get the shot. For birth control."

Luke lifts up on his elbows, the intensity of his gaze reflecting all the emotions that come with being this vulnerable with another person. It's perfect and scary and overwhelming and steamy and awkward, all rolled into one. A moment so right, so sublime, I can't bear to look away. He threads his fingers into my hair as he aligns himself with my entrance, whispering, "I love you, Tessa," as he slowly pushes into me.

I'm soaked from all his attention, but he takes it slow, easing in a little at a time. Once he's in to the hilt, there's a twinge of pain, and I wince. He whispers *I'm sorry* over and over, planting kisses on my lips, cheeks, and nose between apologies. Then he's tugging at my lips and kissing me slowly, lushly, and that's all it takes for the discomfort to morph into something different completely—an urge for him to move. I buck my hips a little to send the message.

Luke responds instantly with a roll of his hips. It's so good, so very different from that first time all those years ago. The way his pelvis is aligned with mine as he finds his rhythm.

"*Oh*, Luke. Mmm, feels so good."

"You're doing so good, baby. This pussy was made for me, wasn't it?"

I can't form words, just an *Uh-huh* before sounds I've never made in my life escape my lips. I swear I sound like a cat in heat or something. So I clamp my lips shut, embarrassed by the outburst.

But he doesn't allow it. "Nope. Don't you hold back. I want your neighbors to hear how good your man fucks you."

Oh. My. God. Luke Shipley's dirty talk might be the death of me.

Our bodies meld as he grinds his hips into mine, roll after sensual roll.

His breath is hot in my ear when he whispers, "Been driving me crazy with wanting you, Tessa. Now that I've had a taste and know how well you take my cock, I'm gonna need some of this pussy every. Damn. Day."

"Luke!" My climax builds again, that throbbing growing more and more intense with all his delicious manly weight pinning me to the mattress, anchoring me to this moment. I clamp my hands around his biceps and dig my fingertips into the muscle as I wrap my legs around him and pull him as close as I can.

"You close?" he forces out. "God, you feel so good." The rolling of his hips picks up speed, the pressure on my pelvis so intense I know my climax is imminent. "So fucking beautiful," he rasps out in time with his thrusting. "So. Fucking. Mine." Each word is punctuated with a hip grind that makes my eyes roll back in my head.

"*Unnhh,*" is all I can manage as that bomb detonates again, forcing my eyes to close in ecstasy. As the throbbing waves retreat, I tighten my inner muscles, and then he's pulsing inside me, reaching that peak moments after I do, groaning and swearing as it happens.

His hips slow their rolling motion, but he doesn't pull out. Instead, he lifts up onto his elbows again and rests his forehead against mine; our mouths are so close we share the breaths we're trying to catch.

Luke kisses me. Once. Twice. Three times.

"Holy shit, Ivy," he says, still panting. "That was fucking amazing."

"Yeah," I agree, my smile wide and happy. I run my hands up and down his back, not wanting him to pull away just yet.

"Thank you," he says earnestly, his wide-eyed expression full of wonder.

"What for?" I laugh out.

"For that. For letting me be the first one to give you that pleasure."

"You're really good at it." I giggle. "I think I'll let you do it again."

"Baby…" Luke buries his face between my neck and shoulder. "I'm gonna need to do it again. All the time."

We lie like that for several minutes, basking in each other, sated and peaceful. I'm so blissed out that my eyelids grow heavy, but one thought rings out in my mind, clear as a bell: *This is what I've been missing all this time. This all-consuming, can't-live-without-you, scary-but-exhilarating, intense, passionate feeling.*

This is love. And I'm in it so deep.

Luke finally lifts his head with a groan. "Let's get cleaned up." Before I can respond, he's on his feet and scooping me up into his arms, bridal style.

I let out a surprised whoop and link my hands behind his neck as he carries me into the bathroom. He sets me down gently, and I wait for the bashfulness to hit me—because here I am, *totally naked* and about to pee in front of Luke Shipley. But that feeling never comes. Instead, an odd sense of comfort washes over me, even in such a vulnerable state. While I'm taking care of my business, he finds a washcloth in the cabinet and then holds a hand under the faucet, waiting for the water to warm up. Once the cloth is wet, he waits for me to flush before he tenderly cleans between my legs.

Just when I think he couldn't get any more perfect, he raises his own bar.

Back in bed, I rest my head on his chest and run my fingers up and down the tattoos on his left arm. "Tell me about these," I say softly. "I know the significance of some of them. But what made you choose the rest?"

Luke kisses the top of my head before answering. "Each part of my design represents something special in my life."

"*Your* design?"

"Yeah. I drew it."

"Luke, you're so talented. You should be creating art somehow, some way."

He huffs out a laugh.

"I'm serious."

"You're sure sweet to say so, Ivy, but it's not in the cards."

We'll revisit this conversation another time—when I can discuss all the avenues he can venture down to pursue a creative career. Not that he needs to change what he's doing; if he's happy, then I won't push the issue. But he has options. Especially now that his reading ability has improved.

"Why the rose?" I ask, rubbing at the image nestled on his forearm near Hannah's name.

"It's for my mom. Rose is her middle name."

"Sweet." I place a kiss there. "And the compass?" This one is farther up on his bicep; I've never seen it before.

"To remind me of my true north…my folks, Hannah, Cordell, this town…and now—you."

My heart swells and tears wet my eyes, but I blink them back to press my lips to his skin where the compass is inked.

"The anchor is for my grandfather—my mom's dad. He was in the Navy. Passed away about a year after Hannah was born."

I kiss the anchor, then rest my head back on his chest, waiting for more.

"This part is actually kinda a joke," he says, showing me a small peanut shell high up on his shoulder. It's so interwoven into the rest of the design, I hadn't noticed it.

"When I was drawing out what I wanted, I asked my dad what I should include to represent him. Said that since his favorite thing in the world is boiled peanuts, that I should make a big peanut the focal point of the whole design. He didn't think

I'd have a damn peanut tattooed on my skin." He chuckles. "Showed him, didn't I?"

I push myself farther up Luke's body to place a kiss on his shoulder, and he takes full advantage of my new position by pulling me on top of him so all my soft parts nestle perfectly into his solid ones. From here, the happiness and love shining in his eyes is obvious, even in the dark.

It's time to take the biggest leap of my life.

Because I've never felt safer than I do right now.

I cup his cheeks, his day-old scruff tickling my fingertips. Then I brush my lips across his tenderly and will my breath and my heart to remain steady. And before I can overthink it, I say it.

"I love you, Luke Shipley."

His mouth drops open before a slow smile spreads across his lips. "Say it again," he whispers.

"I love you."

This time he closes his eyes, almost like he can't believe he's hearing the words I've been holding in for weeks, guarding them like a secret in my heart.

"You love me?" he questions, his attention focused on my face now.

"Yes."

I barely have time to appreciate the devastating grin he gives me before his mouth is on mine. And then we get lost in each other again, the action of our bodies a testimony to the love shared between us.

I wake with the sun peeking around the edges of the drawn curtains that cover my bedroom window as snapshots of the night before flash through my brain. With a contented sigh, I reach out, but all I find are cool cotton sheets.

Did he leave already? Did I do something wrong? Does he regret last night?

My heart rate accelerates as panic reaches out with jagged talons, taking my mind captive. But then I register the faint sound of the shower running through the closed bathroom door.

He didn't leave, I tell the traitorous voice in my head. The relief that floods me is palpable. I rest a hand on my chest, my heart rate calming with each passing second.

Just as I'm calm enough to snuggle back into the sheets, the water shuts off and the shower curtain slides along its rod. I sit up in alarm, wondering what the heck I should be doing when he comes out of the bathroom. What's the protocol here? Feign sleep? Prop myself seductively against the headboard? I frantically search my bedroom, as if the answers will be blatantly on display. I spot Luke's T-shirt from last night on the floor beside the bed, and I hastily snatch it up and slip it over my head.

Now at least I won't be totally naked when he catches me scrambling. All the confidence and boldness of last night has most assuredly disappeared, evaporated like drops of dew in the morning sun.

My head's on a swivel, and I'm still scanning the room for some kind of buffer or distraction when the bathroom door opens. I grab the first thing my hand can close around on my bedside table—a bottle of pale pink nail polish. It's the color I used on my toes. I left the bottle here so I could touch them up a few days ago, but I never got around to it.

No time like the present, right?

I'm just twisting off the top, leaning back against the headboard, wearing only Luke's Eagles alumni shirt, when he appears in my bedroom doorway.

Wearing nothing but a towel and a smile.

He props himself against the doorframe and crosses his arms over his bare chest. I don't let my eyes linger on him, but I know —*I know*—there are still droplets of water clinging to his skin, like he was in a hurry to get back out here. I can feel him watching me as I attempt to act like I'm engrossed in the task of touching up my toenail polish.

As usual, he sees right through me.

"Hey," he says cautiously.

"Hey!" I chirp a little too brightly.

You weirdo, you are so bad at this.

He pushes off the door and saunters toward me. I keep my eyes on my toes, trying my darndest to not spill the bottle of polish on the bedsheets. Then he's beside me, towering over me and letting out a soft, exasperated sigh. Wordlessly, he takes the bottle of polish from my hand, seats himself at the foot of the bed, and takes my foot in his large, capable hand. He plants a kiss on the inside of my ankle before he settles it in his lap.

And then?

He proceeds to paint my toenails, a look of pure concentration on his face.

We're quiet for a while. I can't come up with a comment to break the silence that doesn't sound awkward or cringey. But Luke's repose is another example of how he shows his love for me in little ways—how he gives me space to process my feelings but stays close so I can reach out if I need him.

Finally, I can take the silence no longer. "You're really good at that."

He hums in agreement. "Not my first rodeo. Although Hannah prefers sparkly purple polish."

Then, like an idiot, I blurt out, "I'm keeping this shirt."

My face blazes, and I resist the urge to face-palm. Instead, I choose to keep my gaze on Luke. I want to see his reaction.

With a shrug, he says, "Looks better on you anyway," as he finishes the pinkie toe on my foot. When he hunches over to softly blow on the wet polish, a shiver racks through me. At my reaction, his cocky grin returns. "Ivy, seeing you in my shirt is second only to seeing you in your birthday suit. I'll give you every damn T-shirt I own if you'll wear them." Taking up my other foot, he turns serious. "Tessa, you don't feel weird about last night, do you?"

Do I? I do *not* regret it. Not for a moment. But *feel weird*?

I always feel weird.

I give him the most honest answer I can articulate. "It's just new for me. I don't regret it. Please don't think that."

"All right. I won't." So matter of fact and sure.

I relax at his candor, a tiny weight lifting off my shoulders.

He finishes up the toes on my other foot, again blowing on them to drive me wild. When he hands the bottle of polish back to me, he asks, "Will you read to me?"

Of course. Of course this man would use my comfort activity to distract me from the doubt plaguing my mind.

He's so good at this. At being my *person*.

There are five or six books stacked on my bedside table. Being a mood reader means I keep different genres at my fingertips at all times to satisfy any kind of whim. I strategically choose the second book in the stack—*Beach Read* by Emily Henry, a favorite.

So that's how we spend the next couple of hours before we finally drag ourselves from the comfort of the bed and each other. With Luke's head resting in my lap while he listens to me read a story about two perfectly imperfect people who spend their days lost in words, falling in love.

LUKE

The past two weeks have been heaven on earth.

Tessa.

Her luscious thighs cradling my hips as I make love to her.

We've been fucking every chance we can. In my bed, long after we've tucked Hannah in for the night. In her bed, on those weekend nights my parents babysit. Once, in my truck, parked on the riverbank where we had our first date, steaming up the windows as Tessa straddled my lap and I dug my fingertips into her hips.

We can't fucking get enough of each other.

Since her birthday, Tessa's only grown more confident, participating more and being more vocal about what she wants. And I eat that shit up. Like a lifetime of pent-up needs are finally being fulfilled.

And I'm the lucky idiot who gets to fill them.

Like this morning, when I woke her up with my head between those delicious thighs.

Damn. Her taste. The way she moans my whole first name when my tongue flicks just right. What I'd give for a repeat—

"You are not focused, mister." Tessa smacks my arm, using

the bossy librarian voice she doesn't know turns me all the way on. Those green eyes are narrowed into slits as she scolds my inattention.

It's Saturday afternoon, and we're sitting at the one and only concrete picnic table at the park downtown. Though *park* might be generous. It's really a patch of grass with two swings, a slide, and a climbing structure that is currently keeping Banana occupied while Tessa forces me to practice. Nestled catty-corner from the library, it's become a favorite place for us to meet now that the spring weather is cooperating. We stopped the regular sessions a couple of weeks back, now preferring to get practice in whenever and wherever we can. I've started reading the book that Tessa gave me for Valentine's Day aloud to her; it's so slow-going I'm shocked she hasn't ripped it from my hands and chucked it across the room. But not my Tessa. She listens with infinite patience as I stumble and backtrack over the words, helping me decode when I'm really at a loss and praising all of my efforts.

"Can't help it, ma'am. You're so damn distracting." I'm straddling the bench, my knees pressed to the side of Tessa's thigh as she faces the table with her head bent over a yellow legal pad. I scoot closer and press my nose to the soft skin below her ear. A spot I know makes her weak. I stay like this for several beats, breathing her in. Breathing in the scent that's filled my truck and embedded itself in my bedsheets. When she drops a hand to my thigh and digs her nails into the denim, I know I have her.

"Luke, you promised." She's not mad. She sounds more like she's scolding a beloved child who just can't help but get into mischief.

"Hmm. Did I now?"

"Yes! You promised me thirty minutes of hands-off working."

"Maybe you haven't noticed," I say, "but I *am* hands-off at the moment." I hold my arms up, palms facing her, to emphasize my point. My nose is still pressed against that sensitive spot, my breath sending a shiver down her spine. "But it seems like you can't keep your hands off *me*."

She's still gripping the thigh I've got lodged against her ass.

She huffs out a small sigh. "Here. Split these into syllables and code your vowels." She pushes the legal pad in front of me on the table. Now it's my turn to sigh as I force myself to sit up and take the pencil she's holding in the air. On the page, Tessa has written a list of several multisyllabic words in her precise handwriting.

"I like it when you're bossy," I mumble under my breath, scanning the words on the page. Then I get to it. I break the first one apart with lines and swoops. Tessa taught me how to code words with distinguishing marks so I can figure out what they are if they're not immediately familiar to me. Of the twelve words she's written, I can read eight of them with ease. I still mark them like she wants, though, trying to earn bonus points for later.

"Done," I say after a few minutes. I've double-checked the marks on all words, and I'm ready to read them to her.

Tessa slips the index cards she's working on under a heavy book so they won't blow away, then shifts her body in my direction, giving me her full attention. "Let's hear them, then."

My lips twist up in a smirk as a brilliant idea comes to mind. "How about we make a deal?"

She squints at me, but intrigue shimmers in her irises. "A deal?"

"Yep. How about for every one of these words I read correctly, I get to give you a kiss in a location of my choice?"

She raises her brows. "Location of your choice, huh? We're in public, Lucas Shipley."

"I'm aware, Tessa Burton."

My favorite shade of pink creeps up her neck and settles in

her cheeks. I have to restrain myself from leaning over and planting a kiss on one.

"What do I get if you get them wrong?"

I gasp and bring a hand to my chest. "You'd rejoice in my mistakes? What kind of girlfriend does that?"

She playfully swats my thigh.

"All right, if I miss the word, then you can give me two new ones in its place." I only offer this because I know without a doubt I can read all twelve words.

What a difference seven months and a persistent champion can make.

"Deal," she says, sticking out her hand to shake on it.

"Daddy, will you swing me?" Hannah shouts from where she's hanging upside down on one of the climbing bars.

"Give us five minutes, Banana!" I call back and watch my little girl pull herself up and go back to playing.

Then I turn my attention back to the notepad. "First word —instructional."

"Correct," Tessa says, blushing again because she knows what comes next.

I make a big deal of choosing where I want to place the first kiss, then finally push one of her sleeves up and plant it on her elbow, which makes both of us laugh.

She recovers quickly. "And what does the word root *-struct* mean?" she questions.

"If I get this bonus question right, will I get a bonus kiss?"

"Nope."

"Aw, hell." I sigh. "Fine. It means *to build*." I angle in to drop a kiss to her cheek anyway, but she turns her head, and my lips catch her hair instead. I let out a low growl that makes her wink at me.

God, I love this woman.

"Next word, please."

"Abbreviation," I say, no hesitation.

"Yes!" Tessa's sunshine smile flashes brighter than the rays shining down on us. This time, my kiss lands on her denim-clad knee. She laughs again, a soft, happy sound that makes me feel like I'm walking on air.

We continue this way, with me reading the words correctly and then finding random places for my reward kisses—her eyebrow, her shoulder blade, her ring finger.

Okay, so *that* one wasn't so random.

As I'm placing my last kiss—on the inside of her wrist—Hannah scrambles up the bench on the other side of the table, climbs across, and plops her bottom down so her feet are wedged between Tessa and me. Her hair, which was in a smooth french braid when we left the house, now has strands sticking out all over, and it's loose and sweaty from all of her hard playing.

"Hungry, Jelly Bean?" Tessa asks, offering her one of the granola bars we threw into a bag before we left.

She shakes her head but takes a big gulp from the water bottle Tessa offers her next. She swallows before asking, "Is it my turn to do the words?"

Since we've started tutoring outside the library, Hannah has taken it upon herself to join in, asking Tessa to "trick" her with hard words. She's never questioned why Tessa works with me; she takes it all in stride like a five-year-old whose main concerns are playing and avoiding bedtime. And Tessa has never hesitated to include her in our study sessions. She makes Hannah sets of words to decode on index cards and has her practice her own sounding out. She also plays listening games with her. They play all the time—setting the table for dinner, watering the flowers in Hannah's garden, getting ready for bed—rhyming words, breaking words into single sounds, counting sounds, you name it.

I fall even more in love with Tessa every time I observe a quiet moment shared between them.

It's like she's the perfectly shaped piece I didn't even know our family was missing. And she's locked in place now, filling our days with words and love.

"After my words, you'll swing me, Daddy?"

"You got it, Banana."

My daughter's brows pinch in concentration at the first card Tessa holds up, and her little mouth works out the sounds. It takes a few seconds, but she finally shouts, "Best!"

"Yay! Good job!" Tessa praises. "And which letter is the vowel in the word *best*?"

Hannah answers correctly and gets more praise before Tessa hands her the next card.

After nine more correct words, Tessa packs up our study materials while I push Banana on the swings, to shouts of "higher, Daddy!" and childish laughter. My fearless girl likes to swing as high as she can. So high her little body bounces off the seat when she reaches the ends of the arc and gravity takes over.

Tessa's cheering stops abruptly, drawing my attention. She pulls her phone from her pocket and holds it to her ear. Her face instantly morphs from happiness to pure dread. Then she stands and strides toward the tree at the edge of the park.

I'm certain I know who's on the other end of that call.

It's written in every muscle in her body as she holds herself rigid beneath the tall oak. Her shoulders are pulled up to her ears and her free hand fidgets with the hem of her shirt while the other grips the phone so tightly I'm sure her knuckles are white. I can't hear what she's saying, but the way she's pacing in the shade of the tree tells me I'll have to do some damage control when she hangs up.

Shit.

I want to throat punch the person on the other end of the line for ruining her perfectly happy Saturday.

After a few minutes, Tessa ends the call and slides her phone into her back pocket. But she doesn't come back. She stays under the tree, facing the street with her back to us. And by the way her hands keep swiping at her face, there's no doubt in my mind that she's crying.

"Hey, Banana, can you swing by yourself for a minute?"

"Okay, Daddy."

I jog to the tree, reminding myself to remain supportive and quelling the urge to bash her parents. It's a damn tightrope I'm sick of walking. What I really want to say is that she needs to tell her parents to fuck off.

When I'm a couple of feet away, Tessa turns. She lets me wrap her up in a hug and presses her face into my chest.

I drop my chin to the top of her head and rub comforting circles across her back. We stand that way for a while before I clear my throat. "What do you need?"

"This" is her only reply.

So I hold her, letting her process her feelings and collect her thoughts until she's ready to express them. I turn us so I can keep my eye on Hannah, who's abandoned the swings for the slide.

"Bet you can guess who I was talking to," Tessa finally says, her face still buried in my chest.

"Mm-hmm."

She sighs heavily, her shoulders sagging. "I made the mistake of sending them the link to a house that's for sale here."

This is the first I'm hearing about a house, but I stay quiet.

"Mel sent it to me yesterday. It's really cute, and it's in my price range and only a couple of blocks from the library. Just went on the market." She pulls her phone out, and once she has the listing pulled up, she hands me the device and takes half a step back so I can scroll through the pictures. I can feel her eyes on my face, watching for my reaction.

How *do* I react to this? Tessa is thinking about buying a house here in Bennett. I know which house it is when I see the first shot. It's a bungalow on Mills Street, close to Central and the downtown area. Really close to the library. Ms. Daisy, my mom's boss, lives a few houses down and across the street. Two bedrooms, one and a half baths. Exterior painted a light, friendly yellow.

It looks like Tessa.

My gut reaction, which I keep from showing on my face, is devastation. Simply because I've been picturing Tessa making herself at home in the white house on Thigpen Road—her clothes hung next to mine in the closet I only use a quarter of, her books stacked on every flat surface, her scent in the air in every room. I've already mentally started plans to build her a wall of floor-to-ceiling bookshelves in what's currently Hannah's playroom. Won't even mention the plans I have for the other spare bedroom…

On the other hand, if she wants to buy this little house, that means she wants to stay in Bennett. Put down roots here. So I should count that as a win, even though it's not the location I prefer.

After I've scrolled through every picture, I hand her phone back, force a smile, and tell her honestly, "Looks like it was made for you, Ivy."

The unsure look on her face transforms into a relieved smile, and her big green eyes shine brightly up at me.

I'd give my right kidney to keep this look on her face always.

"I think so, too," she murmurs. "But, of course, my parents don't agree. They think it's a bad idea to invest in property here because they're still convinced I'm not staying. No matter how many times I tell them I'm happy here. Why can't they just accept that?" She's asking herself that question, not me. But it's time for me to step onto that tightrope once again.

"Maybe purchasing that house would go a long way in showing them you're serious about staying here."

"Maybe." She doesn't sound so sure.

"Listen, if buying that house makes you happy, you know what I say, right?"

"Yeah—do it."

"If it makes you happy, do it," I repeat, cupping her beautiful face in my hands.

She circles my wrists with her slender fingers and presses into me.

"It's okay for you to not give a shit about what anyone thinks about your life choices."

"But they're my *parents*, Luke."

And right there is the core of this issue. I want so badly to tell her that it doesn't matter whether they raised her or provided for her in the past if they can't love and accept who she is in the present. To tell her that she doesn't need them or their judgment to live a full, happy life. However, I'm worried that if I push too much and Tessa does tell her parents to take a hike, she'll resent me later for costing her that relationship.

"I know, baby. But you can't make decisions for your life based on someone else's expectations." All I can do is support her and hope that one day, she'll realize that in order to have a lifetime of happiness, she might have to cut some ties to her past.

"I know." And there goes the shoulder slump again.

All I can do is hold her a little tighter. And then my sweet girl is here, her little arms looping around my legs and Tessa's.

"Group hug!" she cheers, unaware of the solemn moment she's stumbled into. But, like magic, her innocence and joy bring light back to Tessa's eyes.

She laughs at the five-year-old clinging to her leg and rubs a hand down her hair affectionately. "I've missed you, Jelly Bean!"

"But I've been here the whole time!" Hannah giggles.

"Have you really?" Tessa asks, her voice full of pretend wonder.

"Yes, silly!"

"Well, I missed you, nonetheless."

My baby girl's face scrunches up. "What is nonetheless?"

"It means anyway. Like, 'I missed you anyway,'" Tessa explains.

"Oh." Satisfied with the explanation, Hannah lets go of our legs and shouts, "Piggyback, please!"

"Since you said please. Hop on." I crouch down so she can latch on to my neck. She giggles like crazy when I stand to my full height.

"Can you give Ms. Tessa a piggyback next?" she asks, innocent and unaware. I turn and walk backward a few steps so I can take in the way the blush spreads across Tessa's face and down her neck. She's making a don't-you-dare face at me, knowing I'm about to say something naughty.

I grin and give her a wink. "Oh, I can give Ms. Tessa a ride for sure."

She closes her eyes in exasperation, but her lips twitch like she's trying hard not to grin. I spin quickly, making my baby girl cackle, and head to the picnic table so we can pack up. It's almost suppertime, and I promised my girls I'd make fajitas tonight.

My right hand finds Tessa's thigh as soon as we get buckled in, and I give her reassuring squeezes every so often. She's quiet on the ride home, though Hannah's voice fills the truck as she chatters about school and asks questions about anything and everything.

After dinner, Tessa offers to clean the kitchen while Banana and I play outside, taking advantage of the longer day and the cool spring temperature. Once she's finished, Tessa takes a seat on the wooden porch swing, a glass of wine in one hand and a cold beer waiting for me in the other.

"She needs a dog," Tessa says when I join her on the swing.

She settles into me once I'm seated, nestling close as I wrap an arm around her and kiss the top of her head. Hannah's still in the yard, which is littered with hula-hoops, plastic horseshoes, glittery batons, and a pink motorized Jeep she's almost too big to fit in. I'm tempted to tell Tessa that we'll get a dog as soon as she moves in to help us care for it, but as much as I want that, she's not ready, so I bite my tongue.

Instead, I clink my beer against her wineglass and take a swig. We're quiet for a minute, soaking up the end of the day.

Then, so soft it's almost a whisper, Tessa asks, "Will you go with me? To see the house?"

I force down a swallow and clear my throat before answering. "Sure, Ivy. When do you want to go?"

"This week, for sure. Mel said to call her dad to set it up. I'll make sure it's after you get off work."

"That's fine, baby. I could get away during lunch one day, too. The site we're at this week is close."

Hannah runs at full speed up the porch steps and dives into her favorite rocking chair. She starts a rhythmic back-and-forth, stifling a big yawn. This kid has played hard today, so she's fading fast.

"Banana, how about we get your bath ready?"

Surprisingly agreeable, she hops to her feet. "Ms. Tessa, I want you to pick out my bedtime story while I get my bath."

"I'd love to." She'd give this kid anything she asked for.

This kid.

Our kid.

That thought brings that chest tightness back full force. It's so powerful, I forget to breathe for a few seconds, causing me to gasp for air, which makes me cough like I'm choking my damn self.

"You okay?" Tessa asks, taking my empty bottle so I can carry Banana up to her bathroom.

"Yeah. Just swallowed wrong." I play it off. But the idea of Hannah being Tessa's as much as she's mine runs on a loop all the way through bath time, pajama selection, teeth brushing, and bedtime storytelling.

I could give a flying fuck that Tessa and my girl don't share

DNA. She's become more of a mother to Hannah than Shelley ever was.

As if I needed even more convincing, Tessa whispers, "Love you, Jelly Bean," against Hannah's cheek when she leans down to kiss her goodnight.

And my little girl murmurs, "Love you, too," in response.

Fuck.

These girls are *everything* to me. All my needs, desires, and dreams—right here. I'm afraid to blink; I don't want to miss a damn second. With either of them.

Tessa and I stand in the doorway until Hannah's asleep, which only takes a handful of minutes, then I tug Tessa into the hall and close the door halfway. Still holding her hand, I lead her silently to my bedroom.

What I hope will one day be *our* bedroom.

"Got something in mind, Mr. Shipley?" she asks once the door is closed behind us.

Her flirty voice makes me tighten in anticipation. "Well, Ms. Burton, I believe I promised you a ride."

I spend the next hour worshipping the body of the girl I'm madly in love with.

The girl I want to spend the rest of my life with.

And as we come together, we prove our love for each other with soft kisses and tender touches. No words necessary.

CHAPTER TWENTY-TWO

"You know we'll only be gone for two nights, right?" Luke gives me that smile that makes my knees week. He's standing on the sidewalk in front of my place, staring down at the three overnight bags and the heavy backpack resting at our feet.

I *may* have overpacked for our weekend camping trip.

Last weekend, over slices of pie at Ruth's, Mel announced that she'd bought a pop-up camper. When asked why, she shrugged and said, "Why not?" And when Luke asked her where she bought it from, her cryptic response was "I know people." She then begged us to plan a weekend getaway to "break Betsy in." And here we are. Standing on the sidewalk at the crack of dawn with Betsy hitched to the back of Luke's truck.

Hitched to Luke's truck because Mel's little convertible cannot haul Betsy. He agreed to haul her new toy, but only if Hannah and Cordell could come along.

So the five of us are set to spend the first weekend of spring break at Chattahoochee Bend State Park, a little over two hours from Bennett. The pop-up only has one bed, a queen-size that the girls will share, which means Luke and Cordell are going to rough it in a tent.

Luke did a *lot* of grumbling about that. When I teased him about a weekend without my company, he cocked a brow. "Oh, I'm not going the whole weekend without," he rasped, affecting the gravelly tone he knows makes my insides quiver.

Secretly, I'm just as bummed about having to sacrifice together time for this trip.

"When are we leaving?" A sleepy Hannah is already snuggled into her booster in the back seat of Luke's truck.

"Soon, Banana," he promises her through the open window, giving my backside a playful swat before he hoists my luggage into the truck bed and secures it with the rest of the gear.

Cordell's Land Rover pulls up to the curb behind Betsy, and he exits his vehicle looking bright-eyed and fresh, carrying a duffel bag, a travel coffee mug, and a small white paper bag.

"Greetings, fellow campers!" he calls.

Clearly, this man is a morning person.

Luke huffs out a reply and takes his bag from him while his best friend gives me a friendly side hug, then greets Hannah at her window. "Banana, good morning. Just for you," he says, handing her the paper bag.

When she peers inside, her whole face lights up. "Holes!" she exclaims, pulling out a donut hole to shove into her mouth. "Thank you, Uncle Dell," she says through a mouthful of fried dough.

"Didn't bring enough to share with the class, Coach Watkins?"

The three of us startle at Mel's sudden appearance. I didn't even hear her pull up or shut her car door.

Cordell turns from the truck, his hand on his chest like he's trying to calm his spooked heart. "Ms. Marshall, giving people heart attacks your new side hustle?" he questions.

"Ha. Funny." She sounds anything but amused. She's

wearing cut-off denim shorts and a navy T-shirt that reads *Camping is In-Tents*. A bright green bandanna holds her lavender pigtails back, and she's got hiking boots laced over colorful polka-dot knee socks. She has a backpack on one shoulder and a hot pink overnight bag slung over an arm.

Mel, by the way, is *not* a morning person.

Cordell holds an arm out in offering, but she steps around him with her nose in the air and instead hands her stuff over to Luke, who wordlessly takes it and adds it to the rest.

When I tug on the handle of the back door, Luke grabs my arm. "What are you doing?"

"Mel and I can ride in the back. It'll be too cramped for Cordell back here."

"But—" Luke whines.

"Don't be a grumpy bear."

"Can't help it, Ivy. I'll miss you." He gives me a shy, boyish smile and tugs my T-shirt, pulling me closer so he can kiss me.

Once. Twice. Three times.

"Let's go, lovebirds! We've got lots of nature-ing to do!" Mel appears beside us and gives me a playful push, urging me into the back seat, next to Hannah's booster. The guys settle in the front, and once we're all buckled in, our weekend camping adventure begins.

Hannah's out cold by the time we leave Bennett city limits, her little head propped on a small pillow so she won't wake up with a sore neck and the empty donut bag still clutched in her hand.

Cordell's taken over DJ duties, much to Mel's chagrin. And Luke keeps making eyes at me in the rearview mirror, so intense at times that it sets my skin on fire. Now and then, he reaches back between the front seats and caresses my knee or calf or ankle. And every time, Mel waggles her brows at me, which only causes my blushing to intensify.

The trip is uneventful, except for Mel shouting out "Veto!"

every time Cordell starts a song she doesn't like. Once we arrive at the campground, the guys set up camp while we take Hannah to scope out our surroundings. The pop-up has a wet bath with a plastic curtain for privacy, but we check out the park's amenities anyway. The public bathroom is older but clean. After taking care of our business, we trek back to the campsite to find the pop-up secure and ready.

"Betsy!" Mel shouts, like she's greeting a long-lost friend. "You're lookin' good, old girl!" She runs a hand over the side appreciatively before stepping inside.

Hannah's so excited, she's bouncing all over the site, touching everything. It's her very first camping trip, and I'm thrilled that I get to witness her experience it.

"Come meet Betsy, Jelly Bean!" Mel calls from inside the camper.

"Daddy!" she calls within seconds of entering. "The toilet's right by the table!" She's so loud, I'm sure the people three sites over can hear her.

Luke smiles and shakes his head as he pulls a plastic tote from the back of his truck. "Weird, yeah?"

"Yeah!"

Everyone is occupied setting up the site—Mel getting Betsy's bed prepped and Cordell securing the tent's rain fly—when Luke snags my arm. "Wanna make a run for it?" he asks, tugging my hips to his. "I need some alone time with you." His words are hot and breathy in my ear.

Popped up on my tiptoes, I loop my arms around his neck and angle in like I'm going to kiss him, but as my lips are about to brush against his, I swipe the cap off his head and place it on mine backward.

His eyes narrow, but he leans back to check out my new look. "Mmm, yep. I think you should wear this when I get you alone later." His mouth finds my ear again, and he whispers, "Nothing but this."

I kiss his cheek and say, "We talked about this, handsome."

"And I told you"—he grasps my chin—"I'm not going all weekend without being inside you. Don't worry. I'll find a way."

His wicked promise sends tingles coursing through me. He winks and kisses me softly before stepping away. Yeah, he knows exactly what kind of effect he has on me.

I keep his Braves cap firmly on my head. Serves him right.

After a hike and lunch, the guys want to head down to the river to fish for a while, so Mel and I take Hannah to the playground. We settle on one of the metal benches to watch Hannah play, and in true only-child fashion, she makes a friend. Though as an only child myself, I never made friends as naturally and as effortlessly as she does. I was always on the outskirts, wishing I could join in with the others but not sure that I would be welcomed. Too afraid to take a chance. Too worried that I would do something wrong.

"Ms. Tessa! Watch this!" Hannah shows off her climbing prowess and hangs upside down on one of the monkey bars.

Her fearlessness is inspiring. Still, I can't help but call out, "Cool, Jelly Bean! Be careful, okay? Don't get too high!"

"She's crazy about you," Mel states, bringing her legs up to sit crisscross on the bench next to me. "So is her daddy."

The genuine joy she radiates makes tears well in my eyes, but I shake my head to keep them at bay.

"I'm crazy about them, too."

"Happiness looks good on you, T." She playfully jabs her elbow into my arm. "You know it's okay to feel happy, right? To chase after this feeling and never let it go?"

Somehow, I find my voice. "I don't think I really knew what true joy felt like until I moved to Bennett. Until I met you. And Luke…"

"Yeah, love will do that to you—make you feel like everything before was a pale imitation of the magic that life has to offer." She's scanning the playground, a wistful look on her face.

"You sound like you know from experience." Not once in the months I've known her has she alluded to a past love. In fact, she acts like dating is a big adventure and that men are simply fun distractions.

"Yeah" is all she says.

I want so badly to pry. But if I've learned anything about my best friend, it's that she likes to keep people on their toes by only revealing a layer of herself at a time.

She shakes her head like she's clearing cobwebs, that wistful look replaced by her usual casual indifference. "I've been wanting to ask you for *weeks*, so be honest with me. The sex— it's fantastic, right?"

I gape at her for a long moment, then whip my head back and forth to make sure we're out of earshot of other campers.

I find my wits and demand, "Who says we're having it?"

"Pfft. Please." She snorts. "Everyone in Bennett knows you're having it. On the regular."

"What?" I squeak. "No they don't."

Mel just gives me a good-natured eye roll. "Tessa. Seriously. Luke's walking around town, looking like a man who is *very* satisfied. And you? You are effing *glowing*, my friend." When I shake my head in denial, she splutters again. "You are! You've got that O-glow."

The *what*? I give her a puzzled look.

"O-glow. That *glow* that can only *come*"—she winks to make her point—"from having a good *O*."

I'm certain my face is as red as the slide Hannah's racing down. Backward.

"Spill the deets, girl."

God knows I love her, but she won't quit until I give her something. So I scan the park again and say, "It's freaking amazing, okay? I want to jump his bones. All. The. Time."

Mel squeals with delight. Loudly.

So loudly that Hannah darts over, thinking she's missing out on something exciting.

Saved by the Jelly Bean.

Her cheeks are flushed, and strands of her hair escape the pigtails that hang down her back. She plops down between us on the bench, then leans against my arm, her head hot and sweaty. When I pull my arm out to wrap around her, her little body melts against mine.

This tiny human has my heart.

"You having fun?"

"Yep." She takes my hand and plays with my fingers, weaving her own between them affectionately. Mel makes an *aww* face at me over her head.

"Who's your new friend?" Mel asks.

"Her name is Chloe. She's six. I will be six in…" She turns to me. "How long?"

"Less than two months."

"Daddy said that I can have a fairy birthday. You'll come, right, Ms. Mel?"

"'Course, JB. Wouldn't miss it."

The way Luke's face lights up when Hannah and I return to the campsite hand in hand takes my breath away.

I love this man so much it terrifies me.

This thing we have, this love we share, feels so precious—in a once-in-a-lifetime way. I'm scared of it. I'm scared of messing it up. Because if anyone's messing up something this good—it will be me.

I feel like I'm hard-wired to disappoint.

Working on that with the therapist, for sure.

Luke meets us near the truck and sweeps Hannah up into his arms while leaning in to plant a kiss on my lips.

Hannah rubs his cheeks with her tiny hands and singsongs, "Hairy-Face Daddy," while he leads me to the picnic table near the grill.

"No fish, I see," Mel says, her attention locked on Cordell, of course.

"No fish today. They must've heard you're here. Gone into hiding." He's busy prepping the grill so we can cook hot dogs for supper.

"Har har." She moves her camp chair so that her back is to him. I swear, these two. Luke gives me a *why did we do this to ourselves* look that I can only shrug at.

To ease the tension, I fetch two beers out of the cooler and give one to Luke and the other to Cordell. He smiles appreciatively at me, then resumes his grilling duties.

Mel occupies Hannah until dinner with a couple of rounds of Uno at the picnic table while I settle into a lawn chair and listen to the guys spin tales about their high school football days. I love getting little glimpses of Past Luke; they're like little puzzle pieces I savor, hoping to one day fill in the whole picture and know every last part of him.

Shortly after dinner, Hannah's day of hiking and playground time catches up with her. Luke gives her a quick wash-down and gets her ready for bed, tucking her into the camper bed where Mel and I will join her later. She's out as soon as her stuffed otter is snuggled tightly in her arms. Cordell lights a citronella candle to keep the bugs away and sets it on the ground in the center of the circle of lawn chairs. Mel passes out another round of beers, and we all sit quietly for a while, content to enjoy the last moments of light as the sun starts its descent.

"Favorite movie villain." Mel takes a swig of her beer and points her bottle to me.

I hate going first.

Luke knows this, so he calls out his answer. "Darth Vader."

"What, no second choice you wanna sneak in there, Shipley?" she asks, surprised.

"Nope. You go, Marshall."

"Okay. I'm going with Thanos. He wipes out half the planet."

She gives a pointed look to Cordell, like she thinks he will dispute her. He doesn't. "Your turn, T."

"I guess I'll go with Voldemort."

"Of course you will, you adorable book nerd," Luke says, tapping my foot with his.

"So, who's it gonna be, Watkins?" Mel asks.

"The correct answer is: Hans Gruber. *Die Hard.*"

"Never seen it," she states, her nose in the air.

The guys shout out their bafflement simultaneously.

Cordell can't stop gaping at her. "Best Christmas movie ever," he declares.

Mel just shrugs like she can't be bothered to care. But a second later, she perks up. "Speaking of Christmas," she turns to me, "it's a shame you didn't get the house on Mills. It has the perfect Christmas tree window."

Stomach sinking, I glance at Luke, then back again. He knows I put an offer in on the house last week, after visiting it three times and nearly having a panic attack over the prospect of having to tell my parents about it. But I haven't had the chance to tell him that I was outbid, even though I found out yesterday.

The look in his eyes when he processes the information makes my lungs seize up.

It's relief. Pure, unrestrained relief.

It's only there for a moment, a blink-and-you'll-miss-it fraction of a second, but it leaves me feeling all sorts of confused. Especially after he encouraged me to go for it. His exact words flash through my mind: *It looks like it was made for you, Ivy.*

So I don't know whether to believe him when he says, "Aw, that's a shame." But I won't question him in front of our friends.

Who are you kidding? You won't confront him about it when it's just the two of you either.

The conversation drifts to other topics, but I can't keep the questions from plaguing my mind: Luke didn't want me to get the house? Did he think the asking price was too high? Does he doubt that I'm truly happy in Bennett? That I want to stay? Does he think my parents will eventually wear me down, and I'll go back to Atlanta?

But the ones that scare me the most, the sharks circling their kill: Have Luke's feelings about me changed? Does he no longer see us having a future together? Maybe he doesn't want me to stay.

Here's the thing about anxiety: once an anxious brain starts down a rabbit hole, it's very hard to find an exit. It imagines so many scenarios, so many possibilities. And no matter how far-fetched or ridiculous they may be, it's very hard to talk oneself out of believing them. Therapy has given me practical strategies for dealing with these intrusive thoughts, but it hasn't erased them completely.

The thought that Luke's feelings have changed hits me like a punch to the gut. The conversation continues around me, but I can't focus on it. It takes all of my willpower not to go into full-blown meltdown mode.

No, I have to play this cool. Make sure I don't give away the panic raging inside. Like a duck, gliding serenely through the water, while under the surface, its feet are paddling like crazy.

I offer smiles and laugh when it's appropriate until bedtime. But I didn't figure Luke's intuitiveness into the equation. As soon as Cordell and Mel say goodnight and retreat to their sleeping areas, he pulls me up from my chair and hovers close.

"What's up?"

"What do you mean?" I school my features and plead with my body to remain neutral.

Luke's not buying it. "Tessa. C'mon, baby. I know when something's bothering you."

I force myself to swallow and look up into those brown eyes so full of concern.

"Is it about the house?"

Direct hit.

But should I go *there*? Question his reaction to the news?

He speaks up before I can talk myself into it. "I know you're disappointed. It's a great house. But things happen for a reason. Just take this as a sign that there's something better out there for you." His words are so earnest, so confident, that I find myself wondering if I misinterpreted his look earlier.

"You're right," I croak, burying my face in my favorite spot on his chest, where I can breathe him in and feel the solidness of him beneath me. His hands find my bottom, cupping me and pulling me closer. The way he holds me—and holds me up, no matter what—goes a long way in making my earlier intrusive questions melt away. Plus, I find myself the good kind of distracted when he puts his hands on me.

"Tomorrow, Ivy. You and I are sneakin' away," he whispers into my ear, then kisses that spot beneath it that makes me tingle all over.

"Hmm. We'll see, handsome."

Luke's deep chuckle makes me smile.

"Wrap it up, Shipley," Cordell's gruff, sleepy voice calls from inside the tent.

Luke heaves a big sigh, then moves his hands so they're cradling my cheeks. He watches me for a long moment before he gives me a scorching good night kiss that leaves me breathless.

"'Night, Tessa."

"Good night, Luke."

Snuggled up with Hannah and Mel, I fall asleep relatively easily, despite the doubt that's taken root inside my mind, thoughts of Luke's warm embrace and Hannah's sweet laughter lulling me into a deep, dreamless sleep.

CHAPTER TWENTY-THREE

LUKE

At the sound of crunching gravel, I look up from where I've been sanding the same stretch of wood for far too long. It's beyond smooth now, but I've been lost in my thoughts.

"The girls aren't back yet?" My dad ambles over to my workstation inside the garage as soon as he climbs out of his truck.

The girls. I shake my head and go back to sanding, my gut twisting. Because something has been wrong with *my* girl since that damn camping trip earlier this month, and for the life of me, I can't shake this sense of dread that's consumed my thoughts since then.

Of course, every time I've asked her about it, she plays it off. I haven't pushed her too much, though I've wanted to. Badly. It's like I'm back to dealing with that skittish animal—one wrong move, and she'll bolt for good. So when she tells me that everything's fine, that she's happy and things are good, I sit back and take stock of all the things that are, indeed, good—we see each other almost every day; she kisses me until we're both breathless; we fuck like we can't get enough of each other. She smiles that sunshine smile every time she sees me, showers Hannah with her time and affection.

Tells me she loves me.

But there's still something wrong. I'm as certain of it as I am my own damn name. I know Tessa Burton, every inch of her body, all of her tells and poker faces. I know her. *I know her.* And something isn't right.

Gonna give myself a damn ulcer if I don't figure it out soon.

"Looking good, kid." Pop's standing beside me, running a hand down the back of the bench I've been working on for the last several days. I can only grunt a response as I continue, my hands still sliding along the wood aggressively in hopes that the movement will calm the dread in my gut with the repetitive motions.

"This for Tessa's new place?"

"Yep." One-word answers are all I can muster at the moment. My pop, bless his soul, lets me get away with it.

Another thing that's changed since the camping trip: Tessa's future living situation. She found out a few days after we got back that the buyer of the bungalow backed out, so she put in another offer, and it was accepted. My performance when she called to tell me the news could probably earn me a freaking Oscar.

Of course, I *am* pleased that she's standing on her own two feet despite her parents' disapproval. And it makes her happy. So I'm happy.

Sorta.

It means she's staying put in Bennett, but I can't shake the disappointment that there's no way I'll convince her to move in with us anytime in the near future. I know it's too soon. I know others would say we're rushing things. But I don't give a fuck.

I want to build a life with her. I want my ring on her finger and her in my bed every damn night. I want to get started on our future, because I don't want any part of a future where she's not in it with me. With us.

"What time you expectin' them to get back?"

"Soon. Tessa texted about an hour ago. Said they were heading back." Mom, Tessa, and Hannah took a day trip to Albany for lunch and to take advantage of after-Easter sales to get a dress for kindergarten graduation.

My little Banana is so close to finishing up her first year of school.

"You wanna talk about what's eatin' at you?" Pop pulls a stool down from where it's flipped upside down on my workbench. He settles in and crosses his arms, giving me time to collect my thoughts. Part of me wants to deny anything is wrong, but I swore to myself I'd stop keeping secrets from my parents after I finally set the last one free.

I huff like an ornery kid but spit it out anyway. "Something's up with Tessa, and I don't know what it is. Or how to fix it." I don't look at him, just continue making my way down the back of the bench with the sandpaper.

He's quiet for so long, I wonder if he's dozed off. When I glance up at him, he's got his head tilted back and he's focused on the ceiling, deep in thought.

Thomas Shipley is a man who thinks before he speaks.

"Hmm," he finally responds. "And you've talked to her about it?"

I fight the urge to roll my eyes. "'Course I have. She says nothing is wrong. Says she's happy. She doesn't *act* any different, per se. But I *know* her. I can tell something's up."

"Did I ever tell you about when I asked your granddaddy for permission to marry your mama?"

I shake my head. I've heard the story of his proposal several times. But I can't recall this one.

"You know full well your granddaddy could be damn scary."

I huff out a laugh, nodding at the truth in that statement.

Never to me, never to the family he loved so much, but my mom's dad could certainly be a hard-ass when the occasion called for it. He was a Navy man, regimented and tough.

"I was terrified of that man back then. Hell, I was terrified of him for the first five years we were married, too. So imagine me, a nobody punk, wanting to marry his only daughter. His only daughter who had just graduated from high school." He lets out a big sigh. "But gosh, was I gone for her. Would've done anything to make her my wife. So I went to my own dad to get his advice before I had to face William Elton. He knew the man. Knew how much of a hurdle I was facing. He also knew how much I loved your mama. So he gave me some of the best advice I've ever received. And now that you've found the one you can't live without, I'm gonna pass it on to you."

I look him in the eye and swallow past the lump in my throat. "I want to marry her, Pop." I've never said those words to another soul. Have thought them dozens of times over the past few months. But I've never voiced them.

"I know, kid," he says. "Your papaw told me that if I wanted something I've never had before, I would have to do something I've never done. If the thing you want so bad is worth it, then you'll find a way to make it happen."

I stop sanding again and survey the tree line across the way, thinking about his words. Thinking about the things that I've truly gone after in my life: Being the best father possible to Hannah. Working hard to learn how to read. Pursuing Tessa.

That woman is worth every single ounce of my courage.

"You'll find your way with her, kid. Just be there for her. Be patient. Lettin' her work through it herself might not sit well with you because you're a fixer. But that might be what you have to do in order to keep her."

Taking a deep breath, I nod. Maybe I can't fix what's bothering Tessa, no matter how badly I want to step in and be her hero. I'll just have to have faith in what we have and trust that she'll work it out for herself.

More tires crunching on gravel pulls our attention to the road that leads from my folks' place. Sure enough, my mom's sedan is creeping up the drive. My hands itch with the need to get them on my girl, to assess her demeanor this afternoon.

As soon as Hannah's released from the back seat, she's dashing up to us in the garage. I brace myself just in time to catch her as she leaps into my arms.

"Daddy, we got me a dress for graduation!" She plants a kiss on my cheek before rubbing at the stubble with her little hands.

"That's awesome. Can't wait to see it."

Pop holds up his hand so Hannah can give him a high five, and we wander out to where my mom and Tessa are collecting bags from the trunk.

"Looks like y'all bought out the shops," I say, taking three shopping bags from Tessa. "Hey there, Ivy."

"Hey, handsome." She leans in for a quick kiss, then ducks her head when she remembers that my parents are nearby.

I do a quick scan of her face but don't see any sign of stress or worry. Then I can't help but give her a once-over, taking in the floral shirt and the jeans that hug the curves I love so much.

Jeans that I can't wait to peel off her later.

Where Hannah's perched in my arms, she's at the right height to brush her hand down Tessa's silky hair. The way she leans into my little girl's touch makes my chest squeeze in that familiar way. Next to us, my folks watch the interaction with hearts in their eyes.

Damn. This feels fucking right.

I clear my throat before my emotions get the best of me. "You gonna show me this dress, Banana?"

"Yep! It's *so* pretty!" She kicks her legs, a clear signal that she wants down. Once she's back on her feet, she takes a bag from my hand and pulls out a hanger that's holding a white

Banana-sized dress. It's sleeveless with ruffles at the shoulders and the bottom hem, and it has a wide white sash tied in a bow at the back. It's innocent and sweet and perfect. Damn, I have to blink back tears when I picture my little girl wearing this when she walks across a stage to get her tiny kindergarten diploma.

Shit. Get it together, Shipley.

"Ms. Tessa's dress is gonna match," Hannah cheers, taking Tessa's hand.

Tessa's cheeks instantly flush, but she smiles down at her little bestie. "Well, it's similar," she explains, her eyes darting up to mine like she's worried about my reaction.

I fight the urge to tell her that I'm all-in for *all* the family matching moments. Vacation T-shirts, Halloween costumes, Christmas pajamas—I want it all.

"Can't wait to see my two beautiful girls all dressed up," I say.

Tessa's relieved smile makes my heart hurt a little. She helps Hannah put the dress back into the shopping bag carefully. "Let's make sure we hang this up in your closet so it doesn't get even more wrinkled."

When we head toward the house, my mom zeros in on the wooden bench I've been working on. "Ooh, this is going to be perfect!" She turns to Tessa, wearing a huge smile. "You're going to put this in your entryway?" she asks. "Such a lucky girl to have a handy boy to build you anything you want!" Mom squeezes my bicep affectionately.

"Oh, he's very handy."

I waggle my brows at Tessa, and her face blooms with color when she realizes why. She recovers quickly, though.

"I think he should set up a page on Instagram where he can show off his pieces. It would drum up more business for him."

I've never bothered with any kind of social media before. Why would I, when I couldn't read setup instructions or captions? But I'd love to offer my custom-built pieces to a wider clientele. I've sold plenty of items to folks here in Bennett, and my job with Statler Construction offers me other opportunities to connect with people who are looking for handcrafted furniture. But the reach that an Instagram page would have could be a game changer.

"That's a great idea, kid," Pop offers.

"Yeah, we'll see." I smile at Tessa only to find her watching me carefully, like she's waiting for me to reveal something. What that something is, I'm not sure, and that twist in my gut flares up again. Instead of dwelling on it, I pull her into my side and press a kiss to her temple.

"Miss June Bug, you ready to grab your stuff? Papaw is taking us to dinner at Ruth's." My mom offered to keep Hannah tonight, leaving Tessa and me totally alone for the first time in weeks.

And I've been making plans all damn day.

She cheers—probably knowing her grandparents won't say no when she asks for a chocolate milkshake with extra whipped cream—and skips off.

We say our goodbyes with quick hugs and good-night kisses and the pinkie promise that's become a ritual, then they're off.

As soon as the door is closed behind us, I'm all over Tessa. My hands running through her hair, gripping her ass, tugging her closer. My lips on her skin, her mouth, my tongue meeting hers in a long, hot kiss that turns into several more.

"I need a shower," I say between kisses. "Wanna join me?" When I pull back so I can see her face, I groan at the sight of her swollen lips, and my dick grows harder in anticipation of having her all to myself for the rest of the night.

She gives me a coy smile. "As tempting as that sounds, why don't I fix supper while you get cleaned up?" She pops up on her toes to give me a sweet, soft kiss, like an apology for not jumping at my shower suggestion.

"Damn, Ivy. I didn't even think—do you want me to take you out tonight? We can go anywhere you'd like."

"Oh, no. I'm fine with staying in. Really."

I search her face for any tells that she's just being agreeable, but her features reinforce her sincerity. "I'm being a crap boyfriend, aren't I? Our first night alone in weeks, and all I can think about is getting between these gorgeous thighs."

"Luke." She slides her hands from where they've been resting on my ribs and brings them up to cup my face. "You are not a crap boyfriend." Her words are fierce, and she shakes my head a little to make sure her message sinks in. "You are the perfect boyfriend, and I'm so incredibly lucky that you're mine." Her words are going a long way in calming that feeling of dread that's been a constant gray cloud hanging over me for the past couple of weeks.

Tessa's big green eyes are warm and loving as she keeps them locked on mine. At this moment, at least, she's sure of me. Of us.

Tessa's already at the table, omelets plated and ready, when I jog down the stairs. She watches my approach, homing in on my bare feet and skimming up my plaid pj pants and T-shirt. I have to tell my dick to calm the hell down before I spread her out on the table and forget all about supper. I brush my hand down the back of her head when I sit, and then we eat in silence.

After several minutes, Tessa sets her fork beside her plate and drops her hands to her lap, where she twists her fingers together nervously. "I have some news." Gone is the heat from before dinner, replaced by a wariness that stirs the ache in my gut.

"Is it about the house?" I blurt before I can think better.

"*No*," she says, searching my face, her eyes frantic and her chest rising and falling rapidly.

Well, shit. This is *not* how I'd hoped to get her heart racing tonight.

I tug one of her hands and pull it to my mouth to kiss the back. "What is it then, baby? You can tell me anything."

She smiles weakly, then continues. "My parents. They're coming for a visit."

Now it's my heart's turn to beat like crazy.

"Not here, in Bennett. In Albany. My dad is meeting up with one of his buddies from law school to play golf, and the country club just *happens* to be in Albany, which just *happens* to be relatively close to where their only disappointment of a daughter *happens* to be living. Convenient, huh?"

"Hey, you are not a disappoint—"

"They want to meet you," she cuts me off, the words hitting me like a bucket of ice water. "They *expect* to meet you, to use their words."

Fuck.

I've been living in this happiness bubble and putting out the parental fires from a distance. But now I'll have to face these people.

"Of course I'll go with you. When?"

Tessa's sigh of relief loosens the panic gripping my heart just a little. "Next weekend." She winces when I choke on a piece of omelet. "I'm sorry! They ambushed me right before your mom picked me up."

"It's fine, beautiful." I affect the most self-assured expression I can to help ease her panic.

She nods and picks her fork back up, relief evident on her face.

"Hey." I wait until she's looking at me again. "I love you."

There it is—that sunshine smile that lights up my world.

"Love you, too."

After supper, once the dishes are all clean and put away, I get to follow through with my plans for the night—peeling Tessa's jeans off and losing myself between her thighs. Our coupling is slow and sweet, and I make sure to whisper *I love you* in her ear every chance I get.

After, when she's sound asleep in my arms, I make a silent promise that she'll always know exactly how precious she is to me. That she will never doubt that my heart belongs to her.

I almost pull my truck to the side of the road to lose my breakfast in the grass lining the highway. Twice.

That's how nervous I am about this country club lunch.

I'm dressed in a pair of khakis that rarely see the light of day and a long-sleeve button-down so my tattoos will hopefully go unnoticed today. As much as I loathe the idea of meeting these people, I want to make the best impression I can, for Tessa's sake.

I want them to like me, because I'm ridiculously in love with their daughter.

Tessa's already in Albany. She drove over this morning to meet her mother for breakfast and a manicure while her father golfed. Even though they've been in town since Friday morning, this is the first time they've made an effort to see Tessa. She even invited them over to Bennett to tour her new hometown, but they fed her a bunch of excuses.

Today she's going to tell them about the bungalow. I'm sure it'll go over about as well as the news that she's dating a construction worker with a kid and an armful of tats who's only recently learned to read. That old list of reasons has ticked through my mind the whole way here. In the country club lot, I avoid the valet parking in favor of the side lot that is situated next to the clubhouse.

Shit. I've never been to a country club before.

When I told my folks where I was meeting the Burtons today,

all my mom said on the matter was "you're just as good as any of them, Lucas" as I slipped out the door.

The waffles I made this morning are *not* sitting well.

Just inside the glass doors of the pristine white clubhouse, my girl is waiting. She doesn't see me at first, so I take a minute to drink in the sight of her. She's wearing a dress that's more fitted than what she usually chooses, the color a weird pinkish-orange I've never seen her wear before. Her hair is pencil-straight, not in the soft waves I'm used to running my fingers through.

She looks as nervous as I feel.

When she sees me striding her way, her face lights up in a relieved smile. But it's not a sunshine smile, and that alone makes me cautious as hell.

"Hey, beautiful," I say before pressing my lips to her cheek.

"Thank you for coming," she says woodenly, like she's thanking a guest at a funeral.

I take her hand in mine, and she returns the gentle squeeze I give her, but she quickly lets go. Ducking my head, I try to get some steady eye contact, but she won't return it. Instead, she glances at me, then scans the room like she's taking in the surroundings.

"Of course," I tell her. "Hey."

She finally looks at me for more than half a second.

"We can leave right now if you want." It's obvious this morning hasn't gone well, and I'm willing to do anything I can to fix it for her. Even if that means abandoning ship and making her parents hate me even more than they probably already do.

"No. I don't want to make it worse," she says softly, almost to herself. "I made the mistake of telling my mom about the house while we were getting our manicures. She immediately called my father, and they had this long discussion on the phone about it. With me sitting right there."

She's mentioned that she sometimes feels invisible when she's with her parents. Now I know why.

"Whatever you need to do, Ivy, I'm here. Okay?"

"Okay." She finally takes my hand in hers again and doesn't let go this time. And a little piece of my soul slots back into place. "Let's get this over with."

She leads me through the foyer and into an elegant restaurant tucked into the side of the building that overlooks the golf course and is filled with men in sports coats and women in fitted dresses like Tessa's.

The only time I've felt this out of place was during those days at school when I had to hide my inability to read.

As we approach a round table in the back corner, an older couple stands from their chairs.

Patrick and Kathleen Burton.

Mr. Burton is a few inches shorter than me, with salt-and-pepper hair and a slight paunch. He's clean-shaven and slightly sunburned, and his jaw is set as he squints disapprovingly at me. So I slide my attention to Tessa's mother. She looks a lot like her daughter, but her hair is blond and cut in a short bob without a single hair out of place. They're dressed in clothing that probably cost more than my entire wardrobe.

"Mom, Dad. This is Luke."

As Tessa introduces us, I shake their hands with way more confidence than I'm feeling.

"So, Luke," Tessa's father begins in a booming voice once we've settled around the table. "My daughter failed to mention what it is you do for a living." It's more of an accusation against Tessa than a question, which pisses me right the hell off.

"I work in construction, sir." I don't miss the little side glance Mr. Burton gives his wife after my answer. The action sends my damn knee bouncing under the table.

"Luke also builds custom furniture. He's working on a bench for my new—" She cuts herself off abruptly, probably realizing that bringing up the house again won't go over well. Her face turns a bright red, and she ducks her head.

This whole damn thing has already gone off the rails.

I reach under the table to place a calming hand on her thigh.

"Buying that house is a mistake, Tessa," her mother says as she's reading over the menu. Thank fuck I can actually read the damn thing myself.

"Mom—"

"Your mother's right. It's not a prudent financial decision. If you want to invest in real estate, there are plenty of properties in the Atlanta area."

I clench my free hand on my leg, reminding myself that I can't give these two a piece of my mind. Yet.

Next to me, Tessa's shoulders are slumped and she's wearing a devastated look. And that shit makes me want to rage at these people.

Instead, I force my voice to remain calm. "It's a great property, sir. I know Bennett is small potatoes compared to Atlanta, but it's a friendly, safe community full of hard-working folks."

Tessa's mom gives me a condescending close-lipped smile before turning her attention back to the menu.

"Son, I mean no disrespect," Mr. Burton starts, using the exact phrase that signals that he's about to disrespect me, "but you have no idea what's best for my daughter. You've been dating for, what, a few weeks? I'm sorry that you'll be a casualty in my daughter's futile quest to prove that she's Miss Independent, but we all know how this story ends." His sunburned cheeks grow redder as his temper flares.

"Patrick," Mrs. Burton chides, but there's no real feeling behind it.

"How does it end, sir?"

He smirks. "It ends with my daughter back home where she belongs, and you—"

"Dad, please listen—"

He interrupts her again. "No, young lady, you listen. Your mother and I have given you the best all your life—the best upbringing, education, opportunities. Yet you've squandered it all. For what? What career advancement opportunities do you have as a librarian in some backwater town?"

"It's not backwater, Dad. And I have plenty—"

"No. I'll tell you what you have here—nothing. I'm wondering when my daughter, who was *so* aspirational in high school, decided to give up on creating a bright future for herself."

Shit. He won't even let her get a word in to defend herself.

"That was all for you, not me," Tessa whispers, so softly I wonder if her parents even heard it.

The scowl on her father's face and the deep frown on her mother's tell me they did.

I look over at the girl I love, certain she'll give me a can-you-believe-this-shit look or maybe a weak, watery smile—I'd take it and kiss away each tear that fell. But instead I see the girl who's given me the whole damn world with her head down, refusing to make eye contact with any of us. She's mentally building walls around herself. Walls I've spent months razing to the ground. She twists away from me so my hand drops from her thigh. The movement is physical proof of this magical, once-in-a-lifetime connection slipping from my grasp.

No, Ivy. Don't shut me out.

Please.

Mr. Burton clears his throat and continues with his rant. "You see, Luke, Tessa has no reason to stay in your town. This little act of rebellion is a result of us giving in to her too much over the years. But soon she'll realize the error of her ways and decide she wants a *real* future, and she'll come on back home."

A *real* future. The words hit me like a physical punch to my gut. My jaw clenches so tight in response I swear I'll need dental work.

Why isn't she speaking up for herself? For *us*?

Next to me, she looks embarrassed. But is it because of her parents? *Or me?*

"Baby," I whisper, angling closer. "Tell them you're happy."

Because that's ultimately what all parents *should* want for their kids.

"Tessa Diane, don't string this young man along," her mother scolds.

What the actual fuck is happening right now?

Then her father goes in for the death blow. "We can all be adults here and chalk this"—he waves his hand at the two of us like he's swatting away a fly—"up to being a fling, right, darling?"

We're being ambushed, and the person who's supposed to have my back no matter what has gone radio silent.

Fucking fight for us, damn it!

There's a long silence, one I'm aching to fill with words that will convince these awful people to give us a shot. To give their daughter a chance to choose the life she wants. Tessa curls in on herself, and a deep wrinkle settles between her eyebrows while she wrings the napkin in her lap with both hands. Then, with her eyes on the table, she says the words that completely crush me. "I, uh...I don't know what I was thinking..."

I mentally fill in the blank at the end of her sentence: I don't know what I was thinking getting involved with *him*.

And all at once, that damn list comes crashing back.

She was my tutor. *I'm stupid to think it was ever more than a fling.*

She's too young for me. *She would rather be with someone her own age, someone who doesn't have a kid.*

She's probably not looking to settle in Bennett long-term. *Her parents will make sure of that.*

She's not going to date a tattooed construction worker. *She'll want someone who can provide the kind of lifestyle she grew up in. Not a blue-collar loser.*

She's never going to want someone who can't read well. *Who never went to college. Who doesn't have a country club membership. Who her parents don't approve of.*

What a fucking fool I am.

My chest is heaving when I finally force myself to stand, my fists clenched at my sides. But I don't storm off. No, I wait like the lovesick bastard I am, hoping with everything in me that Tessa will take it back. That she'll stand up with me so we can storm out together.

It doesn't happen. She doesn't even look at me.

So I leave with the shred of dignity I can muster. I walk away from the love of my life, knowing she's chosen the parents who've made her life miserable over the man who loves her completely.

As I stomp to my truck, the pain that lances through me is unlike any I've ever felt before.

My heart is breaking. My heart is breaking in the middle of a fucking country club parking lot.

And as I'm doing my best to keep my shit together, to keep from falling to my knees and sobbing, it hits me: I've been so busy taking care of Tessa's heart, that it never even occurred to me that she could break mine.

CHAPTER TWENTY-FOUR

TESSA

Oh God. What have I done?

No, no, no, no, no, no, no…

The panic that courses through me when Luke stands from the table is enough to knock the air right out of me.

The pain that slices into my heart when he turns away is enough to break me.

Get up. Get up and fix this.

My eyes are locked on the white tablecloth in front of me. I don't want to see the looks of smug satisfaction on my parents' faces.

Minutes. We haven't even ordered. That's how long it took for my whole world to come crashing down around me —minutes.

For me to ruin the best thing that's ever happened to me.

I'm paralyzed. Unable to spring into action like I desperately need to do. To say the words that need to be said to the two people who've continually tried to mold me into someone I'm not.

But then my mother clears her throat and says, "Well, that was unpleasant, but it's for the best."

That does it.

"For the best?" I croak out, my voice full of more venom than I knew I possessed. "The best for whom? Because it sure as hell isn't what's best for *me*." I finally look up, tears swimming in my eyes, my parents blurry and distorted.

Just like our relationship.

"Tessa, language—"

"No. I'm done. I can't do this." I push back from the table on shaky legs. If I don't fix this right now, I might as well crawl into a dark space and stay there forever. Alone.

Oh God, what have I done?

Somehow, I get my legs to move. Careless of how I look, what others in this upper-crust place might think of me, I take off running, hoping to heaven that I can catch Luke before he drives away.

Every step closer to him is synced with the one thought flooding my mind: *Fix this, fix this, fix this, fix this.*

When I get outside, I frantically scan the parking lot, searching for his broad shoulders and dark hair. When I spot him, just feet away from his truck, I kick my uncomfortable wedges off and take off in that direction, shouting his name at the top of my lungs.

"Luke! Wait!"

He freezes but doesn't turn. His shoulders are bunched tight and his hands are clenched into fists at his sides.

Oh God, please let me fix this.

When I reach him, the tears are already coursing down my face. I'm out of breath, broken, and so sick with worry that I'm afraid I might throw up right here. That familiar heaviness settles in my chest, that warning that comes with a panic attack, but I ignore it.

"Luke, please…I'm sorry."

I want so badly to go to him, wrap my arms around his waist and hold on tight. But his closed-off stance keeps me in my place. He doesn't make a move to turn around or say a word.

"Please, Luke. I didn't mean it. I don't even know where that came from…"

The look on his face when he turns on his heel makes me want to sink to my knees and beg for his forgiveness.

His jaw is set tight, and his brows are so low they practically hide his eyes. I've never seen him look this angry—not when he stormed out of the library that first week, and not when he was so frustrated at his reading progress that he pushed the table in the study room.

I've never seen this look before. And it terrifies me. Because I'm afraid I've ruined our relationship for good.

Behind that anger is heart-wrenching devastation. Hurt. And I hate myself so much for putting it there.

"Luke—"

"Stop." His voice is cold. Hard. "I'm so sorry you feel like you've been slumming it with me, Tessa." The words slice me open, but I deserve them. "Not once have you made me feel like I'm less-than or beneath you…until today." When his voice breaks at the end, I instinctively reach my hand out, wanting to touch him, to make this right. But he takes a step away from me.

"Luke…" I'm crying so hard now I can barely speak, having to suck in lungfuls of air between words. "Please. I'm sorry. I've never thought that before, not today or ever—"

"But it's there. Deep down, isn't it? Shit, Tessa." Luke runs a hand through his hair and pulls in frustration. Even now, so angry at me, he's the most devastatingly handsome man I've ever seen. "You let those people fucking dictate your life. So I guess they win. Again."

"No! I-I don't care what they think—"

"Bullshit. God, I'm such a fucking idiot!" He turns sideways, like he's looking for something to punch, something to take the brunt of his rage. "And here you are, crying your eyes out. And it's killing me, *killing me*, that I can't give you the comfort you need. God, I would've burned down this fucking world for you. But apparently, I'm not good enough."

"Luke, no, please. Please…" I can't even string together coherent thoughts. "I'm sorry. I'm so sorry. Please forgive—" My words stop when he turns to me again, the look on his face rigid and harsh. I know I don't deserve his forgiveness. I don't deserve him. Or Hannah. Or the Shipleys.

I'm the absolute worst. A waste of their time. A waste of their feelings.

How can I ever come back from this?

"I'll tell you one thing," Luke says, so coldly that I wince. But I force myself to maintain eye contact, knowing that what he's going to say will gut me. But I've earned every bit of his vitriol, so I'll stand strong and take what I deserve. "I won't fucking be treated like I'm second class. Not by you. Not by anyone. Especially now that I know my own damn worth. Ironic that it was *you* who showed me that, huh?"

And with that, Luke Shipley storms to his truck and drives out of my life, leaving me a broken mess in the middle of a parking lot.

Mel finds me sitting on the curb at the edge of the lot, shoes in hand, eyes swollen so badly I can barely see, all my tears cried out. I've been here for hours. I didn't even see my parents leave. They must be gone, because, like I said: hours. Did they even notice their only daughter sitting out here, broken-hearted and all alone? Or are they so self-absorbed that my presence didn't even register?

I bet it was the latter.

They haven't tried to call me. Not once. Meanwhile, I've dialed Luke's number at least twelve times in the past hour alone. I've left five teary voicemails, repeating how sorry I am over and over. I've sent two texts:

I'm sorry.

I love you.

But I've gotten no response. Not that I thought I would, but I had to try. Try to save the beautiful, once-in-a-lifetime relationship that I so carelessly wrecked.

After wallowing in my much-deserved misery for a long while, I worked up the courage to call Mel for a ride. Even though my car is sitting in the lot, I'm in no state to drive the sixty miles back to Bennett. When she answered, all it took was my distraught, teary "Can you pick me up? Luke and I—" before Mel said she was on her way. No hesitation. No further explanation needed.

I'll worry about my car tomorrow. Or never. Another Future Tessa problem.

At the sound of a car idling in front of me, I lift my head and come face to face with my sympathetic best friend. Seeing her makes the waterworks start all over again. I was sure I'd cried myself dry, but they fall steadily, nevertheless. Mel rolls down the passenger window and waits patiently for me to gather myself.

I don't deserve her.

I've been sitting on this curb so long my backside has gone numb, so it takes me a couple of tries to stand. My silk sheath dress is stained and snagged from the rough concrete; it's an awful salmon color, so I get a sick satisfaction out of destroying it. Every time I dress for my mother's liking, I feel like an impostor. I only wore it today because if I didn't, she'd complain about how I never wear the things she buys for me.

We're silent for a while as she steers the car back toward

Bennett. Silent tears stream down my cheeks as I tip my head back and watch the scenery through the window and reflect on how different this drive is from the one I took this morning. On my way to Albany this morning, I was scared and nervous, yes, but hopeful. So, so hopeful that my parents would see all the good in Luke. See all the aspects of him I've fallen in love with. Hopeful they would, just once, accept something that I've chosen for myself.

You are so, so stupid, Tessa.

"Do we need alibis?" Mel finally breaks the silence, but she doesn't take her eyes off the road. Then it dawns on me: she thinks Luke is at fault.

She thinks he broke my heart, instead of the other way around.

"It's my fault." My throat is scratchy from all the crying. The words are barely loud enough to hear over the car's engine.

She scoffs. "No, really, T. What did he do?"

I'm loath to explain how the fault is totally mine because it'll change her opinion of me. She's going to see me as the villain in this story.

Rightly so, I guess.

But I don't hold back. I tell her every excruciating detail. When I confess the awful words that escaped my mouth, her eyes widen for a mere second, but she shows no other emotion. No disgust or anger or pity or judgment. When I have to relive Luke's hurt and anger in the parking lot, she takes my hand and doesn't let go until every last word has been wrenched from my depths. Then it's quiet, and I begin to think she's going to remain silent until we return to Bennett. But I desperately want her advice, a nugget of wisdom that will give me hope about all of this.

Finally, she blows out a deep breath. "You've royally messed up."

Those words, and the truth in them, make my eyes well once more.

"Hey. T," she says, softer than I've ever heard her speak. "We'll fix it, okay? We'll find a way to fix it."

All I can do is nod and try to believe my best friend.

The past four days have been the worst of my life.

Luke's absence is so profound that I feel physically ill. So ill, in fact, that on Monday, I called in sick for the first time since I started working at the library last July. I locked myself in the bathroom at work on Tuesday morning to stave off another panic attack. And just yesterday, Shanice took one look at me when I came in from lunch at my apartment and called Mr. Weaver and told him I was going home early.

I've taken so many morning pictures this week, it's ridiculous. Because the morning pictures have now turned into afternoon and evening pictures as well. My camera roll is full of shots of my front door, my straightener, the coffee maker, the knobs on my oven, the latches on my windows. It's like all the coping strategies I've learned over the years have left my brain.

So, yeah. This week has been brutal.

Luke has woven himself so seamlessly into every aspect of my life. And now that he's gone, it's like I've lost a limb. Several limbs. All the limbs.

He still won't answer my calls.

Or respond to my texts.

If I thought he'd forgive me—and it wouldn't traumatize Hannah—if I bled myself dry on his front lawn, I'd do it in a heartbeat.

My thoughts have taken a very dark turn this week. Obviously.

But today is Friday, the best day of the work week, right?

At least, that's what I'm choosing to believe. Because today is the day I try to win back the man I love more than anything in this world.

Mel and I hatched this plan on our way to Albany to pick up my car. Though calling it a *plan* is generous. It's the best we could come up with that didn't involve renting a billboard or hiring an airplane to drag an apology banner.

In my heart of hearts, I know I don't deserve Luke's forgiveness. He is terribly hurt, and it's going to take a lot for me to repair the damage I've wrought. But I have to try.

I've done a lot of soul-searching over the past few days. A lot of questioning myself and wondering where the heck those words came from at lunch on Sunday. I absolutely did not mean them. And I'm so ashamed that I let my parents' negative feelings about my life choices hurt the man who has treated me with nothing but kindness, respect, and love. I'll probably hate myself forever for that one awful moment.

I miss everything about Luke. His smile. His scent. The tender way he brushes his hand down the back of my head. How safe and secure I feel when he wraps me up in his strong arms. The way he calls me "Ivy."

And I miss my Jelly Bean as much as I miss her father. I miss our listening games and bedtime stories and pinkie promises.

If Luke refuses me, I don't know that I can stay in Bennett. I won't turn tail and run back home to my parents, who still haven't called me after that train wreck of a lunch. But I can't stay here, where I'd be forced to see Luke all the time. Where I'd have to watch Hannah grow up from afar and miss being a special part of her life. Where I'd watch Luke meet someone new and give her everything I once had.

I stand in front of the mirror and scan myself from head to toe, lingering on my face, taking in the dark circles under my eyes that no amount of makeup can hide, then continue down to the green wrap dress. It's the one I wore on my birthday. Luke's favorite. It's fitting a little looser this week since I haven't had much of an appetite.

"You look like you're trying too hard," I say to my reflection. But I can't find it in me to change. And I *am* trying too hard. I'd try anything to fix my mistake at this point.

Like she knows the exact moment I need a pep talk, Mel's name lights up my phone.

"Hey," I croak.

"Buck up, buttercup. It's game time."

"What if—"

"Nope." She cuts me off before the negative thought escapes my lips. "We are not going there, T."

"Right." I nod at my reflection. My eyes fill with tears, but I blink them away as best I can. "Right. You've confirmed the site with Cordell?"

"Ugh. Yes. And don't ask what that information cost me. All I'll say is that you owe me big time."

"Thank you for being my friend." I don't know what I would've done without Mel this week. She's kept me company and let me cry as much as I needed to. And she's never once berated me for being an idiot. She's just loved me through this, like a true best friend would.

"Are we still positive that going to his jobsite is the best idea?" I ask, doubt and worry creeping into my voice.

Mel sighs. "We talked about this. He's not answering your calls or texts. You could try to talk to him at his house—"

"No. I don't want to chance upsetting Hannah."

"So that leaves us with talking to him on his lunch break."

"Right." The word is shaky.

"You're ready. Go big or go home."

At Mel's unwavering confidence, I pull my shoulders back and stand a little straighter on legs that haven't stopped trembling since Luke walked away from me.

On the way to the construction site, I'm so violently racked with nerves that I worry I'll have to pull the car over. But I make it there in one piece, and I stay put in the car for a moment after I park, desperately searching for Luke amid the flurry of activity outside my windshield. I finally spot him, and my mouth instantly dries up.

The material of his neon yellow Statler T-shirt clings to his sweat-soaked frame. He lifts a corner of the shirt to wipe across his brow, unwittingly teasing me with his taut abdominal muscles.

I close my eyes to calm both my nerves and the fluttering happening down deep. Of course he looks like a distracting beef-cake at the exact moment I'm going to have to bare my soul to him.

When I open my eyes again, I focus on Luke, greedily soaking in his broad shoulders, strong chest, tan skin, and the tattoos I've missed so much this week. Making sure I have what I need, I take a deep breath and whisper, "Here goes nothing."

The wooden framing of the bank building on the outskirts of Bennett looks to be almost complete. And at first, I go unnoticed as I stand amid the chaos and watch Luke, admiring the way his arm muscles bunch and strain and flex as he grabs a bottle of water from a cooler. A sharp catcall whistle sounds from some-where to my left, and then all eyes are immediately on me.

Including Luke's.

A furious blush heats me from the inside out, but I step up to where he's standing with two other men.

Several emotions pass over his face as he stares at me, drinking up every inch of me like he's been dying of thirst. But then he forces a swallow and clenches his jaw, and coldness washes over his face.

I can't let that deter me.

"Hey," I say softly.

"What are you doing here, Tessa?"

The frostiness in his tone makes me wince, and the use of my first name instead of Ivy makes my heart sink. The guys standing with Luke just watch us, their heads swiveling back and forth like they're invested in some drama. I give them a tentative smile and forge on.

"I want to talk to you. Please hear me out."

Deep brown eyes that hold so much hurt and pride find mine. "I don't really want to hear anything you have to say. Especially at my job. Why on earth would you come here?"

I couldn't stop the tears even if I tried, so I let them fall as I answer. "You won't take my calls. Or respond to my texts. Please, Luke." My voice breaks, but I wipe a stubborn hand across my cheeks and take another step closer.

He doesn't say anything, and he doesn't back away, so I take that as a sign to continue.

"I know I hurt you. And you're the last person I ever, *ever* wanted to hurt. But I made a mistake by not standing up to my parents. I catastrophically messed up. I let them turn their awful attitudes and opinions about *me* on you. You, the one person who's accepted everything about me without question." I press my lips together and summon the courage to keep going. "You have to know that I don't share my parents' opinions about anything or *anyone*. Especially you. I don't care what they think anymore. I'm sorry I didn't realize that sooner, that I didn't just cut them out of my life after all the things they've put me through. But most of all, I'm deeply, *deeply* sorry that I hurt you."

Movement has picked up around us, except for the three men standing in front of me. Luke's staring a hole in the ground at my feet.

"You have my whole heart, Lucas Shipley. And I'm so"—I take a fortifying breath and blow it out slowly to hold back another onslaught of tears—"I'm so incredibly sorry that I ever made you doubt my love for you."

Taking another step closer to where he's standing with his

hands on his hips, I hold out an envelope with his name on it. It contains a letter I spent hours on last night. It explains, much better than my shaky words could, exactly what he means to me and how sorry I am for hurting him. Luke glances at the letter and then my face and back again. He doesn't make a move to take it.

"Will you please read it?" I hold it a little higher, hoping he'll reach out, meet me halfway.

He doesn't.

Finally, one of the guys who's been watching the exchange steps up to put me out of my misery. Manny. Luke introduced me to him at Fuzzy's months ago. He gently takes the envelope from my shaking hand and gives me an apologetic smile.

"Okay, then. I guess I'll go. Thank you for listening to me."

Luke's expression is icy again, and he still doesn't say a word. I want to reach out to him so badly, to rest my head against his chest, feel the weight of his arms around me.

Instead, I force myself to say, "Bye, Luke." Then I shuffle back toward my car.

Halfway back, Luke grunts out, "Toss it."

It takes every ounce of pride and self-preservation I have to make it back to my car before I burst into deep, heavy sobs. And now I know, without a doubt, that it is indeed possible for a heart to break twice.

CHAPTER TWENTY-FIVE

LUKE

It's agony, watching Tessa walk away.

Every damn cell in my body screams at me to run after her, to sweep her into my arms and fucking kiss the breath right out of her. I miss her. Every damn thing about her.

Every damn thing about *us*.

Five days without her have felt like absolute hell. There's nowhere I can go to escape her, because every single place in this damn town reminds me of her—even dropping my kid off at school in the mornings has been torture. Her scent lingers in my truck and on my sheets. She's burrowed so deep into my heart I might as well carve it out and lay it on the ground at her feet.

Then she showed up here in that dress. That fucking green dress she wore on her birthday, a day full of so many firsts for us, a day that will forever be etched in my memory.

God, she looked beautiful standing there. Beautiful and sad.

I tried so damn hard not to look at her, but it was almost impossible; my eyes have always been drawn to her, like they're addicted to the sight of her. It was clear to me, in the few glances I allowed myself, that she's taking our separation about as well as I am. The dark circles under her eyes prove that she hasn't slept much.

It took all my self-control not to reach out to her—I swear I don't think I've ever denied myself something like I denied myself *her* today. I want to run my fingers through her silky strands, breathe in her scent, brush my lips over her soft skin.

But those words still haunt me. The words she tossed out so carelessly. They made me feel like I've never been good enough for her. Never will be.

And yet…there are other words, new words, that swirl in my mind as I finish up my Friday shift.

"You have my whole heart, Lucas Shipley."

Hell, the bravery it took for her to even come here, to stand before a group of perfect strangers and apologize. To confess her feelings. I know full well what that cost Tessa. How deep she had to dig to get her anxiety under control enough to follow through.

And then that letter.

The letter I told Manny to toss like yesterday's garbage.

Shit.

A part of me wanted to let her words be enough to heal this rift between us.

But there's also a part of me that wants her to hurt as much as I do.

What the hell kind of man *wants* to hurt the woman he loves?

One who's had his heart fucking broken.

Even though it makes me seven kinds of an asshole, I just couldn't take that envelope from her trembling hand. A hand I had hoped to someday put a ring on.

After Tessa finally left the jobsite, I found myself seriously distracted. Usually, the familiar routine of this job allows me to zone out and forget the rest of the world, but this afternoon, after I dismissed the woman I desperately love, I couldn't get one fucking thing right. Now, as I check over the area and pack up for the weekend, I find I need to take a minute before I head home to Hannah.

Hannah, who's hounded me with questions about Tessa all damn week. She hasn't gone this long without seeing her bestie in months, so I keep making excuses to explain her absence. I don't have the heart to tell my daughter that we're done.

But are we really *done?*

My brain and my heart refuse to accept that we're through. What does *that* mean? It means I'm fucking confused and angry. Angry at her. Angry at myself. Pretty much angry at the world. Just this morning, I snapped at Hannah for wiggling during our hair and story routine. She made sure to call me "Grumpy-Face Daddy" when I dropped her off at school.

And I deserved it.

Most of the guys have started for their vehicles, but I lag behind, settling my weary, sleep-deprived body on the concrete slab where the bank's front doors will be. A few buddies holler out their goodbyes, and it's all I can do to lift my hand to acknowledge them. With my elbows on my knees, I'm watching the trucks and cars peel out of the dirt-covered parking area when I feel a presence behind me. When I crane my neck, I find Manny looming over me. He's focused on the departing crew, too.

We've worked together for years. He's met Tessa before, but I've kept our separation private until now. Only my parents and Cordell know. And Mel, I'm sure. No doubt that's how Tessa knew where to find me today. Mel's like a bloodhound when she needs to be.

"Your girl, she messed up?" he finally questions.

I can only nod, not wanting to share the messy, painful details.

"She cheat?"

"No," I growl, not wanting anyone to think badly of Tessa, even if she did break us.

"Hmm." He pauses for a beat. "Must have been pretty damn bad if that heartfelt speech and those big tears weren't enough to make it right."

My muscles tense, and the urge to defend washes over me. Defend my decision not to give in to Tessa's tears. But defend her, too. To explain how damn beautiful she really is, inside and out. Even if she fucked up. I'm just about to open my trap to tell him off when he holds his hand out to me.

"Maybe this will be enough to make it right, then."

It's Tessa's letter.

He didn't toss it.

The instant relief that floods my body is alarming. I didn't know how badly I wanted it until I was certain he'd gotten rid of it. Tessa's visit was hours ago. Hours in which I've cursed myself for being a jackass. For telling him to trash it to begin with, knowing damn well she heard me say it.

That's the real reason I've been worthless this afternoon—the woman I love heard me demand her words be thrown away. Words that came from her heart in an effort to fix us.

I take the envelope and nod my thanks, the lump in my throat too big to speak over.

Without a word, Manny starts toward his truck, but a few steps later, he turns and squints into the afternoon sun. "A little bit of advice from an idiot who's messed up before. You don't let a girl like that get away, Shipley. I've seen the way she looks at you—like you're the answer to her every prayer." He lets out a low whistle and gives me a huge grin as he waggles his brows. "Ooh, boy. That's some true love shit right there."

I huff out a laugh at his goofy expression and stand, then shove the envelope addressed to me in Tessa's precise cursive in my back pocket. I swear I can feel it heating my skin through my clothing, like she's woven the warmth of her touch into the paper.

I'm desperate to read it but pledge to wait until after I get

Hannah tucked into bed tonight. Just so I can't rush out and go to Tessa, like I already know I'll want to.

Hell, I've wanted to for days. But my hurt pride hasn't allowed it.

At home, I can't help but rush things along so I can finally get to the letter. Hannah gives me a *look* at supper when I tell her to hurry up with her lasagna. Then she proceeds to eat even slower just to spite me. I have to stifle my smile so she doesn't know I'm on to her.

God, I love this kid. Even when she acts as stubborn as her old man.

And like she's done every night at supper this week, Hannah asks about Tessa. My "she's really busy at work this week" excuse is wearing thin, if Hannah's crossed arms and narrowed eyes are any indication. I distract her by asking about Chase, her little frenemy, and she launches into a lengthy story about gym class and an obstacle course, which she calls an *osticle course.*

After our nightly routine, Hannah's all snuggled in bed, waiting for me to read her bedtime story. And like I've done every night since I started reading to my daughter months ago, I silently give thanks for Tessa and her insistence that I could learn how to do this. For her unfailing confidence in me.

When I drop onto the mattress beside her, she's holding her book and her chosen sleeping buddy for the night—a blue narwhal. When I see the cover of the book she's chosen, the knot in my gut twists tighter. "*Happy Halloween, Biscuit*?" I question. "Banana, Halloween is months away."

"I know," she says, hugging the narwhal tighter to her little body. "But Ms. Tessa gave me it, and I miss her."

I can't hold back the deep sigh that escapes.

"Daddy, when will we see her again?" My daughter's eyes fill with tears, splintering my heart. "Are you mad at her?" She studies me, her little lips trembling.

I've put this off long enough, I guess.

"Sometimes grown-ups have disagreements, and they need to take, like, a time-out from each other. That's what Tessa and I are doing. Taking a time-out." I'm kind of proud of myself for finding words that she'll understand to explain the situation. But that feeling quickly deflates.

"But how long is the time-out? My time-outs are only five minutes. It's been way longer than five minutes."

I gently wipe the wetness from her round cheeks. "I know, sweetheart. It feels like it's been too long to me, too."

She squeezes her eyes shut and cries in earnest now. "I want her out of time-out. Please, can't you let her out? I love her and I want her to come o-over."

I scrub a hand down my face. This escalated quickly.

I let her feel these big emotions, not really sure how to make it better. All I can do is murmur soothing words as I brush my fingers through her hair. After a few minutes, her heaving sobs become the shuddering breaths that come after a big cry.

Damn it. I hate all of this shit. Hannah's tears, Tessa's tears, my own fucking tears. All the hurt feelings and painful aches and bruised hearts. This week has been exhausting. But even though we're here now, dealing with the fallout, I don't for one second regret letting Tessa into my daughter's life. If I was truly done with her, wouldn't I feel that regret? Wouldn't I curse the way I let them become so close, so quickly?

"Please get her back, Daddy. We need her. She's ours."

"I know, Banana," I whisper, dropping a kiss to her forehead. I carefully ease off her bed when her little eyes can no longer fight the sleep that's been chasing her the past few minutes.

Then I have my own meltdown in the shower, letting the hot water wash away the pain and sorrow and anger and numbness that have eaten at me since Sunday. When I'm done, the confusing feelings haven't completely gone, but I feel more clearheaded than I have in days. I take a seat on the edge of the bed, on the side Tessa sleeps on, and pick up the envelope from the nightstand where I placed it after changing out of my grimy work clothes.

I take a deep breath and open it, unfold the single piece of paper covered in Tessa's words, and hope like hell this nightmare is almost over. The paper is from the legal pad we used during our tutoring sessions. It's a reminder that the only reason I can read the words on it is because of the woman who wrote them.

Dear Luke,

I am so very sorry that I hurt you, and I can't tell you that enough. I understand why you won't answer my calls or texts; I don't deserve even a moment of your time anymore. But thank you for reading these words anyway. This letter is the only way I can communicate all my thoughts to you now, and after you read it, if you still want nothing to do with me, I'll understand that, too.

But you need to know this; I would never choose my parents, or their lifestyle, over you. I know it feels like I did last Sunday, but I didn't, and I never would. Those awful words were my insecurities coming out, the feelings of inadequacy I've let my parents corner me into my whole life. I can promise you this: I won't let them have any influence on the decisions I make for myself ever again. I choose you, Lucas Shipley. I chose you months ago, I choose you today, and I'll choose you for the rest of my life if you'll give me another chance.

You have my whole heart. You collected a little piece of it the day we faced off in the library parking lot; I saw your vulnerability and knew you were a man who isn't afraid to feel real things. Another piece was yours when I saw you with Hannah for the first time at the fall carnival. I knew right then that you are the best daddy to her, the kind of daddy I want my future children to have. All those nights we worked together at the library, when you showed me your determination and grit, you took fragments of my heart with you. On Halloween, when you smiled up at me from the sidewalk—another piece. The puppet theater at Christmas. When you showed me your thoughtfulness and generosity, another portion became yours. Every time you called me Ivy. The night at the library when you confessed your feelings. That day in the parking lot at Hannah's school when you comforted me and kissed my socks off. The night I saw the beautiful home you built. Our first date. You took pieces of my heart with you after all of these. And on my birthday, when you told me you loved me, then showed me how much, the very last piece became yours. You've been collecting pieces of my heart the whole time I've known you, Luke.

I love you. I want to be with you. Forever, if you'll have me. Please forgive me.

Tessa

Well, shit.

Fuzzy's on a Monday afternoon is the perfect place to drown one's sorrows. It's empty, except for my sorry ass. It's been welded to this stool since before noon, when my boss sent me home for the rest of the day because, to quote him, I'm "not good for anybody in this state."

What state is that, you might ask?

Fucking misery.

I've been in fucking misery since reading Tessa's letter Friday night. Hannah spent the weekend with my folks, thank goodness, so she didn't have to witness the absolute terror I've become. I've read that letter so many times, I practically have the thing memorized. I've driven myself crazy since, and my thoughts and feelings have bounced from one extreme to the other. I've snapped up my keys, ready to haul ass to Tessa's apartment countless times, ready to take her back and end this damn time-out. But then, when I'm about to follow through, the look on her face when she was staring at that damn country club table comes slamming into my brain like a bolt of lightning. Can she really promise that something like this won't happen again? I have my daughter's heart to consider.

I have my own fucking heart to consider.

I'll be man enough and admit it: I'm fucking terrified to trust her again. All the whiskey and beer must be making me *real* self-aware today.

There's no way I'll survive another time-out from Tessa Burton. I love that woman with every fiber of my soul, and if we can't make this work, if our love isn't enough to get us through, then I'd rather not get back together.

But the thought of not building a life with her guts me.

All I know for certain is I want off this ride.

The door to Fuzzy's opens, letting a patch of afternoon sun light up the floor in the otherwise dark room. Cordell strides in and wordlessly takes the stool next to mine. It vaguely registers that he should be at school right now, but then I remember that his last class period of the day is football, so he probably left the assistant coach in charge.

"How'd you know?"

He doesn't need anything more than that; he knows exactly what I'm asking. "Gordo called Mrs. Marj."

I lift my chin to give Fuzzy's owner a death glare, but he's nowhere to be found. Convenient.

"What're you doing, man?" Cordell asks, swiveling on his stool to face me. "This is not Luke Shipley behavior."

No shit. I didn't even do this when things with Shelley were unbearable.

"This is 'Luke Shipley's had his fucking heart broken' behavior," I grit out.

He knows all the ugly details of this past week. Even Tessa's visit to the work site and the letter I almost didn't get a chance to read. I haven't shared the contents of that letter with him yet, though. He hasn't given me a bunch of advice, hasn't resorted to trash-talking Tessa or her mistake. He's been a listening ear as I've poured every ounce of hurt and anger in his direction.

"What do your folks think?" he asks quietly.

I snort at my empty rocks glass. "They're firmly Team Tessa. They agree that she messed up and that I have a right to feel angry. But they think I'm being a stubborn ass for letting this drag on. Say she's paid her dues. Now it's time to put it behind us." My folks love Tessa like she's theirs. "What do you think?" It's the first time I've asked him that point-blank.

Cordell watches me closely before responding. "I think I've never seen you like this. I think you love that girl so deeply that you put her on a pedestal, making her into this perfect version of a woman who's not allowed to make a mistake. But when she finally *did* make a mistake, when she proved that she is indeed as fallible as the rest of us, you didn't know how to handle it."

I swallow roughly at the truth in his words. Deep down, I know he's right.

"You've let your former inability to read convince you that you aren't good enough, for her or for anything new and wonderful in your life. But I'm here to tell you, you idiot, that you are *more* than fucking good enough."

I can't look at him as I fight the tears that threaten to spill over.

"Tessa's the best thing to ever happen to my best friend, save for his daughter. And I think that if he doesn't get his head out of his ass, he's going to regret it for the rest of his life."

I finally look up at him. "You're not pulling any punches, are you?"

"Let me ask you this," he says, his expression full of wisdom and care. He's let me have my days of wallowing in my feelings, but now he's doing his best friend duty, setting me straight. "How are you going to feel if you let Tessa go, and somewhere down the line, she finds somebody new? Falls in love with someone else?"

"Over my dead fucking body." The violence in my tone catches even me off guard. The thought of Tessa with someone else, *anyone else*, sends a red-hot rage coursing through me.

That girl is mine, *damn it.*

He raises his brows and lets that thought simmer for a while before speaking up again. "When are you going to stop punishing her?" he asks softly. "Stop punishing yourself?"

He's absolutely right, as usual. I'm not only punishing Tessa; I'm punishing myself by letting my anger and hurt over one mistake win out against all the love I feel for her.

And it's time for me to get my head out of my ass.

"I need you to drive me home," I confess. "Pop can bring me to pick my truck up later."

"Can do," he says, waving at Gordon, who's magically reappeared, to close out my tab. "And then what are you going to do?"

Pop's advice from a couple of weeks ago surfaces right then: *If you want something you've never had, you might have to do something you've never done.*

"I'm going to get my girl back."

CHAPTER TWENTY-SIX

"Come on, T. Just pick something. It starts in fifteen minutes."

It's Tuesday. My least favorite day of the week. And somehow, my best friend has talked me into a night out—how, I'll never know. But she's incredibly convincing. Mel's sitting on my carefully made bed, scrolling on her phone, as I stand inside my tiny walk-in closet and stare forlornly at the selection. Not one item appeals to me at the moment. Nothing feels right against my skin. Not one piece offers the comfort I need.

Nothing fits my life the way Luke did.

It's been four days since I last saw him. Four days since he told his friend to toss my letter.

Which means I'm on day four of absolute despair. Before the letter incident, I was miserable and everything was horrible, but there was still a teeny-tiny glimmer of hope that kept me buoyed, that kept me from sinking into this deep, dark abyss that's taken root in my soul. That whole "When you hit rock bottom, the only way to go is up" mentality? Total crap.

There's a whole sub-layer below rock bottom.

When I turn from my closet, Mel's watching me with a

sympathetic look on her face. She joins me where I'm standing in jeans and my favorite comfortable bra. Which I stopped wearing once Luke and I slept together that first time because it gives off real grandma-beige vibes.

"Sweetie, just pick something. Shanice is saving our table, but they'll make her move if her team is not there when it starts."

My eyes well with tears once again. I think this is the third time I've cried since Mel arrived twenty minutes ago.

"Oh, T. Don't start again," Mel says, but her tone is soft and gentle. She takes my face in her hands, and her hazel eyes search mine. "Hey. You're going to be okay. It's all going to be okay." This has been Mel's go-to line since Friday. And maybe if she says it enough, I'll eventually believe it.

All I can do is nod, which loosens the tears that were flooding my eyes, causing them to spill over. "S-sorry." It's all I can choke out.

She slides her hands to my shoulders and squeezes them before giving me a quick shake. "Clothing, Burton. Now." Bossy Mel has entered the chat. "How about this one?" she asks, blindly taking hold of a long-sleeve shirt hanging at the front of the closet.

I wipe my cheeks and shake my head, then reach around her to pull out a black three-quarter sleeve boatneck top. Simple. And the color matches my mood. Maybe I'll dress in black every day like I'm a mourning widow in a Victorian novel.

Gordo started Trivia Tuesdays at Fuzzy's a few months ago, and it's become a hit. The place is packed every week, but tutoring with Luke, and then spending every minute with him, has kept me from giving it a try. When Mel mentioned it last week, I immediately shot her down. But then she got Shanice on the case, and before I knew it, I was somehow agreeing to join them.

But I drew a line at the team name she picked out. No way was I going to be on a team called "Quiz on My Back." When I flat-out refused, she rolled her eyes and said, "Fine. We'll be something boring. Like…The Library Girls Plus Mel."

The other caveat I would not back down from? Luke absolutely could *not* be there.

"Ready?"

Begrudgingly, I slink from my hiding spot in the closet. "As ready as I'm going to be."

"Good. Let me tell Shanice we're on our way." She types out a quick message, a tiny smirk curving her lips as she does so. After she sends it, she gives me a grin. "Let's do this."

The crowded parking area at Fuzzy's makes me itch all over. I scan the vehicles carefully to make sure that familiar navy truck isn't among them. Every table in the place is occupied, and the bar is standing room only. Gordo sits in a folding chair on a small stage set up next to the jukebox. Shanice waves to us from one of the high-tops in the center of the room. On our way through the crowd to reach her, I clutch the strap of my purse to keep from fleeing the scene. The panic that overtakes me as I brush against one person, then another makes it hard to breathe. That feeling only intensifies when I notice Marjorie Shipley sitting in a booth with Cordell's mom and Ms. Daisy. I freeze in place when we lock eyes across the space.

"Mel," I call, but she doesn't hear me over the noise. My breaths pick up, becoming more strained when Luke's mom rises from her seat and heads directly for me. I drop my attention to the sticky wooden floor as she approaches. I deserve the harsh words she has for me after hurting her son, so I steel my spine, readying to take every verbal slap she gives.

Yet when she reaches me, she wraps her arms around me in a tight, motherly hug. It takes me a couple of seconds to register what's happening, but soon her warmth and floral scent overwhelm me, and I hug her back as tears slide down my cheeks once again.

My body spasms with sobs as I choke out, "I'm s-so s-sorry."

She pulls back and smooths my hair with one hand and wipes at my cheeks with the other. "Hush, now. You made a mistake. Lord knows, I've made plenty myself."

I'm struck with the realization that I can't remember the last time my own mother comforted me in this way. The last time she gave me a *real* hug, not a perfunctory one. And once again, the stark difference between my childhood and Luke's hits me firmly in the chest—I was expected to be my parents' legacy. He was expected to be his parents' kid.

"I love him," I tell Marjorie, my voice wobbly.

"I know," she says. "And he loves you, Tessa."

When I shake my head, she takes my face in her hands to stop my denial.

"He does," she urges. "He's being a stubborn ass right now, but mark my words, honey. My boy loves you something fierce. This will all be over soon." She leans in to kiss my cheek. "Now. Go have a fun night with your friends."

"Yes, ma'am." I sniffle like crazy, reeling from her words.

Luke still loves me.

And just like that, the teeny-tiny glimmer of hope sparks in my heart once more.

"But I gotta warn you. Rhonda is a trivia beast. And Daisy has lived a lot of life and knows some pretty random stuff." She steps back as I offer her a weak smile. With one final squeeze of my hand, she returns to her table.

Mel's watching me closely as I wobble to our table. "How was that?" she asks gently when I slip onto the stool beside her.

Shanice gives me an encouraging smile and hands a stack of papers to Mel.

"Better than I thought it would be."

"Good." Mel scribbles our team name on the papers. "I'm telling you, T, it's going to be okay."

I lean over her arm to make sure she didn't go back on her

promise about our name and let loose a breath of relief. *The Library Girls Plus Mel.*

Shanice hops up. "I'll tell Gordo our team name."

I slowly start to relax after the face-to-face with Luke's mom, letting the crowd's nearness and volume settle in the back of my mind. I'll stay focused on my friends and the trivia questions. *I can do this.*

Once Shanice is back, Mel shoots off another text, but before I can be nosy and ask who she's talking to, Gordo rattles off the first trivia question. We record our answers to turn in at the end of each round. We're just finishing our debate about the answer to question four when Shanice grabs Mel's arm and nods at something behind me. When Mel follows her line of sight, a triumphant grin breaks out across her face.

All of a sudden, I have the urge to use the restroom—and then escape out the back door.

I refuse to turn. I know who I'll see there, and I can't handle it if he looks at me with the scowl he wore at the construction site. That will break me all over again; I'm in so many pieces as it is, I'm not sure I'll ever feel whole again.

"Tessa," Mel says, resting a hand on my forearm, like that touch will keep me from bolting. My heart is beating so fast I bring a hand to my chest and suck in a deep breath to stave off the panic racing through me.

"You promised," I whisper, unable to look up from the wood grain on the tabletop. The teams around us are noisy as they work through their trivia answers.

But she hears me loud and clear. "I know. I'm sorry," she replies, not a bit contrite.

"Got room for two more?" It's Cordell behind my left shoulder.

Behind my right, that presence I've been craving hovers. He's so close. If I leaned back, I would probably bump against his broad chest.

Cordell pulls an empty stool from a surrounding table and settles it between Mel and Shanice. "How you girls fairing tonight?" he asks, taking a real interest in the answers on the paper in front of Mel.

I chance a glance up at him and get a genuine smile in return. Not a trace of anger or dislike on his face.

He's smiling at me like I never broke his best friend's heart.

What is happening here?

The solid presence at my back disappears for a moment, but then he's there again, setting a stool next to mine.

I've still got a hand pressed to my chest where it feels like my heart is recovering from a sprint down Central, but I'm back to examining the tabletop. I'm terrified to look at him. Luke sits so close I can smell his freshly showered scent and feel the warmth of him. His thigh pushes lightly against mine.

Close. He's so dang close.

Mel, Shanice, and Cordell occupy themselves with the next trivia question, but I'm consumed by the body next to me.

Luke angles closer, then his warm breath is in my ear as he demands in a low, gravelly voice, "Look at me, Ivy."

Ivy?

Chicken that I am, I shake my head, scared I'll break the spell or wake up from what must surely be a dream.

"Please."

The desperation in his voice that time does the trick. I turn, bracing myself for disgust or anger or hurt or disappointment. But what I see in his handsome face takes my breath away.

Because Luke Shipley is looking at me like he used to—with affection and desire and longing. With love. He searches my face so intently I feel it like a caress. Those dark brown orbs I love so much linger on my lips before returning to my own tear-filled ones.

"Is this really happening?" I ask in a whisper as tears slide down my cheeks yet again.

Luke brings those strong hands I've missed so much to my face, cradling my jaw and smoothing under my eyes. I lean into one of his palms as he brings his forehead to rest against mine.

"It's real, Ivy."

"Luke—"

"Shh. I know." He pulls away to place a gentle kiss on my forehead. "We've got a lot of making up to do. But I gotta do something first. Something that might make you a little uncomfortable, but I promise it'll be worth it. And I need *you* to promise that you won't freak out, okay?"

"O-okay," I croak, slowly becoming aware that our friends at the table are watching. Mel and Cordell wear satisfied smiles, but my attention is quickly back on the man who's still holding my face in a grip that's both reverent and possessive.

"These people here," he says, indicating the crowd with a tilt of his head. "They're *your* people now. They know you; they like you. You're one of them. You feel that, right?"

I quickly scan the crowd of Fuzzy's patrons, the townsfolk who call Bennett *home*. No judgment, no haughtiness. I'm safe here, with these people. *My people*.

"Y-yes."

"Good. Stay here," he says, his voice lifting at the end as if he's asking, a hint of vulnerability in his tone. He's still scared that I'll run. That this will all be too much—too overwhelming, too emotional.

But I'm done running away from what I want.

At my subtle nod, his face lights up into that devastating smile that never fails to launch a swarm of butterflies deep in my stomach. After a quick kiss on the tip of my nose, he strides to the table where Gordo is busy scoring round one answers.

"What is he doing?" I question, but when I look to my friends for answers, Mel and Cordell eye each other with small, knowing smiles but don't respond. I drag my attention back up to the stage, where Luke is speaking to Gordo. Then he claps the owner on the back and takes the microphone from the table.

I spin on my stool, seeking out the table where Luke's mom is sitting, but when we make eye contact, she just smiles and gives me a wink. I turn back to demand an answer from Mel, but before I can, Luke's voice rings out through the bar.

"Hey, um, good evening, everybody." He clears his throat and looks as nervous as I'm feeling right now.

My hand instinctively shoots out and grabs Mel's in a death grip. But my eyes are riveted on the man standing in front of most of the town of Bennett, wearing those just-right jeans and a soft navy T-shirt I've slept in on numerous occasions.

"I guess I'm the intermission entertainment while Gordo tallies up the scores. Um, I'm Luke Shipley, as most of you know."

There's a collective chuckle from the crowd.

"But what most of you don't know is that I've kept a big secret for most of my life."

My chest rises and falls in rapid succession. Is he really doing this? In front of the whole town? The mic trembles in his hand a little, but when his eyes find mine in the crowd, he heaves a deep breath, and that hand holds steady. I refuse to look away, hoping I can provide him with the encouragement he needs.

"That secret was so shameful to me. It made me so embarrassed, made me feel like a failure. See, until recently, I couldn't read."

The crowd grows even more silent at his admission.

"But this story has a happy ending, folks. So if you'll bear with me, I'd like y'all to hear it." He nods a couple of times like he's trying to convince himself to continue.

"My daughter Hannah is the reason I confessed this secret and started the process of learning how to read. At the beginning of that journey, I met someone who's become very, very special to me—and I hope she doesn't kill me for doing this in front of everybody."

There are more lighthearted chuckles around the room, and several heads swivel in my direction, but I find I'm not panicked —I'm just desperate to hear what he has to say.

Luke continues, "This person believed in me, became my champion, put up with my moody ass."

More chuckles.

"And with the most patience I've ever witnessed in my life, she taught me how to read."

A few *aww*s float through the crowd.

"I fell in love with her," he explains, his voice cracking with emotion.

Now there are even more *aww*s and a whistle that I'm almost positive came from Ms. Daisy.

"I'm not so ashamed of that secret anymore. One, because I fixed it. And two, because look what it brought into my life." He gestures in my direction with his free hand. "She opened up the whole world for me when she taught me how to read. How could I not fall in love with her and want to keep her forever?"

I swear I don't think I'm breathing as the words pour from him. I'm sure Mel's poor hand will be bruised from the way I'm clutching it.

"Recently, we sorta hit a roadblock." Luke's eyes never leave mine, even while a couple of soft *boo*s ring out through the room. "We've both done some dumbass things lately."

Someone from the back hollers out, "Been there!" and more laughter resounds from all around me.

Luke shakes his head, fighting a grin. But then he turns serious again. "All relationships go through hard times, but the great ones come out the other side stronger than ever. So if you'll indulge me, I've written a few words for that special person. To let her know how much she means to me."

He swallows deeply as he pulls a folded piece of paper

from his back pocket. Images of him doing the same on the night of Valentine's Day flash through my mind. I can't look away.

He studies the paper he holds in one hand, and someone in the crowd hollers out, "You got this, Luke!"

He smiles and then begins.

"Dear Tessa," he says, and I swear my heart gives a lurch. "I'm choosing you, too."

Tears stream from my eyes again as realization sweeps over me.

My letter. He read my letter.

Luke's deep voice keeps me grounded, keeps me in this moment. "I'm choosing you for a million reasons, so I thought maybe you'd like to hear a few of them. I'm choosing you for the way you never let me give up on myself, even though there were so many damn times I wanted to. You never doubted that I could do it. And look. Here I am, reading these words to you— from my heart to yours.

"I'm choosing you for the way you love Hannah. The love and pride you have for *our* girl knocks the breath right out of me. You were meant to be a part of her life, to be a mama to her and help her grow into the person she's supposed to be.

"I'm choosing you for all the little things that make you who you are. Your kindness. Your quirks. Your love of chocolate pie." Luke looks up and gives me a big grin before continuing. "The way you melt into me when I hold you. The passion you have for your job. How you treat my folks with love and respect. The love and care you have for your friends."

He takes a deep breath and looks at me again. "But most of all, I'm choosing you for the way you love *me*. The way you've trusted me with your heart. Because I can't imagine my life without you in it."

Then he folds the paper and returns it to his back pocket. When his eyes find mine again, they're shining. "I love you so damn much, Tessa Burton. And I want to be with you forever, too."

The crowd erupts into cheers and whistles as Luke hands the mic back to Gordo and strides to our table. Somehow, my legs hold me up as I stand. And then he's dragging me into his arms and kissing the breath out of my lungs. God, I've missed kissing this man. I've missed the taste of him, how his lips are both gentle and demanding, the way his tongue flirts with mine, how he angles my head just the way he wants it. The audience at Fuzzy's Tavern is going nuts, but my only focus is the man holding me tight.

The man I love with my whole heart. Who just put all my pieces back together.

When he finally pulls away so we can catch our breath, I can't help but repeat the words I've been thinking since that fateful Sunday lunch. "Luke, I'm so sorry—"

"Enough," he growls. "We're done with sorrys. We're putting it behind us, Ivy. You got it?"

"Okay."

Gordo announces the start of round two, and the teams surrounding us dive into discussions as the two of us hold tight to each other.

"Good. Now, let's get out of here. I'm dying to peel your clothes off and kiss every inch of you."

My cheeks heat, but I let Luke rain kisses all over my face, even while standing in the middle of a crowded bar.

"We're taking off," he says to our friends, his attention never leaving me. He laces his fingers with mine and tugs me toward the door. On our way, several people give him high fives or offer words of encouragement. It makes me fall in love with this town even more. I'm so proud to claim Bennett, Georgia, as my hometown.

Almost as proud as I am to claim the hunk of a man who's all but dragging me through the parking lot to his truck.

But—

"Wait!"

Luke jerks to a halt and spins to face me. "What's wrong?" He steps up and grabs my shoulders, ready to slay whatever is holding me back.

I'm thankful the parking lot is empty as I lean in to confess my dilemma as softly as I can. "I'm wearing a granny bra."

Luke stares at me for a moment, then he drops his head back and guffaws. His laughter is so full of joy and relief that I can't help but grin back at him.

I never want to go a day without seeing this kind of happiness lighting up his handsome face.

Luke's laughter dies, and he turns serious once more. "Ivy," he says gruffly, grabbing my hips and pulling me into his body so I feel how much he's missed me for the last several days. "I don't give one fuck about what kind of bra you're wearing. I'll be tearing it off you so fast, it won't even register."

Those words spark a flame deep in my core. "Take me home then, handsome."

On the short drive to my apartment, Luke doesn't let go of me. And when we're parked in front of the house, he kisses my knuckles. "So your first public love declaration in Bennett, Ivy. Everything you hoped it would be?"

"More," I respond.

Then I let the man I'm desperate for take me upstairs so we can spend the night getting lost in each other, letting our love heal us and wipe the slate clean.

Three days later, I'm standing in the back of a crowded elementary school gymnasium, searching for my people.

My people.

I'm so honored to have the privilege of calling them that. To know, without a doubt, that these sweet souls are the ones who will stand beside me for the rest of my days.

I finally spot Luke's dark hair four rows from the front and shuffle down the aisle. He's saved a seat for me between him and his mom. Past her is the rest of Hannah's fan club—Luke's dad, Cordell, Ms. Rhonda, and Mel. I drop into my seat and place a quick kiss on Luke's cheek, then breathe out a sigh. I'm later than I intended to be.

Probably because the man to my right kept me up late last night. He looks fresh as a daisy, though.

In my periphery, he's giving me a once-over, so I send him a little smirk in return. He knows exactly why I'm running late.

"Ooh, Tessa, you look beautiful!" Luke's mom gushes. "June Bug is going to brag to all her friends about your matching dresses."

I broke down in tears when I slipped the white eyelet dress over my head, so grateful to be wearing it for Hannah's special day. Just a week ago, I sobbed on my closet floor, certain it would never see the light of day.

"She does look beautiful," Luke agrees, then drops a kiss to my temple. He laces our fingers together and places our joined hands on his thigh.

I've never felt anything so right in my life.

For about the millionth time since Tuesday night, I say a silent prayer of thanks and gratitude that I've been given a second chance to have this love and vow to never take it for granted. I'll try every day for the rest of my life to deserve it.

"What did she decide on?" I ask Luke quietly. This morning, he called me so I could discuss hair options with Hannah. She was being indecisive and giving her father a hard time about it.

"Down, but with that side barrette swoop thing you do." He rolls his eyes good-naturedly. "After talking with her bestie, she didn't want the braid. She wanted 'Ms. Tessa hair' instead."

"Aw, I love my little Jelly Bean."

"I know you do, baby." He brings our joined hands to his lips. "But she wants you to be surprised by her choice, so…"

"Got it. I'll be sure to rave about it."

We settle in to be charmed by the most adorable kindergarten graduation ever. There are cute songs and lots of waves and even a few tears when one kid forgets which side of the stage to stand on. The two kindergarten teachers take it all in stride, and overall, it's a smashing success. Hannah grins and waves big at us as she walks across the stage to accept her diploma. Our whole row stands and cheers when we hear "Hannah June Shipley." I'm so proud of that girl I could burst. I can't help the tears that flood my eyes. And beside me, Luke's fighting his emotions, too.

After the ceremony, we're invited to a small reception for the graduates and their families in the school cafeteria. They're serving punch and cookies shaped like little mortarboards. When Hannah finds us in the crowd, she launches herself into Luke's waiting arms.

"Did you see me, Daddy?" She pats his cheeks.

"I did, Banana. You're a kindergarten graduate, and I'm so proud of you."

She kisses his cheek and my heart squeezes. When she notices the rest of her fan club, she wiggles to be put down. As soon as her little feet hit the tile, she's reaching for me. I crouch and clutch her to me in a tight hug, fighting back another round of tears. I came so close to missing this moment with her.

"Your hair is beautiful, Jelly Bean. The perfect style for your big day."

She nods knowingly. "It's just like yours." Then she grasps my hand and tugs me over to where Cordell and Ms. Rhonda are watching us. "Uncle Dell! Look! Ms. Tessa is out of time-out!" she announces.

Our friends chuckle, and my face turns beet red, but her innocence and enthusiasm make up for the awkward moment.

Ms. Rhonda quickly changes the subject, and once again, I give thanks that these are my people.

After we've taken pictures with our little graduate in every grouping we can configure, Hannah's teacher pulls Luke to the side. I can't hear what she's telling him, but I'm sure I know the gist. He's wearing a modest but pleased smile, and hers can only be described as jubilant. When Mrs. Gibson leans in to give him a hug, I can make out the words "I'm so proud of you" on her lips.

When he returns, I wrap my hand around his bicep. "Big day, Mr. Shipley. Lots of feels."

"Don't I know it," he says with a wry smile. But the emotion is there, just beneath the surface. I get what a full-circle moment this is for him. I'm so dang proud of him.

And because I know how powerful words are, I make sure to tell him as much.

He leans in to brush a quick kiss on my lips and says, "Thank you, Ivy. Your confidence in me got me here."

"Your hard work got you here."

"It was both," he insists.

"You kids gonna head straight home?" Luke's mom asks as our group meanders toward the exit. The proud grandparents have a family gathering planned at their place to celebrate Hannah. We're meeting there after Luke stops in the office to check Hannah out for the afternoon.

"Sure thing," he says. "I know Pop is dying to get the grill fired up."

"Grill master, reporting for duty!" Mr. Shipley calls.

We hug and kiss our goodbyes, even though we'll see each other in a little while, and the three of us make our way to the front office to sign her out. As we're standing at the front office window, Luke pauses, pen in hand, at the clipboard holding the sign-out page.

"You okay?" I ask gently.

He grins at me and says, "So damn grateful, that's all." Then he fills out each of the columns to check Hannah out for the day.

On our way to the parking lot, he takes my hand on one side, and his sweet girl's on the other. We smile and laugh as she regales us with a graduation story about Chase and the rest of her friends.

I tip my face to the perfect spring sky and thank the heavens for this moment.

The three of us. Hand in hand. Walking toward all our tomorrows.

EPILOGUE
LUKE

The hot May sun beats down, making my hard hat feel like an oven. I check my phone for the time and holler at the guys to wrap it up for the day. All over the residential site, the guys on my crew begin closing down. They're as ready for the weekend as I am. This place is a good thirty minutes outside the Bennett town limits, and I can't wait to get home to my girls.

"Hey, boss man, we're headed to Fuzzy's. You in?"

I shake my head at Manny's use of the title, something he's taken to calling me since Mr. Statler promoted me to construction manager a year ago. I never take him up on the offer, but I appreciate that he asks just the same.

"Nah, man, I've got an eager young wife waiting on me at home."

A lot has changed in the two years since Hannah graduated from kindergarten. For starters, Tessa's last name is Shipley. I put a ring on it the Christmas of Hannah's first-grade year, and we were married a month later in a small ceremony at the library —one of Tessa's happy places, and the place we fell in love. It felt right for us to begin our lives as husband and wife there, too.

Tessa moved into the bungalow on Mills not long after

Hannah finished kindergarten, but six months later, I finally convinced her to move in with us. We kept the property, though, as a reminder of Tessa's independence and as a real estate investment.

Not much has changed with Tessa's parents. They didn't attend our wedding, though they sent a gift, and they even sent Hannah a Christmas present this past year. Tessa talks to them every few months, and although the lack of relationship makes her sad, she's no longer the ball of anxiety she was when we first met. Sure, she has moments, but she's continued her therapy sessions, and they've helped tremendously. Panic attacks are very rare these days. And my folks love and cherish her like their own daughter, so there's no shortage of people around who care for her.

I park next to Tessa's small SUV behind the garage. We'll be forced to continue parking out here until I can get started on a workshop of my own. Our garage is full of in-progress custom-furniture orders and others that are complete and awaiting pickup or shipment. Once Tessa set up an Instagram account for my furniture business, it took off just like she thought it would. Shipley Custom Furnishings now ships to places all over the southeast.

As I exit the truck, laughter and voices from the backyard have me tempted to change direction. I can't wait to wrap my girls up in big hugs and start our weekend together, but I force myself to take a quick shower before I join them.

Once I've thrown on a pair of jeans and a T-shirt, I find Tessa standing on the back porch. She's got one hand shielding her eyes from the sun as she watches Hannah trying to teach our year-old boxer how to shake.

Yep, we got a damn dog.

Tessa and Hannah finally wore me down, so last August, for my birthday, no less, Chipper Shipley joined our family. My girls even let me choose his name. And though I tried not to fall in love with him, he made that a challenge. He's a damn good dog. He loves Hannah like mad, is devoted to Tessa, and tolerates me.

I wrap my arms around my wife and rest my hands on the small swell of her abdomen—our baby, growing for the last five months. I kiss the side of her neck, and she lets out a soft sigh, like she's been waiting for me to do that all day, then sags into me.

We fit each other perfectly. Every damn time.

"How was your day, Ivy?" I ask as she drops her head to my shoulder.

"It was good. How about you?"

"It was fine, but it's better now."

We stand in silence, watching our daughter try like hell to get a sixty-pound dog to roll over and play dead.

"Your mom called. She wants to know if Cordell is bringing anyone on Monday."

"Is Mel coming?" I ask. I'm pretty certain my wife's best friend wouldn't miss my parents' annual Memorial Day cookout, but then again, Mel Marshall can be a mystery.

"She is," Tessa replies.

"Then Cordell isn't bringing anyone."

Tessa sighs as I rub her belly. "Those two, I swear…"

"I know," I chuckle.

"Mama," Hannah calls, drawing our attention, "did you see that?" When she looks up to the porch, she finally notices me. "Dad! You're home!" She beelines for us, her long brown braid flying out behind her as Chipper chases her, barking all the way. When she reaches the porch, she wraps her arms around Tessa and me, then leans in to place a kiss on Tessa's rounded belly, where her little brother or sister is snug and safe.

"How was your first official day of summer?"

Hannah finished second grade yesterday, making the honor roll for the whole school year. She spent today at the library with Tessa, where she'll spend several of her summer days. She'll rotate between there, Ms. Daisy's flower shop, and Ms. Rhonda's house. I am so damn proud of the girl she's become, but I've never been prouder of her than I was the night she worked up the courage to ask Tessa if she could call her "Mama." The two of us had discussed it for weeks before she finally took the plunge. I'll never forget the look on Tessa's face or the emotions that choked all of us up that night.

"It was good. I found a new series at the library. It's about dragons."

"Dragons, huh? Maybe you can read a chapter to us at bedtime."

My kid loves to read as much as Tessa does. And I've slowly learned to love it myself. Though these days I'm mostly reading about baseball, not dragons.

"Wash up for dinner, Jelly Bean." Tessa tilts forward to kiss the top of our daughter's head. "The roast should be done in a few minutes."

She nods without argument and heads for the door, patting her leg so Chipper follows.

Yep, the damn dog is allowed inside.

My beautiful wife turns in my arms. "I've missed you today, husband," she says sweetly, then she places a kiss on my chest, right where her initials are tattooed. The letters are surrounded by an outline of an ivy leaf, the vine of which connects seamlessly with the sleeve that covers my left arm.

I glare playfully. "Hmm. How much, wife?"

"So, so, *so* much," she answers, as I rake my fingers through her hair. We get lost in kissing each other for a few minutes, Tessa fisting my T-shirt on either side.

When we finally break apart, I make a growly noise in the back of my throat. "Tonight, wife," I tell her passionately. She just turns that adorable shade of pink and gives me a knowing smile.

"You love me?" I ask her, just as I've done every day since she became mine forever, when she took my last name.

"An infinite amount," she replies, the way she always does.

With that, I give her perfect, round ass a playful slap and take her hand to lead her into our home.

Our home—the place that holds all I'll ever want or need for the rest of my days.

Tessa's always saying that words are powerful, but in my limited experience, I haven't found one that comes close to describing how perfect our life is these days.

So I guess *blessed* will have to do.

ACKNOWLEDGMENTS

I sat down in front of a new laptop on July 5, 2022 in hopes of publishing a book. I had no idea how to even go about it, but I believed in this story. So I began writing…

Here we are, almost a whole year later, and you're holding the finished product in your hands. And I'm so grateful that you've taken a chance on a total rookie. So my first thanks goes to you, dear reader. Thank you for buying or downloading my very first book. Thank you for reading the words I poured my heart and soul into, and thank you for spending time with characters who are so precious to me. You're literally making my author dreams come true.

To all the authors whose words have inspired me, and frankly, have saved my life: I always read every word of your book acknowledgments every time I finish one of your books. I love to recognize all of your hard work and all of the special people who made your books' journeys possible. It also makes me feel like I know you as a *real* person, like I could possibly be one of you someday. Thank you for filling my life with your beautiful, funny, snarky, spicy words.

To Beth, my editor, thank you so much for taking my words and making them shine. Your patience with my newborn author status was so fantastic; sorry for all the *justs* and *-ly* adverbs. I'll remember to limit those next time!

Mel, developmental editor extraordinaire, your insights were invaluable. Thank you for your detailed notes on the plot and characters. I loved chatting with you and I hope we get to do it again soon! (*cough-Mel and Cordell-cough*)

To Sam with Ink and Laurel designs, thank you for designing the book cover of my dreams. It is perfection, and I love it so much.

To Kristen, thank you for making my words look like a real book! You were so accommodating while formatting this; thanks for being patient with my indecisiveness.

My alpha readers are some of my very best friends, and this book wouldn't have happened without them. Charlotte, you have the distinct honor (ha!) of being the first person to hear this book idea (over mimosas and chicken and waffles!) and the first person to see the cover. But more than that, you're the One to my Four, and I love you endlessly. Lisa K, you've been such a champion of this book from the moment I shared the idea. Your cheerleading and demand for me to "write the effing book" kept me excited and accountable. Leigh, thank you for cheese fry therapy, for Mel and Cordell's character names, and for making me laugh when I need it the most. (L.H.W.A.S.O.W.F.W.S. 4-Eva!!) Jocelynn, thank you for your PR expertise and for talking out dialogue and ideas with me and for being a ride-or-die friend. And for being prompt about responding to my "does this sound okay" texts! Love ya mean it!

To all my peeps I teased with chapter one: your reactions were everything! Erin, your Mariah Carey comment might be my favorite; you are an amazing hypewoman and an even better friend. Lisa W, thank you for "Peer Pressure;" it was my Luke and Tessa anthem the entire time. Matt, thanks for the "coach speak" and sports input. Sarah and Brianne, thanks for being encouraging early readers. Michaela, thank you for planning an unforgettable book release party. I have so many amazing friends, and I wish I could thank all of you individually, but this book is already long enough! Please know that your encouragement and support mean the world to me. Thank you for listening to me talk ad nauseum about all the bookish things.

To my teachers who taught me how to read, thank you for opening up the whole world for me.

To my family, thank you for loving me.

Finally, to Clara Jean Bennett Brown, who raised me to be an independent woman who goes after what she wants. There are traces of you throughout this story. I hope you're proud. And I miss you every day.

AUTHOR'S NOTE

The idea for this book came to me when I was watching a documentary about reading instruction in America. Sources differ when searching for statistics, but one claims there are thirty-two million illiterate adults in the United States. As a reading interventionist, I am passionate about working to ensure that we have fewer kids who grow up unable to read like Luke did. If someone in your life wants to learn how to read, help is available. A Google search for local literacy volunteers will provide a list of organizations with adult literacy programs.

ABOUT THE AUTHOR

Brandy Pelletier spends her days as a reading specialist and her nights and weekends reading anything she can get her hands on. She's wanted to become a published author ever since second grade, when her original story "How the Giraffe Got Its Long Neck" was published in her school district's annual writing anthology.

When she's not blasting Taylor Swift or attempting to tackle her ridiculously long TBR, she can be found dreaming of living in a witch cottage with her miniature schnauzer, Pippa. *Between the Lines* is her debut novel. Follow Brandy on Instagram @thebrandyland.